A Pri...

of Wales

The Saga of Roland Inness
Book 5

Wayne Grant

FIRST EDITION

ISBN-10: 1979319472
ISBN-13: 978-1979319478

A Prince of Wales is a work of fiction. While some of the characters in this story are actual historical figures, their actions are largely the product of the author's imagination.

*Cover Art by More Visual, Ltd.

For Tony and Artie
There are no friends like old friends...

Contents

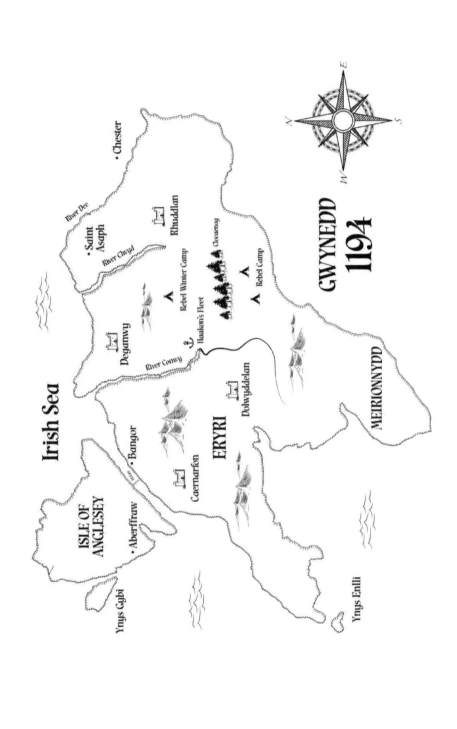

A Prince of Wales

Wayne Grant

Prologue

*T*he boy should have been home by sunset. His father had demanded he muck out the cow's pen before dark, but he would rather throw stones in the river. He climbed down the bank to the gravel bar and searched between the little fishing boats there until he found the perfect projectile. It was shaped like a flattened egg and had been worn smooth by the flow of the River Conwy for a thousand years. The boy hefted his prize and felt sure he could get a dozen skips or more from this beauty. He shifted weight to his back foot, extended his arm behind him, cocked his wrist—and froze.

In the fading winter twilight, he saw boats on the river—ten of them. These were nothing like the little boats that belonged to the village fishermen. They were long and low, with a single row of oars on either side and a long, curved prow rising gracefully from the bow of each. He watched, mesmerized, as hundreds of oar blades moved as one, dipping into the dark water and propelling this flotilla upriver against the current.

The boy had never seen boats such as these, but he knew what they were—had heard the terrifying stories passed down from father to son for generations. He reflexively looked toward the fortress across the river. The castle at Deganwy sat on a rocky crag looking down on the mouth of the river where it spilled into the Irish Sea. From this stone and timber fortress, the princes of Gwynedd had guarded a strategic avenue of invasion into the north of Wales for over five hundred years.

1

There should have been a warning fire lit on the heights but the boy saw none. There should have been soldiers streaming down from the fortress to confront this horror, but he saw not a one! He dropped his rock and ran faster than he had ever done to the little house at the edge of the town. His father looked up, annoyed, as he burst through the door.

"Yer late!" he said and reached for a strap, then noticed the terror on the boy's face.

"What is it lad? What's put the fright into ye?"

The boy stood there, bug-eyed and fighting for breath. Finally, he blurted out the terrible warning.

"Northmen!"

***

Haakon the Black watched the boy drop his stone and run away as though he'd seen the Devil. Snorri, his helmsman, gave a little laugh at the sight and nudged him.

"Shit his pants, I'll wager."

Haakon nodded. He'd seen this before.

"The whole village will, once the boy spreads the word."

Snorri grunted. It was good to be feared. Frightened men put up less of a fight. He looked behind him at the longships that followed in their wake—ten crews in all, manned by four hundred mercenary Danes—something to be feared, indeed.

These were the Dub Gaill, descendants of the Danish invaders who had dominated Ireland for two hundred years. The name was from the Gaelic and meant "dark foreigners." Snorri glanced at the tall man standing next to him. Their leader fit that description well. He had fair skin, but coal-black hair, worn long and loose to his shoulders. There were blue rune signs tattooed on one cheekbone and bands of silver around heavily muscled arms. He was every inch the Viking.

Haakon the Black.

That name marked his reputation more than his colouring. Operating out of Dublin, Haakon was a throwback to an earlier time when Viking longships ruled the northern seas unchallenged. He was a pitiless warlord whose band of hardened

2

warriors struck fear from Cornwall to the Orkney Isles. Now they had come to Gwynedd.

He was here at the behest of his old patron, Ragnvald, King of the Isles, who ruled a domain from the Hebrides to the Isle of Man. But it was not Ragnvald who was paying for his services. The King had family connections in Wales and it was they who had promised silver for his Dub Gaill swords—a lot of silver.

Haakon looked up at the castle on the hill. It had been built there to guard against ships such as these and men such as those he led, but he could see that no alarm had been raised. He expected none. He had been assured that the garrison at Deganwy Castle would let them pass unmolested up the River Conwy and into the very heart of Gwynedd.

As the longships slid quietly by the fishing village, Haakon watched its inhabitants streaming out of the tiny hamlet and running for the surrounding hills. Upstream, the river narrowed, and the longships fell into a single line with Haakon's in the lead. As full night fell, torches were lit and a lookout perched at the bow watched for shallows and sandbars, calling directions back to Snorri at the helm.

For twelve miles, the boats moved against the current, until rounding a bend, they saw a bonfire on the bank and a wide bar where they could safely ground the boats. One by one, they slid up on the gravel of the bar like hunting hounds, come to sit at the feet of their master. Haakon leapt onto the gravel, sword in hand, and strode up toward the fire. Waiting there was a tall man with a short black beard and fine clothes. He was surrounded by a score of warriors in mail.

In the glow of the bonfire, Haakon could see a huge herd of horses grazing in the meadow that spread back from the river's edge. He nodded in satisfaction and bowed to the man by the fire. This was the man who would pay them their silver.

"Lord Roderic, King Ragnvald sends his regards," Haakon the Black announced in serviceable Welsh. He had made it a practice to learn the tongues of the peoples who bordered the Irish Sea. It was good for business.

"Lord Haakon, you are most welcome here," Roderic said, stepping forward and offering his hand. "When next you greet my father-in-law, give him my fond wishes, but first, I have some Welshmen I need for you to kill."

Treachery

*T*he ravens that circled above the far ridge were the first warning. Wherever these scavenger birds gathered, there was death. The birds had likely been drawn to the valley beyond the ridge by a dead deer or some other forest creature that had perished in the cold. It had been a hard winter after all, but Griff Connah knew that men had a way of dying in the forests of Gwynedd at any time of year. A day ago, they had left a score of their men camped in the valley beyond the ridge where the carrion birds circled. And ravens would feast on dead men as happily as dead game.

He scanned the ridgeline, searching for any hint of trouble, but saw none. He glanced at the rider to his left. His companion was a striking young man, handsome after a fashion—or at least the women seemed to find him so. He was a big man with a russet beard and sat his horse with an easy grace. Even after a long day in the saddle, he rode erect, like the prince that he was, a thick mane of brown hair whipping behind him in the freezing wind. He was Llywelyn ap Iowerth, rebel leader and one day, God willing, Prince of Gwynedd.

They were returning from a parlay with Llywelyn's uncle, Daffyd ap Owain, the man Llywelyn had been in rebellion against for seven long years. Lord Daffyd had ruled Gwynedd east of the River Conwy for twenty years, but had been unable to snuff out Llywelyn's growing strength in the backcountry. The invitation to talk had come from Lord Roderic, Llywelyn's other uncle and Daffyd's younger brother. Roderic, who ruled

5

Gwynedd west of the Conwy had offered to serve as intermediary between the warring parties and had pledged hostages to guarantee the safety of both men.

Now the talking was done and the hostages returned. Like all land east of the river, the land they now rode through was claimed by Daffyd, though the wilder parts of Gwynedd were under no firm control. And whatever peaceful overtures had been made at the talks, the bloody civil war was far from over. He saw that Llywelyn's eyes were also fixed above the ridgeline ahead. He had seen the birds too.

It was probably a dead animal—nothing more, but they had not survived seven years as rebels in this wilderness by ignoring warning signs. The prince edged his mount close to Griff.

"See anything?" he called, just loud enough to be heard over the horses' hooves. No one in Wales had keener eyes than Griff Connah.

"Just the ravens."

"Worried?" Llywelyn asked.

"Always."

***

Griff had been with Llywelyn since shortly after the young nobleman arrived in Gwynedd at the age of fourteen to claim his share of an illustrious, and dangerous, inheritance. The boy's grandfather, Owain, Prince of Gwynedd, had been the ruler of this region of northern Wales for over thirty years, controlling much of the rest of the country as overlord to lesser princes. The old man had seven acknowledged sons, Llywelyn's father, Iowerth, being the second oldest. He also sired countless bastards and died without officially naming an heir. It was a failure that would drench his patrimony in blood across two generations.

The killing began within months of the old Prince's death. Daffyd and Roderic, sons of Owain's second wife, killed Hywel, Owain's oldest son, in battle. They would surely have done the same to Llywelyn's father, Iowerth, who was next in line of seniority, had he not retreated to his fortress at Dolwyddelan, deep in the towering peaks of Eryri.

There he stayed, far from the intrigues of his half-brothers, and there he sired a son, Llywelyn. But the fortress proved no refuge for Iowerth, or his family. In a calamity for his line, Iowerth died of a fever, leaving only his wife and infant son to face the ambitions of Daffyd and Roderic. The wife was no fool. She fled east to Powys, the land of her kinsmen, and raised Llywelyn there, safe from the boy's ruthless uncles.

While Daffyd and Roderic split Gwynedd between them, Llywelyn lived as an exile in Powys. There, the boy was raised to understand his noble heritage and to hate the men who had stolen it from him. For, by right of primogeniture, Llywelyn had a legitimate claim to the rule of all Gwynedd. His line, through Iowerth back to Owain, was senior to that of the brothers Daffyd and Roderic, but in the brutal world of northern Wales, rules of succession bought the boy little.

As he grew older, Llywelyn chafed in exile and dreamed of glory. When he was fourteen, he gathered a small band of maternal cousins and, against his mother's entreaties, rode west into the land of his father to claim his inheritance. He was not warmly received.

Llywelyn had been hunted relentlessly for months by his uncle Daffyd when he stumbled wet and exhausted into Griff Connah's village. He had only one man with him, his cousins having fled back into Powys. The young noble's cause seemed hopeless, but Griff had seen something in the gangly boy, a burning intensity in his eyes, that had drawn him to this royal pretender.

Connah became one of Llywelyn's first adherents and, in the hard years that followed, rose to become the rebel prince's most trusted lieutenant. He was tall and lean, with heavily muscled shoulders that marked him as a bowman. He commanded the archers of the small but growing rebel army that had come to dominate the wilder tracts of land east of the Conwy River—the part of Gwynedd claimed by Daffyd.

In the past year, Daffyd's forces had retreated to the coastal plain, leaving the hinterland to his nephew. Llywelyn used his light cavalry and archers to control the narrow roads and forested hills inland, but dislodging Daffyd from the richer lands on the coast had proven to be another matter. Llywelyn had neither the force to assault nor lay siege to the string of fortresses that protected the lowlands.

And so there had been stalemate.

The first snows brought an end to the seventh year of campaigning and both sides settled into winter quarters. Then the unexpected offer of parlay arrived during Christ's Mass. Surprisingly, the message had come not from Daffyd, but from Roderic. The messenger said that Daffyd was ready to recognize Llywelyn's claim to some part of Owain's old domains and had enlisted Roderic as a go-between. Roderic had agreed to arrange a meeting between his brother and his nephew and guaranteed the safety of both men.

The meeting would be held in an open field on the eastern bank of the River Conwy, a few miles upstream from the castle at Deganwy. This was Daffyd's land and his men garrisoned the castle, but Roderic had substantial forces just across the river and had promised to provide hostages to insure there would be no treachery on either side.

"Why would Daffyd offer a deal now?" Griff asked after the messenger had left their camp. "I don't like it."

Llywelyn shrugged.

"Perhaps he grows weary of the fight. He's no longer young and I hear he's grown fat. He knows we are winning."

Griff gave a quiet hoot.

"Your uncle is feasting before a roaring fire this Christ Mass, snug in his fortress at Rhuddlan, while we huddle in these timber huts against the cold. I'm not sure it looks like we are winning."

Llywelyn laughed and shook his head.

"True enough. Perhaps he will offer me half of his lands and name me his heir so he can live out his life in peace."

Griff shook his head.

"I don't think his son, Owain, would appreciate that!"

Llywelyn laughed again.

"No, I suppose not. Owain bears my grandfather's famous name and I hear he harbours ambitions to one day rule himself. Alas, he has not the brains or the balls to do so."

The two grew quiet for a long moment watching the snow fall around the primitive hill fort that was their winter quarters. Finally, Griff spoke.

"So, my lord, in the unlikely event Daffyd should offer you half of his land now and all upon his death—in return for peace—would you accept?"

Llywelyn grinned and swung his arm in an arc taking in the cold grey woods around them.

"And give up all this, Griff?" He paused and looked at his friend and follower. "Perhaps I would."

***

Two weeks later, they made the hard, two-day ride from the hill fort to the edge of the high country that looked down on the coastal plain. Llywelyn left a score of his personal guard behind in a sheltered valley and rode on with only six men, all that either party was allowed to bring to the parlay. As they approached the meeting place, two riders came out to meet them, one of middle years and one a mere boy of no more than six years—though he sat his horse as though born to it.

The older rider greeted Llywelyn.

"My lord, I am Andras, sworn man of Roderic, Prince of Aberffraw and Lord of Anglesey and Eryri. He bids me welcome you to this parlay, which he prays will bring peace to Gwynedd and his own dear family."

Llywelyn reined in his horse and gave a quick nod to the man.

"We all hope for peace," he said blandly, then turned to the boy. "What is your name, lad?"

The older man started to speak, but Llywelyn cut him off.

"I'm addressing the boy, not you. Let him answer."

The boy was fair-haired and a bit wide-eyed, but he spoke up readily enough.

"I am Rhun ap Thomas ap Roderic, my lord," he announced proudly. "I am your hostage. Are you Llywelyn?"

"*Prince* Llywelyn to you, lad. Roderic is your grandsire?"

"Aye, Llywelyn...Prince Llywelyn. He is my father's father."

Llywelyn turned back to the older rider.

"Tell your master the hostage is acceptable."

The rider turned his horse's head to go, but Llywelyn spoke again.

"And tell him my man will slit the boy's throat if there is treachery."

The messenger gave a grim nod and rode off. Llywelyn pointed to one of his men who rode up next to the boy and took the horse's reins in his hand. Llywelyn spurred his mount and followed Roderic's man along with Griff and his four remaining men. The boy watched them go, then turned to his guard.

"Did he mean that? If things go wrong…you'll kill me?"

The man thought to frighten the lad, but saw the boy was frightened enough already.

"No, lad. No need to fear. Prince Llywelyn does not kill children, but I hope your kin folk don't know that."

The boy sat silently contemplating his situation for a bit.

"I hope they don't either."

***

The parlay was held in a large white tent erected in the centre of a broad meadow that sloped down to the river. Behind the tent were half a hundred well-armed men, brought by Roderic to ensure there would be no mischief at the gathering. As Llywelyn rode up, he saw Daffyd and his entourage sitting their horses near the tent.

Llywelyn had only seen Daffyd once and that had been as a child, when his uncle had travelled to meet with the ruler of northern Powys, who was brother to Llywelyn's mother. Daffyd had been filled with familial affection at that meeting and invited mother and son to return home, but his mother, Magred, was no fool. The invitation had been ignored.

His uncle had, indeed, added much to his girth since last they had met, but Llywelyn had no trouble recognizing him by his air of command. He had more recent recollections of the young man mounted next to Daffyd—his cousin Owain. Owain had made a lightning strike against another of Llywelyn's hill forts two years ago and had almost destroyed his rebel band. Only the unexpected arrival of Roland Inness and the Invalid Company

10

had saved his cause that day. Llywelyn could see by the smouldering anger in his cousin's gaze that Owain had not forgotten how that triumph had been snatched away.

The two groups eyed each other suspiciously, hands on sword hilts and, for an awkward moment, it appeared they might come to blows. It would have only taken a spark to set things off between these warring kinsmen, but Roderic chose that moment to step out of the tent with his constable.

"Welcome brother!" he called cheerily to Daffyd, then turned toward the new arrivals.

"And welcome to you, nephew! I'd recognize you anywhere, for you look strikingly like your dear mother. I am glad to make your acquaintance."

Llywelyn smiled at his uncle, determined to give away nothing in this dangerous company.

"And I yours, uncle. Let us hope our meeting is profitable for all."

"Well said, sir. Now, I would ask all to lay aside your arms before entering the tent. You each hold one of my grandsons hostage and I am fond of the boys. I would not like some misunderstanding here to bring any harm to them."

With wary eyes, the men dismounted and filed into the tent, dropping their swords, dirks and axes at the entrance. Once inside, Roderic, so lean and dark next to his corpulent brother, directed the two principals to a small table with chairs. Retainers stood back as Llywelyn and Daffyd sat down and took the measure of each other.

"Llywelyn," Daffyd began, "we have fought for many years and are no closer to a final reckoning. I believe this bad blood between us has been stoked by your kinsmen in Powys, who fear the power of a united Gwynedd. Let us set aside our differences and join together. Together, we can strike fear into those who wish Gwynedd ill."

Llywelyn gave a noncommittal smile.

"My kinsmen in Powys have no role in this, uncle. It was I who begged them to join me when first I came to claim my birthright. Some did, but they soon grew weary of being hunted like hares by you and your men. But I am heartened by your

11

sincere wish to reconcile. So, tell me, what do you offer me for peace between us?"

Daffyd leaned forward eagerly.

"I offer you the largest cantref in my domain—Tegeingl—a good third of my land! You will, of course, do homage to me for that grant of land, but I will let you rule there as you see fit."

Having laid his offer on the table, Daffyd sat back and waited for a reply from his young nephew. Tegeingl lay between the Clwydian hills and the River Dee. It had been fought over between the Earls of Chester and the princes of Gwynedd since the Norman Conquest. It was largely abandoned and gone to wilderness.

Griff, who had listened to the proceedings in silence, leaned in to whisper to his master.

"He thinks to have you buy a pig in a poke, lord, but we have lived in that land. It's shit."

Llywelyn nodded, then smiled back at Daffyd.

"A reasonable offer, uncle. I will need a day to think on it and confer with my men."

Daffyd frowned and gave Griff a dark look.

"You should not trust this rabble you've surrounded yourself with, Llywelyn. Let us settle this…among family."

Llywelyn nodded.

"If you can't trust family, my lord, who can you trust?" he said, with no trace of sarcasm. Daffyd looked at him hard for a long moment, then shrugged.

"My offer stays open for one day. I would have your decision before then. Let there be an end to the blood. It is time we made peace."

Llywelyn nodded as he rose from the table.

"Peace unto you, uncle."

***

No one spoke as Llywelyn's party rode away from the meadow and back toward the hills that rose from the coastal plain. There was no point. Daffyd's proposal was laughable on its face, but the meeting had served a purpose. The fact that his uncle had made *any* offer confirmed the weakness of the man's position.

By his own reckoning, Llywelyn felt he would have the strength to march on Daffyd's great fortress at Rhuddlan within a year and roust the old goat out. There was no need to make a poor deal now. His uncle would know Llywelyn's answer when he failed to return to the meeting place in the morning.

Rhun saw Llywelyn approach with relief. The little boy loved his grandfather, but the man who rode up to him truly looked like a prince. Llywelyn hailed his man and gave the boy a grin.

"How fared our hostage?"

"Very bravely, my lord. I was ready to slit his gullet, but he showed nary a qualm. He'll make a good fighter someday. Maybe we should keep him!"

For a moment, under the smiling gaze of Llywelyn, the boy thought it would be a very fine thing to ride off with these men. He loved his grandsire, but there was *something* about this Llywelyn!

"No, I cannot break my word. You know the way home, boy?"

Rhun nodded and gave his horse a jab with his small heels. As the animal started back toward the river, the boy turned and waved.

"Goodbye, Prince Llywelyn!"

Llywelyn returned the wave, then turned his horse back toward the hills above the coastal plain.

***

It was nearing sundown when they approached the sheltered valley where his personal guard camped. A score of picked men had come with him from winter quarters, but had been left behind in the hills, their safety vouched for by Roderic. It was clear and cold and the air was still. With no breeze, Llywelyn would have expected to see smoke rising from campfires beyond the ridge, but the only thing in the blue sky were the ravens. The Prince dropped his eyes back to the road as a hare flushed from the underbrush thirty paces ahead.

Trap!

Llywelyn and Griff reined in instantly and this saved them. A dozen arrows flew from the woods on their left, taking down three men to their front.

"Back!" Griff shouted, and wrenched his horse's head to the rear. Llywelyn had already turned his mount and dug his heels into the animal's flanks. He heard a cry and saw another of his men fall with an arrow in his back. More arrows buzzed by as the two men frantically whipped their horses into a gallop. A shaft struck a glancing blow against Llywelyn's steel helmet and almost unhorsed him, but he was a superb rider and stayed in the saddle. Both men bent low along their horse's necks to make a small target for the men trying to kill them.

They were almost out of the killing zone of the ambush when a score of riders came charging around a bend in the trail less than two hundred yards to their front. They were armed for battle. Daffyd, or Roderic—or perhaps both brothers—had planned this ambush carefully. No doubt the men he'd left in the valley were already dead—a meal for the ravens. Now they were cornered, front and back, and hemmed in by wooded slopes on both sides.

"The trees!" Llywelyn shouted and turned his mount to the left.

In only a few bounds they reached the bottom of a steep slope and leapt to the ground. Llywelyn wrenched his shield free of his saddle and Griff did the same with his longbow and quiver of arrows. Together they began to scramble up the densely-wooded ridge as the thunder of hooves drew near. Below them, there were shouts and curses from the valley floor as the horsemen dismounted and began to climb uphill after them.

The two men reached a false summit and paused to look behind them. At least fifteen armed and mailed men were struggling up the ridge in their direction. Further down, archers who had missed their mark in the initial attack joined the pursuers. Llywelyn was bent at the waist, trying to catch his breath.

"Can we outrun them?" he managed between pants.

"Maybe. That first lot…are but…lowland horse boys," Griff managed as he too gasped for air. "They won't have the…wind."

Llywelyn gave him a sour look.

"Perhaps…we've spent too much time…in the saddle as well," he said.

Griff gave him a faint grin, then loosened the ties on his mail jerkin and pulled it over his head.

"Won't be of much help if that lot catches us," he said, nodding downhill. Llywelyn returned his grin, then shucked off his own heavy mail.

"What of the archers?" he asked as his breath began to steady.

Griff smiled as he drew an arrow from his quiver and nocked it.

"They don't worry me none. If they could shoot straight, we'd both be dead now."

In one swift motion, he drew his longbow, calmed his breathing and released. A yelp from below told them he had not missed his target.

"That'll slow 'em down," he said, as the men below all went to ground. Llywelyn slapped the tall archer on the shoulder and turned back uphill.

***

For an hour, they scrambled up and down the sides of steep ravines, finding game trails where they could and clambering over rocks and deadfall when no path led them away from their pursuers. The sound of the chase grew slowly faint, but it was still there when Llywelyn stopped at the top of a sawback ridge and looked down on their back trail.

"Rest here," he said and sat down heavily on a flat rock. Griff slumped against the trunk of a deadfall oak and looked up at the sky. It had grown dark through the late afternoon as they fled through the woods and now there were scattered flakes beginning to fall. He grunted.

"It's going to be a cold night, but the snow will cover our tracks."

Llywelyn looked up as the sky grew darker and the flurries multiplied, but did not reply.

"Who was it, ye think? Roderic or Daffyd?" the archer asked.

Llywelyn shrugged.

"This is Daffyd's realm, so more likely it was him, but I would not discount Roderic."

"Why would he attack us? We've stayed clear of that bastard's lands all these years—just a few cattle raids."

"My uncle Roderic plays a long game. He has been well satisfied for me to be a thorn in his brother's side for these many years, but now…"

"He thinks you might win."

"Aye. He has no fear of Daffyd, who had grown fat and contented with his lot. Daffyd is no threat to him, but I am. He knows I will not be content with but half of Gwynedd."

"So now we will fight both uncles?"

Llywelyn gave an emphatic nod.

"Both will have to go if Gwynedd is to be whole. It was always going to come to that, old friend. But if we are to see that day before we are both too old to enjoy it, we will need help."

"Help?"

"Aye. I have been in contact with my cousins of late."

"Which ones?" Griff asked. "You have so many—and all of them scheming bastards to my knowledge."

Llywelyn laughed aloud.

"You are right enough there. The spawn of Owain Gwynedd have multiplied like hares, and most are treacherous as snakes. The key is to cultivate the snakes who will find it in their interest to support me. Then watch them like hawks."

"So which cousins are you enlisting?"

"Gruffydd and Maredudd."

Griff couldn't suppress a groan.

"You're jesting."

"No."

Griff shook his head.

"I can see your logic. They occupy the cantrefs of Meirionnydd and Dunoding and unlike your other cousins they can actually put fighting men in the field, but, my lord—by all accounts—including your own—they are crazy."

"Aye, you are right about that," Llywelyn said with a wry grin. "They once came to Powys when we were all boys. By the time they left, I had a broken arm and a furious mother! But perhaps ruling their little patches of ground these past years has sobered them a bit. And those little patches of ground are south of Roderic's land. They can threaten him from there. Crazy or no, they are the only players on the board who have something to offer me and who might have an interest in undoing our uncles."

Griff looked sceptical but held his peace. Llywelyn rose from the rock he had been sitting on and cocked his ear. Faint sounds of men could now be heard on the ridgeline behind them. It was time to move on. He turned back to Griff.

"There is also the debt owed me by the Earl of Chester. We harboured him when he was outlawed and gave him men—you included—to take back his city. Ranulf swore he would repay the favour. I think it's time he did."

"I was wondering when you would remember our friend, the Earl. What will you ask of him?"

Llywelyn grinned.

"It will be you who does the asking, Griff. Whoever planned this ambush will not be sitting idle. Unless they are utter fools, they will already be marching to strike at our winter camp. My place is there. Earl Ranulf knows you. You will take my demand directly to him."

Griff frowned. He did not fancy the idea of leaving his liege lord alone to make his way back to their camp. It was a good two-day ride through rough country to get there and they had abandoned their horses in the ambush. Still, he knew it would do no good to object simply on grounds of danger.

"Ye'll steal a horse?"

"Aye, and so should you. I'll want you back within a fortnight. If I'm not at our winter camp, seek me at Dolwyddelan."

Griff nodded. Their last place of refuge was the fortress in the high mountains of Eryri, where Llywelyn had been born.

"And what, exactly, shall I demand of Ranulf?"

17

"Men—at least a hundred, and not those poxy town boys he has manning the walls of Chester. Make that clear, Griff."

"You'll want the crippled lads then."

"Aye, the Invalid Company."

"They can fight."

"That, they can, and, Griff, I will need a man to lead them—a man we can trust."

Griff gave him a quizzical look, then broke out into a broad smile.

"Roland Inness?"

Llywelyn nodded.

"None other."

Danesford

A thick line of mounted men moved out of the shadows of the wood line and into a cleared field. Steam rose from the nostrils of warhorses as they stamped the frozen ground. A thin winter sun glinted off sharpened lance points. The man standing alone in the centre of the field felt hope die. On the far side of the open ground lay a patch of forest land, a place where he might elude his pursuers, but he knew he could not reach it in time. Still, he would not simply stand still and be ridden under. He turned and ran.

Behind him, a command rang out and he felt the ground tremble as iron-shod hooves pounded the icy ground. Without breaking stride, he reached for the quiver over his shoulder and found it empty. Somewhere in the running fight with his pursuers, he had loosed his final arrow. He ran harder, but the safety of the trees seemed no closer and the pounding of the charging horses swelled behind him. In a few seconds, they would be on him.

Roland Inness sat bolt upright in the bed, his chest heaving, the thunder of charging warhorses dissolving into the hammering of his own heart. *A dream. The damned dream.*

He looked to his right as he fought to settle his breathing. His wife had not stirred.

Must not have cried out. Good. It worries Millie when I do.

He slid quietly out of bed, the pounding in his ears growing quiet as his heart slowed. He did not often have these dreams, but when they came, they were vivid. Sometimes his pursuers were Flemish mercenaries and sometimes Saracens with their wicked curved scimitars. Sometimes both pursued him, which made no sense. But when did dreams ever make sense?

Tugging leather breeches on under his night shirt, he slipped out of the small room. Wooden stairs led down to the hall where he found a bench and pulled on his boots. Embers from the night's fire still glowed in the hearth.

He tried to shake off the effects of the dream, but it seemed to cling to him. He had fought in pitched battles from England to the gates of Acre in the Holy Land and had survived those fights, but they had left a mark. It was a price paid by men who took up arms as a soldier. He supposed shepherds dreamt of being savaged by wolves and seamen of being devoured by creatures of the deep. .He wondered for a moment what nightmares farmers and shopkeepers might have. No doubt some sort of unpleasantness troubled their sleep.

He looked around at the rough-hewn timbers of the house— *his* house—and had no regrets about the life he had chosen. A small smile tugged at the corner of his mouth. *Chosen* was not the right word. He had been a farmer and a hunter once; then a fugitive on the run from the Earl of Derby after poaching a deer. He'd been a green squire to a Norman knight and been knighted himself for a bloody day atop the crumbled walls of Acre. He had fought under Earl William Marshall at Towcester where they had routed the mercenaries that threatened Richard's throne and sometimes troubled his sleep. Very little of it had he chosen. Still, none of it had he refused.

Behind the door at the top of the stairs, Millicent Inness slept. They had married less than a year ago. *That* he had chosen and he still could not believe she had made the same choice. Millicent was…the star upon which he guided. All that had come before—the good and the evil—had led him to her and to this home they had built together. For that alone, he would have fought all the Saracens and mercenaries on earth. Dreams? They were nothing.

He walked to the big oak door of the hall and swung it open. A frigid blast of air swirled through the opening, causing the coals in the hearth to flare. He stepped outside and looked to the east where the sky was beginning to lighten. Dawn was coming, but he could tell snow would come with it.

It was light enough for Roland to see the rough wooden palisade that surrounded his timber house—the place could scarce be called a keep. The house and its defensive wall sat atop a small ridge overlooking the River Weaver. Timbers had been cut over the summer and driven into the rocky soil on the hillside. There was a single gate and a single watch tower. It was a primitive fort and reminded him, for all the world, of a brigand's fortress in the Clocaenog Forest where he'd once had to rescue Millicent.

His wife had named this little fort Danesford, to honour the thousand Danes who had fled across the river at the ford below to escape the Earl of Derby and Prince John's Flemish mercenaries. The Danes were Roland's people and had once ruled a third of England before the Normans came and drove them into the high country of Derbyshire. There, they had become a thorn in the side of the Normans. When Earl William de Ferrers was given command of Prince John's mercenary army, he seized the chance to finally rid Derbyshire of the troublesome Danes.

But the Earl of Chester had other plans. He stood with King Richard and against Prince John in a growing civil war, but lacked the men to withstand John's mercenary army. He had sent Roland Inness, his young commander, to seek an alliance with his fellow Danes and a deal had been struck—the Danes of Derbyshire would fight for Earl Ranulf in exchange for good farmland along the Weaver. And they had fought.

They'd defended Chester during a long siege and marched with Ranulf to the aid of William Marshall at Towcester. On that bloody field, their longbows had felled hundreds of Irish and Flemish mercenaries and turned the tide of battle. That victory had ended Prince John's efforts to usurp the crown from Richard and, with the King's return to England, there had been peace at last.

The Earl had kept his promise to the Danes. Each man who had fought for him was given a hide of good farmland. In the spring, they had put aside their longbows and happily hitched ploughs to oxen to break ground in their new steadings. By autumn, the harvest had come in bountiful and there was an air of contentment in the valley of the Weaver.

Roland raised his eyes to the timber watchtower by the gate and noted with approval that the guard was awake and alert. Peace might be upon the land, but it was a fool who thought it would last. The man in the tower was Gurt, one of his fellow Danes who had entered Roland's service as one of ten men-at-arms. A few of the younger Danes, finding soldiering to their taste, had taken service directly with the Earl of Chester, but the rest had happily settled on the land promised them and had gone back to farming. All looked to Roland Inness for leadership in their new home.

Roland took a deep breath of the cold air and went back inside, his head feeling clearer. He saw Millie, a shawl wrapped around her shoulders, coming down the stairs. He smiled at his young wife and quickly grabbed an armful of firewood to stoke the hearth back into life.

"Good morning," she said brightly. "Sleep well?"

"Very well, indeed, my lady," he replied, as he used a small bellows to help the logs catch.

"Liar!" she said.

Roland sighed and looked over his shoulder, as she drew up a bench behind him.

"You heard."

"Aye, I did. Was it the horsemen again?"

He laughed.

"It was," he said, "and I almost made it to the woods this time."

"You're getting faster then, husband," she said and laid a warm hand on his arm. "I think the day you outrun the horses, the dreams will be done."

She smiled as she spoke, but Roland could see the concern in her eyes.

"I expect you're right, but till then—they're only dreams." He gave the coals a few pokes with an iron and turned toward her as the fire began to crackle. She rose and he pulled her in close.

22

She gave a little squeal as he buried his face in the crook of her neck. She smelled of wood smoke and love.

Millicent reached up and ran a hand along his cheek, brushing the raised scar left by an arrow that had ploughed a furrow there the night they had taken Chester back from William de Ferrers. When she reached his jawline, she stopped and drew back.

"You're growing woolly in the cold, Roland!" she said with mock sternness. Roland raised his own hand to his chin and felt the stubble there.. Millie had never liked him bearded. He would have to take a blade to the growth before the day was done. He made as though to rub his bristles on her cheek and she pulled away laughing, just as the door swung open. Through it came Sir Edgar Langton, a mountain of a man with a tangled black beard that preceded him like a storm cloud. He saw the two embracing and hesitated.

"Beggin' yer pardon, Roland...my lady," he managed. "But there's a rider crossing the ford and headin' this way."

Millie smiled at the big man and beckoned him forward. "Come warm yourself, Sir Edgar. Roland just stirred the coals."

Looking at the two with their arms around each other, Sir Edgar thought to ask what sort of coals, exactly, his young master was stirring, but he held his tongue and strode over to the hearth. It was one thing to poke fun at Sir Roland, but Lady Millicent was quite another matter. The big knight was just a little overawed by her.

"Obliged, my lady," he said and stretched out his huge paw-like hands toward the growing blaze.

Roland crossed the room and took his heavy wool cape from a peg on the wall. He pulled it over his shoulders and headed for the door.. Sir Edgar paused one more second to soak up a bit more heat then followed him, limping just a bit on his one bad leg.

Roland and Millicent had met the big man years ago in a tavern in Towcester. They'd been travelling to London to seek out the Queen when they'd met Sir Edgar, a bitter veteran of the King's great Crusade.

Sir Edgar had taken a wound on the walls of Acre—in the mad charge up the rubble strewn breach with the first wave of the

English assault. Few men survived that charge and those who did knew they owed their lives to a young squire who had rallied them just below the top of the breach. A horde of Saracens had counterattacked the exhausted English and the Crusader line began to break and stumble back down the slope. Had the rout continued, slaughter would have surely followed, but the squire had refused to run.

Roland Inness had shouted at them to form a shield wall and they had scrambled into a tight-packed line as the enemy wave crashed into them. As men hacked and thrust desperately at each other, their shield wall bent but did not break. Roland and Declan O'Duinne had been knighted by the King for their actions that day.

Over a year later, Sir Edgar had recognized the two young knights cross the tavern floor. He was drunk and penniless that night, but he did know the whereabouts of the Queen. For the price of a new horse, he had pledged his service to Roland and had not wavered since. He had fought beside his young master in the wilderness of Wales and in the high country of Derbyshire. He had helped to break the last desperate charge of Prince John's mercenary cavalry at Towcester.

When peace had finally come, he had been made Master of the Sword for Danesford and had proven more than up to the task, training Danes and local boys to become men-at-arms. As they left the hall together, Sir Edgar jabbed Roland in the ribs.

"I'd a waited a few minutes if I'd known ye were romancin' the missus," he said and laughed at his own joke. Sir Edgar might be big and have a forbidding countenance, but there was something playful beneath that frightening appearance. Roland grinned.

"I'll tell Lady Millicent that you apologize."

Sir Edgar scowled. Fun was fun, but there was a limit.

"No need to bring her in ta' it!" he grumped as they trudged down to meet the approaching rider.

A few white flakes drifted slowly onto the dirt courtyard as Jamie Finch rode through the gate. Finch looked younger than his nineteen years, but appearances deceived. He had been raised in the back alleys of London where every day was another chance for a young boy to take a wrong turn. He had survived to his fourteenth year when he managed to convince a sceptical sergeant that he had soldiering experience. He'd sailed with King Richard's army to the Kingdom of Palestine where he'd fought bravely, until grievously wounded by a Saracen spear.

He'd been sent home and, unlike many injured veterans of that brutal war, had found a welcome waiting for him in his old haunts. He'd taken to picking pockets and occasional armed robbery—all skills he had learned as a boy, but found these old pursuits had paled after his time in the east. Neither money, nor drink, nor women, had filled an odd void inside.

Finch knew of the Invalid Company. They were men who, like him, had come home damaged from the Crusade. Some were missing limbs. Some had hideous scars. For some, the scars of war were not visible to the eye. Few had been able to take up their old lives upon their return to England. The King had ordered that they be provided for, and many had gathered in London where they were billeted in a rank barracks outside the Ludgate and given a small stipend. With nothing to occupy them, they had fallen into indolence, drunkenness and violence. Londoners, Finch included, had looked on these men with a mixture of pity and disgust.

It had only been out of desperate necessity that Earl William Marshall, Justiciar of the Realm, had mustered the Invalids at Oxford to go in search of the Earl of Chester who had fled a trumped-up charge of treason and was a fugitive in Wales. They'd been put under the command of the incompetent Sir Harold FitzGibbons who fled at the first sign of danger. But Roland Inness had rallied the Invalid Company and they had decimated a troop of Flemish mercenaries lying in ambush.

When news of this reached London, these broken men, so recently objects of disdain, became instant legends. Drunken men sang rousing songs of the band of cripples who had beaten the hated mercenaries. For Finch, the Invalid Company seemed to offer him a way to fill the void. He had ridden the breadth of England to find them in Chester and soon thereafter had returned to London where he had helped Lady Millicent ferret out a

French spy. Jamie Finch looked like a boy, but all who knew him, knew he was a steady man and deadly in a fight.

Finch swung out of the saddle and Roland clapped him on the shoulder.

"Good to see you, Jamie! What news from Chester."

Finch smiled at Roland and nodded a greeting toward Sir Edgar.

"Doubt you'll like it, sir. The Earl requires your presence. He says you are to come with all necessary gear to take the field."

Roland furrowed his brow.

"That's it?"

"Aye, sir. He said he would have need of your services for some length of time and you were to pack accordingly."

Sir Edgar shook his head.

"Just like an Earl to be uselessly vague."

"When am I to report, Jamie?"

"He says you're to come with 'due haste', sir."

Roland sighed.

"Very well. Come along. Lady Millicent will be happy to see you. Are you hungry?"

"Aye, sir. Rode most of the night, till the track got too rough for the horse in the dark—and took no time for breakfast when it started to show light. The Earl said I was to make haste."

Roland draped an arm over the tired young man's shoulders.

"We'll leave in an hour, but have some breakfast first. Edgar, have the stable hand saddle The Grey."

Sir Edgar nodded and trudged off toward the stables.

The grey gelding had been a wedding gift from Lady Millicent and Roland had come to appreciate the choice over the past year. The animal was no warhorse and he was glad of it. The gelding was smaller than the massive destriers and could outrun any of those big brutes, but he was big for a palfrey. What's more, the horse had proven to be even-tempered, sure-footed and tireless.

Roland had never sat a horse until he was fourteen and had learned to ride as a squire from an expert—his own wife-to-be. He had not been an apt student, but, of necessity, had grown competent enough in the saddle, learning to fight from horseback, as any knight was expected to do. But at heart, Roland would always be a bowman. And for that, the big steady gelding was perfect. Over time he'd come to love the good-tempered horse, but had not come up with a suitable name for the animal. After a while, the gelding became known simply as "The Grey" to everyone at Danesford. He thought the name suited.

***

Millicent was happy to see her old friend Jamie Finch, but not happy with the news that he brought. Roland could see the tightness at the corners of her mouth that gave her away. She had Cook bring an extra plate to feed the young messenger and, for a few minutes, the two cheerfully recalled their adventures together in London trying to flush out a French spy in William Marshall's household. It had turned out that the spy was real enough, but had been only a cat's paw for a more dangerous agent close to Archbishop Walter of Coutances.

"Master Finch had to drag me though a bawdy house to finally run the treacherous clerk to ground," she said and laughed. Roland grinned at her. He had heard the story before, but he was pleased for anything that would lighten the mood of his leave-taking.

Breakfast and packing took little more than an hour. Finch left to see to a new mount and Roland lingered at the door while Millie stuffed a final pair of woollen stockings into a bag. Leaning against the wall were two unstrung warbows he'd fashioned with his own hands and a quiver with fifty good arrows—half with bodkin heads that could rip through mail or plate armour at close range.

He had already belted a short sword around his waist and, in his boot, was a long dagger with a small ruby in the hilt—a long ago reminder of an assassin sent by Earl William de Ferrers to kill him. Ivo Brun's bones were somewhere at the bottom of the Thames now, but the Earl still lived—a fact that nettled the young knight whenever his mind touched on it.

On the floor at his feet was his mail jerkin, rolled and secured with a leather strap. He had not worn the mail in a year and was surprised to find it glistening.

"Lorea and I took it down to the bar on the river a week ago and scoured it from one end to the other," Millicent said. "It was fearfully rusted." Her words had been spoken lightly, but with an unmistakable hint of sadness. "Perhaps I should have taken it as an omen."

Roland looked back at his wife and for the thousandth time thought what a lucky man he was. He walked back to her and gently grasped her hands, which had been aimlessly sorting through his kit. She looked up at him, her eyes shining. He pulled her close

"I won't cry," she murmured into his shoulder.

"I know you won't. You are a soldier's wife."

Roland stepped back and reached inside his tunic. He pulled out a silver talisman with a spreading English yew carved on its surface. It had been a gift from a twelve-year-old Millicent de Laval to remind him of home—the day before he followed her father off to the Crusade.

"This has always brought me luck, Millie. It won't fail me now."

***

Roland sat astride The Grey and looked down at his wife.

"Millie, I'll send word to you when I know where I'm bound. Tell Oren and Lorea I'm sorry that there was no time for farewells."

His brother Oren's farmstead was an hour's ride to the west along the Weaver. Like every man among the Danes who had wielded a bow in the defence of Chester, Oren had been given a hide of good farm land in the river valley. Roland's sister, Lorea, lived here at Danesford and had attached herself tightly to Millicent since she had arrived, but just the day before they had left her with Oren for a long-planned visit.

Jamie Finch was already edging his horse toward the gate. Roland leaned down and grasped Millicent's hand.

"Trust to Edgar and to Oren while I'm gone and you'll be all right."

Millicent Inness gave him a little smile.

"And what of you?"

28

"I'll be back. I promise."

These were the words soldiers always spoke to their wives when they were leaving for a fight—and where else would a soldier be going?

Not to pick daisies, she thought.

Millicent let her hand fall away and watched her husband and Jamie Finch ride out. She ran across the small dirt courtyard and climbed the ladder to the wall walk on the south side of the palisade. A cold north wind blew her long brown hair across her face, and she snatched it back in time to watch Roland and The Grey disappear into the valley of the Weaver. Only then did she cry.

Chester

*T*he winter sun had passed to the west of the Northgate tower when the two riders neared Chester. Roland looked around him as they approached the walls of the city from the north. Much had happened in this innocent looking patch of cleared ground. It was here that he and his Danes had rained fire down upon the siege engines of the mercenary force that besieged the city for months. Here it was that he had unhorsed Earl William de Ferrers with a bowshot that men still spoke of in awe. The distance had been over two hundred yards and his arrow had struck the Earl's helmet as he fled the field. The blow rendered the nobleman senseless, though the wound was not mortal.

As he rode past the spot where de Ferrers had been struck and unhorsed, Roland thought of the other chance he had had to kill the man who had murdered his father. De Ferrers had fled the field after the battle at Towcester, but he had ridden the man down. All that saved the Earl that day was ancient custom. The coward had thrown himself on the mercy of the King and Earl William Marshall had ordered that he be spared and face the King's judgement.

To everyone's shock, Richard had simply banished him from England. De Ferrers was now somewhere in Brittany, living comfortably through his exile. In three more years the banishment would end and until then, Roland's oath to kill him would likely have to wait.

The two guards who stood watch at the Northgate recognized Jamie Finch and waved the riders through. The men were unfamiliar to Roland, but it had been over a year since he had led the men of Chester in defence of their city. New members of the garrison were to be expected. The two riders clattered through the arch of the gate and into the city.

It had been six months since Roland had seen the Earl and on their several visits to Shipbrook since then, he and Millie had skirted Chester. It was not out of any desire to shirk his duty to his liege lord, but the Earl was always surrounded by men of substance who still found Roland's hill country accent amusing and who constantly jockeyed for favour. He felt ill at ease in such company and understood why Sir Roger de Laval had always steered clear of Chester when he could. Roland knew that if the Earl had need of him, he would come when summoned— as he had this day.

Once inside the walls, Finch took his leave, his task complete. Roland had come to know the city like the palm of his hand and needed no directions to the Earl's dwelling on the south side of the town. More guards met him at the entrance to Chester Castle and a stable boy took the big grey gelding to be fed and watered. As Roland entered the bailey, he was hailed.

"Sir Roland Inness, bless my soul!"

Coming across the cobbled courtyard, swinging his wooden leg as he hurried along was William Butler, know to all as Sergeant Billy. Roland grinned as the man drew near.

"Billy, good to see you! I see you are as nimble as ever!"

Sergeant Billy smiled at the young knight.

"Aye, sir. Fit as a fiddle, though getting a little thick in the middle." Then he frowned. "Garrison duty, ye know."

Roland leaned back and assessed the bulk of the man.

"We could use a man like you out on the Weaver, Billy. You'd soon be thin as a rail and healthy as an ox. The country air would be good for you."

The man lowered his eyes and shook his head.

"Ye know I'm a city lad at heart, sir. A campaign is one thing, but takin' up, permanent-like, out in the country? It's not for me!"

31

Roland laughed.

"Well the offer stands, but we can discuss it over an ale. For now, I've been summoned by the Earl so I must be off."

He started to move toward the keep, but Sergeant Billy touched his arm.

"There's been rumours about, Sir Roland. Trouble across the Dee. Are we bound for a new adventure?"

Roland shook his head. He had heard of no trouble in Wales, but it was not likely he would at his small outpost in the north of Cheshire.

"I suppose I'll know after I see His Lordship, Billy."

***

"Sir Roland! How fare my Danes up on the Weaver?" Ranulf de Blundeville, the Sixth Earl of Chester, slapped Roland on the back. The young Earl appeared to be in high good humour as he greeted his young vassal—and well he should have been. The man's stock had risen markedly since King Richard had been ransomed from the Holy Roman Emperor.

Richard's return had transformed the political landscape of the island realm. Only two years before, Ranulf had been ousted from his lands by William de Ferrers and charged with treason by Prince John, all part of the Prince's grand plan to usurp the throne from his brother. And the plan had come very near to succeeding.

While the Earl fled to Wales to escape the headman's axe, John drained the Midlands of its wealth to buy the support of key barons and to pay the wages of a mercenary army that had marched and plundered across the land unchecked for two years. Throughout, Ranulf remained steadfastly loyal to the King and in a lightning stroke had retaken his city of Chester from de Ferrers, with the help of Roland Inness and the Invalid Company.

Having retaken the city, Ranulf had to hold it as John turned his fury on the place. Chester was besieged and almost starved into submission, but the Earl would not yield. When John's mercenaries lifted the siege and marched on London, he followed, shadowing them relentlessly. His timely arrival on the field outside of Towcester to bolster William Marshall's small force had tipped the scales in that clash and dealt a death blow to John's ambitions.

Ranulf's emergence as a military leader and a man of absolute loyalty had elevated his standing in the King's eyes. When Richard began his campaign to take back the English lands treacherously seized by Philip of France during his long captivity, the Earl of Chester had been pointedly exempt from the levy of troops and left to prosper in peace—if peace could be maintained along the border with Wales.

Roland smiled at his liege lord. He had watched Ranulf grow from a pampered and indecisive young nobleman into a credible leader. Adversity had a way of paring away the surface of a man and laying bare the character beneath and Ranulf had faced adversity aplenty. The Earl might never be a great warrior like William Marshall or the King himself, but he was steady and had courage to spare. Roland liked the man.

"My lord, the Danes are content with their lot. With the Earl of Derby in exile, a few—a very few—have drifted back to the high country. Leaving behind the ground that their sires are buried in has been hard for them all, but most are well pleased with the land you have given them. The harvest was bountiful and that's all that farmers can ask."

"Good, good! I can tell you, it makes me sleep well at night knowing I have a hundred men with longbows I can call upon if my need is dire. And how does work on your fort proceed? I'm told you've named it Danesford."

"Aye, my lord, it was Lady Millicent's choice of names. The fort is complete now and sits on the only high ground near the ford. One day we hope to replace the timber palisades with stone, but for now it is secure enough to watch over the crossing of the Weaver. You must come be our guest."

The Earl smiled a genuine smile. It was useful to have the Danes with their lethal bows only twenty miles away, but it was the young knight before him that put him most at ease about his northern lands. Since first they'd met at the great archery tournament celebrating Richard's coronation, he had taken the measure of Roland Inness many times and never found him wanting. He trusted the young man completely.

"I will make a point of it! It will be a pleasure seeing Lady Millicent again. You know my head would have been on a pike above the Northgate were it not for her seeing things more clearly than I."

It was a story Roland had heard many times—of how Millicent had led the Earl out of Chester in the dead of night, just ahead of William de Ferrers' men. It was a grand tale and all too true. If caught, Ranulf would have been a dead man.

"She will be most pleased to see you as well, my lord."

"Excellent, but my visit must wait until some pressing business is attended to." The Earl's voice grew serious, indicating an end to pleasantries. Roland waited patiently to finally hear why he had been summoned.

"Your Welsh friend, Griff Connah the archer, appeared at our gates two days ago with an urgent request from his master. It seems things are coming to a head on the other side of the Dee, though Connah was not inclined to provide many details. The man's message was clear enough. Lord Llywelyn is calling in the debt I owe him. He has asked for the Invalid Company."

Ranulf did not have to explain the debt owed to Llywelyn. The Welsh rebel had sheltered him as well as Millicent and Lady Catherine for a year when there was a price on the Earl's head. He also had provided eighty Welsh longbowmen to support Ranulf's attack on Chester. Llywelyn had taken a huge gamble and made powerful enemies by supporting Ranulf against Prince John—all in the hope that Ranulf would someday repay that support in full. It seemed that day had arrived. Llywelyn had kept his part of the arrangement. Now it was Ranulf's turn.

Roland nodded.

"And I'm to go with them, my lord?"

"You will command them, Sir Roland. Llywelyn asked for you by name, but I would have sent for you in any event. The men trust you and so do I."

"I am honoured by your trust, my lord—and by theirs. I will do my best."

"I'm certain you will, sir, but it is no simple task I am giving you. To begin with, there is the current situation with the Invalid Company."

"Situation, my lord?"

"Aye, situation indeed. It seems the men of the Invalid Company are not so well-suited for garrison duty. The bishop was just in to see me a week ago. There's been a bawdy house opened but a block away from St. Mary's on the Hill and by all accounts their profits come entirely from the Invalids. His excellency is most put out. And there have been other—*incidents*—here in the city." The Earl made a face.

"The upright folk of Chester have started to complain. It's to the point that I was seriously considering dispatching the Invalids to France. No doubt the King would make good use of them, but I doubt I would ever have got them back. And who knows when I might have need of men such as they again?"

The Earl paused for a long moment, then spoke again.

"Never doubt my regard for the Invalids, Sir Roland. You brought these men to me in my hour of greatest need and they proved their mettle more than once. There are none like them anywhere in England. But, I must say, this request from Llywelyn is timely. I can discharge my debt and get the Invalids back into the field where they belong, but have a care. I would not have the Invalid Company, *my* Invalid Company, destroyed to serve a Welshman's ambitions. Is that clear?"

"Aye, my lord—clear enough."

Earl Ranulf put a hand on Roland's shoulder.

"I know you will be anxious to make your preparations, but before attending to your duties, I must confide something else to you. My spies tell me that Llywelyn's strength has grown. He now commands over seven hundred men. His uncle, Lord Daffyd, has retreated from the interior of Gwynedd to the lowlands. It seems our bold young prince may be winning his long war, though this new request leaves some room for doubt. Daffyd has ruled the lands that border my own for ten years now and he has shown no inclination to directly threaten my interests. In many ways, he has been as good a neighbour as an Earl of Chester could hope for."

The Earl paused to let the young knight absorb the point he was making.

"I would not like to see all of Gwynedd ruled by one man, Sir Roland. Owain Gwynedd, Llywelyn's grandsire, did so in my father's time and gave Earl Hugh nothing but trouble. So, you can appreciate, I'd not want an ambitious man as my neighbour. And there is always the possibility that, even with your aid, Llywelyn may not prevail. If that is the case, it would ill serve me with the victors to have taken the field in his support."

Roland did not respond at once. This was no straightforward mission his liege lord was handing him. He was being ordered to aid Llywelyn, but not to sacrifice his men and not to do it so well that the Welshman became a threat to his own lord— that was plain enough. How to do all that, without revealing Ranulf's involvement, was not clear at all.

"I will do the best I can, my lord," he said, trying to conceal his unease.

Earl Ranulf cocked an eyebrow, but then smiled.

"You remind me of your old master, Sir Roger. There is a man who hates politics—and I see you like it no more than he. But don't worry—just trust to your judgment and bring me back my Invalids."

Roland managed a weak smile.

"Aye, my lord."

The Earl slapped him on his shoulder to signal the end of the meeting and together they walked toward the door.

"I've promised the man Connah that you would be prepared to ride in two days. He has remained in the city and will be your guide when you have the men ready."

***

Sergeant Billy was waiting for him outside the keep, anxious to hear the truth behind all the rumours that had been about.

"Are we to march?"

Roland nodded curtly, still trying to sort through the tangle of advice his Earl had just given him.

"Aye, Billy. Where will I find Patch?"

Patch was Thomas Marston, a veteran of the crusade who had lost an eye at Arsuf and who was something of an unofficial leader of the Invalids. Sergeant Billy looked up at the sun and mumbled something under his breath. Roland turned on him and saw an abashed look on the man's face.

"Well? Out with it. Where is he?"

Sergeant Billy cleared his throat, resigned that he must now reveal his comrade's whereabouts.

"I'd expect, this time a' day, he'd be over to the Ram's Head."

Roland knew the place. It was the foulest tavern within the walls of the city. It favoured sour ale and rancid food, but it was cheap.

"For God's sake, Billy, it's mid-afternoon."

Sergeant Billy shrugged sheepishly.

"Aye, sir. I know it and so does Patch, I imagine."

The Earl had warned him that the Invalids had not adapted to the tedium of garrison duty, but if Patch was drinking at midafternoon....

Roland headed for the main gate of the bailey. The Ram's Head was just down the hill toward the Shipgate. He beckoned for his companion to follow.

"Let's go get him, Billy."

***

Patch was not fully in his cups when they arrived and seemed only mildly surprised to see Roland and Sergeant Billy forcing their way through the crowded, dim interior of the Ram's Head.

"So, the rumours are true!" he shouted as the two men approached. "We are off to Wales!" This announcement he punctuated by upturning a mug of ale and draining it.

Roland stood in front of the man for a long moment. The tavern stood a stone's throw from the Bridgegate. Patch had been with him the night they had stormed the Bridgegate tower and hauled up the portcullis, opening the way for Ranulf and a hundred armoured horsemen to thunder into the city. A better fighter and braver man he did not know. He owed the man much, but this....

"Tom, I'm going to the barracks now."

37

Patch started to reply, but saw the look on Roland's face and fell silent. He set the mug on the table and his shoulders sagged.

"Roland, I...ye'll not like what ye see there."

"Don't like what I see here either, Tom, but let's be off."

Patch gave a great sigh and stood up—a little unsteadily.

"Aye, sir."

***

The first thing that struck him was the smell. The gutter outside the barracks stank of piss and vomit and the aroma did not improve as he entered the dim interior of the place. From somewhere near the far end of the building, he heard a woman shriek and then laugh. He turned and glared at Patch.

"What's all this, Tom?" he asked, a wave of his hand taking in the squalor of the scene.

Patch had a pained look. The walk up the hill from the tavern in the cold air had done much to clear the man's head.

"It's the duty, sir. These ain't garrison troops. Too much temptation, and guardin' the walls of Chester ain't kept 'em sharp. A few have soldiered well enough, but the rest...? I gave up a couple a' months ago tryin' to keep 'em in line."

Roland felt his temper rise. These men had once been scorned as cripples and drunkards by their countrymen, but in the recent civil war, they had gained a reputation as the most feared unit loyal to the King. Time and again, the Invalid Company had faced and defeated mercenaries paid for by Prince John.

Now this.

In the first alcove he came to, a man lay face down, snoring. He kicked him in the backside and the soldier simply groaned, curled onto his side and returned to snoring. Roland turned back to Patch.

"Turn them out! Now!" he snarled.

"Aye, sir!"

Roland stepped back outside and moved up the street away from the stench. From the barracks, he could hear Patch roaring his orders and, after a bit, men began to stumble into the street, blinking in the midday sun. From a side door, he saw two women fly into an alley and quickly disappear. Slowly, men formed into two ragged lines, some leaning on each other for support.

This was the feared Invalid Company.

It looked more like a gathering of beggars than a band of warriors to be feared. Roland let them stand there in the cold for a long time. He counted heads—ninety-two. He knew some would be missing from the muster, either on guard duty, if that was still expected of this rabble, or more likely in a tavern or gutter somewhere within the walls.

"Sergeant Billy, I will want you to see to horses. We'll need good ones where we're going and mules as well, enough to carry a fortnight of rations. I doubt there will be much forage south of the Dee. We will ride out at dawn."

"Aye, sir."

Having shouted the men into some semblance of order, Patch presented himself to Roland. There was no longer any sign of drunkenness in his bearing.

"You will see to these *men*, Patch. Any one of them not ready to mount and ride at first light will be left behind. I do not think the people of Chester will be hospitable to stragglers."

"Aye, sir."

"That's all."

Roland turned on his heel and walked away.

***

He found Griff Connah in a more respectable inn near the Eastgate. He hadn't seen the Welshman since Griff had made a surprise appearance at his wedding the year before. But he had no trouble spotting the tall, rangy archer sitting alone with his back to the wall and his eyes on the door. He walked over and pulled up a stool.

"Welcome back to England. Stolen any cattle?" he said as he sat.

Griff laughed. The Welsh were infamous for coveting and carrying off English cows.

"Thank you for asking! I intend to gather a few fat heifers on the ride out!"

Roland grinned and extended his hand, which the Welshman grasped and pumped vigorously.

"How is it with the marriage, young English?" he asked. "Good?"

Roland smiled. Griff liked to refer to him as English, though many Englishmen would think of him as a Dane first. To the Welsh, anyone from beyond the Dee was English.

"Very good, Griff. You should try it."

The Welshman hooted.

"Not for me! Certainly, not until all the fightin' is done."

"Then you'll go to your grave a bachelor, my friend, for when is the fighting ever done?"

Griff shook his head.

"Never, and a good thing too, or men like you and I would be forever stuck behind a plough."

"I'd be happy to be back behind a plough, but that is not what the Earl has summoned me for. Perhaps you can shed some light on what we are to do for your lord."

Griff looked to his right and left, then leaned in.

"Too many ears hereabouts," he said, sliding out from behind the table. "Walk out with me."

The inn sat near the eastern wall of the town and the two made their way up stone steps to the wall walk. Over the rooftops of Chester, they could see the Earl's castle perched on its hill to the southwest and the tower that overlooked the Watergate opposite them. They began a slow stroll north along the wall.

"So, what is the situation with Lord Llywelyn?" Roland asked. "We all knew he would one day call in Earl Ranulf's debt, but why now?"

"Because things have now reached a tipping point," the tall Welshman answered without breaking stride. "We have grown stronger in the last year. We've driven Daffyd from the interior of his lands to a strip along the coast. He knows we are winning and ten days ago he offered Llywelyn land for peace."

"And Llywelyn refused his uncle's offer?"

"The offer was shit. You know the land along the west bank of the Dee could be rich farmland, but the Princes of Gwynedd claim it as do the Earls of Chester. Much blood has been spilt between them over this land. No plough turns the earth there."

"And that's what Daffyd offered."

"Aye."

Roland nodded.

"Not a very valuable parcel under present circumstances and it would place your master squarely between his uncle and our Earl of Chester. It's a good place to get trampled upon."

"Yes."

"So Llywelyn said no."

"He did not give them an answer, and maybe they didn't expect one, for they tried to kill us shortly after the offer was made."

"They?"

"Aye, Llywelyn believes that Roderic, who rules west of the River Conwy, has decided that we are now a threat to him and has thrown in with Daffyd. The men who ambushed us flew no banners, so we can't be sure…"

"Roderic and Daffyd are brothers, are they not?"

"Aye, and half-brothers to Llywelyn's father."

"It's a complicated family."

"Ye've said a mouthful there, English!" Griff said, with a rueful laugh.

Roland stopped and gazed over the battlements toward the west. The sun was creeping toward the Irish Sea and the breeze was stiff from that quarter. He thought about all the blood that had been shed in the dispute within England's own royal family. Richard had risen twice against his father, King Henry, and his final rebellion had driven the old man to his grave. Then, Richard's own brother had come within a hair's breadth of snatching the crown from his head while he was a prisoner of the Holy Roman Emperor. He looked back at Griff.

"Fights between blood kin tend to spill a lot of unrelated blood."

"True enough," Griff said, "and there will be no end to it in Gwynedd until Llywelyn rules all—or is dead."

"What would he have us do?"

Griff shook his head.

"He didn't say. I'm not sure he knows yet. Before we parted, Llywelyn told me his uncles would likely move against our winter quarters, expecting the Prince to be dead or at least on the run. He hoped to reach our men before they did."

"And if they have done as he expects?"

"Then he will have beaten them or, failing that…" The tall Welshman paused for a long time before he spoke again, as though unwilling to consider this possibility.

"There is a place in the mountains to the south. It's remote and almost impossible to attack. I've been there, but in the seven years we've fought the uncles, we've never had to rely on it. I'm praying it's not that bad, but we won't know until we are back in Gwynedd."

Griff paused again, gathering his thoughts.

"Whatever we find over the Dee, English, I know this. Our need is urgent as was your Earl's not many years ago. You and your Invalids could tip things in our favour. How soon can you ride?"

"We will ride at first light."

Griff arched an eyebrow.

"I've seen some of the men of the company. They looked…"

"Unfit."

"To put it kindly."

"I *will* have them fit before we cross the Dee, Griff, but they will not improve here in Chester. Too much to tempt them, so we will ride at first light. But I'm curious—why did Llywelyn ask for me?"

Griff laughed.

"He likes you!" the Welshman said and slapped Roland on the shoulder. "And he well remembers the charge you led with your Invalids that saved us in the Conwy valley. He thinks you are a man who understands war—and he thinks you are lucky."

Roland wondered at that. In his short life, he had survived fights with Welsh raiders, Saracens, Moors, Berbers and mercenaries, but did he truly understand war?

Or had he just been…lucky?

42

Muster of the Invalids

The sky was still pitch black when Roland rose and gathered his weapons and kit. He had taken a room at the inn where Griff was quartered, but saw no sign of the Welshman as he came down the stairs and made his way through the darkened tavern to the street. Connah knew where and when the Invalids were to assemble and Roland didn't doubt he would be ready to ride when the time came to depart the city.

The Grey was stabled around the corner and the horse's ears perked up when Roland came to his stall with a saddle. He patted the gelding on the neck as he threw a light blanket over its back and secured the bridle. Once saddled, he led the animal out into the dark lane. He held the reins loosely and The Grey followed obediently as he headed toward Northgate. The streets were empty at this hour and the sound of the horse's iron-shod hooves echoed sharply from the buildings crowding in on both sides.

The wind that had blown steadily the day before had died completely and the night was still and cold. No sign of dawn showed in the east and brilliant stars hung in a clear black sky. He looked overhead and saw the pattern in the star field that his father had called the Plough. His eyes travelled in a line from two of its bright points toward the north wall of Chester. There, hanging high above the Northgate, was a star brighter than the rest. The sight was comforting. Many things were uncertain in this world, but the northern star stayed steady and true.

He had ordered Patch to have the Invalid Company mounted and ready to ride from the Northgate at first light. He rounded a corner onto Barn Lane and stopped. A hundred yards to his front he saw a column of mounted men.

The Invalid Company had mustered.

Given what he had seen the day before, Roland had wondered if Patch could actually assemble the men, but here they were. As he drew nearer, he saw that it wasn't a pretty sight. Riders slumped in the saddle and one man leaned over and retched on the cobbled street without dismounting. He felt the heat start to rise in his face as he watched this display.

Roland stopped The Grey and mounted. Near the head of the column, he could see Patch and Sergeant Billy in deep conversation just inside the arch of the Northgate. The two men looked up as the sound of hooves on cobbles reached them, but Roland ignored them as he rode past. He walked his horse slowly down the length of the column, looking at each man as he passed.

These were men who had been the scourge of Prince John's professional mercenaries. Englishmen sang songs of their deeds in taverns. He wondered what songs would be sung if their countrymen could see them now?

As he rode slowly along the line, he saw many familiar faces, but there were some newcomers. Halfway down the column he came to a giant of a man—bigger even than Sir Edgar—with one side of his face deeply scarred from burns.

Greek fire.

He'd seen men die screaming before the walls of Acre when they had been engulfed by that strange flame that clung to whatever it touched. Somehow this man had survived, though with a fright mask for a face. Unlike most of his fellow Invalids, the big man seemed fully alert and ready to go on campaign. Across his saddle rested a five-foot long pike with a wicked-looking axe blade on one end. Roland had never seen such a weapon. He made a mental note to acquaint himself with this new man.

A few ranks behind the giant was another stranger. This man met Roland's gaze with a dark look. He was missing an arm at the elbow, which was not unusual among the Invalids, but everything else about this rider set him apart. He did not slump in the saddle and sat astride a beautiful black warhorse that could only belong to someone of substantial wealth. His mail was of exceptionally fine quality and the helmet on his head had been buffed to a high sheen. Obviously, this was a man of some means, but something in his look spoke of a simmering anger.

Another man to get acquainted with.

As he completed his circuit of the column, only a few of the other men met his gaze and no more than a dozen looked prepared to go to war. Jamie Finch was one such, though he looked a bit shame-faced at the company he was keeping. Roland nodded at the young Londoner as he rode by. His inspection complete, he guided his mount back to the Northgate and dismounted. Patch stepped forward and waited nervously.

"How many?" Roland asked.

"One hundred seven, sir. Six men could not be accounted for."

Roland nodded.

"We'll leave them behind."

He turned to Sergeant Billy.

"How are we on mules and rations?"

The one-legged veteran took out a small scroll and handed it over. He could not read, but had the Earl's steward write down the supplies he had been issued. He might not be able to decipher the writing on the scroll, but he had counted things himself.

"Nine mules and dry rations for two weeks, sir."

Roland unrolled the parchment and saw that Billy's count agreed with that of the Earl's man. He turned back to Patch.

"Weapons? Mail?"

Patch still looked uncomfortable.

"Every man is armed, Sir Roland, but I cannot speak to the condition of their weapons. Haven't seen a blade sharpened for months. Most have mail, though it be rusty, and all but a few have shields." Roland looked back down the long double column of men that disappeared into the gloom of Northgate Street and was at least comforted to see that every man had a helmet, of sorts, on his head.

He gave Patch a curt nod and was about to give the order to move out when a man came clattering up from the rear of the column on a tall, spindly horse. The rider was a match for the horse—tall and bone-thin and wearing the robes of a monk.

"My lord!" he called out cheerfully, a gap-toothed smile plastered across a face that was as sharp as an axe blade. He hauled in the reins of his mount and the horse proceeded to skitter across the cobbles and almost trample the men standing beside the column. The cheerful grin turned to a look of stricken horror as Patch and Sergeant Billy scrambled for safety.

"Oh damn!" the man cried as the horse managed to regain its footing and stop six feet from the scattering men. Accident averted, the tall monk slithered down the side of the horse and onto the street. He hurriedly crossed himself and turned to Roland.

"I beg pardon, my lord," he said, a little unsteadily. "My mount is a bit too spirited."

Roland looked sceptically at the bony nag, then turned his attention to the priest.

"Come to see us off with a blessing, father?"

The man nodded his head vigorously.

"Yes…eh…no."

"Well, which is it?" Roland asked with just a touch of irritation in his voice. Over the man's shoulder, he could see the first lightening of the sky above the eastern wall. It was time to ride.

The man smiled sheepishly.

"I will of course provide a blessing, my lord, but I will be riding with you. I am the company chaplain."

Roland turned and gave Patch and Sergeant Billy a look.

"Chaplain?"

Billy shrugged, but Patch spoke up.

"This is Friar Cyril, Sir Roland. He appeared among us last spring and has provided spiritual counsel to the men."

Roland arched an eyebrow.

"Do you say Mass for the men, father?"

The churchman looked at the ground and rubbed his hands nervously.

"Mass, my lord? Well, no. Not for some time. Attendance has been…sparse. But I have found a way to serve God and be useful to my comrades—I hope."

Sergeant Billy eased up beside Roland and whispered to him.

"Father Cyril patrols the taverns and helps the boys find their way home by morning, sir. He also intercedes with the Bishop when…complaints are lodged."

"Why does he do that?" Roland whispered back.

Billy shrugged.

"Never got a clear answer from him, sir. But the boys like the fellow."

Roland turned back to the skinny monk.

"You should stay here, father. There's no place for a priest where we are heading."

The man stiffened.

"You go to fight, do you not, my lord?"

Roland nodded.

"Likely."

"Then where better for a priest to be than where men are about to meet their maker."

Roland gave the man a long look, then shrugged.

"Suit yourself, but if you don't keep up, or if you cause any trouble, we will leave you wherever we are. And you do not want to be left behind in Wales, Friar."

The man smiled broadly.

"I'll be no trouble, my lord. You'll see."

Roland once more surveyed the column. The entire length of it, stretching down Northgate Street, was now visible in the approaching dawn. He looked to the front of the line of riders and saw a man holding a staff. At its top, a black banner stirred, as a stray breeze found its way through the open Northgate.

"What is that?" Roland said pointing at the flag.

Sergeant Billy stumped over to the rider and took the shaft from him, lowering it for Roland to examine. Emblazoned on the black field was a grey wolf's head. The beast's face was fixed in a snarl with bared fangs and there were deep scars around its muzzle. One ear was half gone.

"It's our banner, sir," Billy said proudly. "The men wanted one of their own to take into battle. Seamstress over on Eastgate Street did the head."

Roland took the black cloth in his hands. The wolf's image was finely done. The animal's red eyes seemed to look right into his own. He handed the banner and staff back to Billy.

"Put it away."

"Sir?"

Roland looked once more at the men lined up in the dawn. Another leaned over and tried to heave, but nothing was left to come forth. He started to speak, but Patch spoke first.

"You heard Sir Roland. Put it away, Billy."

The old sergeant gave a little sigh, but did not protest. He unknotted the cloth from the shaft, carefully folded it and tucked it inside his tunic.

Roland turned to Patch.

"Lead them out," he ordered.

"Bound for?"

"Shipbrook," he said, nodding toward the column of half-awake men. "This lot isn't ready for Wales."

***

Griff was waiting just outside the Northgate when the Invalids rode out of Chester. No doubt, the Welshman had seen the men groaning and puking in their ranks and had not wished to embarrass his English friend by being present for such a spectacle.

"We go to the crossing at Shipbrook?" he asked, as Roland reined in beside him and let the column ride past.

"Aye, but we won't cross this day—or the next."

Griff started to protest, put Roland raised a hand.

"I know your master would not have sent for us unless the need was urgent, but you saw the men. They are useless in their present condition."

"But…."

Roland turned on the Welshman.

"Understand me, Griff. We will pay the Earl's debt and with interest I expect, but these men," he said, nodding toward the

48

column as it passed them by, "must be ready to fight. If they are not, they will die and be of no use to Llywelyn or the Earl."

Just then a man in the column almost toppled out of his saddle but managed to grab his horse's mane and pull himself back up. Griff shook his head.

"I take your point, English. But we can't tarry long."

"That's why we make for Shipbrook, Griff. It won't take long for Roger de Laval and Declan O'Duinne to reacquaint these men with soldiering."

***

Roland sent Jamie Finch ahead with a message for Sir Roger and when the Invalid Company emerged from the trees east of Shipbrook just before noon, Roland's old master was there to greet them. By his side was his Master of the Sword, Sir Declan O'Duinne. Roland ordered the column to halt and spurred forward to meet the man who had saved his life—many times over. Griff followed close behind.

"My lord, you look well!" he called as he reined in.

Sir Roger was mounted on his new warhorse, a young roan stallion with thick muscled shoulders and haunches. The animal pricked up its ears as Roland came near and gave a warning snort for The Grey to stay clear. Roland laughed as he halted the big gelding a respectful distance away.

"I see Tencendur's mood has not mellowed."

Sir Roger reddened as the warhorse fought against its reins and edged toward Roland's mount, malice in its white eyes. The roan's sire was a magnificent warhorse that Roland had taken from a dead Flemish mercenary. Declan had dubbed that horse "The Surly Beast" for its foul temper, but Llywelyn had been smitten the moment he saw the animal. It mattered not to him that the horse was truculent. He cared only that it was a fighter and a proper mount for a prince. Roland had been happy to throw the unruly stallion into a bargain with Llywelyn for eighty Welsh archers to help retake Chester for Earl Ranulf.

The year before, Llywelyn had presented Roland and Millicent with the first foal sired by The Surly Beast as a wedding gift. Roland had gladly gifted the animal to his old master, who

49

had lost his beloved horse, Bucephalus, to a farmer in the high Alps. Sir Roger proudly named the little stallion Tencendur. It had been the name of Emperor Charlemagne's great warhorse. The big Norman lavished attention on the young horse, but it seemed Tencendur had inherited his sire's truculent temperament.

Sir Roger hauled back harder on the reins. Tencendur nickered at the other horses, but finally settled. Declan O'Duinne sat his horse casually and tried to suppress a laugh. The horse under control, Roland made his introductions.

"My lord, may I present Griff Connah. He and his Welsh archers helped us take back Chester from de Ferrers."

Sir Roger nodded at the newcomer.

"Yer welcome here at Shipbrook, Master Connah, and my thanks for your service to my Earl. There was a good deal of mischief done in these parts while I was away with the King on Crusade. I appreciate the help ye gave these two lads," he said, gesturing to Roland and Declan.

"Thank you, Sir Roger," Griff said. "I but served Prince Llywelyn. I am happy to see Shipbrook has been rebuilt. It was a shame what they did to your home."

The big Norman knight frowned at the memory.

"Aye, those were bad days, sir, but better ones are ahead, I pray." Greetings dispensed with, he turned back to Roland.

"It's good to see you, lad. How fares my daughter?" he asked, trying not notice his young mount had curled its upper lip and was showing white teeth at the other horses.

"She is well, my lord, and sends you her warmest greetings."

"Good, good."

Never one for dawdling over pleasantries, Sir Roger turned to business.

"You can billet the men on either side of the road outside the gate. Not nearly enough room inside to hold 'em. I gathered from your message that they have lost their edge." The big knight paused and looked at the ragged column drawn up behind his son-in-law. "I see I was not mistaken! When would you wish Sir Declan and I to commence our ministrations on this sorry looking lot?"

Roland looked over his shoulder at the men of the Invalid Company. They were about to receive a rude reminder of what it meant to be a soldier.

"Straight away, my lord. I will have Patch detail a few of them to make camp. The rest...they are at your disposal."

"Good! Have the lads dismount and join us over to the northwest field. We have a pile of good ash staves there. Just the thing to get them back in a fighting mood!"

Roland nodded, then turned to signal Patch forward. He issued quick orders then edged his horse toward Declan.

"Don't go easy on these boys, Dec. They are good men all, but seem to have forgotten who they are."

Declan reached over and clasped hands with Roland.

"I'll sweat the ale out of them, even in this cold, Roland. Ye can be sure of that. Then I'll be wanting all the news from Danesford."

"And you shall have it, but for now, I must go pay my respects to Lady Catherine."

Behind him Patch was bawling orders. Men dismounted stiffly and led their horses to a chest-high picket line that was stretched between poles off to the left of the road. Sergeant Billy and the most fit men were detailed to make camp and rode off toward the gate of Shipbrook, with the supply mules in their wake. On foot, Patch led the Invalids toward the frozen, stubbled field that lay off to the northwest.

None looked eager to get there.

***

Lady Catherine de Laval greeted Roland at the top of the stone steps that led up to the fine wood frame manor house near the south wall of Shipbrook. The place had been burnt to ashes by William de Ferrers two years before, but a new structure had risen over the old foundations, grander than the original. Roland always felt a rush of fond memories anytime he passed through the gates of this place. He had been brought here five years ago as a fourteen-year-old fugitive on the run from the Earl of Derby. Sir Roger and Lady Catherine had taken him in and had made Shipbrook his home. It was a kindness he would never forget.

The mistress of Shipbrook had a warm smile on her face as she watched him bound up the steps. Roland noted a few more fine lines around her eyes, but she remained a handsome woman and no doubt as formidable as ever she was. One did not cross Lady Catherine de Laval without consequences.

"My lady," Roland said and gave her a deep bow. "It is good to see you."

Lady Catherine extended her hand and Roland took it in his.

"Sir Roland, you are looking well! Marriage seems to agree with you."

Roland couldn't help but flush a bit.

"Aye, my lady, it does. Your daughter sends her fond greetings."

Lady Catherine nodded and withdrew her hand.

"Come inside. This wind is chilling and we have much to discuss."

Roland followed the tall woman into the manor house as she called for a servant to bring food and ale. The table in the main hall was larger than the one lost in the fire, but she brushed by it and led him to a set of chairs arrayed in front of the hearth. A low fire was crackling there, keeping the chill away. Roland settled in and looked up at the high timbered ceiling.

"It's a grand home, my lady."

Lady Catherine laughed.

"The King and the Earl have been generous, but I miss the old place. This one has no memories yet."

"You will make new ones here, I'm sure, my lady, but, tell me, how are things with you?

Catherine smiled.

"It is always well with me when my husband is home and safe—at least as safe as he can be along this border. All of the strife in Wales has begun to spill over onto our side of the Dee of late. I've heard that our friend Prince Llywelyn is winning, but with Daffyd losing his grip along the border, the old habits of the Welsh have reappeared. Roger and Declan have had to chase cattle thieves back across the Dee twice in December and once already in January. They are hungry over there, Roland, and men need to feed their families. So the raids will continue until some kind of peace can be found in Gwynedd."

Roland listened carefully. Lady Catherine was a dedicated collector of information flowing across the borderlands and all such news would be helpful where he was going.

"How fares Sir Roger?"

A fond smile played across Lady Catherine's face.

"He is not a young man any more, Roland. He leans a bit more on Declan for the patrolling these days. His years in the east aged him—aged you all, I would guess—and the arm he broke the day he fought his way back to Chester still troubles him." She paused for a second, then arched an eyebrow. "But I'd not bet against him in a fight."

"Never," said Roland with a smile.

Lady Catherine chuckled, then leaned toward him.

"So, what are you about, Roland? What brings you here with the Invalids—you're too late for the Twelfth Night celebration!"

"No, my lady, there will be no celebrations where we are going. You know well the debt owed to Llywelyn by the Earl. We are payment for that."

Lady Catherine gave a little sigh.

"I guessed as much. Armed men do not come to Shipbrook lest they are going to Wales or coming from there. What is your charge?"

"The Earl said that I was to lead the Invalids in support of the Prince, though even Griff Connah does not seem to know his master's plans for us."

"Is that all that Ranulf told you?"

"No, my lady. He reminded me that there has been peace between him and Lord Daffyd along this stretch of the Welsh Marches for years and that Daffyd is no threat to his interests. He is not so sure about Llywelyn."

Lady Catherine rose and stepped toward the fire. She stretched out her long slender hands to the warmth and looked over her shoulder at the young knight. He'd changed much since she'd first met him as a ragged, skinny boy trailing after her husband like a stray dog. She had been sceptical of his loyalty and his worth, but Roland Inness had more than proven himself in her eyes. Now the young man was about to step into very murky water.

"Roland, you and I spoke many times when you were a squire about the nature of the Welsh. My family has been bound up with them since the time of my grandsire, Edric the Wild. The Welsh are brave and passionate folk, Roland, poets and warriors, but…"

She hesitated for a long moment, searching for words, then continued.

"Let me tell you two stories that might be of help to you. After King William slaughtered so many of your people in the harrowing of the north, Edric allied himself with the Welsh to resist the Normans here in the west. Together, they held back the Conqueror's armies for over three years. But in the end, the Welsh betrayed my grandsire to the Normans, who took him in chains to London. There, he wasted away and died in prison."

Roland nodded. He thought back to the many lessons he had received from Lady Catherine on the history of this land—none of which he had known of as a boy in Derbyshire. Everything the woman taught him had helped him survive in a brutal world. And, with Lady Catherine, there was always a lesson within the lesson.

"So, the Welsh are not to be trusted…"

Lady Catherine sighed.

"You will have to judge that. Alwyn Madawc was a Welshman and I trusted him with everything dear to me. We have much we owe Llywelyn and he strikes me as a man with some honour, but ambition can make men forget themselves and Llywelyn is ambitious."

"Aye, he is that, my lady. But what of the other tale?"

Lady Catherine moved away from the hearth and sat opposite him.

"Roland, you should be aware that our Earl Ranulf's ancestor, Hugh of d'Avranches, once enticed Llywelyn's great grandsire, Gruffydd ap Cynan to a parlay and treacherously seized him. Gruffydd was imprisoned in Chester Castle for ten years before finally escaping."

Roland furrowed his brow. This was a story he had not heard before.

"So, the Normans are not to be trusted…"

Catherine smiled at this.

"Excepting my husband—of course not. I'm a Saxon and you are a Dane. We understand this in our bones."

She stopped and turned serious.

"Roland, there is much history between the Princes of Gwynedd and the Earls of Chester, little of it pleasant. Earl Ranulf is a good man, but no less ambitious than Llywelyn. His honour compels him to pay this debt, his interests compel him to weigh the price. I would not like for you and your Invalids to be that price. My daughter should not be made a widow so young."

***

As he walked out of the gate of Shipbrook, Roland considered all that Lady Catherine had told him. It was troubling. War was complicated enough without the politics—though he knew the two were always bound together. He wished he had Friar Tuck along to help him sort it all out. The monk had an uncanny knack for knowing where all the pieces stood on the chess board.

Tuck had journeyed to Danesford a week before Christ's Mass to pay his newlywed friends a visit. After the King had been ransomed, he'd gone back to ministering to his flock of outcasts in the wilderness areas of Derbyshire and seemed happy with his lot. Roland had asked after Sir Robin of Loxley and that had brought a rueful laugh from the monk.

"Gone to France to join the King," Tuck said. "I knew Robin was never suited to be a peaceable country nobleman—told him that straight out when we came home from the east. He'll be happier fighting the French, if he's not killed over there. Nothing ever happens these days in Nottinghamshire. He'd be miserably bored."

The friar had spent three days with them and had delighted in playing games with Lorea, Roland's young sister. Millicent had shaken her head in wonder as the retired Knight of the Temple got down on hands and knees to whisper stories to her seven-year-old charge. The girl, who had been raised for three years by the monks of Saint Oswald's priory, would cackle with laughter and the burly monk would fairly beam with joy. In truth, Roland knew he would miss Tuck's buoyant spirit as much as his wise counsel in the days ahead.

Outside the gate, there was a buzz of activity as Sergeant Billy's detail was busily setting up camp for over a hundred men. Lady Catherine had dispatched her kitchen staff to try to make an evening meal out of the field rations the Invalids had procured. They brought root vegetables and dried beans to add to the salted meat already in the stew pots. The Shipbrook men-at-arms made themselves useful carrying wood for the cookfires and fodder for the horses. Sergeant Billy saw his commander coming and limped over to report.

"All will be ready before sundown."

In the distance, Roland could see two lines of men being led through the old sword drills he had once learned from Alwyn Madawc. No doubt Declan and Sir Roger would push those poor souls to the limit. He noticed with satisfaction that Patch had chosen the men who had been most sober at the dawn muster to make camp and escape the ordeal of the others.

"Who is the one-armed fellow with the fine clothes, Billy?" he asked, nodding toward a man using his good arm to chop wood for one of the dozen cookfires dotted around the camp. It was the finely-dressed man Roland had seen mounted on the expensive charger at the dawn muster. "Another new recruit?"

"Aye, sir. That is Sir John Blackthorne. The men call him Fancy Jack behind his back. Always looks as though he's spoilin' fer a fight, but has started nary a one. He's the best horseman in the Company and dead frightening with a blade."

"So, no one calls him Fancy Jack to his face."

"Aye, not a one. He joined us just a little after ye left with Lady Millicent for the Weaver. Bit of mystery exactly where he hails from. Keeps to himself and doesn't say much. Hasn't made any friends to speak of, but no one fancies being his enemy either. He does his duty and he stays out of trouble, which is more than I can say for a lot of the boys of late." This last he said with a jerk of his head toward the men thrusting and parrying in the far field.

"Carry on, Billy. I think I'll have a word with Fancy Jack."

Sergeant Billy arched an eyebrow, but held his tongue and stumped off toward a knot of men arguing over where to set up the one tent that had been provided to shelter supplies. Roland walked over to where Sir John was, quite efficiently, turning sizable logs into firewood. The man looked up as he approached, but did not interrupt his labours.

"Sir John, a moment, sir."

The man finished a stroke with his hand axe, and looked up.

"You are Sir Roland Inness," he said simply.

"Aye," Roland replied.

The man took a clean white cloth from inside his tailored wool shirt and mopped his brow. Then laid on with his axe once more.

"What can I do for you?" he asked as he chopped.

"In a few days, we will be crossing the Dee. I've ridden with, lived with and fought with most of the other lads in the Invalids, but you I do not know. I thought it best to remedy that before swords get crossed."

The man nodded, then wrestled another piece of wood into position.

"What would you like to know?"

"Your story. I do not recall seeing you in King Richard's camp during the late crusade. Is that where you got your wound?" he asked pointing to the missing arm.

The man shook his head.

"No, I did not take the Cross. Never left England. Is that a problem?"

There was challenge in the man's voice.

"Not to me."

The man paused from his work for moment and glanced up at Roland.

"Perhaps it would have been best if I had gone crusading."

"How so?" Roland asked, his curiosity about this man growing.

Sir John seemed to attack the log at his feet with a new fury.

57

"The rest of these boys," he said, gesturing to the small figures still at sword drill in the far field, "at least took their losses in a cause—whether it be holy or otherwise. My loss was from pure stupidity."

The man stopped for a moment to adjust the log with his foot, then spoke again.

"I am from Sheffield, Sir Roland. You know of it?"

"Aye, it's in Yorkshire, near the border with Derbyshire."

"Aye, that's the one. You know what happened at Sheffield?"

Roland nodded slowly.

"John's mercenaries pillaged the place. I was close enough to see the smoke. You lost your arm there?"

The man gave a bitter laugh.

"Arm?" he said raising the stump. "That was the least of what I lost at Sheffield. You say they pillaged and that's true enough, but first they raped and murdered. I was a fool to stay, but I was the constable of the town. It was my duty to stay. Over my protests, the burghers ordered me to open the gates. As soon as I did, those Flemish bastards cut me down with my sword still in its scabbard. I near bled to death I'm told. The surgeon took the arm but I have no memory of that. I took a fever and lay senseless for five days. So I did not see what they did to the town. When I finally managed to get to my house I found my wife…dead."

Sir John punctuated his final word with a savage blow from his axe, splitting the log cleanly in two. When he looked up, Roland could see pain and fury in the man's eyes. He recognized that pain and fury.

Was this how I looked, when my father's death was fresh?

"My pardon, sir. I did not know."

"None here do—save you, now."

The man dragged another log into place and laid a first stroke into the wood.

"So, you joined the Invalids."

"Aye. There was nothing left for me in Sheffield. No one wanted a one-armed constable and the place…I just could not stay there. I went to London. That's where I heard the stories of men—damaged men like myself—who killed mercenaries. That was good enough for me."

"But the mercenaries have sailed back to Flanders and Prince John is in exile."

"Aye, but they'll be back," he said, pure venom in every word, "and I will be waiting."

Roland did not reply at once. His own anger over the murder of his father had once burned this hot and his determination to one day avenge that crime had never waned. But time and the new happiness he'd found with Millicent had banked the fires— enough for him to have a life. In Sir John Blackthorne, he sensed a kindred spirit, if the man did not let his hatred consume him. Such a man could be dangerous and not just to his enemies. He needed to know what was at this knight's core, beyond a thirst for revenge. He cleared his throat and Sir John looked up.

"Did you know the men call you Fancy Jack?"

Sir John struck one more blow with the axe, then laid it beside the neat stack of firewood. Something akin to a smile played across his face.

"Of course, I know. Did you think these drunkards could keep a secret?"

"Sergeant Billy says they are just a bit afraid of what you can still do with your good arm."

Sir John's smile grew broader.

"Well they should be."

"One day, one of the men will have the nerve to call you Fancy Jack to your face. What will you do when that day comes?"

"It seems that day just came, Sir Roland, and you look none the worse for having done it. To be honest, I rather like the name, but let's not tell the lads that."

Roland smiled. He had his answer about Fancy Jack.

***

Satisfied with the organization of the camp, Roland rode out to the northwest field to see how the Invalids were faring. Griff rode with him and, from a distance, they could hear Sir Roger's shouted commands.

"Make ready!"

The men of the Invalid Company were arrayed in two rows facing each other. Roland watched as a hundred wooden staves were raised to a guard position. More than a few wobbled in the frosty air.

"Hold 'em steady, damn all!" he heard Sir Roger curse.

As he dismounted, he saw the big knight stomp over to where one of his charges seemed unable to hold the stave up without trembling. With a gloved hand, he wrenched the wood from the man's grasp. Unbalanced, the man staggered backwards and sat down hard on the frozen ground.

"I've seen milk maids with stronger sword arms than you men!" Sir Roger roared.

Across the way, Declan O'Duinne walked slowly along the line, shaking his head and correcting mistakes. The men of the Invalid Company knew O'Duinne well. They had followed him and Roland Inness into five battles since first laying eyes on the two at Oxford. None of them, veteran soldiers all, would have challenged the Irishman's skill with a blade.

Near the end of the line nearest him, Roland saw the giant he had first glimpsed at dawn by the Northgate. Now that they were both on foot, the true size of the man made him blink. He stood at least six and a half feet tall, had legs like tree trunks and arms like saplings. He held the stave out before him like it was a twig.

Roland walked over and stood in front of the man and could more clearly see the hideous scar that covered the left side of his face. It was as though the skin had melted like candle wax and hardened into a terrible mask.

"What is your name?"

The big man had been looking straight ahead, which is to say, well over Roland's head. He glanced down.

"Murdo, lord, Seamus Murdo."

Roland recognized the name as Scottish and the man had more than a trace of that northern accent.

"How came you by your wound, Murdo?"

The big man screwed up his face in thought.

"Which one?"

Roland wondered what other, hidden wounds, the man bore, but touched the side of his own face in answer.

"Oh, the face. Greek fire at Limassol. Never made it to the Holy Land. I'd liked to have seen the walls of Jerusalem."

"How did a Scot come to fight for an English King on crusade?"

Murdo furrowed his brow and did not answer right away. Roland waited. Finally, the man spoke.

"Had to leave the Highlands, lord. Done some things I shouldn't of."

Roland nodded. Few of the men in the Invalid Company had spotless records and it was not his business to dig up bones.

Roland studied the giant of a man. He was truly fearsome looking, but his voice was soft, almost gentle.

"Why join the Invalids?" he asked

Seamus Murdo shrugged.

"Where else could a man such as I go?"

***

As Sir Roger moved from one man to another, he had worked himself into a high dudgeon.

"Staves up! Who told ye to rest? I thought I was gettin' the Invalid Company here, not some poxy boys who can't hold up a stave!"

All the staves came up.

"Now...fight!" he roared and the field echoed to the sound of oak on oak and occasionally oak on muscle and bone left unguarded.

Roland turned to Griff.

"Seen enough?"

The tall Welshman shook his head glumly and the two mounted their horses and rode back to camp. As the sun set, Sir Roger and Declan rode in from the far field. Behind them, the Invalids straggled in on foot, bruised, sweat-soaked and weary. A few limped and more than a few cursed under their breath as they saw to their horses and gathered their kits. A dozen fires glowed in the chill air and cooks from Lady Catherine's kitchen scurried between stew pots, judging when their contents would be ready.

"How'd the men fare?" Roland called as his old master and friend dismounted.

Sir Roger laughed scornfully.

"Can't go t' Wales with this lot," he barked. "Not yet."

Declan shook his head.

"I've never seen so many men puke in a single afternoon, Roland," he said, then brightened as he sniffed the smells coming from the cook fires. "But a few good bowls of stew and a night's rest should put most of them right."

Roland nodded.

"Griff is not happy that we stopped here, but he saw what we all saw today. He will want the Invalids in full fighting form when we cross the Dee. Still, I think we can spare only one more day to sweat out the drink and knock off the rust, so don't spare the lads on the morrow."

"Wouldn't think of it," said Sir Roger.

***

Roland took the evening meal in the new great hall of Shipbrook and, despite the feeling of homecoming, the gathering had a melancholy tone. For a while, all ate in silence until Sir Roger finally spoke.

"I should go along," he declared, simply.

"I, as well," Declan chimed in.

Roland sighed. He had expected this and, in truth, would have welcomed turning command over to the older man and having Declan's steady nerves and unmatched sword arm to rely on, but he knew it would be a shirking of his own duty.

"My lord...and my friend, I thank you for the offer, but I must say no. Your duty is here, where I believe the Welsh are back to their old profession of stealing our cattle. Am I not right?"

"Right enough," Declan admitted grudgingly. "With things as they are over there," he said gesturing with his knife toward the west, "they can't very well farm, so new raiding bands have formed. They aren't very practiced yet, but they are nettlesome."

Sir Roger scowled, but knew he could not gainsay anything his Master of the Sword had just said. Still he was unwilling to let the matter lie.

"Declan can handle the raiders. I can come."

"And serve under Roland's command, Roger?" Lady Catherine asked. "The Earl has given this task to him—not you! Would you not bridle taking orders from your former squire—and even if you did not, would not Roland defer to you out of respect? It is not a good arrangement, husband. You know that."

Sir Roger groaned.

"Damnit, Catherine, you can talk circles around any subject!"

The mistress of Shipbrook gave him a withering look.

"Roger, you only speak to me so when you know I am right, but don't like what I say!"

Roland broke in.

"My lady, my lord, I owe everything to Shipbrook and the de Lavals, but I am the Earl's oath man now and he has given me command of the Invalids. Sir Roger, it would be passing strange for me to be giving you orders. I know you are a soldier above all and don't doubt you would obey me, but the trouble would be with the men, not you. They know well who you are and your reputation. I may have led them into battle, but you commanded the King's own cavalry. They will look to you in any moment of doubt. Lady Catherine is right, my lord. It is a bad arrangement."

Sir Roger muttered something no one could hear, then went quiet. Declan returned to sawing on a chop of meat, but finally broke the awkward silence that had fallen over hall.

"Sooo, how fares Millie?" he asked innocently.

***

Before dawn the next day, Patch marched through the camp bawling at the men to rise. They rolled out of their blankets onto hard frozen ground with a thick coating of frost. The fires they had drawn close to for warmth through the night had burned down to coals and a brisk north wind made men stamp their feet and clap their hands to get feeling into them.

"It's a grand day to be a soldier!" Patch shouted as he moved among them and a few managed to laugh and return a vulgar reply. Many groaned and nursed injuries from the day before, but all moved with a purpose once they caught the smell of hot pottage in a large cauldron near the edge of camp—courtesy of the Shipbrook cooks.

"Eat up, lads!" called Sergeant Billy as he stood by the food. "It's going to be a long day!"

Before the sun rose above the trees, all the Invalids, including those excused the day before to make camp, were mounted and ready to move. Sir Roger de Laval, on Tencendur, rode out of the gate of Shipbrook and reined in midway along the column. Men turned their mounts to face him. Unlike the previous morning, none slouched in the saddle or emptied their stomachs on the ground.

"Today is mounted drill," Sir Roger announced. "I know that not all of ye have been trained as cavalry, but ye may have need to fight as such where yer goin', so best ye get the basics here and not in the middle of a bunch of Welshmen."

Most of the Invalids knew Sir Roger de Laval and the newer men knew of him. One or two had been under his command in King Richard's heavy cavalry at Arsuf and others had ridden with the big Norman knight to the bloody field outside Towcester when they had faced John's mercenaries. After the brutal drilling the man had administered the day before, all waited with nervous attention.

"Face right!" the big man bellowed and a hundred men yanked their reins to the right—but they had not kept a proper interval and there was little room for their horses to turn. It took a full minute of cursing and manoeuvring to get the double ranks into a column.

"Lesson one, keep…your…interval!" Sir Roger roared. "Now, by twos, forw'rd!"

This order was simple enough and the double column of riders moved off toward the far field. For the remainder of the morning, Sir Roger and Declan put the men through cavalry drills, beginning with simple manoeuvres then moving to more complicated tactics. Columns turned about, formed line, wheeled and charged—again and again.

The drills began raggedly. Roland, Declan and the lord of Shipbrook shouted and cajoled their charges until, by noon, the experienced riders began to recall old habits and the newer men began to shadow them. The formations slowly started to resemble proper cavalry. After a brief respite for a noon meal, they were back at it. Toward late afternoon, Sir Roger summoned his two former squires to his side.

"They are good men, Roland, and a few days in the saddle will improve their horse handling, but it would take a week or more to turn them into decent cavalry. If it comes to it, line 'em up and point yer sword where ye want 'em to go. They'll figure out how to kill the other fellows."

***

Their last night at Shipbrook, the Invalids seemed to be changed men. A few days of good food, hard work and no spirits had worked wonders. All through the camp could be heard the sound of men laughing and jesting with each other. And there were other sights and sounds that made Roland smile.

Near the gate of the fort, the smith had dragged out two grinding wheels and two long lines of men stood waiting to put new edges on their swords, axes and spears. In another part of the camp, a huge barrel had been filled with sand and rusty hauberks. Men shouted and laughed as the contraption was rolled between the fires, scattering men and providing entertainment while scouring the rust from the mail inside. Roland saw the skinny priest, Friar Cyril, scampering around and cackling with the rest and wondered if the churchman had any notion of what he would be facing in the days ahead.

After a time, the activity quieted and Roland strolled through the camp. He hadn't gone far when he was intercepted by Patch.

"Sir Roland, a word—if ye've a moment?"

Roland nodded and the two walked together to the edge of the camp.

"What's on your mind, Tom?"

"Chester, sir…what I done there…or more like what I didn't do. I think you should pick someone else to lead these men. I'm not fit to."

Roland said nothing for a long time as they walked past the last fire and out into the dark beyond the camp. Finally, he spoke.

"Perhaps I should, Tom," he said coldly. "I'll not judge a man for liking drink or women. I like them both myself, but men like the Invalids have none of the moorings that most have—no wife to comfort or scold them, no children to support, no land to tend and no trade but fighting. Such men need something to bind them to their duty. They need a leader and you failed them there."

"Aye, sir, I did," the one-eyed soldier said mournfully.

Roland looked up into the night sky, but there were no stars to be seen.

Storm coming.

"Tom," he said gently, "reputations are hard won, but easily lost. The Invalid Company was once an object of pity and scorn. Men like you and Billy made it an object of fear and respect. That reputation has suffered of late, but not beyond repair. You let them slide back into the gutter. I will look to you to lead them back out—if you are up to it."

Patch drew in a sharp breath.

"My thanks, sir, I won't let you down."

Roland turned back toward the camp and together they walked among the men. For the first time since he had entered their barracks at Chester, they did not cast their eyes down as he passed. It had taken two days of brutal training and the prospect of a fight for these men to right themselves. Across the Dee, he would find out soon enough if they were still the Invalid Company.

Crossing the Dee

After two days of cold but clear weather, the Invalid Company broke camp at dawn as a winter storm struck the valley of the Dee. At first light, a stiff wind blew dark clouds in from the northwest. Then came slanting bursts of sleet that stung the men's faces and caused the horses to turn toward the south.

"A good day for a ride!" Patch bellowed, as he walked among the men clapping his hands together. Roland stood with Sir Roger and Declan beside the last fire still burning in the camp and watched as the men, in surprisingly good spirits, readied their gear.

"I think they're happy to be done with Sir Roger and myself," Declan observed and his master snorted.

"They're just happy t'be soldiering proper again and not drunk in some bawdy house in Chester," the big Norman said. "Only way to keep a soldier on the straight path is send him to war!"

"Or have him marry a proper woman!"

All turned to see Lady Catherine striding toward them, wrapped in a long cape with a hood pulled over her head against the weather.

"Cathy, ye'll catch a chill out here!" her husband scolded her. She just shrugged.

"I've spent days out in worse than this, Roger. I can see my son-in-law off, I think."

Roland gave her a small bow.

67

"Thank you for coming, my lady."

Lady Catherine de Laval looked out over the preparations for the march and gave a little sigh.

"I always come when one of my men goes off to war."

***

In the driving sleet and dim light of early morning, it was hard to see more than a few yards ahead as the Invalid Company was ordered to mount. Patch unfurled the standard of the Earl of Chester with its golden wheat sheaths on a blue field. The proud banner snapped in the wind. Roland rode up beside him.

"We leave that here, Patch. The Earl is not anxious to proclaim his hand in what we do across the river."

"I reckon we must look to ourselves, then," the one-eyed veteran said as he handed over the banner, which Roland passed to Sir Roger.

"That we must," Roland replied. "Now, let's get on with it."

Griff rode up and joined Roland at the head of the column.

"Ready to move, English?"

Roland just nodded and gave Patch a hand signal. The column headed west on the well-travelled road to the old ford. As the riders left Shipbrook behind, he felt a strange sense of loneliness. He was going into harm's way with a hundred men, but never more alone. No Sir Edgar. No Declan. No Sir Roger. His fate and that of the Invalid Company would be on his head alone. It was a daunting thought.

He had already dispatched two men to scout the opposite bank of the Dee on the slim chance that a hostile force might lay in ambush. As they approached the ford, his outriders signalled from the opposite bank that the Welsh shore was empty.

Little wonder in this weather.

Griff had sketched out the route they were to take and it was one that Roland knew well. The first twenty miles followed the rough path that led to Llywelyn's old hill fortress where Earl Ranulf and the ladies of Shipbrook had been given shelter and protection in the bitter days of 1192. The trail branched south from there for another dozen miles to reach the place where

Llywelyn's main body of rebels had made their new winter quarters.

He looked out on the river where the sleet was roiling the placid surface. A thin layer of ice had formed along the bank and extended for two feet into the swirling water. He had crossed this ford many times, and never without apprehension, but at this hour, the tide was low and water would only reach a horse's chest.

He stood up in his stirrups and looked back at the long line of men that disappeared into the gloom behind. In this weather, he would have to take it on faith that there were no stragglers. He eased back into his saddle and clucked to The Grey. The animal did not hesitate and plunged into the icy water. Behind him the Invalids followed.

At the far shore the gelding scrambled up the frozen bank and Roland kept the animal moving until he reached a small rise overlooking the ford. There lay a stone-covered grave, rimed with frost. It was the resting place of Alwyn Madawc, the first and best Welshman Roland had ever known. Sir Alwyn had fallen on this very bank saving Lady Catherine and Millicent from William de Ferrers' men. He wondered what the old Master of the Sword would think of this expedition back into his native land. He said a quiet prayer over the grave, then turned to watch the last of his men cross the Dee and ride into Wales.

The track that led up toward the hills beyond the river valley was rough under the best of conditions. It was now coated with a slick layer of ice, making progress painfully slow. With the arrival of the early winter sunset, Roland was forced to halt the march well before they reached the branching of the trail. They had extra horses back with the mules, but not enough to risk losing one to a broken leg.

On his orders, they made a cold camp. Their forward scouts had seen no sign of trouble, but a blazing fire in this wilderness would be visible for a long way. Men wrapped themselves in their cloaks and huddled in bunches like dogs against the cold. In the night, the storm broke and, at dawn, the men awoke to a cloudless sky, though the wind still blew cold. They took a few mouthfuls of breakfast, mounted, and resumed the march.

With the sun not yet high in the east, they came to the old hill fort but did not tarry at the place. It had been abandoned long ago and they still had a dozen miles ahead to reach Llywelyn's new camp. The path led south and as the morning warmed they pushed the pace. Near noon, there was movement on the road ahead and Roland halted the column.

It was Jamie Finch, one of his advance scouts, coming back to the column at a gallop. Slumped ahead of him in the saddle was a boy who could not have been more than eight or nine years old. As Jamie reined in, Roland and Griff dismounted and helped the child down from the horse. His lips were blue and he was shivering.

"I know this lad," Griff said, tersely. He turned and shouted over his shoulder.

"Build a fire before the boy freezes!"

Half a dozen men leapt from the saddle, some fumbling for flint and tinder and others gathering wood. The boy was trying to speak but his teeth were chattering too much to be understood. As they waited for him to recover, Jamie Finch spoke up.

"Sir Roland, we come across sign ahead. A road comes in from the west and meets this one. Lots of horses passed that way. Can't say when, with the ground frozen, but probably within the last week. A little way beyond, we saw a hill fort. Everything inside was burnt. Found this lad wanderin' around the ruins."

Roland turned to Griff.

"It looks like your prince had the rights of it."

"Aye, it looks bad. Maybe the boy can tell us what we'll find ahead."

It took only a few moments for the half-dozen men to light a flame and get a credible fire started. Friar Cyril had ridden up from the rear with a woollen blanket to wrap around the boy. Griff sat down by the fire and pulled the boy into his lap. Slowly some colour returned to his lips and the shivering began to subside.

"Master...Griff..." he croaked.

"Aye, Pedr, it's Griff. Warm yerself, boy. Yer with friends now."

The boy settled back against Griff's chest and looked as though he might drift off to sleep. Roland was now joined by Patch and Sergeant Billy, as they crowded around the newcomer. Friar Cyril made long, fervent prayers for the boy's recovery until Patch shushed him.

Griff shook the lad and his eyes popped open.

"Tell us, Pedr. Tell us what happened," Griff asked gently.

The boy squirmed around and reached his hands toward the fire.

"The Prince, Lord Llywelyn, came in t' camp five nights ago. He was on a lame horse and alone." The boy was speaking in Welsh, which Roland understood well enough. Having managed a few words, Pedr was promptly overcome with a fit of coughing. He recovered himself and continued.

"There was alarms. Everyone was runnin' about and shoutin'. I heard a horn sound from back along the track where the Prince had come. Lord Llywelyn said something—I couldn't hear what, but some men ran down that way with bows. The others saddled the horses and headed off south. Lord Llywelyn stayed at the camp for a long time. He saw me and told me to fetch my pony and follow the men south. I was right scared, Master Griff."

"Ye should a been, lad," Griff said softly. "But what happened then?"

The boy hung his head.

"I got on my pony, but with all the noise, she spooked and threw me. Weren't her fault. She was scared, too. I must've hit my head when I landed in the bushes. Didn't know where I was when I woke for a bit, but I could hear men talkin'. They spoke a strange tongue—not Welsh or English, but I'm not sure. They wore strange dress too."

Griff stole a glance at Roland, then turned back to the boy, who had climbed out of his lap and was now standing by the fire.

"How many were there, Pedr?"

The boy looked at the long line of men who had dismounted on the trail and were waiting patiently for their orders.

"Many more than ye have here, Master Griff. I kept hid and I saw what they did."

71

"What did they do?"

The boy suddenly shuddered, as though the chill had gone back into his bones.

"The caught two of our lads, Griff—Gwilyn and Caden. They…they hurt em' awful." The tears welled up in the boy's eyes. "I couldn't do nothing. I put my hands over my ears. I couldn't stand the sounds."

"It's alright, lad. Ye did right to stay hid. Is there naught else ye can tell us?"

The boy scrunched up his face in thought.

"Yes! I saw a big man with an axe. He was givin' the orders."

"Did you hear a name, lad? What was he called?" Roland asked in the boy's native tongue.

The boy glanced at Griff, who nodded.

"They called him Haakon, my lord."

***

They found the bodies beside the trail. The freezing weather had preserved the corpses and it was plain to see that young Pedr had not exaggerated the grievous treatment these men had received. They had died hard. Roland had seen such as this, and worse, on Crusade. In the holy wars in the east, men were killed in ghastly ways, but it was a shock to see such wanton cruelty so close to home.

"Gwilyn and Caden," Griff said grimly. "They were two of my bowmen—two of the best and good lads both." The tall Welshman clinched his fists as he stared at the scene. "I swear on my mother's grave I will cut this bastard's heart out and piss on it," he snarled.

Roland stood quietly as Griff fought to control his rage. Friar Cyril hurried forward and said a quick prayer over the maimed bodies and organized a burial party. Sergeant Billy and the giant Scot, Seamus Murdo, gently carried the frozen remains of the young Welshmen to a small clearing away from the road, while other members of the Invalids began to gather stones for a hasty grave.

"This Haakon—is he Roderic's man or Daffyd's?" Roland asked finally. "The name doesn't sound English."

"Roland doesn't sound English either," said Griff, "but this was no Englishman, I think. If it is who I believe it to be, he is neither Daffyd's man nor Roderic's, unless he's been bought. There is a man known around the western seas as Haakon the Black. He and his men are mercenary Danes from Dublin. They call them the Dub Gaill. Dublin is now ruled rather loosely by Normans, but the Danes held that town for centuries and many still operate from there. Some, like Haakon, still hold to the old ways. He is a freebooter and a mercenary, but mostly takes his pay from Ragnvald, the King of the Isles."

"There's a name fit for a Dane," Roland said.

Griff shrugged.

"The Isles were taken by the Northmen three hundred years ago. Ragnvald and his kin rule the western seas and spring from the same root as you, Roland. Their grandsires were Danes. They speak that language still on the Isle of Man, I'm told. Perhaps that's why their speech sounded strange to Pedr. By reputation, Haakon is a man who knows his business. He is a bold one and men flock to him from all across the Northern Sea."

Griff turned and took a last look at the bodies of Gwilyn and Caden.

"By reputation," he said pointing at the two broken bodies, "he is a man who would do this."

"You think Daffyd or Roderic has bought his services?" Roland asked.

"Yes, but this could be more of a family matter than a simple bit of commerce."

"Family matter? For God's sake, speak plainly, Griff. What makes the hiring of these mercenaries a family affair?"

"King Ragnvald is this Haakon's chief patron and Ragnvald's oldest daughter is Lord Roderic's wife."

Roland furrowed his brow.

"Ah…"

"Yes, Ragnvald is Lord Roderic's father-in-law, which makes this…"

"A family matter." Roland shook his head and laid a hand on Griff's shoulder.

"Your Welsh politics put ours to shame, my friend."

Griff pulled away.

"This is no longer politics," he growled, pointing to where his dead bowmen were being covered in stones. "Gather your men, English. It should not be hard to follow the trail of these vermin. We must track them down and make them pay!"

Roland shook his head again.

"No."

Griff blinked.

"No? You saw what they did! Or do you fear crossing swords with these bastards?"

"You would call me a coward, Griff?"

"I...no...you are no coward, Roland," he sputtered, "but this...," he said looking again at the graves, anguish in his voice.

As Roland stood there and looked into the Welshman's eyes, he was tempted to relent. He knew well the thirst for revenge, but William de Ferrers still lived and he had learned to keep that fire banked. And at moments like this, the voice in his head was that of Sir Roger de Laval.

"Don't do anything stupid!"

It was a simple admonition he'd heard many times in his years of service to the big Norman and it had always proven good advice. Striking at this new enemy, without knowing his strength or intentions, would be stupid.

"Griff, if there is a just God, we will have our chance to make this Haakon pay, but I have only one hundred men. I won't throw them away. I led the Invalids here to help your master win his war, not to settle scores. How best can we do that?"

The question seemed to draw Griff back from his seething rage. He muttered a final curse under his breath then nodded at Roland.

"We find Llywelyn."

"Good," said Roland.

"But, English, you must understand that, in Gwynedd, politics *is* settling scores."

74

***

After scouts were dispatched to find where Haakon's men had gone and sentries were posted on every trail leading into Llywelyn's ruined winter quarters, Roland called a council of war. Griff, Patch and Sergeant Billy were there and Roland was surprised to see Sir John Blackthorne as well. Patch pulled him aside and whispered in his ear.

"Fancy Jack is the best horseman in the company, sir, and maybe the best swordsman as well. The men respect that and will follow him." Roland gave a small nod and the promotion was approved. John Blackthorne was now an officer of the company. When all had gathered, Roland spoke first to Griff.

"How many men did Llywelyn have in this camp?"

"Three hundred, give or take a score, and it looks like most got away clean or there'd have been more bodies to bury. We have two camps a little smaller than this farther to the east. I have no notion if they've been attacked."

Roland nodded.

"The men who came here had the advantage of surprise, but I expect they outnumbered your people as well. Else your lord might have stood and fought. What is the strength that the two uncles can bring to the field?"

"Our spies have counted five hundred for Daffyd," Griff said. "As we have not fought with him in the past, I am less sure of Roderic's numbers, but I'd guess near a thousand."

"Add say, four hundred or more Danes, paid by Roderic, and the uncles have a formidable force."

"Aye," Griff said, "I doubt we can field more than eight hundred, if you count your Invalids."

"That makes the odds steep," said Roland.

Griff looked at the small knot of men gathered around him. It would not have surprised him if these English, seeing what had happened here and considering the forces arrayed against them, had wheeled their horses around and headed back to Cheshire. But he saw no sign of quit in any of their faces.

"We've faced steeper odds and won," the tall Welshman said simply.

"As have we," said Roland.

Griff gave him a wan smile.

"Aye, ye have," he said, remembering their midnight assault on the Bridgegate at Chester.

The sound of hooves made the men in the circle look up as two scouts rode in, dismounted and hurried to report to Roland.

"Sir, all of the tracks we saw leaving this camp followed a good path headed due west. Lord Llywelyn must have fled that way. It looks like the men who attacked him here followed."

"That road leads to a good ford on the Conwy and to the main pass into the mountains on the other side," Griff said, rubbing his chin. "It's the road Llywelyn would take if he's making for Dolwyddelan."

"Dolwyddelan?"

"Aye, it's the fortress in the mountains I spoke of back in Chester. It is a difficult place to get to at this time of year, with snow in the passes, and impossible to reach if those passes are defended. It would take more than his uncles and a band of Northmen to roust him out of that place."

"Should we follow?" Patch asked.

"No," Griff said, with an emphatic shake of his head, "the Danes won't likely venture into the pass. They are mercenaries, not fools. But they may settle themselves at the ford to block any attempt by Llywelyn to come down from the hills. I would dearly love to strike them there, but as your commander advised me," he stopped and looked toward Roland, "we haven't the strength."

"What do you propose then?" Roland asked. "Ride east to reach the other winter camps?"

Griff shook his head.

"I think not. The last thing the Prince told me was to find him at Dolwyddelan if he was not at our winter quarters. He has fled in that direction, and while the direct route is blocked, I know of another way. It will not be pleasant, but there is a backdoor into Dolwyddelan that should avoid these Danes."

"Then we shall take it," Roland said.

Nearby a party of the Invalids trudged back from the clearing where they had finished covering the dead men in stones. He turned to Patch.

"Mount the men."

Eryri

*T*he clear weather held for most of the day as Griff Connah led them on a rough path to the southwest. Near sunset, darker clouds appeared to the north as they reached a wretched little hamlet that overlooked a ford on the River Conwy. Across a frozen field, Roland could see the poor inhabitants of the place disappearing into a patch of barren trees, driving a few sheep and a pig with them. He didn't blame them for fleeing at the approach of a hundred mounted men.

Of more concern were the three riders they saw spur out of town at their approach. The men galloped off to the north on a well-travelled road that disappeared into dense woods. Roland reached for his bow and quiver, but they were out of range and it would have been a waste of a good arrow.

Griff gave a short curse.

"I'd hoped they wouldn't know of this route. If those be Haakon's men, he is as careful as he is bold."

"At least they haven't fortified the place," Roland said. "We won't have to fight our way through."

"Not this time," the tall Welshman conceded, "but now they've seen us cross, they'll have more than three scouts here in a day or two."

There was no denying this. Should they need it again, the back door to Dolwyddelan would be closed to them. But for now, they splashed across the ford, its waters shallow and swift. They scarcely wetted their stirrups, and found a rocky path on the far shore. It ran up from the ford, then bent to the southwest, following the river's course into high hills that were covered in snow. Griff reined in his horse and looked ahead as Roland joined him.

"Eryri," the tall Welshman said, looking toward the looming hills. "We follow the Conwy for ten miles or so, until it is no more than a rivulet. Another dozen brings us to the pass at Bwlch y Gorddinan. Men do not use it in winter—at least not in winters such as this one—but it is the back way into Dolwyddelan and that is where we must go. Can yer Invalids manage it?"

Roland shrugged.

"I grew up in hills such as these. If you can manage it, so shall I, and the Invalids will follow."

Griff turned in his saddle and looked at the tall young knight. Roland had his hood pulled back and gusts of cold air had blown his long dark hair in tangles across his face. The commander of the Invalid Company still looked a bit like a boy, but Griff had seen him lead men in more desperate conditions than these. An image came to him of Roland Inness climbing over the parapet of Chester's Bridgegate tower in pitch darkness to open that gate on the night they had taken the city. The lad might be young, but Griff had seen how men looked to him in a fight. He nodded.

"Aye, I expect they'd follow you over the edge of the world, English. But if the snow is deep enough, neither man nor beast will best that pass. Are your hills in Derbyshire higher than these?"

"Higher than those I can see ahead, but I'm told there are true mountains somewhere further south."

"Aye, and great jagged crags they are—their tops as high as the eagle flies." He stopped and then spoke wistfully. "I saw them only once, as a boy. One day I hope to go back."

"Perhaps in summer."

Griff gave a barking laugh.

"Aye, summer for certain, Sir Roland. They say the snow there can be higher than a man's head at this time of year, so summer it shall be. Perhaps you'd like to see them as well."

"Aye, I'd like that. I saw true mountains once, as we passed by Italy, but only from the deck of a ship. I'd like to walk among the high peaks here."

"I will be happy to be your guide, if we live. You may trust that if the weather turns, we will have challenge enough just reaching Llywelyn's fortress in these hills."

"If we live," Roland agreed with a smile.

As the sun fell behind a hill to the west, the dark clouds reached the valley of the Conwy. It began to snow.

***

By nightfall, the light snow became a howling blizzard. Roland called a halt two miles beyond the ford. Men did their best to fashion crude windbreaks to protect them from the onslaught of the storm. Darkness brought a sharp drop in temperature and permission was granted for fires to be lit. No enemy force would venture out in these conditions.

The men of the Invalid Company huddled near the flames or stood to stamp their feet against the cold, as drifts piled up wherever the wind chose to blow the snow. Roland made his way to the picket line with a blanket he had fetched from his kit. Millie had a soft spot for horses and had packed the extra covering against just such a storm as this. The Grey nickered as he approached and swung his head around to rest it on his master's shoulder. Roland rubbed the gelding's jaw then draped the blanket over its back.

"Courtesy of Lady Millicent," he whispered as he secured it with a length of sturdy twine tied at the corners. He gave the horse a pat and walked back through the blinding swirl of white toward the crackling fires of the encampment.

"Come warm yerself, sir," a voice called out as he approached. It was the big Scot, Seamus Murdo. Beside him at the fire were Sir John Blackthorne and the cadaverous priest, Friar Cyril. That these men shared a fire did not surprise him. He had seen this on Crusade when fresh troops had arrived from Europe during the great siege of Acre. New men had to earn their way into the bonds of trust that knit together any company of fighting men. The Invalid Company was no exception. All at this fire were newcomers, yet to prove their mettle with the veteran Invalids.

Roland stepped between the big Scot and the Friar and warmed his hands. On the other side of the flames, Fancy Jack did the same. Roland noticed that the driving snow did not seem to cling to the man's cape, which was fashioned from some kind of tanned leather.

Fancy indeed!

"I seen blows like this many a time in the highlands of home," Seamus Murdo declared, slapping his massive hands together to keep the blood flowing. "Won't last long."

Roland glanced over at the priest who had his robe pulled tight around his neck but stood in the storm bare-headed. In the fire's glow, he had a far-away look on his face.

"I've seen frozen mountains, floating in the sea," he said.

"Mountains in the sea?" Fancy Jack said. "You're telling tales now, Friar."

The man shook his head.

"No. They were made all of ice and were huge. At least the size of some of these hills."

"And where did you see these wonders?"

"Far to the north, Sir John." Off the coast of a great island the Northmen call Iceland and others call Thule."

"I've heard of it," Murdo said, "far to the north of Scotland?"

"Aye, Seamus, very far to the north."

"What took you there?" Roland asked, genuinely interested.

"I was a slave, my lord—taken by Ivar Longbeard, when he raided my village in Northumbria. Ivar had settled in Thule with many of his kinsmen."

"I know Northumbria," Seamus put in.

"Aye, Seamus, I've little doubt. Scot's love to raid there, though I don't remember seeing you among those who paid occasional visits to our village."

The big Scot scowled.

"We only raided into Cumberland and only when provoked by the English!" he said sulkily.

"This Longbeard—he enslaved a priest?" Fancy Jack asked, surprised.

"I was no priest back then," Friar Cyril said, "but he thought I was. My family possessed a scrap of parchment. The priest who visited our village claimed it had the words of the Pater Noster written on it."

"The Lord's prayer," Roland said.

"Aye, or so the priest said. None of us could read and none knew how this relic had come to us, but that parchment was our most precious possession. I was clutching it when they took me out to slaughter. Ivar took the parchment and demanded to know what it said. I knew the words in Latin by heart and, believe me, I was praying with all my heart when I recited them. Thinking I was a priest and could read, he decided to take me back to Thule to teach the skill to his children."

"What happened when they found you could not read?" Seamus asked, taken up with the friar's story and over his pout.

"They never found out."

"You escaped?" Roland asked.

The tall friar shrugged his bony shoulders.

"In a manner of speaking. We were drawing near to Thule when a mighty storm blew up—not unlike this one," he said, as a swirl of icy air sent embers from the fire flying upwards. "Our ship was driven upon rocks and sank. All were lost, save for me and Ivar. The two of us grasped a broken spar and were washed up on a shore of black sand."

"Then what?" asked Fancy Jack.

Friar Cyril's shoulders slumped.

"Ivar was near senseless, but starting to come around. I found his dagger and I slit the man's throat. I dragged his body back into the waves to let the sea take him."

There was shocked silence around the fire.

"It was a mortal sin, I know, but Ivar had killed all in my family save me, whom he enslaved." The friar paused, then spoke with uncommon ferocity.

"I am no man's slave!"

Again, silence fell on the small group around the fire.

"I'd have done the same, Father Cyril," said Fancy Jack, gently.

"The man deserved to die," said Seamus, poking at the fire with a stick.

"Vengeance is mine, sayeth the Lord," the monk said with simple conviction.

The churchman's words took Roland back to the dark day he had killed his first men in a rage of vengeance on the heights of Kinder Scout. Friar Tuck had quoted the same scripture to him that day and he understood it well enough. But it took a humbler soul than his own to follow God's admonition against revenge. His rage might have grown cold in the years since he had first been driven to kill, but his desire for vengeance—on a man no doubt taking his comfort in Brittany—had not waned. He wondered if Friar Cyril had truly found the humility to abide by God's law.

"I was found a day later by some of Ivar's kin and passed myself off as a shipwrecked priest," the monk continued. "It was easy enough. My parchment had been lost in the wreck, but I could recall many passages of the Bible in Latin from years of attending mass. It was enough to convince these folks. I lived among them for months before finding passage back to England. They were decent people, not monsters. In all that time, they had no idea that their kinsman was dead and that I had done the deed. The guilt gnawed at me. When I came home, I made my way to Alnwick Abbey where I took priestly vows. Passing as a priest had saved me. Being one is my penance."

"But why do ye minister to the Invalids?" asked Seamus. "After all, we are killers of men."

"And all the more in need of grace!" the friar said brightly. "That too is part of my penance."

"Best of luck with that," said Fancy Jack with a sly smile, as he tossed another branch on the fire.

***

In the small hours of the morning the snow stopped, though a raw wind still blew from the north and the few trees along the river were coated with ice. When dawn came, it was hard to tell which of the white lumps scattered across the encampment were drifts and which were men covered with a layer of snow. A few of the Invalids were already up at first light, having taken the final shift feeding the fires to ward off the bitter cold of the night.

Now, Patch and Sergeant Billy roused those who still slept. Men shook out their blankets and cloaks, wolfed down cold hard biscuits and saddled their horses. There were more than a few soft curses at the harshness of the weather and the unappetizing breakfast. The Invalids grumbled as they broke camp and Roland watched it all with satisfaction.

Start worryin' when a soldier stops complaining.

It was advice he'd heard often from Sir Roger. In his own experience, he'd found it sound. He had seen men grumble endlessly during the campaigns in the east—and with good reason. Fleas, vermin, rotten food and insufferable heat had been the order of the day in the trenches before Acre, and men had cursed the wretchedness of it all in every language native to Europe.

But there were also units that slowly fell into a sullen silence under the unrelenting harshness of that siege. Some had refused orders to take up their arms and stand their watch. In the end, these men were often shipped back to Tyre, where they fell prey to drink and the fleshpots of that city.

During the siege of Chester, the Invalids had grumbled colourfully about the food, drink, and women of that city, but never complained when it was time to cross swords. It had now been almost a week since he had rousted them, indolent and drunk, out of their barracks in Chester. They were complaining, but every man moved with a purpose on this frozen morning. Roland smiled.

They were becoming the Invalid Company again.

***

The day's march was hard, with new flurries swirling in from the northeast. The trail narrowed and the men rode single file. Always on their left, the River Conwy leapt and plunged down the ever-steepening valley. As the light faded, they made camp in a sheltered ravine near a small village. With nightfall, the last of the snow ceased and the high grey clouds that had spread sullenly over the high country all day drifted off to the south. A crescent moon rose above high hills to the west and its light gleamed off the white blanket newly laid down in the valley.

Griff rode ahead to let the inhabitants of the village know of their approach. These were farmers and freemen who seldom saw armed groups at any time of year, particularly in winter, but they were in the ancestral lands of Llywelyn's father and were willing to part with some bread and cheese for men loyal to the Prince.

The Welshman returned to the encampment leading a pack horse with the proffered food stuffs and sought out Roland. He signalled for him to follow as they walked to the edge of the encampment. Across the valley and beyond the nearer hills, higher peaks loomed jagged and white in the moonlight. Griff pointed to them.

"The pass at Bwlch y Gorddinan begins three miles beyond this valley," he said. "The villagers tell me the way is bad—waist deep on a man since the storm and icy beneath the snow. We will have to lead the horses on foot. Dolwyddelan is but a mile beyond the top of the pass, if we can reach it."

Roland nodded.

"The pass—how long is it?"

"Six miles—six very bad miles. But the villagers also told me five men had ridden into the pass two days ago, before the storm, and had not returned. That could be a good sign."

"Unless we find their bodies up there," Roland said quietly.

For a moment Griff looked stricken, then he barked out a laugh and slapped Roland on the shoulder.

"I'm never sure when yer jesting, English!"

Roland returned the man's smile, but he hadn't been jesting.

Fugitive at the Ford

Declan O'Duinne swung into the saddle of his dun palfrey and looked over his shoulder at the six men already mounted in the courtyard behind him. Most wore rough woollen cloaks around their shoulders against the biting cold wind that swirled through the gate of Shipbrook. It had been three days since Roland Inness and the Invalid Company rode off to Wales and it was time to resume the routine duties of patrolling this stretch of the border.

Declan heard a hound bark and looked up to see Sir Roger de Laval emerge from the timber and stone hall that took up almost half the space within the walls of the little fortress. The big Norman knight hurried down the steps to the cobbled courtyard and headed straight for his Master of the Sword. O'Duinne had to smile.

Still nimble for a big man...

"My lord," he called. "Will ye be joinin' us this morning?"

Sir Roger scowled as he approached.

"Nay," he growled. "Would if I could, but Catherine is insisting that I sit with her while she goes over our accounts. God knows, I've avoided it as long as any man could, but she has me cornered."

Declan wanted to laugh. Sir Roger de Laval, Lord of Shipbrook and lately commander of the King's own heavy cavalry, loved peace, but hated attending to the business of peace.

"My sympathies," offered Declan—and he meant it. The young Irish knight had spent a few years as Sir Roger's squire and had been taught to read and to do sums by Lady Catherine de Laval so that he could assist her in the management of their lands. The woman could be very demanding when it came to such things as counting heads of cattle and bushels of barley. Now that he had been elevated to the position of Master of the Sword, Declan had other duties to attend to and was glad of it. He did not miss those sessions with Lady Catherine. "You'll be missing a fine ride, though. Cold as hell, but look at that sky, blue as a maiden's eye."

Sir Roger laid a hand on the neck of the palfrey and looked up.

"Indeed, it is," he said, wistfully, then lowered his eyes to meet those of the young Irish knight. "But you, Master O'Duinne, do not get drunk on the beauty of the day. I had reports of strange riders to the north yesterday. Probably nothing, but these patrols have a purpose and it's not to take a fine ride. Be on your guard."

Declan pulled back his cloak to reveal a mail shirt beneath.

"I always take precautions, my lord."

Sir Roger gave him a wide grin and slapped Declan on the thigh.

"You've had good teachers! Enjoy your ride."

***

The men seen north of Shipbrook the day before turned out to be two wealthy merchants from Runcorn who had managed to stray from the Chester road and get hopelessly lost. After an uncomfortable night in a peasant hut, the two had managed to find their way back to the proper path and were long gone.

"Likely warming their bums at the Ram's Head about now," said Baldric sourly, his cheeks a bright red from the blustery cold.

Declan nodded. Baldric hated the cold and was over-fond of ale, but he was a good man in a fight. He had proved his mettle a year ago, when he had stood in the line at Towcester. The Irishman expected no trouble this day, but was glad that Baldric was one of his six.

Its work done to the north, Declan led the patrol on a wide swing south and west heading for the ford of the Dee. No patrol from Shipbrook would be complete without a check of this shallow crossing. There, an ancient trail made its way across the river from northern Wales and into Cheshire. The small fort of Shipbrook existed to keep watch over this path that brought trade, but more often trouble, from the untamed lands of Gwynedd.

The day was still cloudless and a bit warmer by the time the patrol reached the river at mid-afternoon. Off to the west, the tops of the hills that separated the valley of the Dee from the valley of the Clwyd glistened white in the sun, the remnants of a fierce winter storm that had blown through the day before, leaving a good deal of snow at higher elevations. Roland and the Invalids were off somewhere in that direction and he hoped they were keeping to the lowlands.

Here at the Dee, Declan studied the bank where any riders would have exited the ford. There were some old tracks frozen in the mud, but no sign of any recent activity. Even with the hard freeze, any passage of mounted men would have made some mark upon the path, but he saw none. He looked at the thin crust of ice forming along the bank.

Too cold for traders or raiders, he thought.

A sound from the far shore interrupted his inspection. He looked across the river to see a horse and rider gallop over the low rise that ran down to the ford. The rider whipped the horse frantically and urged it into the water, but the animal balked and almost threw his passenger at the river's edge. Without hesitating, the rider leapt off the animal and plunged alone into the freezing water, which quickly rose to his chest as he struggled against the current toward English shore.

Declan looked at Baldric.

"What do ye suppose this is?"

Baldric just shrugged.

As the figure in the river reached mid-stream, all could see that it was a boy in the water, not a man, and that he was terrified. A moment later, the reason for his fear appeared on the far bank. Ten mounted men came over the rise and began shouting and pointing at the boy in the river. Their mounts did not hesitate, plunging into the waters of the Dee in hot pursuit.

87

Declan looked at Baldric and sighed. He gave a hand sign to the patrol to stay where they were, then dug his heels into the flanks of the dun and splashed into the river. He reached the boy well ahead of the pursuing riders. The lad was a strapping youth with long brown hair and a broad chest, but his face was very young and there was a nasty gash from his hairline to just above his right eye that still showed crusted black blood. The boy's lips were blue from the cold and there was entreaty in his eyes.

"Helpa fi!" he cried out.

Declan's passable understanding of Welsh wasn't really needed to grasp the boy's plea.

"Why should I?"

"They come…come to kill me," the boy said, struggling a bit with English, his voice wavering as the cold caused his teeth to chatter.

The Irish knight would have questioned him a bit further, but the other riders were coming on and a big man in the lead drew his sword. The boy yelped and resumed his struggle toward the English side of the river. Declan watched the armed riders draw near and slowly drew his own sword. The man in the lead reined in just ten yards away.

"Stand aside!" he barked.

Declan smiled at the man.

"No."

The men behind the leader began to edge forward. Behind him, Declan heard Baldric give terse orders to the Shipbrook men and heard the splashing as six horses entered the ford from the English bank. He swung around in his saddle and held up his hand to halt them, then swung back to the front.

"Give us the boy!" the Welshman snarled.

"Why do you want him?"

The man hesitated for a second.

"He's a thief," he said.

Declan could see the lie in the man's eyes.

"It didn't look like the lad had anything of value on him when he passed by me," Declan said, still smiling. Then he edged his horse forward, his smile gone. "Turn around and get back to your own side of the river. We of Shipbrook do not let armed Welshmen cross the Dee."

The big man's face grew red and he spurred his horse forward, raising his sword to strike. Declan watched him come and waited. The man stood in his stirrups, leaned over his horse's neck and swung his sword in a vicious downward arc. It would have been a killing stroke against a lesser swordsman.

Declan rose in his stirrups and used the tip of his blade to deflect the slash harmlessly to the side. The Welshman found himself off balance and in the next instant had the tip of a sword pressed at his throat.

"Drop it in the river!" Declan ordered and pressed the point into the man's flesh. A thread of blood trickled from where the blade touched. The man tried to lean backwards, away from the threatening blade, but Declan clucked to the dun and the big horse edged forward, keeping the point under the Welshman's chin. The man locked eyes with the Irish knight for a moment and did not like what he saw there. His jaw clinched, but he opened his hand and the sword disappeared into the brown water. Declan clucked to his horse again and it edged back a few feet.

It had all happened so fast that the riders behind had not been able to react, sitting as though frozen in the cold river. Their leader, now a safe distance from the point of Declan's sword, twisted in his saddle and snarled a command. They now surged forward as though released from a spell.

Declan gave a signal to his own men who lowered their lances and moved forward to meet them. The Welshmen reined in without the need of a command from their leader. With no room to manoeuvre, their swords would be no match for lances. The big man who led them cursed and gave a command through clinched teeth. The men behind wheeled their horses around and made for the Welsh side of the Dee. When they had scrambled back onto dry land, the leader turned.

"You will regret this, Englishman," he shouted and spit in the swirling water between them.

Declan gave him a friendly wave and called back.

"Actually, I'm Irish!"

***

The patrol clattered through the gate as the sun dipped below the horizon. Declan had hauled the wet, shivering boy up behind him and thrown his own cloak over the lad's shoulders to keep him from freezing on the ride back to Shipbrook. As soon as he reined to a stop, his passenger slid to the ground and offered the cloak back.

"I am…obliged, sir."

Declan dismounted as Sir Roger appeared at the top of the steps. The big Norman knight looked at the wet boy, then at Declan.

"What have ye brought me now, Sir Declan?

"My lord, I have a fugitive to be sure. A band of unsavoury types thought to cross over the Dee onto your lands—apparently to seize this lad. Claimed he was a thief, but I've seen naught of any value on his person. Young fellow threw himself on my mercy. That is all I know, my lord. I thought it best to bring him here straight away before he froze solid."

Sir Roger inspected the new arrival closely. The boy did not flinch.

"We'll need to have that gash seen to," he said, leaning in to look at the wound on the boy's forehead, "but it's not bleeding." Finished with his inspection of the injury he leaned back.

"What brings you across the Dee, lad?" he asked in Welsh.

The boy hesitated for a long moment, then spoke, in passable English.

"I come to find…my father, my lord."

"Father? I can tell from yer speech, yer Welsh, sure enough, but there are few Welshmen that I know of hereabouts. Why do ye think yer father would be here in Cheshire?"

"My mother, lord. She told me, before she died, that he had found a place for himself here by the ford of the Dee. She said he was at a place they call Shipbrook. Is this that place?"

Sir Roger arched an eyebrow.

"Shipbrook, you say?"

"Aye, it's the name she said."

90

"Well, this is Shipbrook, sure enough, lad, but I'm afraid she was mistaken. For certain, there are no Welshmen here, but what is yer sire's name? Perhaps I know of him."

"His name is Madawc, my lord—Alwyn Madawc."

***

Declan and Sir Roger lounged on a nearby bench as Lady Catherine hovered near the boy as he wolfed down two bowls of mutton stew and an entire loaf of black bread. She had taken him into the kitchen where the cook fire would warm him and where she could get a better look at the gash in his head.

"It should have been stitched days ago," she said, as she held a candle near the boy's forehead to throw more light on the wound. "It will heal, but there'll be a considerable scar."

"No matter," the boy mumbled.

He flinched just a bit as the mistress of Shipbrook began dabbing carefully at the wound with a wet cloth, but did not pull away. One of the servants was sent to fetch dry clothes, while Lady Catherine finished her ministrations. Once done, she sat back and let him eat in peace until he had used the last of the bread to sop up the last of the stew.

"What's yer name, lad?"

"Rhys, my lady—Rhys Einion."

Sir Roger and Declan exchanged glances. The name meant nothing to either of them, nor it seemed to Lady Catherine. It was not a name they had ever heard Alwyn Madawc speak. Still, the boy seemed very certain of his connection to their old friend, so he must be told. Sir Roger cleared his throat.

"Master Einion, I will want to hear the circumstances of your birth and what led you here in search of Sir Alwyn Madawc, be he your true sire or no. But it would be...unkind of me to withhold the news that the man you seek died three years ago."

He watched the boy freeze, a look of incomprehension on his face.

"Died?" he whispered, his voice hardly more than a croak.

"Aye, I'm sorry, lad. Sir Alwyn Madawc was my oldest and dearest friend—a friend to all here at Shipbrook. He was a great warrior and the bravest man I ever knew. He died saving the life of my wife and my daughter. He killed many men the day they brought him low. We have mourned his loss every day since. He is buried on the Welsh side of the Dee, near where you crossed."

The boy gave a small, animal groan as his head sank to his chest.

"Dead. Alwyn Madawc, dead," he mumbled. "I've come fer nuthin'."

Sir Roger placed a hand on the boy's shoulder.

"Time will tell if yer journey was for naught, lad. Whether Alwyn Madawc was your father or no, he was the best man I ever knew and I'm sorry ye've come too late to make his acquaintance. But tell me, why do ye think he was yer sire? Sir Alwyn never spoke of a son and the man I knew would not have kept such a thing secret. If ye be his child, he knew naught of ye. But you say your mother told you this?"

The boy looked up. His eyes were glistening and there was a weariness in his slumped shoulders.

"Aye, m'lord. She told me this on her deathbed—told me she had once loved a man named Alwyn Madawc, and that he was my true sire, not the man I called father."

"You say she named Alwyn as your sire, but whose name do you bear?" Lady Catherine asked gently.

The boy's jaw tightened.

"Until my mother revealed her secret, I took her husband, Talfryn Einion, to be my father, though he barely acknowledged me. Now I understand why. Our small corner of Wales is a poor one, but Talfryn Einion governs it with a fist of iron—a fist I felt many times, as did my mother. He must have suspected I was not his get from the start. My mother feared what would become of me after she passed—feared what Talfryn might do. That's why she told me of Alwyn Madawc."

"And what was yer mother's name?"

"It was Derryth, lord, though all called her Derry."

Sir Roger stole a glance at Catherine, who looked stricken. Long ago Alwyn had told them the story of his flight from Wales. He had fallen in love with a young woman—a woman married to a powerful man.

The girl's name had been Derryth.

92

He had told the basics of the tale to Sir Roger and, as his friendship with Lady Catherine grew, revealed more of the story to her. Derryth had been high-born and beautiful. She was betrothed as a child to Talfryn, the eldest son of the local ruler. But as she grew into her beauty, she caught the eye of young Alwyn Madawc, who was smitten. The story should have ended there, but against all odds, beautiful Derryth was equally taken with young Alwyn. In despair, Derryth had confessed her feelings to her mother, but the woman had been unmoved by such youthful yearnings.

In Alwyn's telling, the girl had to choose between her family and all she had ever known—and him. With a broken heart, she went through with her marriage, but not before giving herself one secret night to her young lover. Soon after the wedding, rumours began to spread that Talfryn Einion had been made a cuckold.

When word reached Derryth that suspicion had fallen on Alwyn, she begged him to flee, knowing that neither her husband, nor his powerful kin would brook any tarnish to their family name. Alwyn recognized the danger and begged her to come with him, but she would not, could not, bring herself to leave the only home she had ever known.

He had no choice but to run or die and made it over the border just ahead of a band of Talfryn's warriors. In the years that followed he had taken service with the Earl of Chester and had become the boon companion of Sir Roger de Laval. He had also made the acquaintance of many of the maids in Cheshire, but had never taken one to wife. Those who knew him well, knew why.

Sir Roger gave the boy's shoulder a pat.

"There is much to tell about the man you've named father, lad, but first tell us what happened after yer mother passed."

"I did not run!" he said, defiance in his voice. "My mother told me that Talfryn never had any real proof of her betrayal and with Alwyn Madawc gone, the rumours finally faded away. But Talfryn never forgot! I believe he would have denounced her and cast me out, had my mother's family not been nearly as powerful as his own. So, he swallowed his bile and took many mistresses while my mother played the dutiful wife. Me, he mostly ignored, but I knew, even as a small boy, that he hated me."

"So, when your mother passed, you stayed?"

"Aye, my lord, and I would be there still, but the choice was taken from my hands. I ran because Talfryn sent men to kill me."

Sir Roger raised a quizzical eyebrow and pointed to the gash in the boy's head. Rhys nodded.

"Aye, lord, a week after my mother died, I was summoned by Talfryn. He ordered me to deliver his monthly tithe to Saint Asaph's church. It's a half day's ride to the north of our land. I thought it odd that I was sent, for I had never been assigned this duty before. Talfryn usually sent three or more of his men, well-armed, to deliver the funds. It wasn't a fortune, but in those parts, men would kill for much less than what was in that bag of silver."

"In these parts as well, lad," Sir Roger said.

"But I was sent alone, lord. That worried me, so I took my sword and wore my helmet and hoped for no trouble."

"But trouble found you. Talfryn's men, I suppose?"

"Aye, lord. On the loneliest stretch of the trail to Saint Asaph's, they waited for me. I was on my guard, but these were my father's men. I did not know what to do, until they drew their swords. It was my good fortune that the trail was narrow at that spot, for they could not all come at me at once. I managed a lucky blow that unhorsed the first man in, but the second stuck me in the helmet and gave me this gash. I turned and rode for my life, not stopping in our small village as I passed, though I threw the bag of silver to old Tomas the village smith as I galloped past. Still, I have no doubt they will have branded me a thief."

"The man at the ford accused him of that," offered Declan.

"That would be Morgant, Talfryn's right hand. I knew I was pursued, but did not know who led the chase until I made it to the Dee. He is a dangerous man. He would have had me when my horse balked at the river's edge, were it not for yer Irish knight there," he said, giving a respectful nod to Declan.

"My pleasure," Declan said with a grin.

Sir Roger had a few more questions for the boy, but Lady Catherine intervened.

"Roger, the lad is all wrung out," she said sternly. "We will let him rest before there is any more talk. Come with me, Rhys."

The Welsh boy tried to rise but his knees would not hold him and he sank back onto the bench. Sir Roger and Declan did not have to be told to lend a hand. Together they helped him back to his feet and across the hall. There was a small cell there with a cot used for travellers given the hospitality of Shipbrook on their journeys. They lay the boy down and slipped out into the hall. All three exchanged glances.

"His tale rings true," said Sir Roger, as they gathered by the hearth. "Can it be that he is truly Alwyn's son?"

Lady Catherine sniffed.

"Did you even look at the boy, Roger? Did you not see the shape of the chin and the colour of his eyes? There is no doubt what seed this sapling sprang from! He is Alwyn's child," she said with finality.

Sir Roger shrugged.

"You see with a woman's eye, Cathy. I just see a boy in a lot of trouble. But his story persuades me. I concede he is a Madawc, though a bastard."

Catherine had started toward the hall, but swung around and pointed a finger at her husband.

"And what should that matter to you, Roger de Laval? Good God, but you Normans are such prig's when it comes to legitimacy! He is blood of Alwyn's blood!"

Sir Roger had taken a half-step backwards, but stopped with her finger touching his chest, and retreated no further.

"Every race has its customs, Catherine, as you know well," he said calmly. "I can name a few Saxon practices that make what little hair I have stand on end, but you have misunderstood me in this. I intended no disparagement of the boy. He is Alwyn's. I care not how he came to be so. He had nothing to do with his parentage, but his parentage has everything to do with his future. His cuckolded father has already shown his hand. He cannot go home again. We must help the lad find his way."

Catherine lowered her hand and smiled at her husband.

"Then we are of one mind, my lord," she said sweetly.

Dolwyddelan

*T*here were stars in the predawn sky above Eryri when Sergeant Billy roused a few of the men to load the pack horses with their dwindling food stocks. He took special care to inspect the lashings and balance of each animal's pack. An unbalanced horse on an icy mountain track could be lost in an instant and might take a man or two and needed supplies along for the plunge. Satisfied that the loads were well secured, he began to rouse the rest of the men with his usual bluff good humor.

"Up, lads, up! It's cold as a witch's teat and a good day to be a soldier! Up, now!"

Men groaned and a few complained loudly, but all were up in minutes and about their morning duties. Some walked a few steps out of camp to relieve themselves. Others trudged toward the horse line to saddle their mounts. Steam rose all around as the warm breath of horses and men met the bitter cold of the dawn. Roland threw his saddle over the back of The Grey and fed the horse a few handfuls of grain. Other men were beginning to mount and he did the same. Griff came up to join him.

"At least we have clear weather for the attempt," he said, glancing up at a sky that was deep blue and cloudless.

"Aye," Roland said, "but I've wondered—what shall we do if we conquer the pass and reach this Dolwyddelan and find your master is not there."

For a moment, Griff seemed at a loss for words, as though this thought had not once occurred to him. But then he recovered.

"I've followed Llywelyn since he was fourteen, English. I was with him when there were but three of us, then a dozen, then hundreds. If I do not know his mind by now, I am a blind man. He is there alright."

"Then let's go greet him!" Roland said, as he clucked to The Grey and headed down into the valley that led to the pass.

***

The pass of Bwlch y Gorddinan was a nightmare. The storm had added two feet of fresh powder to the half a foot of hard pack that had covered the pass the week before. The villagers had been sceptical they could traverse the thing, but Griff seemed unconcerned. When they reached the bottom of the narrow defile that led up into the hills, the order was given for men to dismount.

A slight depression in the unmarked snow showed where the buried path clung to the eastern flank of the pass. As they started to climb, leading their horses by the bridle, the snow rose to their knees, then to their waists. As men in the lead grew exhausted from breaking through the crusting snow, others moved up the column to take their turn at this arduous task. Seamus Murdo, using his huge bulk to advantage, led the column for most of an hour before finally falling back, drenched in sweat despite the miserable cold.

Early on, the frozen track rose high above the valley floor. One horse, straying too far from the line of march, slid down an icy slope and tangled itself in a maze of boulders at the bottom of the narrow cleft. The animal thrashed and tried to rise, but its leg had snapped. Its rider asked to climb down and put the beast out of its misery, but Roland refused. In his cold calculations, he could lose a horse, but not a man. The march continued until the dying animal was finally out of sight..

All morning and into the afternoon, the long column struggled up the pass until, at last, the slope began to flatten. The path now ran nearly flat along a broadening valley floor, though steep hills still loomed on each side. As the sun began to cast long shadows to the east, the head of the column rounded a bend to see a square stone keep on a high crag that overlooked the valley from the west.

Dolwyddelan.

Lookouts on the ramparts of the castle saw the approach of the column and sounded hunting horns to raise the alarm. Soon a throng of men could be seen atop the stone keep and along the top of a timber palisade that ran around the top of the crag. For the first time in hours, Roland lifted his gaze from the treacherous path in front of him and looked around. Everywhere a blanket of white covered the high moorland, broken only by a few patches of gnarled trees. It was a stark place, but beautiful.

It was Llywelyn's birthplace and the Prince had returned to it in his hour of need.

***

There was a huge clamor as Griff and Roland led the Invalid Company through the arched gate of Dolwyddelan. Some men cheered, others beat swords against anything handy, while dogs barked and ran frantically around the small courtyard. Llywelyn rode down himself to greet the newcomers, convinced they could only be friendlies. Even his bitterest enemies would have thought better than to risk the pass after a blizzard.

Roland hadn't seen the Prince in two years and the man had lost none of his royal bearing. If anything, the extra years had added a note of gravity to the young noble's countenance, though Llywelyn's face this day was split by a huge smile that was a reminder of his youth.

The Prince was mounted on none other than The Surly Beast, the magnificent warhorse that Roland had traded for the use of eighty of Llywelyn's longbowmen. Now, he led a hundred men of the Invalid Company to complete payment for that crucial aid. The Prince of Gwynedd leapt from his saddle to embrace Griff like a brother, then held him out at arm's length.

"I knew you wouldn't fail me! That lot said none could make it up here till a good thaw," he shouted, waving his arm in the general direction of the castle. "But as soon as I heard the horn blast, I knew it was you!"

"I come bearing gifts, my lord," Griff proclaimed with a flourish, pointing to the exhausted column of men strung out behind him. "The redoubtable Invalid Company and their commander, Sir Roland Inness!"

Llywelyn spied Roland and tromped through the snow to embrace him almost as enthusiastically as he had Griff.

"Sir Roland! Well met, sir—though I wish it were under more auspicious cirucumstances."

Roland gave the man a small bow.

"My lord, if circumstances were better, we might have no need to meet. And perhaps we can help, in some small way, to change the current situation. I have come to fulfill Earl Ranulf's debt of honour to you. We are at your service."

Llywelyn clapped him on the shoulder.

"Good! Good! Ranulf can be a stiff one, but never did I doubt the man's honour. Come, walk with me. Your men need food, drink and some warmth as well. They look frozen and hungry and we have much to discuss."

The young Welsh noble took back the reins of The Surly Beast from one of his men, who had been barely restraining the ill-tempered warhorse. He led the way up a steep incline to the castle gate and into the courtyard.

"Quarters will be cramped, I'm afraid. I have eighty men here to garrison Dolwyddelan. It is a small keep."

Roland looked around. For the birthplace of a Prince, it was a very modest place. There was a small stone gatehouse that faced south, connected by wooden palisades on the east and west to a square stone keep at the northern edge of the crag. It was bigger than Shipbrook, but not by much. Quarters would be crowded indeed.

Llywelyn saw Roland assessing the fortifications.

"My father had it built to guard against incursions from the south of Wales. This fort blocked one of the paths into Gwynedd. It's a lonely spot. I was but a babe when last I lived here, but I always thought of it as home."

"It reminds me of my own home back in Derbyshire," Roland said, looking over the walls at the surrounding peaks. "I was raised in high country such as this."

Llywelyn nodded.

"Home has a pull on a man's heart, does it not?"

"Aye, my lord, it does. The Earl of Derby drove my people out of the mountains of Derbyshire and many long to return to it, though the new land granted by Earl Ranulf is rich. I will always hold Kinder Scout dear, but I have found a new home and am contented."

"Lady Millicent?"

Roland grinned.

"Aye, lord. Millicent Inness is all the home I need."

Llywelyn stopped at the arched door to the square keep.

"She's a comely lass and full of spirit—I can vouch for that! You've married above yourself with that one, Sir Roland, and I'll do my best to see you safe returned to her."

"I'd be obliged, my lord."

***

A pen had been built on a level spot below the fortress of Dolwyddelan for the horses Llywelyn had brought with him on his flight from the winter encampment. Men were immediately put to work expanding it to accommodate the mounts of the Invalid Company. Finding lodging for the men was a more difficult problem, as the castle itself could not so easily be enlarged.

Llywelyn's steward scurried about as frantically as the hounds in the courtyard, seeking out any sheltered spot where the tired men could take some rest. Patch and Sergeant Billy kept a wary eye on him as he directed the new arrivals into storage sheds, empty grain bins and every other sort of unoccupied space, until all were out of the weather. The Invalids were simply grateful to escape the bitter cold and settled in next to their fellows without complaint.

Roland followed Llywelyn and Griff into the keep, which loomed three stories above his head. The bottom floor held most of the supplies for the castle along with spare arms. The Prince led them up a narrow stone stairway to the second floor, which was spacious and comfortably fitted-out with tables and chairs.

Two men sat at the table. Both were well into their middle years. One was almost painfully thin, with close-cropped greyish hair and an exuberant moustache that curled up at each end. He lounged casually, with his chair tipped back and his feet up on the tabletop. While his body was spare, his face was oddly round. He had lively dark eyes that spoke of a keen intelligence. Across the table was a man of thicker build, with a fringe of a beard at his jawline that had gone completely grey. His round face and dark eyes marked him unmistakably as kin to the man opposite, though his eyes seemed somehow dull and world-weary.

Brothers, Roland thought immediately.

The thinner man slowly lowered the chair to the floor and stood when Llywelyn entered the room. Seeing his brother rise, the man opposite grudgingly got to his feet.

"My lords, may I present Sir Roland Inness, vassal of Earl Ranulf of Chester, Commander of the redoubtable Invalid Company and proclaimed by King Richard himself as the greatest archer in all of England!" announced Llywelyn. Roland bowed toward the two men.

"Sir Roland, may I present my cousins, Lord Gruffydd," the stocky man gave a slight nod, "and Lord Maredudd," the thin man smiled, "rulers of Meirionnydd—and my allies."

"I am honoured, my lords," Roland said.

"How many men did you bring?" Gruffydd asked, bluntly.

"One hundred seven, my lord."

"Hardly enough to frighten our uncles," Maredudd said, still smiling.

"These are the Invalids," Llywelyn interrupted. "I saw their worth with my own eyes in the Conwy valley two years ago. Had they not cut through Daffyd's best men that day, I would not be standing here now. I'd not trade them for three times their number."

"They are all crippled, are they not?" Maredudd asked, with genuine curiosity.

"All have been wounded—in body or in spirit, my lords," said Roland, a bit defensively, "but not a one is crippled."

"They fought in your King's crusade, did they not?"

"Aye, most did."

Gruffydd snorted.

"As soon as your King set sail in search of glory, or salvation for his soul, we should've invaded and taken back all the land you Normans stole from us—but Daffyd and Roderic did nothing."

Roland bristled. He had ridden through a blizzard and struggled through waist deep snow to reach this place and was in no mood for insults.

"I am no Norman, my lord."

"He's a Dane!" Griff offered, helpfully.

Roland fixed Gruffydd with a stare.

"I doubt you Welsh will ever recover what you have lost and certainly not as long as you busy yourselves killing your own brothers, cousins and uncles...my lord."

For a moment there was a frozen silence in the room, then Maredudd let loose with a cackling laugh.

"That is the truth, sure enough, sir, but you must not begrudge us if we kill just two more of our kinsmen! That is why my brother and I are here. It is time for Gwynedd to be whole. It will never happen with Roderic and Daffyd squatting on the two halves of our land. We are hopeful that our young cousin here," he nodded toward Llywelyn, "can unite us, as our grandfather once did. That will make the English tremble when they look across the Dee."

"But of course, we have no ambitions beyond the natural borders of Gwynedd," Llywelyn added, staring pointedly at his two cousins. Gruffydd snorted again, but Maredudd seemed to suddenly remember that Roland was here as a vassal of one of the great English Marcher Lords—a man who had his own ideas where natural borders lay.

"None, whatsoever," he said hastily.

Roland watched this little drama play out and understood Earl Ranulf's concerns more clearly now. How events played out here in Wales would surely be felt in Cheshire and beyond for years to come.

"And we don't kill all of our kin, Sir Roland," Llywelyn added cheerily. "Gruffydd and Maredudd have managed to avoid killing each other through ten years of joint rule!"

"Though I have been tempted," Gruffydd muttered.

"Now it is time to finally deal with our uncles. Daffyd has hunted me like a dog for seven years and Roderic has kept his thumb on my dear cousins for longer than that. It is time for them to go."

"So what is the plan, my lords?" Roland asked, relieved that his own sharp response had not soured the project from the outset. There was a pained silence all around. Llywelyn finally cleared his throat and spoke.

"We have not...agreed upon a course of action...as yet."

Roland's heart sank a bit at this awkward admission by the Prince of Gwynedd. He had seen how difficult it was to forge a coherent plan between allies during the long siege of Acre. There, the Germans had a plan, as did the French, as did each of the European contingents. Under King Guy's leadership, there had been only loose coordination, at best. It was a situation remedied only when King Richard finally took firm command of the host. It appeared that Llywelyn, in desperate need of aid from his cousins, was in no position to dictate as Richard had done. It was yet another layer of complexity he would have to sort out.

Still, there had to be a plan.

"Tell me what forces you can bring to a fight, my lord," Roland asked mildly. Llywelyn seemed relieved to move the discussion from politics and fratricide to strategy.

"I've eighty men here and I've sent two hundred more on to my cousins' domain of Meirionnydd. I've between four and five hundred men scattered between two winter camps near the border with Powys. Your Invalid Company has one hundred or so and my cousins have another four hundred they can muster in Meirionnydd."

"Over twelve hundred men in all—a formidable force," said Griff.

"Aye, but we estimate Daffyd can bring five hundred of his own men to the field and Roderic, if he takes some men from his garrisons at Aberffraw and Caenarfon, can muster a thousand or more," Maredudd said.

"Then there are the men who attacked us at our winter camp," said Llywelyn. "I had little time to stop and make their acquaintance, but I know they were not Welsh. Word has reached me that there are longships beached on the east bank of the Conwy—down near Llywrst. So they are probably Irish mercenaries."

Griff spoke up.

"Irish, after a fashion, my lord. We found the boy, Pedr, wandering about the ruins of the winter camp. He hid during the attack and was left behind. He saw the leader. They called him Haakon."

A dark look stole across Llywelyn's face and he slammed a fist down on the table.

"Haakon the Black! I should have known. That will be Roderic's doing," he said fiercely. "That man has gone begging to his wife's father for aid and the King of the Isles has sent these Danish scavengers to our shores. No doubt it was Roderic who supplied their mounts and who will supply their silver—for I doubt the King of the Isles is that generous, even for his daughter's sake. My uncle will regret this—I swear!" The Prince's face had turned a bright red.

"They caught two of our lads," Griff said softly. "Gwilyn and Caden. They died hard."

Roland could see Llywelyn's jaw tense as he fought to keep his temper from boiling over.

"If this be Haakon, I will make him rue the day he left Dublin," he said finally and seemed to gather himself. "The last of my spies reached me before the storm came with news of these Northmen. Twenty men guard their boats at Llywrst and the rest have marched upstream to block the valley where the Conwy enters Eryri. They sit there, across our most direct route out of these hills, like a bung in a hole. My man counted four hundred of them."

"We saw riders at the Conwy ford further upstream when we crossed," said Griff. "They saw us as well. I would guess they will be blocking that exit as well."

Silence fell around the room as all contemplated the likelihood that the only two routes back into the heartland of Gywnedd were closed to them.

"So we are hemmed in and the enemy has near twice our numbers," said Roland finally.

Llywelyn nodded.

"Aye."

"But they are scattered, are they not, my lord?"

"Usually they are," said Llywelyn. "Daffyd's men guard villages and forts from the Dee to the Conwy and Roderic has large garrisons at Caernarfon and Bangor, plus troops watching over the isle of Anglesey. But now that they have thrown in together, they have concentrated their men near Deganwy at the mouth of the Conwy, or so they had a week ago when my last spy slipped by the Danes. I think, like us, they have not yet decided where to strike. They cannot assail me here and the rest of my men are scattered to the east near the border with Powys. If they move on them, they'll just vanish across the border. So I present no clear target to march against and they do not know—yet—that my cousins have joined me."

"So we are scattered and they are united."

"I believe that captures the situation."

"Then we must split the uncles and unite our own forces."

"Brilliant!" Gruffydd said, making no effort to hide his sarcasm. "We concluded that two days ago. So how are we to do that Englishman?"

"I don't know," Roland admitted. He did know he was no longer thinking clearly. The struggle up the pass had exhausted him no less than the Invalids who had collapsed into whatever cramped quarters offered them hours ago. Llywelyn seemed to have recognized that his new ally was at the end of his rope.

"Sir Roland, I have been a poor host. I will have food brought to you. You may take quarters with Griff. The room is small, but it is the best I can offer. Let us take up this problem on the morrow."

Roland nodded wearily.

"Thank you, my lord, but let me see to my men before I retire."

He took his leave of the rebel leaders and walked down the stone steps to the first floor of the keep. In a corner he saw Patch and Sergeant Billy curled up and snoring. If Patch and Billy were content, he knew that the men were safely settled in. Griff came down the steps behind him and tapped him on the shoulder.

"Come with me, English. I am dead on my feet."

What to do with a Madawc

They let the exhausted boy sleep until well after dawn, when he stumbled out into the great hall, still a little unsteady on his feet. Lady Catherine put aside a scroll she was working on when she saw him.

"Good morn to you, Rhys. How does the head feel this day?"

The boy raised fingers to the gash and examined the newly-forming scab.

"Passable, my lady, passable. You have my thanks for tending to it."

"Are you able to ride, lad? My husband has the patrol duties today and is already off, but Sir Declan is about and he thought you might wish to visit your father's grave. His men buried him on a rise overlooking the ford."

Rhys nodded.

"I would, my lady, and I'm sure I can sit a horse, though I lost mine at the ford. She ran a good race, she did, but the water just spooked her."

"We have horses aplenty here, son. I'll send a groom to saddle you one and let Declan know you are stirring, but first, have some breakfast."

The boy unconsciously touched his stomach.

"I'm obliged to you, my lady."

Lady Catherine led him back into the kitchen where a small kettle of pottage was warming at the edge of the cook fire. Cook was gone to the root cellar, so she spooned the warm contents into a bowl and handed it to the boy who found a stool and quickly tucked into the meal. After a few bites, he stopped and looked up at her.

Catherine smiled, a little embarrassed that she had been caught watching him.

"I did not mean to stare, Rhys, but you so remind me of your sire. He hunched over his food, just as you do!"

The boy furrowed his brow at that.

"Tell me about him, my lady."

How to tell of Alwyn Madawc?

"Very well, but there is much to tell, so please eat while I tell it. Sir Alwyn was a Welshman through and through, with all of the better angels of that race and only a few of the devils. He was a warrior of renown and my husband's dearest friend—mine as well. He was loyal to his last breath."

"How did he die?" the boy asked, pausing for a moment from his breakfast. "Your husband says he died saving you and your daughter."

"Aye, that's true. You might have heard of the troubles here in England these past few years," she began.

"The royal brothers? I heard they fought."

"Aye, they did and a bloody time it was. Richard was off on Crusade, my husband and his squires along with him. Sir Roger entrusted Sir Alwyn with the duty of defending Shipbrook and protecting me and Millicent."

"That is a lot of trust," the boy said.

Lady Catherine nodded.

"Aye, and there is no other man in England my husband would have given it to. Events proved it to be a greater burden than anyone suspected."

"Events, my lady?"

"Bloody events, lad. We were loyal to King Richard, as was our Earl, Lord Ranulf, but men loyal to the King's brother drove Ranulf from Chester. He sought refuge here, but Shipbrook could not stand against the Earl's enemies. We had to flee in the night. They caught us down at the very ford where you crossed yesterday. Sir Alwyn—your father—defended the southern bank against them while my daughter and I got safe away with Earl

Ranulf. I begged him to come with us, but he knew his business. We would have been run to ground in an hour had he not slowed them at the ford. I am told he killed a half-dozen men before he too fell. It gave us the start we needed to make good our escape, but at a terrible cost."

Rhys gave a small sigh and pushed his bowl away.

"It is hard to hear this, my lady."

Lady Catherine bit her lip.

"It is hard to tell it, Rhys. I am so sorry that he had to give his life for me and mine. Memories of that night weigh heavy on me."

"No, no, my lady, I do not fault you for his death. I can see it had to be as it was. You gave him something worth dying for. He found a family here in this place. Something I never managed in mine. I grieve that I never had that and that I will never know him."

Lady Catherine eyes were brimming as she rose and stood next to the boy. She placed a hand softly on his shoulder.

"Stay here awhile, lad, and I think you will come to know him."

***

Declan reined in at the top of the rise and slid out of his saddle. He raised an arm and beckoned to the boy on the opposite bank. Patrols had seen no sign of the party that had pursued young Rhys, but Declan was not one to take unnecessary risks. He had ridden across first and satisfied himself that the Welsh bank was deserted before signalling the boy to join him.

It was low tide and Rhys splashed easily across to join him. The gravesite was well off the trail and not visible unless you sought it out. The grave itself was well-maintained, with round river stones neatly stacked atop the place where Alwyn's body lay. A handsomely-carved cross stood at one end with Alwyn's name etched in careful script. Among the stones were small bundles of brown and weathered stems, the remainder of flowers left during seasons of bloom.

For a long time, the boy stood over the grave silently. Finally, he spoke.

"It's a nice spot."

Declan looked out over the grave to the ford below.

"I think he would be pleased. He spent many a year watching over this ford."

The Welsh boy found a small stone that had rolled off the mound and carefully placed it back.

"You were off on crusade when he died."

"Aye. Your father was not happy to be left behind, and that's a fact. He did not love war, but war was his business and he never shrank from a fight. He was Sir Roger's Master of the Sword and that title was a good description of the man. He gave me this."

Declan lifted his chin to show a ragged scar beneath.

"And this," he said, sliding the sleeve of his tunic up to reveal another scar above his elbow. "He taught me how to fight and what I learned from him saved my life many times over."

Declan paused and slid his sleeve down.

"None could have imagined that those who went off to war would return unharmed and that Alwyn, who chafed at being left safe here in England, would fall."

"But he did not die in England, did he, Sir Declan?"

"No, he died on his native ground. He died here—in Wales."

Rhys turned away from the grave of the man he had never known and looked up the frozen track that led off to the west and the Clwydian hills.

"It's my native ground as well, and I will be going back."

"Back to your village?" Declan asked, sharply. "Whatever for?"

"I have my reasons."

"Do you seek to settle accounts with your step-father?"

"My reasons are my own," the boy said flatly.

Declan shook his head.

"Listen to me, lad. No doubt, ye have yer grievances, but don't be a fool. A man such as this Talfryn does not rule even a small patch of Wales by being weak—or careless. You said he had this man Morgant as his right hand and he will have other guards. Is he ever alone and unprotected? And, even if you could find him so, would you have the skill to kill him?"

Declan watched the boy, who continued to look off toward the hills.

"Or do you not care if you live or die, Master Madawc?"

The boy whirled around, startled to be called by his true name for the first time.

Rhys Madawc locked eyes with Declan.

"I do not wish to die, Sir Declan, and you are right. Talfryn goes nowhere without his guards nearby and I've seen myself his skill with a blade. He would be a hard man to kill, though I have never said that was my intention."

Declan gave him a sceptical look.

"Whatever your purposes, lad, there is civil war in your country. I don't know your village, but I know Saint Asaph's church sits on land ruled by Lord Daffyd and Daffyd is losing that war. The Earl of Chester just sent one hundred of his best men to aid Daffyd's enemy, Prince Llywelyn. The best man I know leads them. There is going to be blood aplenty spilt before all is done. Whatever your reasons for going back, it will put you in mortal danger, if not from Talfryn, then from one side or the other in this war. I do not wish to have another of your line laid in the soil of this wretched country before his time."

The boy did not answer for a long time, but finally spoke quietly.

"This country may be wretched, Sir Declan, but it is my own and one day I *will* return to it. I know well there is war there. Lord Daffyd calls on Talfryn from time to time to supply men for the fight. I also know that some younger men from the village have slipped away to fight for Lord Llywelyn. Only God can know how it will all end. But, if you feel obliged to keep me from harm, then teach me the things my father taught you. Talfryn never spent a moment teaching me any useful skills. I can ride well enough, but have no training with a sword—or weapons of any kind. I heard one of the men call you Master of the Sword. Do you hold my father's old post?"

"Aye, I do."

"Then teach me how to fight, my lord. Teach me what he taught you."

***

Declan and Sir Roger sat by a roaring fire in the great room of Shipbrook late into the night considering the future of Rhys Madawc. Declan had reported on Rhys' determination to return to Wales and to be trained in arms. The first item troubled the big Norman knight, but the second was welcome news.

"I need a squire, Declan, and I've yet to find a boy among the folk here at Shipbrook who seems suitable."

Declan arched an eyebrow.

"My lord, with respect, you could not swing a cat by the tail around here without hitting a boy who would be an excellent squire! Why, I've nominated three myself."

Sir Roger scowled.

"They all talked too much. A bit like another squire I once had!"

Declan laughed at that.

"So, you think a *Welsh* boy will be more taciturn?"

The master of Shipbrook sighed and shook his head.

"You still talk too much, Sir Declan, and I could well do without a squire, but I confess—the chance to have Alwyn's son in my company…"

"Then we will make it so, my lord," said Declan, rising. "I'll start with him on the morrow."

"Good, and Declan, keep an eye on the boy. There'll be nothing but death for the lad if goes back to Wales."

"Aye, lord, I'll watch him."

***

The next day, the education of Rhys Madawc began humbly enough. He was sent to help the grooms muck out the stables until midmorning and only then did he report to the patch of hard earth set aside within the walls for arms training. Declan O'Duinne was already there, watching carefully as two of Shipbrook's men-at-arms had at each other with wooden swords. He called a halt when the boy hurried up, eager to begin and smelling of horse dung.

"Top of the mornin', Master Madawc. By yer fragrance I can tell yer well on yer way to mastering the first duty of a fightin' man in training—that being shovelin' horse turds. But now it's time for more serious work. Find yerself a wooden sword that suits you in the barrel yonder."

The boy hurried to the barrel that stood in one corner of the practice field. He sorted through the dozen or so carved wooden staves and found one that seemed to have the right heft and feel in his hand. He hurried back, face full of eager readiness.

"So, take up a guard position, if yer familiar with that."

The boy hesitated, unwilling to show his ignorance, then spread his feet and brought the wooden sword up horizontally to shoulder level. Declan just stared.

"Oh, gad! I see we will be beginning at the beginning with you on sword drill. First, ye can't stand stiff-legged like that. Bend the knees—and don't sit back on yer heels. And in most fights, you will likely be moving forward and back, not side to side, so having yer feet square beneath yer shoulders is no good. If ye have a shield in yer left hand, then left foot forward. If no shield, it depends on what the situation dictates."

The boy tried to make all these corrections at once and practically fell over. His face reddened and Declan laughed.

"Let's take it one step at a time, lad. Now, shift yer left foot a little forward. Good. Bend the knees and get off yer heels."

He watched the boy reposition himself and walked ten paces to his front.

"Very well, that's where we start from. Now come at me as though you planned to strike with yer sword."

The boy hesitated, then came forward in a sort of scurrying walk toward Declan.

"Ah, now here is a rule to take to heart, lad. In close quarters, never—and I mean never—let one foot cross the other when ye move. If they tangle and ye go down, ye stay down—for good! Watch me."

Declan took up a guard position with his left foot forward and came across the practice field in a quick series of lunges and shuffles, his rear foot never crossing in front of his lead foot.

"This is most important in a pitched battle, Rhys, where there'll be bodies layin' about to trip over, but even if it's just you and one other man, ye can't afford to lose yer footin'. Clear?"

"Aye, sir. Clear."

Declan nodded.

"Now we practice it."

For an hour, Declan drilled Rhys with no let up, until the boy was dripping with sweat in the cold air. The lad was nimble on his feet and had a natural sense of balance. What's more, he was fast—very fast. But he was unused to these drills and, while he never complained, fatigue began to make his movements slow and clumsy. Declan called a halt.

"We'll finish every day like this, lad. I've seen more men die in a fight from weariness than from lack of skill. Now let's give the legs a bit of a rest and work on yer sword and shield arms."

He handed Rhys a heavy metal bar, twice the weight of a broadsword and led him to a leather bag stuffed taut with hay and rags that hung at one end of the field. He ordered the boy to strike the bag thirty times with the bar using his right arm, then thirty more with his left. Rhys did not complain, but there were small, involuntary groans as he laboured through the drills.

As Declan watched him, he suppressed a smile. It was too soon to offer any kind words to the boy, but he liked what he saw. It was clear the lad had had no training whatever in arms, but he had ample strength in his thick shoulders and he was game.

In time, he might be a dangerous man.

No Simple Plan

*R*oland awoke with a start to the sound of a rooster crowing. For a moment he did not know where he was, then he saw the still-sleeping bulk of Griff Connah curled up on a straw mat across the cell-like room they shared. He arose quietly and slipped from the room, making his way to the keep's entrance where a sleepy guard straightened a bit as he passed by into the courtyard.

He looked up to see another cloudless blue sky, brightening with the coming sunrise. High hills loomed above the wooden palisades to the west, their tops dazzling white with reflected sunlight. It felt as though the bitter cold of the past few days had vanished overnight. There was still a chill in the air, but Roland could see icicles forming at the edge of roofs as the snow began to melt.

Along one side of the stone keep, a shed gave shelter to two cooks who were busily preparing morning rations for the garrison and the new arrivals. Otherwise, the courtyard was empty. An audible growl from his stomach reminded him that it was time for breakfast. He wandered over to the cook pots and was rewarded with a chunk of black bread and small bowl of thin broth. He eyed the pot over the fire.

Rations running low.

He turned up the bowl and quickly drained it. It was hardly more than warm water.

"Good morning, my lord!"

Roland turned to see Friar Cyril approach in his usual jerky gait, all long shanks and elbows.

"And the same to you. Did you sleep well?"

"Well enough, my lord. Jammed in among the lads, but I've fared worse!" The friar looked up at the dripping icicles forming on the cook shed. "Looks like a thaw is coming."

"Aye," said Roland, "and none too soon. It's a thin soup for breakfast and that tells me our stay here will not be long."

"Two days, lord. That's what I heard the Prince's steward tell one of his men—and it's the fodder that will be gone before the food."

"You have sharp ears, Cyril."

The monk grinned.

"All in service to the Lord."

Roland returned the smile. He was warming to this churchman. The friar might be awkward, but he had a keen mind.

"Well then, I'd best fashion a plan before the horses starve."

The monk nodded.

"I'm sure you will make it a good one, my lord, but I'll put a word in with God all the same."

"Amen to that."

***

Roland returned to his small room to find Griff stirring. The tall archer yawned and stretched.

"Morning, English."

"Morning, Griff. I wonder if you could spare me a bit of your time? I'm in need of your help."

"Trouble?"

"None that you don't already know of. I've been thinking on a plan. I have an idea, but it needs meat upon the bones. You've been fighting this war for seven years. I think you can help me."

Griff nodded, fully awake now.

"What is it you need?"

"The uncles have most of their forces concentrated near Deganwy. What will it take to draw one or the other away?

Where are they vulnerable? Where might we pose a threat they cannot ignore?"

Griff furrowed his brow.

"Let's walk while I think. I could use some breakfast."

"I think it will disappoint you."

"Nevertheless, I think better with something in my stomach."

Together they walked out of the keep and Griff took his place behind three other men in line at the cook shed. While he waited, he turned to Roland.

"The place Daffyd values above all is Rhuddlan. It's the only stone fortress within his domain and its walls are tall and strong. Built by a Norman of course," he added sourly. "Rhuddlan gives him a base that we cannot threaten—at least not by assault—and we are in no position to lay siege. He also puts great store in his castle at Deganwy. We believe he keeps half of his treasury there, but it is no Rhuddlan. It sits atop two steep hills, which makes it difficult to get at, but Daffyd has not spent any of his silver maintaining the place. It's built of timber, not stone, and is not in good repair. They've allowed the gorse to grow right up to the base of the walls. With a bit of luck, it might be taken by a surprise assault, but near two thousand men are presently camped within sight of the fortress. We can hardly surprise the castle if we have to pass through an army to get to the gate."

"Hardly, but what of Roderic? What does he value that we could threaten?"

Griff reached the head of the line and accepted a bowl of the thin soup. He slurped it down before replying.

"Roderic's most valued possession is the great castle at Caenarfon. He keeps much of his treasure there. It is stronger even than Rhuddlan and can be resupplied by sea, so you can forget threatening that place. We would be laughed at by the garrison."

"The Prince mentioned Bangor."

"Aye, there is a cathedral there and no fort to speak of, but I doubt seizing church property would cause Roderic to panic. Besides, it lies just a single day's march from Deganwy."

"That's not far enough for our purposes," Roland agreed. "Perhaps we should just surrender to the uncles."

Griff scowled at him, then laughed.

"Don't think that hasn't crossed a few minds these past few weeks!"

Roland grinned.

"So, what of Anglesey? Llywelyn says Roderic has men there. I know little of the place. I believe I must have sailed past it once on my return from the Holy Land, but it was night and I got no view of it.

"Ah, the Isle of Anglesey!" Griff exclaimed, a dreamy look coming over him. "It is lovely flat ground. In truth, it is the best land in Gwynedd. Most of our grain and half of our cattle come from there."

Roland rubbed his chin.

"We could raid the place."

"That *would* cause Roderic to panic, *if* it were harvest time. But as you can see, it is the dead of winter. We might carry off a few cows and burn a granary or two, but the fields are frozen with nothing much to steal or despoil there."

While they spoke, men had begun to rise and stumble out into the courtyard. Some headed for the cook shed, but others began to drift over to where the two men were so intently engaged in conversation. Both noticed the growing interest.

"I could stretch my legs," said Griff pointedly and Roland nodded his agreement. Together they crossed the courtyard and walked out through the arched gate of Dolwyddelan. The sun was fully up now and wherever it struck the drifts, the morning light sparkled like diamonds. Roland looked around.

"It's beautiful up here."

Griff scannned the valley below the fortress as they trudged along.

"Aye, and safe too, but we are short provisions."

"Two days I'm told."

Griff gave him a hard look.

"Our people talk too freely."

"That doesn't change the fact that we will have to move in two days or start to eat the horses. And we have no plan."

They walked along in silence for a while, save for the crunch of their boots on the crusted snow. Abruptly, Griff stopped and grasped Roland's arm.

"Aberffraw!"

The name sounded familiar to Roland, but he could not recall its significance.

"What of it?"

"It's but a small village on Anglesey, but Roderic keeps his Ilys—his royal court—there. Aberffraw holds a special meaning for the people of Gwynedd. The village was chosen by Anarawd, son of Rhodri the Great, three hundred years ago to be the seat of his family dynasty. It's been seen as the centre of royal authority in Gwynedd ever since. Princes of Gwynedd may rule from wherever they choose, but most have recognized the value of ruling from there. At Aberffraw, there is a low stone enclosure and a handsome great hall where Roderic holds court and issues his edicts, but no real fortifications."

"So, we strike at Aberffraw?"

Roland watched, as mounting excitement played over the usually stolid face of the tall Welshman.

"Aye, aye, if Llywelyn seized the royal court and proclaimed himself Prince of Gwynedd from that sacred place…"

"Roderic would panic and march to take it back."

"He would!" said Griff with absolute certainty.

"Then we have at least part of a plan. How do we get to Anglesey?"

Griff shook his head.

"As you know, Anglesey's an island. It is separated from the mainland by the Strait of Menai. The strait is hardly more than the width of a river in places, but it is deep and there are difficult currents. There is a ferry that crosses the narrowest section, but it would take most of a day to get enough men across. And the ferry is less than a day's march from Roderic's garrison at Caenarfon. We would not be able to cross unseen or unmolested."

"We will have to find a way, but there is another problem," Roland said.

Griff cocked his head.

"If we seize Aberffraw, what will keep Roderic and his brother from marching together to meet us there?"

The Welshman rubbed his chin.

"Daffyd would rather stay near his own territory, no doubt of that. But if they thought there was a chance to bring Llywelyn to battle at Aberffraw with their united forces, he would go. So, that *is* a problem. The uncles would still be united and the flat land of Anglesey is no place to fight a battle if you're outnumbered."

By now, they had reached the bottom of the path leading from the castle to the valley floor. The snow still lay deep, but the temperature had continued to climb along with the morning sun and the signs of melting were everywhere.

"What if we seized the fortress at Deganwy? You said yourself that Daffyd keeps half his treasury there, but it might be taken by surprise assault. Daffyd would not march off to Anglesey if we seized his treasury."

"Aye, but I also said we couldn't just parade through the uncles' encampment on our way to attack the fort without raising the alarm."

Roland nodded.

"So, we have a plan—seize Aberffraw, if we can get there, and take Deganwy, if we can surprise the place."

"With that many ifs, it's not much of a plan," said Griff dryly, as they began trudging back up the slushy track to the castle. Roland slapped him on the back.

"It's a beginning, Griff, and I've begun with worse!"

***

"Aberffraw?" Prince Llywelyn snorted. "Why not just take London and declare myself King of the English? Sir Roland, I know you made the plan that took Chester back from the Earl of Derby. It was a brilliant diversion and a bold assault you made to open the Bridgegate, but this is no plan. Roderic's court might not be fortified, but we would need wings to get there! You *do* know it's on an island, do you not?"

"Aye, my lord."

"There is the ferry at the Menai Strait, but we'd need to march thirty miles through mountain passes and slip by the garrison at Caenarfon. Hardly likely."

"Aye, lord," chimed in Griff. "Using the ferry would not be advisable."

"Well, we can't swim the strait!" Llywelyn said heatedly.

"No, my lord, we can't," said Griff. "We will need boats, but cannot use the ferry."

"And where shall we find these boats?"

At this, Griff stood and walked over to the fire burning in the hearth.

Where to find boats...

He looked back at the men gathered around the table and blinked. Then a small grin creased his usually solemn face. He gestured toward Llywelyn's cousins, who had been watching this debate with barely concealed boredom.

"It occurs to me, as I look upon my lords Gruffydd and Maredudd, that there are boats in Meirionnydd," he said, "lots of them."

Gruffydd looked startled, but Maredudd's eyes lit up. He turned to Llywelyn.

"Your man is right, cousin. Recall that Meirionnydd has little farmland. It's why our dear Uncle Roderic gave it to us. But we do have the sea, and many of our folk are fishermen. We have boats that could make the voyage around Llyn and on to Anglesey."

"Fishing boats? How many?" Llywelyn asked.

Maredudd turned to Gruffydd.

"What would you guess, brother. Thirty vessels sturdy enough for such a voyage?"

Gruffydd shrugged.

"About that."

"How many men could we transport?" Llywelyn asked eagerly, his irritation at a foolish plan was starting to turn to enthusiasm.

Gruffydd took a moment to pick something from his teeth.

"Six hundred, give or take a few score. Enough for most of the men here and those waiting in Meirionnydd—but not enough for your men in the eastern camps or these English," he said, jerking his head toward Roland.

"But it would be enough to take Aberffraw with Roderic and his thousand men camped at Deganwy!" Llywelyn said as he rose from his seat and began pacing the room.

"Aberffraw sits hardly a mile up the Ffraw River from the coast," Maredudd said, warming to this new idea, "but the river would be too shallow for our boats. As I recall, there is a fine little bay with a good sandy shore near its mouth. We can beach the boats and reach the town before anyone can prepare."

"They'd hardly have time to close the gate!" Gruffydd added, starting to get caught up in the idea of storming the royal Ilys.

"By God, that would shock my uncle!" said Llywelyn. "He will not sit there at Deganwy while I warm his seat in Aberffraw!"

He turned back to face Roland, a little of the fire going out of his countenance.

"It's a start, sir, but only that. If they think they can trap me on Anglesey, both brothers will march there. Six hundred men could not stand against such a host."

Roland had stayed silent as the idea of a waterborne attack on Anglesey had taken hold of the Prince and his cousins. While the men around the table had exulted at the thought of tweaking Lord Roderic by taking Aberffraw, he had been thinking about the next move.

"My lord, timing will be everything for this plan to work. Your seizure of Aberffraw must draw both of your uncles south. Only then will the way be clear for us to mount a surprise assault on Deganwy Castle. If Daffyd doesn't move, then there is no hope of taking the place. But if he does, we let him march a day south while we take his fortress from him. He will then countermarch, leaving Roderic to face you alone."

"With at least a thousand men, Sir Roland, and perhaps another four hundred mercenaries!" Llywelyn shouted, slamming his fist down on the table. "Of what use is drawing Daffyd back to Deganwy, if Roderic alone can slaughter me and all my men at Aberffraw?"

"But you will not be at Aberffraw when Roderic arrives, my lord."

The room fell silent for a moment as Llywelyn stared at Roland.

"What do you mean?" he asked finally, confusion written on his face.

"My lord, once you are certain that Roderic is across the Menai Strait and marching on Aberffraw, you must take ship once more and sail for the mouth of the Conwy River."

The room fell silent once more. The men around the table exchanged questioning glances. It was Griff who first grasped the logic.

"Deganwy!" he exclaimed and pounded a fist on the table. He looked first at Roland who nodded agreement, then turned to Maredudd.

"How long would it take to sail around Anglesey to Deganwy, my lord?"

Maredudd squinted into the middle distance trying to estimate the distance and time.

"Twelve hours—maybe more, maybe less—depending on the winds."

Griff turned back to Llywelyn.

"And how long would it take Roderic to march back to Deganwy from Aberffraw, my lord?"

Llywelyn was starting to grasp the plan. He placed both palms on the table and leaned forward.

"Two days for cavalry—three for foot! By God, it might work! We draw them both south, then seize Deganwy Castle— Daffyd keeps a horde of his silver there. He will countermarch back as fast as he can drive his men. Griff, you could gather our men out on the border with Powys and when Daffyd returns to Deganwy, he will find that I am not in Anglesey. I will be waiting for him on his own ground along with all of my men. Those odds will be better than even with Roderic two day's march away!"

Again, the room fell silent as all saw the shining possibility of facing Daffyd, alone, in open battle. Llywelyn was the first to break the spell. He turned back to Griff.

"But how do we seize Deganwy Castle?"

Griff shrugged, his face going solemn once more.

"This plan to split the brothers is not my own, my lord. Perhaps Sir Roland can answer that."

All eyes swung back to Roland. Another lesson from Sir Roger came to his mind.

There is no need to coat the truth with honey.

"I don't know, my lord, but if it must be done, we will find a way."

Llywelyn frowned at this.

"Sir Roland, you have devised a clever plan—brilliant even—but dangerous. Still, it is more than any of us have been able to arrive at over the past week. We have two days of food and fodder left, so please tell me how we will take Deganwy Castle before it is gone."

"Aye, my lord,"

***

For the remainder of the day, Roland pondered the nettlesome problem of Deganwy. Deganwy could not be approached until most of the enemy host had crossed the Conwy and it must be taken before they crossed over to Anglesey. But how to do that?

He conferred with Patch, Sergeant Billy and Fancy Jack. All had ideas, but all fell apart under hard questioning. He huddled with Griff for an hour considering whether they could march the men in the winter camps to the fort and seize it, but concluded that the arrival of five hundred mounted men at Deganwy would make a surprise assault impossible and that five hundred were not enough to take the place if the defenders were alerted.

As the sun sank below the hills to the west, Roland ate a quick supper of hard cheese and bread and retired to his cell with a candle to sit and think. Sir Roger had always counselled keeping plans simple, but there seemed no simple answer to scattering the enemy's forces and concentrating their own. Finally, his brain full of cobwebs, he blew out the candle and curled up on his mat.

***

It was well past midnight when Roland arose, his heart pounding and his chest heaving. It was the damned dream again—horsemen on a frozen field thundering toward him. As always, he had turned to run for the woods as the riders drew near. He could hear the horses snort and the men shout. But something was different this time. In this dream, the cries were not in the Gaelic or the Dutch of Prince John's mercenaries. These words he understood plainly.

They were Danish.

"Griff!"

Griff Connah had been snoring contentedly in his own corner and rose in a panic, searching for his sword in the pitch dark.

"Griff, Griff! Calm yourself. There is no danger."

The sounds of the Welshman rummaging for his weapon stopped.

"What then," the man rasped.

"I have the rest of our plan!"

"It had best be good, English," he managed, groggily.

"We are going to steal the boats!"

"Boats?"

"Aye, Haakon's longships! Llywelyn's spy said they were drawn up on the bank of the Conwy with only a score of men to guard them. The Invalids will have no trouble dealing with twenty men. So, we take the boats, row down the Conwy, land at Deganwy and march right up to the gate. The men Daffyd leaves behind when he marches south will think we are their Danish allies. Before they realize we are not, we take the fort!"

Griff did not respond at once and Roland wished fervently that he could pierce the darkness to see the look on his companion's face. Finally, the Welshman spoke.

"I'll grant ye, that you and the Invalids are the only folk we have who have taken and held a fort," he said, "but what of Haakon? He is blocking the road out of these hills with four hundred men."

"Griff, I grew up in country such as this. There are always paths known to folk in the hills that avoid the valleys. For this, we will not need horses. Find me a local boy and he will lead us round the Danes to their boats."

"And how will you be able to convince the garrison that you are Haakon's men?"

"When we arrive in longships, they will think us Danes."

"From afar, no doubt," Griff said in the dark, "but you are leading Englishmen and Welshmen. How will they pass, once you are ashore?"

"They won't need to, not if they are led by a Dane."

There was a long silence, then Griff spoke quietly.

"Of course, English. You are a Dane."

Roland heard him get to his feet.

"There is much that can go wrong with this, Roland, but I like it. Let's wake Llywelyn."

***

Llywelyn did not complain when Roland and Griff roused him long before dawn. He summoned his cousins to a new council and they arrived, groggy from sleep, but alert enough once the plan had been laid before them. All peppered Roland with questions and concerns. He could see them turning the thing over in their minds, like some shiny new play thing.

Roland glanced across the table at Llywelyn and could see in the Prince's eyes that he was torn. It was a perilous plan and one that put at risk the lives and the fortunes of every man in the room, but if it worked, he would rule Gwynedd at last.

If.

When the questions had at last died away, Llywelyn rose.

"This plan will be like a dance—and there can be no missteps. I will lure my uncles toward Aberffraw and once they've committed, Sir Roland will draw Daffyd back to Deganwy by seizing his fort. Before Roderic can grapple with me on Anglesey, I will take ship once more. Griff will gather the men in the winter camps and we will all meet at Deganwy. And that will be the end of Daffyd."

Roland looked around the table and saw Maredudd and Gruffydd nodding their heads eagerly and it worried him. He stood and spoke directly to the Prince.

"My lord, there is much here that can go wrong—there will certainly be some things that *will* go wrong. You are risking all on this plan. Are you sure?"

Llywelyn looked at him for a long moment.

"Sir Roland, I see the risks, not the least of them to you and your Invalids, but for a generation, divided rule has made our country weak." he said, disgust in his voice. "And we have been lucky! Your old King Henry was too busy fighting with his own sons to trouble us and your King Richard occupies his time in France. Otherwise, Gwynedd would already be under Norman rule. Sooner or later, you English will again cast covetous eyes on our country and Daffyd and Roderic are not the men to save it. I am. That is why I fight. I believe God intends for me to rule all of Gwynedd. If that is true, He will not let this plan fail. It is in His hands."

Roland winced at the Prince's words. He had heard other men invoke God's hand in their own causes before. At Hattin, in the Kingdom of Jerusalem, a Christian army had marched into battle chanting "God demands it!" He had ridden over their bleached bones on that field.

"God can be a fickle ally, my lord," he said quietly.

Llywelyn glared at him, then softened.

"Sir Roland, the greatest risk is yours. If Griff and I fail to reach Deganwy in," he stopped, working through the times and distances in his head, "five days time, you could be facing Daffyd alone. Are you willing to risk that? Are *you* sure?"

Roland did not answer at once. Sir Roger de Laval had always said that the best plans were simple, but this *thing* he'd devised was anything but that, and it left him with a kernel of doubt. But he could see no other path forward with any chance of success and he could take some comfort from another piece of his old master's advice.

Even a bad plan may succeed, if boldly carried out.

If the plan could not be simple, the execution would have to be bold. He met Llywelyn's gaze.

"Aye, lord, I'm sure," he lied. There was nothing more to say.

126

Opening Moves

*L*lywelyn sat on The Surly Beast, though he did not call his favourite warhorse by that name, and watched his men ride through the gate at Dolwyddelan and down toward the pass at Bwlch y Gorddinan. Traversing the pass was much less daunting now, since warmer weather had turned the waist-deep powder on the trail into ankle-deep slush.

Gruffydd and Maredudd had ridden out at dawn, anxious to muster their fighting men and assemble their fishing fleet in the protected estuary of the River Mawddach. It was midmorning now and Llywelyn was leading sixty of his own men down to join them. Roland Inness stood beside the big horse that had once been his own and watched the men ride out.

Once agreement on the plan had been reached in the small hours of the morning, there was no more discussion. Orders were issued, cooks were roused, horses were given the last of the fodder and the men were mustered. At Roland's request, a local boy who knew the mountains between Dolwyddelan and the River Conwy and a man who had grown up along the Conwy River were left behind along with twenty of the Welsh longbowmen.

Holding a poorly maintained fort, protected only by a steep slope and a wooden palisade, simply could not be done without archers and Llywelyn had been quick to grant the request. If Haakon joined Daffyd at Deganwy, as he well might in search of his stolen boats, there would be at least eight hundred men trying take back the castle. Twenty longbowmen on the ramparts might just buy enough time for help to arrive.

Roland glanced up at the Prince, keeping a wary eye on the big roan charger, who had a nasty tendency to bite without warning. Llywelyn looked full of confidence, but Roland fretted. The Prince had been fighting for seven long years and was now about to risk all on a complicated plan that Roland himself was not sure would work.

Simple is always best.

Sir Roger's words still gnawed at him, but the die was now cast. As the last man in the column cleared the gate, Llywelyn leaned down and interrupted Roland's thoughts.

"Maredudd has an eye for weather. Before he rode out this morning he studied the heavens and prophesied good sailing. We should reach the Mawddach on the morrow by late afternoon and will load the boats and set sail straight away. Gruffydd says his fishermen are not afraid of the dark. With fair winds, we will land at Aberffraw just before dawn two days from now."

"And I will take Deganwy Castle on the day after, if all goes well."

As they spoke, Griff rode up to join them. He was mounted on Roland's big grey gelding. There was no place for horses where Roland was going and the Welshman had need of a horse with speed and endurance to reach the winter camps out near the border with Powys. He would need to take narrow and steep trails to skirt the Danes, who would now be guarding the main roads out of the mountains. For that, there was no more sure-footed mount than The Grey.

Griff patted the horse's neck and nodded to Roland.

"I'm obliged for the loan," he said.

"I'll need you in Deganwy in five days, Griff. If any horse can get you there, it's The Grey."

Griff smiled.

"I'll not fail ye, English."

"Nor will I," said Llywelyn. "Look for my boats on that day and luck to you both!" The Prince gave The Surly Beast his spurs and the big horse sprang forward. His rider did not look back at his childhood home as he rode through the gate and down toward the pass. A moment later, Griff turned in his saddle.

"Good hunting, English." he said with a growl and dug his heels into The Grey's flanks. As the horse sprang forward, the Welshman called over his shoulder.

"In five days—at Deganwy!"

***

It took Llywelyn a full day to make his way through the mountain passes of Eryri and reach the border of Meirionnydd. Just over the border, he found his two hundred men waiting for him where the River Eden meets the River Mawddach, high in the foothills. Maredudd and Gruffydd had passed their encampment in the night and alerted them that the Prince was not far behind.

Marching at first light, Llywelyn reached the protected estuary of the River Mawddach at noon, where Maredudd and Gruffydd were waiting for him with boats and four hundred men. Llywelyn gave a silent sigh of relief when he saw the thirty large fishing boats bobbing at anchor in the estuary. The brothers had made good their promise of sea transport.

The afternoon was spent in getting the men embarked, so that the small flotilla could get under way before night fell. The boats all reeked of rotten fish, which bothered the men who manned them not at all. For the six hundred fighting men jammed in the holds and crowded on the decks, it was another matter. By the time the fleet of fishing vessels hoisted sail, men were already retching over the sides and into the river.

Llywelyn stood by the helm of the lead craft and tried to take no heed of the smell or the misery of the men. They were soldiers after all and would get used to the stench. Finally, the anchor was weighed and the bow of his small boat turned toward the mouth of the river and the short run down to Cardigan Bay.

The man at the helm was twice Llywelyn's age and as brown as tanned leather. There was not an ounce of fat on his wiry frame and his hair, streaked with grey and flying free in the sea breeze, was in a tangle that showed little acquaintance with a comb. The helmsman's clothes were of coarse, undyed wool that would have been suitable for a pauper, but Maredudd had introduced him as Caradog Priddy, owner of a quarter of the craft assembled for the invasion of Anglesey and a man deferred to by others in the fish trade along the coast.

"Welcome, Lord Prince," Priddy had greeted him warmly enough, when he'd stepped upon the deck of the foul-smelling vessel. "We'll have unfavourable winds for roundin' the Llyn once the sun is down," he announced in a cheery voice, "but never fear—round it we shall! Can't tell as what we'll find beyond that. It will be what it will be."

Llywelyn nodded.

"My thanks, Master Priddy. All of Gwynedd will thank you for what you are doing this day."

"Aye, my lord, and I appreciate that, I do, but it is I who thanks you!"

"Me?" Llywelyn asked, puzzled.

"Oh, aye, lord. There's few fish along this coast this time of year, so the silver you've promised is most generous and very welcome."

Llywelyn furrowed his brow. What had Gruffydd and Maredudd promised this man—in his name? That question was on his tongue, but he bit it back.

Let sleeping dogs lie, he thought.

***

The sun was setting behind the Llyn peninsula as the makeshift flotilla emerged into open water. As Master Priddy had predicted, the winds were blustery and from the south. As the bottom fell away, deep swells formed and the small boat began to rise with each crest and plunge into each trough. Men who had endured the smell stoically, now gave in to the motion and rushed to the edge of the pitching deck to empty their stomachs.

Llywelyn had never been aboard a ship in all of his life. He tried not to watch the wretched display of men heaving on the deck and over the side and he steeled himself against the constant up and down motion of the waves. It was to little avail. Before they were a mile off shore, Llywelyn, Prince of Gwynedd, leaned over the side and vomited into Cardigan Bay. It would take nearly twelve hours to reach Anglesey. It was going to be a long night.

***

Forty miles northeast of the bay, Griff Connah slid out of the saddle and led the big grey gelding off the trail that ran alongside the Conwy. The river, so broad when it reached the Irish Sea, was hardly more than a brook here in the hills. In a few more miles it would tumble out of the high country and bend toward the west. Where the river left the hills was the ancient ford he had crossed with the Invalid Company just days ago. The path he had been following crossed that ford, but he could not. He knew it would now be guarded by Haakon's Danes. He had to find a game trail or some other path that would take him around his enemies unseen.

The sun had already dipped below the high hills to the west and twilight was descending on the broad valley as he surveyed the low ridge that flanked the valley on the east. Somewhere above him he heard a sheep bleat. He followed the sound and was rewarded with a narrow but well-worn trail, no doubt used by local shepherds to move their flocks between pasturages. It was heading due east away from the valley and that suited his purposes. He dismounted and led The Grey on foot up the side of the slope. Sometime in the night, he guided the horse back down from the high hills and into the gently rolling country beyond. Connah mounted and turned the horse's head toward the border with Powys.

The sixty Danes who watched the ford saw nothing.

***

By the time the fleet of fishing boats reached the tip of the Llyn peninsula, Llywelyn had completely emptied his stomach and tried to recover a little of his dignity. It was full night now, and as Caradog Priddy turned his bow to a more westerly course, he nudged Llywelyn and pointed off to the south.

"Ynys Enlli," he said, simply.

Llywelyn stared into the darkness and could see white foam breaking around the shore of a dark hump of an island.

"Twenty thousand holy men are buried there," Priddy said.

Like all Welshmen, Llywelyn knew of Ynys Enlli, though he had never seen it, and would not have this night, if Priddy had kept silent as they sailed past in the dark. He had imagined it to be much bigger.

"Hardly seems they could find room for so many," he said.

Priddy hooted at that.

"Aye, lord. The saints must be cramped. Makes me glad I'm a sinner!"

The Challenge

While other men moved to carry out Llywelyn's plan, the man who devised it sat at Dolwyddelan Castle and waited. It was only a day's march to reach the river at Llywrst, and only hours from there by boat to Deganwy—if they were able to capture the longships. He must not move too soon.

Llywelyn must first strike at Aberffraw and that would take at least two more days. Only then could Roland attempt to bluff his way into the castle and take it by storm. Move too soon, and he would run into the entire force of the uncles when he reached the fortress near the mouth of the Conwy. So he waited.

The Invalid Company made good use of the time to finish honing weapons they had let go to rust during their long garrison duty at Chester. Roland's sword needed no such attention, but he did need to replace a string on his longbow that had been soaked during the blizzard. He had packed two spares and these were carefully coated with a mixture of resin and beeswax to ward off any dampness. He had just begun his task when he saw the leader of the Welsh archers approach. The man stopped and gave a little bob of his head.

"Pardon, sir," he said, "could I see the bow?"

Roland lay down his string. The man before him was short and well-muscled with fair hair and an unremarkable face—save for a look of mischief in his eyes. His words were heavily accented, but clear enough. Llywelyn had recognized the need to provide at least one man among the twenty archers he'd assigned to the Invalids who could speak English.

Roland nodded and stood.

"What's your name?"

"Engard, my lord."

With a few deft moves, Roland attached his freshly waxed string to the longbow and handed it to the man. This bow was fashioned from one of the yew staves Millicent had saved from the flames at Shipbrook. He had crafted it to be longer and stiffer than the first bow he had made as a boy on Kinder Scout. That bow had been lost to one of Saladin's men on a dusty hill outside of Jerusalem. This new bow had a harder pull and greater range than his first, and that suited him. He had put on considerable muscle through his back and shoulders as he'd grown to manhood and valued the greater striking power of his new weapon.

He sat back down and watched as Engard leaned into the belly of the bow and slid the string up and into the horn notch at the top. The stocky Welshman held it horizontally for a moment, inspecting it. He raised the bow to his nose and sniffed it.

"This wood—it is not elm?"

"No. I prefer yew."

Engard looked at him sceptically, but said nothing. He turned the weapon vertically and made a few tentative, shallow draws, then raised it and brought the string back toward his cheek. He gave a small surprised grunt at the resistance but managed to make a full draw then slowly eased it back.

"Stiff," was his assessment.

"It's to my taste," Roland said simply.

The Welshman nodded.

"Griff—he says you are the best archer in all England."

Roland shrugged.

"I make no such claim."

"Griff says you won your king's tournament."

For the first time, Roland noticed a sizable number of the Welsh archers had edged near to listen, as Engard engaged this Englishman they had been ordered to follow. He frowned.

"It was a long time ago."

Engard looked over his shoulder at his fellows and allowed himself a small smile.

"I say the Welsh are better archers than the English."

Roland sighed and stood. For a moment he thought to just agree with the young Welshman and be done with it, but hesitated. These men had been placed under his command and not by their own choice. He had no doubt they would follow him, as Prince Llywelyn commanded, but what would they do when swords were drawn and blood flowed?

They did not know him and had no reason to trust him. In battle, when men are coming to kill you, trust in the man next to you and in the man who leads you can make the difference between standing or running. What he would be asking of these Welsh bowmen in the days ahead would require a great deal of trust. If it took a test of his longbow skills to earn it...so be it.

He held out his hand and Engard placed the bow in it with a triumphant grin. Now the Welsh archers crowded closer and the commotion caught the attention of the Invalids who had been tending to their weapons. They drifted across the courtyard to where the Welsh had gathered around their leader.

"Have you a test in mind?" Roland asked mildly.

"Aye, lord, outside!" One of his fellows had handed Engard his own longbow and the stocky Welshman headed toward the arched gate of Dolwyddelan. Roland followed, with the Welsh archers and a growing number of Invalids in his wake. A little way along the slushy track, Engard stopped and pointed down into the valley. There, some two hundred paces down the track was a target—of sorts. Men had rolled large balls of dirty snow into a vaguely human shape and placed a small peaked cap on top. Clearly this challenge had been carefully planned.

"Three shots?" Engard suggested.

Roland nodded. Someone handed the Welshman three arrows. He pointed again toward the snowman on the track.

"I think it looks like an Englishman," he said with a nasty smile, then turned to his men and repeated his jest in Welsh to howls of laughter.

"It looks more like a cow thief to me," Roland replied.

Engard scowled, but there were howls from the Invalids. Sergeant Billy edged up to one of the Welsh archers and jingled a few silver coins.

"Wager?"

The man knew no English, but silver was a universal language. He produced a few coins of his own and nodded his agreement. A ripple of whispers ran through the onlookers as more side bets were made. Roland couldn't help but smile. He had no trust issues with the Invalids.

Finally, all the wagers had been made and Engard stepped forward with an arrow nocked. His bow was of elm and beautifully crafted. He gauged the distance and the downslope and raised the bow to a sharp angle as he drew back the string. All grew quiet. He released and the arrow leapt into the air, all eyes following its path toward the target.

It struck the bottom of the snowman and there was a murmur of approval from Engard's supporters. He drew another arrow, adjusted his angle by a hair's breadth and released. The arrow struck flush in the center of the target. Small cheers went up from the Welsh. His third arrow bore into the snowman two inches lower than the first. A hit, but very nearly a miss. Engard stepped back, a confident smile on his face. It had been exceptional shooting for a target two hundred paces down a steep slope.

Roland gave the young Welshman a respectful nod and stepped forward. He had grown up hunting in the high country of Derbyshire—a place with little flat ground. It gave him an instinctive feel for shooting on a slope. He gauged the angle and the distance and began his draw. His heavier yew bow allowed him to find a release point lower than Engard's as he loosed his first arrow. It struck the target dead center, only an inch from Engard's second shot. Now the murmur of approval came from the gathered English.

Roland nocked his second arrow and drew the bowstring to his cheek. He felt a light breeze pick up and made a tiny adjustment to his aim. He released and the arrow arced down into the valley, burying itself into the snowman's chest two inches from his first shot.

This brought forth a mix of cheers from the Invalids and groans from the Welsh. Engard had a look of abashed admiration on his face at the accuracy of this shot. Sergeant Billy leaned near to the man he'd wagered with and whispered to him.

"Did I mention, I once saw Sir Roland strike a man in the head on a galloping horse from just about this distance?"

The Welshman scowled and made no reply. He did not understand English, but there was no need to translate the gist of this comment.

Roland had one arrow left. Behind him he heard someone yell out.

"The hat!"

He turned to see Friar Cyril giving him a gapped-tooth grin.

"Your cow thief has no manners, my lord. He should have doffed his cap in the presence of an English knight." That brought amused titters from the gathered Invalids. Then Cyril repeated his jibe in serviceable Welsh—another surprise from this scarecrow monk. The Welsh were not amused.

Roland looked back down the hill. The hat had been blown almost flat by the wind, but clung to the top of the snowman, a small green smear on a field of white. Roland glanced at Engard who had a sour look on his face. The young Welshman met his gaze and shrugged.

"Hit that hat and I concede," he said.

Roland stepped up. The wind had continued to rise and now swirls of ice crystals were being blown into the air from the drifts that still filled the valley. Through this thin white haze, the small hat on the snowman's head looked in danger of blowing away. Roland stood still for a moment, feeling the strength of the wind on the side of his face, then nocked his final arrow. He drew his longbow and corrected for the wind blowing in from his right. He waited a single heartbeat, then released.

The arrow leapt down the slope, slowly being pushed to the left by the wind. In mid-flight, a strong gust swirled through the valley floor, lifting the green cap and sending it dancing high into the air as Roland's arrow plunged down, digging a furrow atop the snowman's head.

On all sides, a clamor went up. Men who had wagered turned to each other and hot words, in two languages, were exchanged. Roland watched it all with growing horror. He waded into the crowd and raised his arms, appealing for peace, but tempers were flaring. Then Engard plunged in, bellowing at

137

his men in Welsh. Finally, quiet fell over the men, though angry looks continued.

The leader of the Welsh archers shouldered his way through the crush toward Roland. When he reached him, he offered his hand. Roland took it. Engard turned to his men.

"By God," he shouted in Welsh, "but for the wind, that was a hit! I now see that at least one Englishman can handle a bow!"

"What'd e' say?" one of the Invalids shouted from the rear of the crowd. Roland caught Engard's eye, then turned and shouted back.

"He calls it a draw!"

Engard nodded and released Roland's hand. A few men on each side grumbled, but all had seen the shot and silver was grudgingly returned to its original owners. The excitement over, men began to drift back toward the castle, but Engard lingered.

"Are you sure you are not part Welsh?" he asked Roland with a grin.

"No Engard, I am English, though many English call me a Dane."

"The boats we will steal—they belong to Danes, no?"

"Aye."

"Are any your kin?" Engard asked, only half in jest.

Roland laughed.

"Perhaps," he said, "but don't fear. I'll have no trouble killing them, if need be."

Engard gave an approving smile.

"If you'd kill your own kin, then you *must* be part Welsh!"

Like Father

Sir Roger de Laval paced slowly along the eastern wall of Shipbrook, stopping every few yards to check for any loose mortar between the stones or to lean over the parapet to view the condition of the ditch that ran along the base of the wall. He made this inspection weekly and was quick to assign men to attend to anything he might find amiss.

It was late January with spring still months away, but the day was one of the warmest in the valley of the Dee since the previous autumn. Looking west, he saw white tops still on the Clwydian hills, evidence of a fierce winter storm that had blown through five days before. It left only a dusting of snow in Cheshire but the high country of Wales would have got much more. He wondered how Roland and the Invalids had weathered the tempest.

Below him he watched a resident robin digging a worm from the softening soil at the bottom of the ditch and made a mental note to have his men clear out a small cluster of brambles that had taken root there. He was nearing the southeast corner of the wall walk when he spied Rhys Madawc. The boy was on the south wall looking off into the distance. So engaged was he in his gazing, that he jumped when he heard Sir Roger's steps behind him.

"My...lord," he sputtered.

"Afternoon, lad. Fine day for a stroll on the walls."

"Aye, it is, my lord."

"Not much to see from here, though. Ye can't even see the Dee through the trees at this distance."

"Well, I can see the hills yonder, lord. Home is that way."

Sir Roger nodded.

"It hasn't been very hospitable to ye, but home is home, I reckon. Sir Declan tells me yer making good progress with yer trainin'."

Rhys gave a rueful laugh.

"Aye, lord. Sir Declan gave me this, just this morning," he said, pointing to an angry red welt behind his ear. "It's only been three days, but he says I'm improving. He said I might not actually hurt myself in a fight, though I was not yet likely to hurt an enemy either."

Sir Roger laughed.

"That's decent praise from the Master of the Sword. Seems I remember a young Irish squire being told much the same a few years back."

Sir Roger paused and for a long moment both the big knight and the young refugee turned back to look at the snow-covered hills of Wales.

"Rhys, I've heard ye've sworn to go back to yer home, but I would ask you to wait a bit to do that. Sir Declan and I have agreed that I have been too long with no squire. Lost my last two when they went and got themselves knighted on crusade. I will be going north to Yorkshire in a month or two to visit our holdings there and will have need of a squire for the trip. We think you would do nicely."

Rhys turned and looked at the big man.

"My lord, I...I'm honoured by the offer."

He looked around the small fort of Shipbrook, then back to the big Norman knight.

"I can see why my father found a home here, but…"

"But?"

"I need time to think on this, my lord. Will you give me a day to decide?"

Sir Roger clapped the boy on the shoulder.

"Of course, of course. You need a bit of time to settle in, lad. Take a few days, and let me know your decision."

"I will, my lord."

***

"Damn the boy! He's gone," Declan O'Duinne muttered, as he hurried toward the main hall of Shipbrook.

He had gone searching for Rhys Madawc to give him a proper hiding when the boy failed to show up for the morning sword drill. His young student had always been in the courtyard and ready for instruction well before the appointed hour and, when that time passed, the Irish knight had a bad feeling. Those feelings grew darker when he found the boy's bed chamber empty and his few possessions gone. Running to the north gate, he hailed the guard. He knew in his gut the answer to his question before he called up to the man.

"Did Master Madawc ride out this morn?"

"Aye, sir. He wished me a good day as he left. Last I saw, he was headed down toward the ford."

Declan cursed. It was common practice for the members of the Shipbrook household to come and go as they pleased, with no challenge from the guards. And while Rhys Madawc had only been among them for a week, he had been accepted as a member of their household—and a popular one. It wasn't just that he was the son of the much-loved Alwyn Madawc. The boy had a natural charm all his own and it gained him friends quickly.

But behind the genial manner, Declan had seen a fierce determination. The Welsh boy had approached his few days of weapons drill with a focused intensity, a fire Declan knew must be fed by a thirst for revenge. It made the lad an adept student, but worried his teacher. Like all important skills, learning to kill took time, and practice and repetition. Rhys Madawc was happy enough with the practice and repetition involved, but less so with the time. Declan had cautioned him from the start that it would be months before he was ready to move from wooden staves to steel blades. He hoped that by the time the boy had attained the skill, his fire would have cooled, but he could see Rhys chafed at the thought.

Now he was gone.

Declan hurried into the hall and found Sir Roger and Lady Catherine discussing plans for the spring planting.

"He's gone," he said simply. He did not have to explain who.

"Damn!" said Sir Roger. "I feared this. Though he had me half cozened that he was growing contented with his place here."

"Roger, they'll kill him. You know they will," said Lady Catherine, with anguish in her voice. "We cannot let that happen. He's Alwyn's..." Her voice trailed off.

Sir Roger turned to her.

"Of course, we cannot," he said with a growl. "Declan, I want six men mounted and ready to ride as fast as the horses can be saddled."

Declan held up a hand.

"My lord, consider. There is war where we are going. If we come in force, we will certainly be met with force—and I doubt eight men would much impress this Talfryn."

"What are you suggesting, Declan?" Lady Catherine asked, harshly. "Surely you won't have my husband go alone..."

"No, no, my lady, I'll be with him."

Sir Roger held up a hand for silence.

"He's right, Catherine. Eight armed and armoured men riding through that bloody land would be seen for what they are—a war band—and would attract the wrong sort of attention. Two men, though, might pass as peaceful travellers."

The mistress of Shipbrook frowned and twisted her hands together. She started to protest, but finally sighed.

"Very well. I won't tell you your business, Roger, but I don't like this at all."

Sir Roger gave her a small bow and turned to Declan.

"No mail, no helmets, no shields—swords only—and we leave the warhorses behind and ride palfreys."

Declan hurried from the hall to order the horses saddled.

"I'll gather your provisions," Catherine said, bleakly. She started toward the kitchen, but he grabbed her wrist and pulled her close.

"Yer a good woman, Cathy de Laval."

"I'm happy you still notice, husband."

142

"Always," he said and gave her a gentle kiss.

"Bring that boy back, Roger."

"If it can be done, I will do it."

Lady Catherine returned his kiss and touched his weathered cheek.

"And yourself as well…"

***

Catherine packed provisions for three days and little time was wasted on further leave-taking. They were now three hours behind the runaway and would need to ride hard to make up that gap. As they mounted, Declan turned to Sir Roger.

"The boy said his village was a half day's ride south of Saint. Asaph's church. I've heard of that church, but have never ventured that far into Wales. How do we find it?"

"I've not been to the church proper," Sir Roger replied, "but I did ride with Earl Ranulf to Rhuddlan Castle, nigh ten years ago, to parlay with Lord Daffyd. I understand the church is just a few miles south of there. That would put Rhys' village in the valley of the River Clwyd. By my reckoning, if we ride due west from our ford until we reach the Clwyd, we would come very near to where the boy said his home was."

Declan nodded.

"And with this thaw, there is a good chance he's left a trail that will point the way. Even I could track one of our horses through mud."

"Let's hope. It will be a rough road through dangerous country, so let's get down to the ford and make up some time. With luck, we'll catch up to the boy before he reaches his village and starts trouble."

The big knight turned the head of his black palfrey toward the gate and applied the spurs, with Declan close behind. The two men rode through the gate of Shipbrook and swung west on the track that led down to the Dee. Catherine De Laval had already found her way up to the wall walk by the gate and watched them until they were out of sight.

As always, her husband did not look back.

***

143

Across the Dee and into Wales, Rhys Madawc reined in his horse at the top of a rise and searched the trail behind him. Nothing moved there. He did not know how long it would take for the alarm to be raised at Shipbrook. The guard at the gate had seemed unconcerned as he departed and, with luck, he wouldn't be missed until he failed to appear for weapons drill. By then, he would have a good head start on whoever might come after him.

He wondered if he would be pursued at all. The folk of Shipbrook had seemed fond of him, for his father's sake, but would they risk chasing him into these wild borderlands? It would hardly make sense, but, then again, he had stolen a good horse and a sword. That thought brought a flush of guilt to his face.

He had repaid the kindness of the de Laval's by robbing them! It was a shameful act and he knew it. He had sworn to himself that he would return to Shipbrook with the animal and the weapon when he had done what must be done, but it was a feeble attempt at justification. He took a last look back to the northeast. Still nothing. He dug his heels into the horse's flanks.

Too late to turn back now.

***

Sir Roger and Declan rode until darkness forced a halt. The ground had been rising for the final hour of the day as they reached the foothills of the Clwydian range. In narrow clefts and shaded slopes, a thin layer of snow still clung to the ground, but the weather continued to be mild. They hobbled the horses and made a cold camp by a small stream, a hundred yards off the track.

"What'll we do if we catch him?" Declan asked absently, as though the question had just struck him.

Sir Roger, wrapped in his winter cloak was leaning on his saddle and chewing a piece of dried beef.

"We take him back with us, whether he is willing or no. I will try to reason with the lad, but he goes back to Shipbrook either way, trussed and bound to his saddle if it comes to that."

"Really, my lord? You do that and he'll just run again when he gets the opportunity—or do you fancy keeping him under lock and key?"

Sir Roger snorted.

"If I must—at least long enough to talk some sense into the boy."

Declan gave a scornful laugh.

"When did ye last talk sense into a Welshman, my lord, or a boy, for that matter?"

Sir Roger did not speak for a long moment, then gave a long sigh.

"I take yer point, Declan, I do, but we must try, for Alwyn's sake. In the end, though, ye have the rights of it. He will do whatever is in his heart."

Declan smiled in the dark.

"As do we all, my lord. As do we all."

***

Darkness forced Rhys to halt for the night. By late in the day the track had started to climb up the flanks of the hills that stood between the river Dee and the river Clwyd. His village was on the far side of the broad valley of the Clwyd and he was anxious to reach it, but he could not risk his mount breaking a leg on the rough trail.

The Welsh boy led his tired horse well off the trail and made camp. He would be up and away before first light and should reach his village just after dark. He'd not brought any fire-making kit when he'd fled, but would have hesitated to start a blaze in any event. Even if no one was on his back trail, there was no profit in announcing his presence with a fire in these parts.

He sat down and leaned against a tree as he munched on a slab of dark barley bread he'd slipped from the kitchen at Shipbrook—another theft! His face flushed as he swallowed the mouthful of black bread. He'd never stolen so much as an apple from a neighbour's tree before and now he was little better than a lowly cutpurse!

But he'd seen no other way. Tomorrow he would reach home and do what he'd come to do. And *that* would be worth this stain on his honour. He finished his bread and tried to sleep.

Almost home, he thought as he drifted off.

Aberffraw

Hova Iwan kept a gnarled hand on the tiller as he gave quiet instructions to his oldest son, Cadugan. The sail on their tiny fishing boat had gone slack in the fluky onshore wind and it was costing them time. They had set out from the beach that lay near the mouth of the River Ffraw just past midnight and had to reach the spawning ground of the herring before first light. The fish schooled up at night and dispersed to feed at dawn. If they arrived in darkness they could fill the bottom of their little boat with herring in an hour. If they were late, they'd likely come home empty-handed.

They'd launched the boat with plenty of time, but the shifting winds were hindering them. No sooner had the boy adjusted the sail to make it taut than it began to flap once more. Hova was about to chastise the lad, when he noticed that his son was no longer watching the sail. The boy swung around with a look of shock on his face.

"Father…"

He did not have to speak further, for Hova saw with his own eyes what had so stunned the boy. Out of the darkness to their front—and to port and starboard—came ships. First two, then four, then more, looming up, then sliding by in the gloom. They were bigger than Hova's little craft and as the first of them plunged by, he saw that the decks were crammed with men— armed men.

The ships kept coming, but seemed to take no heed of the smaller boat. Hova frantically turned the tiller to starboard, then port, then back again to avoid a collision. As the last of the flotilla passed by, a man in a steel helmet leaned over the railing and acknowledged them with a small wave. The gesture did nothing to lessen the dread gripping the man. These ships were heading back the way he had come, back toward his home, and he knew full well what boatloads of armed men meant.

When the last boat had passed, Hova swung his bow around and followed in their wake. They were headed straight for the mouth of the Aberffraw River. Just a mile inland was his village and the royal court. The court was barely defended and the village not at all. Lord Roderic had marched away with most of his local garrison a fortnight ago. Rumours said he was joining his brother to crush the upstart Llywelyn, but that hardly mattered to Hova. What mattered were his wife and younger children, still asleep in the undefended village.

His one hope was the river itself. With a quarter moon in the sky, there was a neap tide. In such a tide, he thought he could navigate the shallow, braided Aberffraw River, but the big ships would run aground if they tried. They would have to be beached down at the bay. From there it was only a short march across the low dunes to the village.

As he tucked in behind the trailing boat, Hova wasn't sure his own craft could manage the shoals in the river, but it had a shallow draft and he would try. He looked up at the sky and saw the first hint of false dawn in the east. The men on the boats would reach the town before sunrise. He tacked off to port to try and gain more speed.

There had been peace for many years here on Anglesey, but Hova had lived long enough to remember when there had been no peace. As a boy, half of the people in his village near the Strait of Menai had been slaughtered by raiders on one bloody night. No one had ever been certain which of the warring royal kin had ordered it and it hardly mattered to the dead or grieving. One more tack to starboard headed him directly into the mouth of the river.

He might have a chance yet.

***

Llewelyn had seen the small boat dodge between his ships, but thought little of it. He was straining to see what lay ahead. There was a bright crescent moon in the sky, but it kept ducking behind clouds. While the moonlight held sway, he could clearly see the mountains of Eryri, rising up to starboard, but Anglesey was low country and not yet visible.

Master Priddy said they were but a few miles offshore, but clouds had again made the night dark and he could see nothing. Long minutes passed until, finally, the clouds parted. Llewelyn saw a dozen ships on either side of his own and more strung out behind. Ahead, the moonlight illuminated a bright strip of white. It was the beach that bounded Aberffraw Bay

As the boats grounded on the sandy bottom of the bay, men leapt from the decks into waist-deep water with swords drawn. Some had been with Llewelyn for many years. Others were oath-men loyal to the brothers from Meirionnydd. In the long years of rule by Roderic and Daffyd, none of these men had imagined a day such as this.

Aberffraw.

It was no great city. Nor did it boast a great fortress, such as the castle at Caenarfon, but it was the home of the dynasty that had ruled Gwynedd for three hundred fifty years. Each of the men who now contended for the rule of Gwynedd were offspring of that royal line and recognized the legitimacy that Aberffraw lent to whoever possessed it.

Both Maredudd and Gruffydd had visited Roderic's court as younger men, but only at the sufferance of their uncle. Llewelyn had never laid eyes on the royal Llys, having fled Gwynedd as a babe and returned only as a rebel.

As the men assembled, quiet orders were given and they began to move off the beach. As the first ranks topped the high dunes that rimmed the bay, someone noticed the small fishing boat tacking into the mouth of the Ffraw River. Maredudd, who had landed with his men closest to the mouth of the river, instantly realized the danger posed by this boat. If surprise were lost, they might still seize the royal court, but casualties would be high. He dispatched a half dozen of his archers to head off the threat.

But Hova Iwan had luck on his side. There was wind at his back and just enough tide to keep his small boat from running aground. With the skill acquired in thirty years of sailing, he coaxed all possible speed from his little boat. Not even Welsh longbowmen could stop him, as a flurry of arrows fell twenty feet behind his stern. When word reached Maredudd that the boat had slipped by, he cursed, then sent a warning to Llywelyn.

The Prince had already started down the backside of the dunes at the head of his men when the news reached him. Looking to his left, he could see the top of the mast of the fishing boat gliding up the river. He turned to his men.

"At the run, lads!" he ordered.

The command did not need to be relayed. Men in the rear and on the flanks saw the tall young nobleman break into a run toward the river and leapt forward to follow him. They reached the eastern bank of the twisting Aberffraw River just as a cock crowed in the sleeping village that lay on the opposite side. Only two hundred yards to the north, the low walls that enclosed Roderic's royal court could be seen.

Llywelyn saw the fisherman's boat pulled up on a mud flat. It was empty. Without slowing, he scrambled down the bank and into the river. This far upstream, the water barely rose above his knees. A hundred yards ahead of this invading host, Hova and his son raced through the alleys of the village. They made no effort to reach the royal court and alert the guards of the calamity about to fall upon them.

Let the royals kill each other! It was none of their concern.

As Llywelyn and six hundred men splashed through the shallow river and streamed into the town, Hova led his wife and children out the far side.

***

In the first dim light of dawn, men slipped silently through the dirt alleyways of Aberffraw. A skinny dog tied up in a small garden snarled as they passed, but none gave it heed. As ordered, they halted at the edge of the village. Across an unploughed field laced with tendrils of frost lay the Llys—Roderic's royal court.

One lookout slouched sleepily against his spear atop the wall near the south gate. He gave no sign he had seen anything amiss.

At a hand signal from Llywelyn, a dozen of his taller men burst from the cover of the village and sprinted across the open ground to the low wall of the Llys. The wall, more ornament than fortification, was only eight feet tall and there was no ditch beneath it. The men reached the wall and sprang forward, planting a foot and hauling themselves over. Before the first confused alarm was raised, a dozen men were inside the court.

Three guards died defending the gate. The sound of their struggle did not go unheeded and men began to stumble out of the low barracks that sat just a few yards from the south gate. The first of these were cut down, but more erupted from the building. They were too late. The first men over the wall had reached the gate and raised the bar. The heavy oak barrier swung open with a groan and a wave of men rushed in, led by Llywelyn.

Without looking to see who followed, the Prince slammed into the defenders who were desperately trying to form a line across the narrow street outside their barracks. He rammed his shield into the face of the man to his front, sending him tumbling backwards, then turned and slashed to his left and right with his broadsword. That quickly, a gaping hole was punched through the line. A few of Roderic's men began to break and run. A feral roar went up from the attackers who surged forward.

Abruptly, Llywelyn turned to face his own troops.

"Hold!" he ordered, then turned toward the wavering garrison troops.

"Yield, and be spared!"

A few of the older defenders, proud veterans, snarled defiance, but most of these garrison troops were green—hardly more than boys—and were stunned at the savagery they had witnessed. They had no stomach for more and began to throw down their weapons. The veterans cursed them, but had no choice but to drop their own swords.

Llywelyn gave a curt order and the prisoners were herded back into their barracks and placed under guard. Patrols were dispatched to search the dozen or more small buildings inside the Llys as Gruffydd and Maredudd forced their way through the crush of men at the gate to join their younger cousin. Maredudd had a gleam of triumph in his eyes and even the dour Gruffydd sported a broad grin as he greeted Llywelyn.

"God's breath! This will upset our uncle!" he growled.

Llywelyn nodded.

"Let us pray, for we need him to be upset! Now let's go see what Roderic keeps in his great hall."

Together, the three men hurried up the centre lane of the royal enclosure toward the large building on the north end. Llywelyn's men fanned out on both sides of the street to ensure no hidden defenders might strike at their Prince. When he reached the front of the hall, Llywelyn stopped and looked up at the stone façade. He dropped to one knee, said a silent prayer and rose. Together, the three grandsons of Owain Gwynedd marched through the arched doorway their grandsire had built.

The guards had fled and no one tried to bar their way. The front entrance led to a large formal receiving room with narrow windows set on either wall and a high-beamed wooden ceiling. Two men stood alone in the room. One was of middle years with a beard that had gone to grey. The second was young—no older than Llywelyn himself. He was fair of face, but his body bent oddly to the left—a sign of some infirmity. The younger man bowed low as the three men entered but the older stayed stiffly erect.

"Who makes war on the Prince of Gwynedd?" the older man asked sternly.

A small smile flickered over Llywelyn's face.

"First, you will tell me your name, old man. I wish to know who asks such a puzzling question—for *I* am the Prince of Gwynedd. You are old enough to have known my father, Iowerth. Mine is the senior line from Owain Gwynedd. Any man who gainsays that is in league with usurpers."

To his credit, the older man did not flinch at this news.

"I am Cadwalader, Seneschal of Gwynedd, my lord, and you must be Lord Llywelyn. I see you have brought your faithless cousins with you," he said and gave Maredudd and Gruffydd the evil eye. "Why have you come to disturb the peace of Aberffraw? I had thought you and your uncles could reach agreement to bring this senseless rebellion to an end. My lord Roderic had high hopes for a reconciliation."

Llywelyn gave a small harsh laugh.

"Your lord Roderic is a dried-up horse turd and I barely escaped with my life from his *reconciliation!*"

The Seneschal was unmoved by Llywelyn's claim and hardly seemed surprised by it, but the younger man looked troubled. He sent a searching glance at his older companion, but was ignored. Llywelyn addressed him for the first time.

"Aye, lad, it's true. Your master set an ambush for me and, when that failed, he sent hired Northmen to hunt me down. Perhaps they should have looked for me closer to home—for here I am. Who are you?"

The older man started to answer, but Llywelyn silenced him with a raised hand.

"Let the man speak."

"I…I am court poet, my lord. I am called Benfras."

"I like poetry, lad, particularly where there is fighting! Are you any good? Spin me a poem to commemorate my arrival at Aberffraw."

The young man looked terrified, but Llywelyn clapped him on the shoulder and spoke quietly to him.

"Do your best, lad. I know not good poetry from bad, so fear no censure from me."

Benfras gulped, then squeezed his eyes shut. Silence descended on the hall as they waited for what he might bring forth. Then he opened his eyes and spoke in a high, ringing voice.

"Oh, proud Llywelyn, of unmatched fame
In the dark of night, to Aberffraw came
Long had usurpers denied his right
But none could stand before his might
While a dried-up horse turd searches in vain
Here stands the true heir of Owain!"

Cadwalader turned and snarled at the poet, but Llywelyn roared with laughter.

"Best poem I've ever heard, lad! You are now my court poet."

He turned and pointed at the Seneschal.

"And you, scribbler, if you do exactly as I say, you may live to see an end to this war."

Gruffydd, who had watched this encounter in silence, came forward and spoke quietly to Llywelyn.

"My men report a rider got out the north gate before we claimed it," he said.

Llywelyn nodded.

"Good! We need word of this to reach Roderic. We must draw him to us in all haste. If he tarries, we must goad him. Roderic must march on Aberffraw and bring Daffyd with him."

"They could be here in three days with two thousand men," said Maredudd who seemed suddenly daunted by what they had set in motion. Llywelyn placed two hands on his older kinsman's shoulders.

"Fear not, cousin! When they come, Roland Inness will take Deganwy and we will have the uncles where we want them!"

***

By noon, a dozen riders on fast horses taken from Roderic's stables rode from Aberffraw. They carried summonses from Llywelyn to the most powerful barons on the island—men who controlled the fertile fields of Gwynedd's breadbasket. Most of these men had marched off with Roderic a month ago, but all the same, they were ordered to appear at the royal Lys at Aberffraw in two days. And while the barons might be gone, a royal summons would certainly stir up the noble families left behind.

Other proclamations asserting Llywelyn's authority were to be posted throughout the island. One rider was ordered to prominently post a proclamation near the ferry landing on the Anglesey side of the Strait of Menai. For years, Roderic had collected a tax on every passenger crossing the waterway. The proclamation abolished the ferry tax and carried the royal seal of the House of Aberffraw. It was signed "Llywelyn, Prince of Aberffraw and Gwynedd."

The Longships

It was a clear night in the valley of the River Conwy, as Ulf Haroldson stroked his long red beard and looked up into the star-filled sky. He often gazed at the heavens as he went about his evening duties and had spent many a night pondering what the spray of light in the night sky meant. He was a Dane and his people had once believed that the stars were the lights of Valhalla.

Valhalla.

The sagas said that warriors who died in battle with a sword in their hand would be lifted up by the Valkyries, winged warrior maidens, to feast with Odin in the great hall of Valhalla. He half believed that himself, though the priests called it blasphemy.

Priests!

They said men must turn their cheeks if slapped. They said men should be merciful and humble. Ulf snorted at that notion. What kind of man let another strike him without killing the offender? What sort of man sought humility? Why a man with no coins in his pockets and no woman in his bed! Just like a priest!

For Ulf, there'd been plenty of coins in his pockets since joining Haakon five years ago and if you had money, the women would follow! It was a good living and one he'd blindly stumbled upon. He'd sailed from Denmark to seek employment in Dublin with nothing in his pockets and little else to recommend him, save a strong sword arm.

After a week, he'd found no work and was in danger of starving. He considered sailing back to Denmark, but had no money for the passage. Someone told him a Dub Gaill chieftain might be looking for men. He found Haakon in a local tavern. He started to approach, but six local men, Irish by their speech, had surrounded the big Dane and were goading him into a fight.

Ulf Haroldson had seen many fights in his day. They could begin with words—and the locals were spewing plenty of those at the big man—or actions. The Dub Gaill sat impassively, while the locals voiced their disapproval of his presence, but then one was imprudent enough to let his hand grasp the hilt of his sword. For this he received a tankard of ale against his temple. The man went down without so much as a groan and his intended victim was up and coming forward with a long straight dagger before the others could react.

Always game for a fight, Ulf had waded in and killed one of the local men. By the time he had laid his man low, the big Dane had killed three of the others with shocking dispatch. He then gave chase as the last man bolted out of the door. Ulf followed out of curiosity. Most men would have been satisfied with the slaughter he had already inflicted, but not this man. The Dane pursued his last assailant relentlessly and finally ran the man to ground halfway across the city. The exhausted Gael had begged for his life—to no avail. Haakon the Black was neither merciful nor humble, but he was a man who would not let a favour go unnoticed.

That same night he'd offered Ulf a place with his raiders. In the five years since, he had risen to command *Wavebreaker*, one of the deadly longships in Haakon's fleet. He was a wealthy man now, with a fine house on the banks of the River Liffey just a short walk from Dublin's port. Life was good.

Ulf lowered his eyes from the heavens and looked down the gravel bar at the row of low-slung boats lined up there. Haakon had left him in charge of securing the longships, not a duty to be taken lightly. A longship was more than sea transport, it was a weapon—one that had helped his ancestors conquer half of Europe. With its banks of oars and shallow draft it had taken entire armies far inland on the rivers of Britain, France and Rus.

It was a swift craft and with a good crew, it could overtake slower trading vessels and outrun any war vessel yet designed by their foes.

But every weapon has its counter and, in time, ways had been found to blunt the threat of the longships. The English and Welsh had learned to build fortifications near the mouth of every major river in Britain to challenge any invaders who came by sea. This had gradually wrung the life out of the raiders from the north. Great fleets of longships no longer set out from the fjords of Norway or the low sandy islands of Denmark as they once had.

But there was still no vessel that could navigate ocean and stream like a longship! The bond between a master and his ship was a strong one. Haakon loved his boats even more than he loved his women or his horses. This, Ulf understood. And if they were no longer the weapons they had once been, these boats were still their only way back home and must be kept safe.

So Ulf dutifully checked the guard postings every evening. No harm would come to their precious longships while he was in charge! In the bright moonlight, he could make out the shape of his friend, Snorri, at the far end of the gravel bar. Snorri was Haakon's own helmsman and no better sailor plied the northern seas. The man saw Ulf and raised a hand to signal that all was well. Satisfied, Ulf turned to look at the river. The bright moon made the rushing water gleam and twinkle as it danced over the rocks in the shallow bed.

He had to admit that Wales was a lovely country. When he'd first heard that this was their destination, he was careful to show no concern, but it had worried him. The Welsh did not have a reputation for humility or mercy. He had heard that they were a fierce and warlike people, though mostly fighting amongst themselves.

But events had proved his worries to be ill-founded. After they'd been given free passage past the castle that guarded the mouth of the River Conwy, they'd been sent to attack the winter quarters of this rebel, Llywelyn. They'd struck near dawn and surprised the camp. A few men, with their damned longbows, had given a good account of themselves—and died painfully for their trouble, but most had been routed. They'd fled into the mountains and had not dared to come back down and face the Dub Gaill who waited for them. It seemed the fearsome reputation of Welsh warriors was an exaggeration.

As he surveyed the gleaming river in the quiet night, this Wales campaign promised to be the easiest money he'd ever made.

***

In the trees on the opposite bank of the Conwy, Roland and the Invalids watched the man stargazing by the banks of the river. All that day, they had followed a local boy along small trails through the high hills, skirting the large force of Danes that sat astride the valley five miles upstream. As they neared the river, another of Llywelyn's men who'd grown up along the Conwy took the lead. They had slipped into trees opposite the gravel bar where the Danish longboats were drawn up like sea beasts come to bask on the shore.

On the bank above the gravel bar, men sat around a fire and told tales and laughed until well into the night. Finally, they had drifted off to a row of low huts and gone to bed, save for one sentry who kept watch down by the river. Roland had been set to signal his Welsh archers to take out the guard, when he saw a second man come down to the bar and look up at the heavens.

His bad luck.

He gave the hand signal and four longbowmen took aim. A small sound to his right caused Ulf to look back down the row of longships. He saw Snorri, clearly illuminated by the moonlight, bend forward at the waist, then straighten up and raise a hand. He started to wave back, but saw the man fall, face-down, onto the gravel.

Ulf was a veteran and not slow to recognize danger. He reached for his sword and crouched low, looking for cover. He ran for the nearest longship but took only three steps before one arrow took him in the back of the neck and another between his shoulder blades. He dropped to his knees, clutched at his throat and joined Snorri, face down on the rocks. One hand clutched desperately for the hilt of his sword, but it lay a foot away on the gravel, forever out of reach. Ulf Haroldson would not be feasting with the gods in Valhalla this night.

The archers' job done, Roland slid down the bank into the river. The night air had warmed considerably since the fierce winter storm the week before, but the Conwy was fed by snowmelt and the water was shockingly cold. He gritted his teeth as the icy stream rose to his knees and then to his waist.

Here, the river shallowed enough for a man to cross on foot—if he could keep his feet against the strong current. Behind him, Seamus Murdo eased into the river and clasped hands with Roland who gingerly searched for a solid spot on the streambed to set his next step. One by one, forty of the Invalids followed, until there was a chain of men stretching from bank to bank. A few slipped on the mossy rocks of the bottom, plunging up to their necks before being hauled back up by the men on either side. Despite the splashing, nothing stirred on the far shore.

Roland reached a small fringe of sand that edged the stream above the gravel bar and ran at a crouch to shelter beneath the deeply cut bank. There he waited as his forty picked men slowly joined him, soaked and shivering beneath the bank. No word of command was needed as Roland led them downstream to the gravel bar then up to a row of four small huts strung out along the bank. The Invalids stationed themselves around the entrance of each hut.

While there had been daylight left, they'd carefully counted the men guarding the boats. With two dead on the bar, there would be eighteen left in the shelters. Roland pulled back the flap that served as a door to the first hut, stuck his head inside and shouted in Danish.

"Up, there's trouble with the boats!"

Men groaned and stirred, slow to rise. Roland stepped inside.

"Up, damn you!" he roared and grabbed the first man to rise by the collar, dragging him out the door. The Dane was knocked senseless by Seamus. Other men stumbled out of the hut to a similar fate, while Roland moved to the next hovel and repeated the alarm. In minutes, it was over. Two of the Danes in the last hut realized something was amiss and came out fighting. These two were quickly dispatched to Valhalla. The rest now sat disconsolately on the ground, bruised and bleeding.

Roland nodded to Patch, who whistled sharply. It was the signal for the Welsh archers and the rest of the Invalids to join them. While they waited for the others to cross the river, Roland ordered the prisoners stripped and bound. He sent men into the huts to gather clothing and any other gear they could find. They were going to have to pass as Danes very soon and it would help if they dressed the part.

Clouds had started to obscure the bright moon by the time the rest of the men reached the Danish encampment. They would not begin their voyage downriver until dawn, which was still hours away. Roland ordered fires built to ward off the chill and dry out the men, many of whom were still trying to get feeling back into their feet from the river crossing. By the light of the fires, the newly arrived Welsh set aside their bows, drew knives and moved toward the prisoners.

Roland stepped in front of Engard.

"No killing," he said simply.

Engard drew back.

"No killing? What sort of trick is this? We know what they did to our lads at the winter camp. Griff told us. These bastards have to die. We will at least make it quick, which is more than they did for Gwilyn and Caden."

Roland looked at the furious face of the young Welshman and sympathized. What these Danes had done to the two archers they'd caught at Llywelyn's winter quarters had turned his stomach. The men had been strangers to him, but for Engard and the rest of the longbowmen, they were comrades and friends.

He looked up to see that the Invalids had edged closer, waiting to see if he would allow the Welsh to have their revenge. None would have challenged him had he done so, but he recalled the revulsion he felt when news reached him of the slaughter of the Muslim captives at Acre on King Richard's orders. That was a stain on the Lionheart's honour he could never wipe clean.

"We will not kill unarmed prisoners while I command," he said quietly. "Or would you wish us to be no better than them?" he said, pointing at the Danes who looked terrified.

Engard spat on the ground.

"You speak their language. Perhaps you're more Dane than English," he said with disgust.

A low growl rose from those Invalids who had overheard the man's insult. Nearby, Fancy Jack and Jamie Finch reached for their sword hilts. Roland gave a small hand signal without taking his eyes off Engard. Hands slid off hilts. Roland took a step toward the Welshman.

"Hear me, Engard. Your Prince knows my heart—even if you do not. Lord Llywelyn gave me this command. Do you wish to challenge that?" For a long moment, the two stared at each other. It was clear the Welshman did wish it, but also clear he dared not. Finally, he dropped his head.

"No, lord. Llywelyn is my Prince."

"And?"

"You command here."

"If it comforts you, Haakon will probably kill these men when he finds his boats gone."

Engard shrugged.

"Maybe Haakon understands this war better than you do...my lord."

***

With the first hint of dawn in the east, the men of the Invalid Company and the twenty Welsh archers began loading their gear into three of the longships down at the gravel bar. The long days of waiting at Dolwyddelan had not been spent solely on weapons' maintenance and archery contests. Roland knew from Llywelyn's spies that the Danes had come in ten longships manned by forty men each. They would need three of those boats to carry them down the river to Deganwy. And three boats required three men who could steer them past the bends and bars of the Conwy and a crew that could row in unison.

Only Friar Cyril had any direct experience on such a craft, having travelled in one to and from Iceland, outbound as a slave and homeward as a false priest. He would man the tiller on one boat. Roland had spent many hours on the steering oar of the Sprite on their voyages to the Holy Land and back. He would steer a second boat. To the surprise of all, Sergeant Billy offered himself as master of the third longship.

"I grew up on the Thames—downriver from London. I know how to steer in a current," he'd said.

"How big was yer boat?" Patch asked.

Billy shrugged.

"Not big…bit of a rowboat really, but I know how to handle a tiller!"

Now that the actual boats had been seized, men assembled around the three helmsmen who would steer them right into the heart of enemy territory. As they gathered round, bits of clothing, weapons and armour belonging to the prisoners were passed out to a few men in each crew. The Dub Gaill armour was distinct. Their helmets, in particular, had an unusual mail coif that draped down over the back of the neck and shoulders. The shields they carried were also uniform—round oak, with red and black designs on the front.

Only a handful of the men would be able to don the Danish gear. The others would be treated as rebel prisoners being transported to Deganwy for confinement. It was not much of a disguise, but it was the longships themselves that gave weight to the deception. No one would expect any but the mercenary Danes to arrive in such craft.

As men began to hoist themselves over the sides and find their places at the oar benches, Roland returned to the captured Danes who watched sullenly. They were happy to be alive, but knew that Haakon would be furious at the loss of three boats. Roland spoke to them in their own tongue.

"Tell Haakon that he should have stayed in Ireland. He will be lucky to leave this land alive."

One of the bolder men spat on the ground.

"You speak Danish like an Englishman," he snarled. "When Haakon learns you have stolen three of his longships, he will come after you. He will hunt you down!"

Roland smiled at the man.

"Then he'd best find a horse or start walking."

The man glared back, unsure of his meaning.

Roland turned to Patch and Fancy Jack who were standing behind him and pointed to the seven boats that sat empty on the bar.

"Burn them."

Both men pulled flaming brands from the one bonfire that still burned. In the night, Roland had ordered piles of dry branches to be stacked fore and aft in the seven boats they were leaving behind. It only took moments for the dry wood to catch and soon long rows of furled sails that lay along the keels ignited and began to burn furiously. When the flames reached the pitch-soaked wool that caulked the hulls, the Dub Gaill longships became infernos that lit up the valley of the Conwy ahead of the approaching daylight.

The bound prisoners looked on in horror—horror at the loss of their beloved vessels and horror at what Haakon would do to them. Some cursed and some wept as they watched the last of their captors shove the surviving longships into the current and clamber aboard. In the hellish glare of the burning boats, the Dub Gaill awaited the dawn with dread.

Riders in the Night

It was past midnight when the rider reined in his horse at the gate of Deganwy Castle and leapt from the saddle. His mount staggered from exhaustion and the man looked in no better shape than the horse. The glow of torches set above the fortress gate illuminated the rider's face, streaked with dust and lined with fatigue. He'd ridden all day and most of the night to get here, ruining three horses in his haste. A sleepy guard heard the commotion and peered over the rampart.

"Open the gate! I've urgent news for Lord Roderic!" the man shouted.

The guard ducked out of sight without replying and the messenger, left standing before the barred gate, began to pace back and forth in agitation. He was about to pound on the unyielding oak of the gate, when it suddenly began to swing open with a loud groan. The sleepy guard appeared, and right behind him came a tall man in mail and helmet, who was anything but sleepy.

"This better be good!" the captain of the watch snarled at the exhausted rider.

The man straightened. He might be of lower rank than this man, but he had ridden eighteen hours to get here and was out of patience. He snarled back.

"Rouse Lord Roderic—at once! Aberffraw has been taken!"

"Taken? What nonsense is this?"

The messenger wanted to scream.

"It's the rebel, Llywelyn, damn you! Llywelyn has taken Aberffraw!"

The captain of the guard blinked, then shook his head.

"That bastard is bottled up in the mountains of Eryri—last I heard."

The rider stepped in close to the captain.

"I was there, and he's not in Eryri anymore! The men coming over the wall of the Llys were shouting Llywelyn's name. This is no mistake. Now, get me to Roderic or answer for it later!"

The messenger's certainty troubled the officer of the guard, but his story seemed far-fetched. Just a fortnight ago, Llywelyn had been routed from his winter quarters and driven into the mountains. Most of his men were scattered out near the border with Powys. How could he now appear at Aberffraw in strength?

But the damn man seemed certain…

"Very well," he said at last. "But if I rouse Lord Roderic and this is a faeries' tale, I'll have yer balls!" He turned and headed back through the gate with the messenger trailing behind. In minutes, he was rapping tentatively on a door on the second floor of the timber keep.

Roderic pulled open the door in his nightshirt. He was a man who slept lightly, an asset in a world full of betrayal and shifting fortunes, and was fully alert, despite being roused from slumber. He looked right past the officer of the guard to the dust-covered messenger standing in the man's shadow.

"What news?" he asked, calmly.

The messenger could read nothing in Roderic's face, as he told of men attacking the royal court in the predawn darkness, scaling the walls with Llywelyn's name on their lips and overwhelming the garrison at Aberffraw.

"I got out the north gate on a good horse just ahead of them, my lord. I knew I had to get to you with this news."

Roderic showed no reaction as the man related the loss of his capital, though the news felt like a gut punch. Aberffraw was a place that conferred great authority on whoever possessed it. Now it appeared his most dangerous foe had somehow snatched it from him. He turned to the officer of the guard.

"Go to the camp and rouse my commanders. We will march at first light." He turned to the sleepy guard, who was now wide awake. "You go fetch my brother and tell him to meet me in the hall."

He turned to the rider.

"You did well getting here quickly with the news, lad. Did you actually see my nephew at Aberffraw?"

The man furrowed his brow.

"My lord, I cannot say fer certain. I've never seen the rebel, but there *was* a tall man there. He was coming right up the street toward your hall and he was wearing a tabard with your arms on the front."

"The arms of the House of Aberffraw?"

"Aye, my lord, the ones with the lions."

Roderic rubbed his chin. All the warring parties in this conflict had some right to wear the coat of arms handed down from Rhodri the Great, Llywelyn included. But cloth was cheap and an imposter could wear the rampant lions of the Aberffraw dynasty as easily as anyone. Roderic held out a small hope that this was the case—some raider posing as the rebel prince, come to loot the place. He turned back to the messenger.

"What else did you see?"

The man squinted his tired eyes and tried to think back on the chaotic scene he'd fled from at dawn that day. Then it struck him.

"Oh, aye, my lord. Your other nephews were there as well— Gruffydd and Maredudd. They were following behind the tall man wearing your arms."

Roderic's shoulders sagged.

Gruffydd and Maredudd—it all made sense now.

His two nephews had once sided with him and Daffyd when they attacked and killed Prince Hywel, Owain's recognized heir. As reward, he had granted them their small patch of land in Meirionnydd, but they had not been pleased with rule over such a minor cantref. The two brothers grumbled endlessly over their poor treatment and had occasionally challenged his overlordship, but he had always whipped them back into line. Roderic knew they held grievances against him, but had not considered them a threat until this moment.

Allied to Llywelyn...

Yes, it made sense. He had sent his hired Danes to bottle up his nephew in the mountains until spring when it would be possible to march against the young rebel. He had forgotten that those mountains had a back door, down into Meirionnydd—and Meirionnydd had boats, boats enough to carry an army to Anglesey!

His thoughts were interrupted as Daffyd arrived in the hall. The man's hair was mussed and he seemed but half awake, but there was worry in his eyes.

"Is it true?" he asked.

"I'm afraid it likely is, brother. It appears our troublesome nephew has found help from Meirionnydd and has taken my court at Aberffraw."

Daffyd shook his head.

"Aberffraw—that's bad, and with Gruffydd and Maredudd you say?"

Roderic nodded.

"I should have killed those two years ago, but they seemed harmless enough."

"I told you they were trouble," said Daffyd sourly. Roderic nodded again.

"You were right, brother, and we will deal with them in due time. I will march south at first light to undo this disaster before Llywelyn starts issuing edicts as Prince of Aberffraw and stirring up half of Gwynedd!"

"How many men does he have?"

Roderic shrugged.

"Our messenger says he saw hundreds streaming over the walls and through the south gate before he took to his heels. He probably exaggerates. Llywelyn only managed to bring a few hundred with him when he escaped into the mountains and Meirionnydd can't supply more than a few hundred to add to that."

Daffyd rubbed his chin.

"You will outnumber him, then, but I have been fighting this bastard, Llywelyn, for seven long years. He's made few mistakes, but now he has and it's time he was crushed! I will march with you, Roderic."

Roderic clapped Daffyd on the shoulder. He had never liked his brother and they had crossed swords more than once, but he was genuinely glad to have this extra strength. He had underestimated Llywelyn to this point. He would not do so again. When they cornered him on Anglesey, it would be with overwhelming force.

***

Forty miles to the east of Deganwy, Griff Connah jerked awake in the saddle. He had nodded off after two days of hard riding with no sleep. Just an hour before, he'd halted at a stream to let the big grey gelding have a drink and to splash icy water on his face, but that had only banished the heaviness in his eyes for a while. The horse had such a smooth gait it had lulled him to sleep, but the animal was so sure-footed, he hadn't been pitched from the saddle as he dozed. He shook himself and patted The Grey's neck.

"You're a steady one," he said.

He wondered if Roland Inness might sell the beast to him, but doubted he could afford the price. He'd seen the Englishman do a horse trade with Llywelyn for the Prince's prized warhorse. Inness had got the loan of eighty men for a month—himself among them—for that single horse, and an ill- tempered one at that! No, he would not horse trade with Roland Inness.

He looked around him. He was in a clearing and had a good view of the night sky. He looked for the bright star over the northern horizon and found it. He had been headed northeast the last time he'd checked, before falling asleep in the saddle, and saw that the track still pointed in that direction. If he had not missed a fork during the night, he should be very near one of Llywelyn's winter camps soon.

He was about to give the grey gelding a gentle nudge in the flanks when two men stepped out onto the road ahead. They had longbows.

Our lads—or I'm about to be robbed, he thought.

He looked over his shoulder and was not surprised to see two more men emerge from the gloom behind him.

"What brings ye out in the middle of the night?" one of the men to his front called to him. The tone was not threatening, but it was a challenge nevertheless. Griff strained to see the man's face, but could not in the darkness. There seemed no point in concealment.

"It's Griff Connah, come on Llywelyn's orders to gather his men. If you be they, then lead me into camp. If yer brigands, I've little to rob."

The man who had hailed him laughed.

"The horse looks to be of good enough stock to steal—but we'd not make the great Griff Connah walk!"

Griff let out an involuntary sigh of relief, as longbows were lowered and men hurried up to greet him. The first to reach him was Gareth Hager. Hager had joined them two years ago, after his father had been dispossessed of his farmstead by one of Daffyd's henchmen.

"What news, Griff?" he asked eagerly. "Last we heard, the Prince had got away into the mountains and a pack of bloody Danes were watchin' the passes."

Llywelyn had sent out messengers to his other camps during his retreat into the mountains, warning them that Roderic and Daffyd had joined forces and were on the attack. The men in the camps had heard nothing more for almost a fortnight.

Griff dismounted and one of the men took the reins of The Grey.

"Aye, the Danes sit at the foot of the mountains, but the Prince has gone out the other side. He's been joined by his cousins, Maredudd and Gruffydd. By now, they will have landed on Anglesey and taken Aberffraw." He said this with more certainty than he felt.

This set off a buzz among the four sentries who had stopped him.

"Aberffraw! Now that is news."

Griff slapped Gareth on the shoulder.

"There's more. We've been joined by five score men, sent by the Earl of Chester. Some of you were with me when we took that city for the Earl and know these men."

"I was at Chester," called out one of the bowman standing in the shadows. "Have they sent us the Invalid Company?"

"Aye, the Invalids are with us and so is Sir Roland Inness. And by the end of this day, they will have the castle at Deganwy in their possession."

An excited growl rose from the sentries at this news.

"What of us, Griff?" asked Gareth.

"How many men have we left here?" Griff asked and braced himself for the answer.

Their rebel army had been growing rapidly over the past year as the people of Gwynedd sensed Llywelyn gaining the upper hand, but a rebel army is a fragile thing in some ways. Suffer a setback and those who flocked to the Prince's banner would start to slink back to their homes to wait to see how the wind blew. For a fortnight, all the men out here on the border knew was that Llywelyn had been routed from his winter camp and pursued into the mountains. Griff feared that many would have lost hope in the face of these blows.

"Two hundred eighty-two at the morning muster," Gareth said, matter-of-factly, "and maybe half that at the camp over near Ruthin—as of two days ago."

Griff wanted to kiss the man. It seems they had lost no more than a handful of their fighters.

"So, where are we headed, Griff?"

He looked up to see that all four of the sentries were waiting to hear where and when they would strike back at the enemy.

"We ride for Deganwy at first light."

***

An hour before dawn, a man banged on the door of a small farmhouse. It was the finest house in a miserable little village that clustered between the surrounding hills, but it was hardly more than a hovel. Haakon the Black had taken it for his own quarters, its owners having fled at the first sight of the approaching Danes. The men Haakon brought with him had found what cramped lodging they could in the lesser dwellings scattered along the river.

Here they had sat for a fortnight, watching the pass that led up into the mountains to the south. A league up that pass was a fortress where they'd been told the rebel Llywelyn had gone to ground. After they had surprised and routed him in his winter quarters they'd chased him into this cleft in the hills, but had been turned back by the steep terrain and the blasted longbows the Welsh were so fond of.

Haakon saw no profit in losing half of his men trying to force his way into the mountains and had pulled back. Their paymaster, Lord Roderic, had been displeased, but after a fierce winter storm blanketed the pass in deep snow even he had conceded that his nephew was, for the time, out of reach. So, they had settled in to watch the pass.

He'd sent sixty of his men to keep watch over another break in the hills further south where one of his scouts had reported seeing a large number of mounted men ride into the hills just ahead of the storm. He'd left twenty more to guard the precious longships they'd beached on a gravel bar downstream. Haakon did not like having his men strung out so in unfamiliar country. Still, the pay was good and these rebels seemed to not have much fight in them.

The pounding on the door had roused him in an instant. His men never disturbed him in the night without very good cause. He leapt from his bed and yanked open the door. Arn, one of his lieutenants who had commanded the night watch stood there.

"What?" Haakon snarled.

"A fire—a big one," the commander of the guard said simply. "Big glow in the sky—some miles north of here."

For a moment, Haakon was confused. Why would he be rousted from his bed for a fire miles away? He looked off to the north and could easily see the yellow glow there. Then it struck him with an icy dread.

"The boats…"

"Could be a patch of woods caught," Arn said hastily, but there was little conviction in his voice. If he had thought it a patch of woods, he would never have awakened his leader. Haakon shook his head.

"Pick six men to ride with me," he commanded. "Leave twenty men here to watch the pass and start the rest on foot north along the river road." He reached for his long mail coat that hung from a peg on the wall, as Arn rushed off to issue his orders. For not the first time, he cursed Lord Roderic's decision to take back the horses he'd provided for their raid on Llywelyn's camp.

"You'll not need mounts to guard these passes," he'd said. That might be true enough, but using his men thus was a pure waste of money. His Dub Gaill were hand-picked warriors, skilled in fighting from horseback or the deck of a ship. If Lord Roderic had left the horses, they could have raided the length and breadth of Gwynedd, until none were left to oppose them. Farm boys with spears could have watched the mountain passes.

But it was Roderic's money and they were his horses, so they had sat and watched. Now, the passes could be damned. They needed to move and, for all but a handful of his men, it would have to be on foot.

He had no lingering effects from being roused from a deep sleep as the dancing yellow glow in the sky to the north held his attention. He felt a burning rage at the thought that his beautiful longships might be the source of that hellish light. Those boats were his most prized possessions and it would take a fortune to replace them. They were also his means of escape, should things go ill on some foreign shore.

The thought that he and his men might not have a ready way to quit this country troubled him. The Welsh had thus far proven no match for his men, but he had no desire to be stranded here. As he strapped on his broadsword and stepped into the night, the anger still coursed through him, but as he looked at the glow to the north he felt something else. For the first time in years, he felt a twinge of worry.

Down the Conwy

By the growing light of dawn and the dying light of burning boats, the men of the Invalid Company shoved their longships into the river and started downstream. Friar Cyril was at the helm of the lead boat, followed by Roland in the second and Sergeant Billy at the helm of the last longship.

While at Dolwyddelan, the Invalids and the Welsh archers had been divided into three crews and spent their last afternoon at Llywelyn's fortress sitting in rows of four on the ground being schooled by Friar Cyril on the handling of oars. The pretend oars they grasped and the pretend boats they rowed had been remarkably easy to manage.

The first hour on the river proved that a day pretending to row a boat had ill-prepared landsmen for navigating the Conwy. The three longships made it round four bends in the river, when a shouted warning from Jamie Finch came too late and the lead boat ploughed into a sand bar on the fifth. The impact nearly tossed the small Londoner from his perch in the bow as Friar Cyril frantically swung the steering oar and shouted commands to the cursing men at the oars.

"Starboard side—lift your oars!" he screamed and some of the men managed to comply. Whether by their actions, or by luck, the current caught the stern and swung it around, dragging the boat free. Now it drifted downstream backwards.

"Port side—pull!" the churchman begged and most of the men on that side did pull, spinning the boat around so that its bow once more faced downstream. Over the next quarter-hour, each of the three longships ran aground at least once in the narrow river channel, as the men struggled to find a rhythm at the oars.

In the second boat, Roland held his tongue as they blundered downstream. In truth, his ship and crew had fared no better than the rest. It was now fully daylight and, even with their clumsy handling of the boats, it would not take long for the current alone to fetch them up at Deganwy. If they could not row together or steer a straight course by then, no one would mistake them for Danes, the greatest sailors in the world.

As they rounded the next bend, the river broadened a bit and Roland ordered Fancy Jack, who had been calling the stroke, to up the tempo. As they closed on Friar Cyril's boat, he signalled the church man to beach at the next gravel bar. Sergeant Billy followed them toward the shore and, surprisingly, all three boats managed to run up on the bar without further disaster. Roland scrambled forward and vaulted over the bow to the gravel. His two helmsmen scrambled to join him.

"This won't do," he said simply. Sergeant Billy and Friar Cyril nodded in sad agreement.

"Not a seafaring man among them," Sergeant Billy said in frustration, gesturing toward his crew.

"Or among us," Roland said, flatly. "The men camped at Deganwy will not be fooled."

"They just need practice," Friar Cyril said, defensively. "Sitting on the ground and playacting at rowing is a far cry from the real thing!"

"Aye, you're right, but now we have the real thing," Roland said pointing at the boats drawn up on the bar. "Get back to your stations and drill the men here on the bank, but with real oars in their hands."

Friar Cyril and Sergeant Billy clambered back aboard their boats and gathered their crews. Roland did the same and stood in the bow. He looked at the ten rows of men at the oars. Many hung their heads. He turned to Fancy Jack who had been calling the strokes.

"Sir John, let's have one stroke, on your command."

The one-armed knight nodded and turned to the men.

"Make ready!" he roared. It was not, perhaps, a proper command, but men knew what was intended and drew their oar handles to within a few inches of their stomachs and held the blades more or less level, a foot above where they would meet the water.

"One stroke, on my command!" he called. Men tensed on the rowing benches.

"Pull!"

Men thrust their handles forward, rotated them up a foot then dragged them back to the start position. It wasn't together, but most of the rowers executed a serviceable pull on their oars. Two men who had been slow to respond to the command almost tangled their blades with the men on the bench behind them. One of those men rose with a curse on his lips, but Fancy Jack leapt forward.

"Sit yourself down!" he ordered coldly. The man muttered, but sat. Sir John turned to the two offenders in the row ahead and snarled.

"This is no game, damn you! We go clumsy with the oars in sight of these Welsh bastards downriver and we'll not even make it to the bank! Now—make ready!"

For the next hour, in each boat, men called the stroke and oarsman repeated the drill, over and over. It was ragged to begin with, but after considerable cursing and finger-pointing, all of the crews began to find a rhythm.

High above the bar, two small boys watched the strange exercise from a grassy hillside, while their sheep pawed the ground looking for anything green.

"What ye suppose they're about?" said one, as they watched the men cursing in a strange language and rowing away on dry land.

"Don't know," said the other, "but I doubt they'll get far that way."

***

Out along the wilderness that separated Powys from Gwynedd, men were rousted from their rough shelters at dawn to begin the long march to the west. They rode out behind Griff

Connah and under the red and gold banner of the House of Aberffraw. Two hours later, they reached a second camp in the valley of the Clwyd. Griff had sent a man ahead to alert the rebels there of his coming and they were armed and mounted when he arrived. The column barely paused as seven score men fell in behind.

Griff pushed the pace hard, for by his reckoning, Roland Inness should be headed down the Conwy River by now in Danish longships to seize Deganwy Castle. As fanciful as that plan still seemed to him, he thought Roland and the Invalids would find a way to make it work. The young English knight's plan to take back Chester had seemed just as fanciful, but in the end, Chester had fallen to them.

Still, if he failed to arrive with his four hundred men in two days, the plan would unravel and Inness and his men would be dead. Speed was required, but as the day warmed, the backcountry roads thawed, turning them into black muck that sucked at the hooves of their horses and bogged down the ration wagons that tried to keep up.

By mid-morning, he ordered bread handed out to the men and abandoned the wagons. But progress was painfully slow and he could not risk ruining their mounts before they reached Deganwy. As he wiped a clot of black mud from his cheek, he saw a horse in the passing column slide back down a hill into the rider behind and knew one thing with a cold certainty.

They were going to be late.

***

On the banks of the Conwy, a stream of curses echoed in the morning stillness as Haakon the Black surveyed the smouldering ruins of his longships. Most were blackened shells, half-collapsed onto the gravel of the bar. A few still fed flames that were completing their work of destruction. He whirled around and faced the men he'd left to guard his precious fleet. He'd found them bound by the huts and had left them that way. They trembled at the fury of his gaze.

"Who did this!" he roared.

No one dared to speak.

"I'll have an answer or, by God, I'll kill every man here!" the tall Dub Gaill screamed.

Finally, a man spoke up.

"It was Englishmen, lord, I swear. Hundreds of 'em! A few Welsh too, but mostly English."

Haakon stepped forward and drove a massive fist into the side of the man's head, toppling him over like he'd been poleaxed.

"Englishmen? Hundreds of Englishmen?" he snarled, as he stepped in front of the next man. "They took but three boats! Can't get hundreds of men into three boats!"

The man before him cringed, but dared not hesitate to speak.

"Wasn't hundred's, lord, not near that. A little over one hundred is all, plus a score of Welsh archers. But they was English, I swear, lord. All save the archers and the leader—he spoke Danish."

"Danish?" This piece of news momentarily cooled the big Dane's fire. "He spoke Danish?"

The man nodded vigorously.

"Aye, lord, but with a strange accent. Never heard the like."

"Did this Dane have a name?"

The bound man screwed up his face as he tried to recall, then brightened.

"Oh, aye, sir. They called him Sir Roland."

Haakon turned the name over on his tongue. Roland was a common enough name among the Danes, but Danish warriors didn't style themselves as knights, as was the custom of the English.

A Danish knight leading Englishmen and Welshmen?

It was a puzzle, but hardly mattered at the moment. Haakon turned away from the bound men and looked back upon the ruins of his fleet. He saw his old companion, Ulf Haroldson, and his helmsman, Snorri, lying face down on the cold stones of the gravel bar. He grunted and turned to his second in command.

"Pick out three of these bastards to kill as a lesson to the others. When the rest of the men come up, we march downriver. I have three boats to retrieve and a Dane to kill."

***

Three miles to the north of Haakon's burnt fleet, an hour of drill with the beached longships had the men pulling on the oars in unison at last. Roland ordered them back into the river. It was now well into the morning and as the three boats slipped downstream, the river widened, allowing some room for error on the part of the helmsmen. Patch, Jamie Finch and Sir John Blackthorne called a steady cadence, while Roland, Sergeant Billy and Friar Cyril kept the longships in the centre of the channel. After a time, the boats began to surge forward smoothly with each stroke.

As they came around a bend in the river, the valley ahead widened further and the hills angled away to the west. The local riverman told Roland that they were now only two river miles from the final ford on the Conwy. It was here that Roderic and Daffyd would have to cross to march south to Bangor and beyond to Anglesey. Roland signalled to beach the boats once more. When they'd been run up on a sand bar, he called together the two other helmsmen along with Patch, Fancy Jack, Jamie Finch and Engard.

"If Llywelyn has taken Aberffraw as planned, word will have reached his uncles sometime in the night. The Prince expects Roderic and Daffyd to move against him as soon as they get this news, but we cannot afford to reach the ford and find a thousand Welshmen still crossing—or still camped at Deganwy."

He turned to Engard.

"I want you and Jamie Finch to scout the ford and the camp below the fortress. I'll not have us blunder into more than we can handle."

The Welshman nodded and turned to Jamie.

"We go on foot, unless we find a horse to steal."

Jamie Finch nodded his agreement.

"And if a thousand men are still at Deganwy?" asked Patch.

Roland shrugged.

"Then we wait."

***

Lord Daffyd stood on a low bluff on the western side of the Conwy and watched anxiously as the last of his men urged their horses into the river. They'd roused the men three hours before dawn and started the foot soldiers marching south from Deganwy an hour later. It had been a race against a rising tide that daily surged from the mouth of the river far upstream. At this time of the month, the ford was impassable by noon. By the time the last of the foot had crossed, the water was chest deep at midstream and still rising.

He watched as the tide forced the last of his mounted troops to swim their mounts across. He let out a relieved sigh when the last horse came splashing onto the bank. He'd brought three hundred men across the Conwy to join Roderic and left two hundred behind in the camp below Deganwy Castle. He was eager to smash Llywelyn on Anglesey, but too cautious to strip his own domain of troops in the attempt.

Satisfied that all his men were accounted for, he mounted and headed north along the track that had been churned-up by the hundreds of men and scores of horses that had gone before. He spurred his horse into a trot, a dozen of his personal guards trailing behind.

He never felt fully comfortable on this side of the Conwy. This was his brother's domain and he had no illusions about the depth of Roderic's affection for him. But Llywelyn had finally made a false step and he meant to make him pay. His nephew had grasped at Aberffraw without the power to hold it. Neither he nor Roderic could ignore this chance to finally dispose of the upstart rebel.

By the time the last horseman had cleared the ford, the head of the column, and his brother, were passing through the little fishing village that sat across the river from Deganwy and nearing the coast road to Bangor. South of Bangor was a ferry that would take them across the Strait of Menai to Anglesey and from there it was a short march to Aberffraw.

Aberffraw.

He had long ago accepted his younger brother's rule over the birthplace of their family's dynasty, but had never liked it. They might jointly rule Gwynedd, but Roderic never missed an opportunity to remind him that it was *he* who ruled from Aberffraw, as had their grandsire. This he had tolerated, but the thought of his *nephew* sitting on Owain Gwynedd's throne drove him to fury.

He signalled his guard to clear a path along the side of the marching column. He was determined to keep a close watch on Roderic and he could not do that from the rear of the column. He urged his horse into a fast canter and his guards surged ahead, shouting at the men on the trail to give way for Lord Daffyd.

***

Atop a high ridge on the eastern side of the Conwy, two men watched the last of the riders exit the ford and disappear into the hills on the far side. The dark, muddy quagmire churned up on either side of the ford below them was clear evidence that a large number of men had passed this way, but how many? To the north, the fortress of Deganwy and the encampment below it were shielded by high hills. Jamie Finch nudged Engard.

"Let's find horses."

***

Sergeant Billy was idly whittling on a stick when he heard the horse coming up the river road. He'd stood watch here, a half mile downstream from where the longships were beached, for three hours. They had seen no enemy patrols and it appeared that any locals were staying close to their hearths on this winter day— a wise course when armies were passing nearby.

The approaching rider was out of sight around a bend in the road, but he was coming at a good clip. The Welsh bowman who stood watch with Billy eased an arrow from his quiver and nocked it. They did not have to wait long. A spavined old plough horse rambled around the bend with two men riding bareback aboard. The scouting party had returned.

Jamie Finch signalled to Billy to follow them back to the boats as he urged the rickety old horse down the lane. Engard sat behind and looked more than eager to dismount. Sergeant Billy hobbled up the road behind the horse as fast as his wooden leg would allow. He reached Roland as Jamie was beginning his report.

"The uncles have marched. We saw the last of their men crossing the ford. We got as near to Deganwy as we could. We couldn't count the garrison troops in the fort, but there are about two hundred men still in the camp down near the river. The road from the landing up to the fort runs right through the camp."

Roland was careful to hide his concern at this news. Two hundred men still in the camp! He had hoped that Daffyd would leave just his garrison behind.

"What could you see of the fort?" he asked.

"It's built on two rocky hills, not more than one hundred paces apart," Jamie said, using his hands to sketch out a picture in the air. "Each hilltop is circled by a wooden palisade and these two strongholds are connected by timber walls on either side, from one hill to the other. They form a kind of bailey in the low saddle between. There's a gate into the bailey that faces down toward the river. We got close enough to see it was open, with two guards on either side and two more on a parapet above."

Roland furrowed his brow. During his time at Dolwyddelan, Llywelyn and Griff had done their best to describe the fort, but they had only seen the place from a distance and had never set foot inside. News of the open gate into the lower bailey was welcome, if it was still open when they arrived. The two hilltop citadels were a problem. These had to be taken quickly once they'd forced the main gate. If Daffyd's men held even one of these strongpoints, it would be impossible to defend the low ground between the hills. If they held both, his men would be cut to pieces from every direction. He turned back to Jamie.

"The forts on the two hills—could you tell how they are entered?

"Couldn't see without going into the fort, sir," he said and glanced at Engard. "We thought that not advisable."

Roland hid his disappointment. They would have to wait until they were inside the main gate to find a way into the forts that overlooked the bailey. That's if they could bluff their way through two hundred of Daffyd's men in the camp. He looked at his two scouts.

"Sensible choice—both of you."

Above him, the sun was inclining toward the west. They had sat on this sandbar for three hours, but he would wait. It would be folly to navigate the river in the dark, but the less light the better once they landed at the enemy camp. He turned back to the men gathered before him.

"Tell the men—we go at sundown."

***

As the afternoon wore on, Roland kept turning the plan over in his mind, looking for weaknesses. There were more than a few. They would present themselves at Deganwy as Danes, bringing rebel prisoners in from the backcountry, but their disguise would be thin. Bits of Dub Gaill clothing, weapons and armour taken from Haakon's men would help as would the longships themselves, but if the ruse failed, things could turn ugly in an instant.

Should that happen, he had no doubt the Invalids would give a good account of themselves, but the clamour of battle would end any chance to surprise the fortress on the hills above. The open gate would be closed and barred against them and the garrison roused. Without surprise, the place could not be taken—not even by the Invalid Company. His men would have to fight their way back to the boats and flee, their mission a failure.

As the only man among them who spoke Danish, Roland was prepared to pose as the leader of this band of Northmen. He would have to put on a convincing show if they were to bluff their way through. As the disk of the sun sank behind the hills to the west, Roland pulled on his steel helmet with the mail coif that hung down to his shoulders. He wore a sleeveless jerkin made of deer hide and a fine woollen cape fringed at the neck with the fur of a fox. Both garments were of good quality and had belonged to one of the dead men they'd left on the gravel bar when they'd taken the boats. As much as anything, the cape marked him as a man of some stature. He hoped no one would notice the hole in the back where the arrow that ended the man's life had struck.

As he walked among the Invalids, he could feel their tension. He'd seen this before. It was an eagerness to get on with a fight

182

they knew was coming. Patch grinned at him from beneath his own steel helmet and hoisted his red and black shield.

"I may keep this," he said admiringly.

Near him, Seamus Murdo loomed like a mountain. He wore a fur cloak that only made him look bigger and he slung his long-handled battle axe over one shoulder. He wore a wool cap, as none of the helmets would fit his massive head.

"Do I look like a Dane?" he asked, as Roland examined him.

"You look like a nightmare, Seamus. I doubt any man will wish to question your nationality."

Murdo grunted and moved off toward the boats. Down on the gravel bar, Engard was collecting his men's longbows and tying them into two bundles. He too was dressed as a Dane, though the rest of his men and most of the Invalids would play the role of prisoners when they landed at Deganwy. The Welshman had a dark look on his face.

They had argued over giving up the bows an hour before, but Engard had finally conceded that his men could hardly pass as prisoners if they openly carried weapons. It was agreed that men who played at being captives would carry concealed blades on their persons—but not bows. Those would be carried in two bundles, wrapped in cloth and only returned to their owners once inside the fort. Seamus Murdo would carry these, and Friar Cyril would carry a large sack filled with arrows.

Roland walked over to Engard and handed the man his own bow. It was not a weapon a Dane chieftain would carry.

"I'll feel naked without my bow, but the big Scotsman yonder," he said, pointing down the bar at Murdo, "will carry them all. I doubt anyone will ask him to unwrap his parcel."

Engard looked over at the giant in the black cloak and nodded reluctantly.

"I'd not do it, fer certain," he agreed.

Roland looked downstream. Visibility was still good, but the light was fading. It was time. He looked along the gravel bar and saw that men had already gathered near their longships.

"Launch the boats!" he ordered.

Deganwy

A bored guard on duty down at the river bank was the first to see the Danish longships come gliding around the bend at twilight. He had heard of such craft, but had never seen one, and now these three boats were coming right at him—moving fast on the last of the ebb tide. All knew that Lord Roderic had hired Dub Gaill mercenaries, but only a few remaining in this camp had seen their longships pass upstream a fortnight ago.

Now it seemed, some were returning. The man wondered what their business might be, but was not alarmed. These were allies after all. He hurried up toward the centre of the half-empty camp and called for Iolyn, the man Lord Daffyd had left in command. He found him hitching up his pants by a ditch where men had been relieving themselves for a fortnight. The smell almost made him gag, but it was just another part of camp life.

"Boats on the river, sir—three of 'em. Look to be Danes."

Iolyn screwed up his face as he tied off the cord that held his pants up. No one had told him there'd be any visits from Haakon's men, but that was nothing new. No one ever told him a damn thing. He looked down toward the river and in the fading light saw the three boats pulling steadily downstream.

Maybe they were heading back to Ireland where they belonged, but he doubted that. Lord Roderic would not be releasing them until Llywelyn was in their hands or dead. That thought had barely registered when the boats began to veer from the centre of the channel and head for the bar that served as a landing for the camp.

"Best pick a few of the lads to form a greeting party, Harri. It looks like we have visitors."

***

Roland's longship was the first to run up on the gravel bar. He turned to watch the others come in and felt an odd surge of pride as he saw them, one at a time, ship their oars and run smoothly up onto the landing.

Nearly as good as any Northmen, he thought.

He made his way forward as the men on his boat secured their own oars. When he reached the bow, he vaulted over the rail and onto the rocks below. A half-dozen men wandered down to the bank to watch them land, more curious than vigilant. Roland saw them gawking and turned back toward the two longships that had followed him in. He took a deep breath and shouted in his best Danish.

"Sikre bådene!"

All around men nodded and scurried about onboard the longships as though they had understood his command. The men on the bank nudged each other at the odd sound of the words, then parted as Iolyn and Harri arrived with four armed men behind them. Roland paid them no attention as he went about hurling orders in Danish at his men as they began to join him on the bar.

"You there!" Iolyn called down in Welsh, the only language he knew. "What's yer business here?"

Roland had spent enough time south of the Dee to understand him clearly. He turned and scowled.

"Fanger!" he called back, pointing at the boats, then paused as though remembering that the man on the bank could not understand him.

"Prisoners," he shouted again in heavily accented Welsh. "Rebel scum. Haakon sends to Lord Roderic."

"Prisoners?" Iolyn said, rubbing his chin. "When did we start taking prisoners?"

"Prisoners," Roland repeated, ignoring the Welshman's question. "Haakon says, take to fort." He motioned toward the brooding timber fortress that coiled around the tops of the two hills that overlooked the river.

By now, most of his armed men had gathered on the gravel bar and the prisoners were being herded to the bow of each longship, their hands bound in front of them and all secured by a long rope linking them together. The first of these had begun to climb awkwardly down onto the landing.

Iolyn eyed all this with mounting concern. It seemed passing strange to him that prisoners were being taken to the fort. There was no good place to secure them there and he could not imagine what use they would be. He could tell by their dress that these bound prisoners were not men of any rank who might be ransomed off.

"Lord Roderic is not here. Understand?" Iolyn said, speaking slowly and loudly—as any man would to a foreign savage who could not speak a civilized tongue. "Ye should load this lot back on ship and go on to Bangor," he added, motioning toward the mouth of the river. "His Lordship will be there by now."

As Iolyn spoke, the last of the prisoners assembled at the landing. Roland ignored the man's suggestion with a shrug of his shoulders.

"Fort," he grunted once more and pointed obstinately toward the two hills to the east. "Haakon say bring there."

The man on the bank shook his head in frustration and cursed to himself. No one ever told him anything! But who was he to know the mind of Roderic or of Haakon the Black? He had no wish to cross either man. He looked around and saw that half the men in camp had found their way down to the bank to watch the show. Most of them had not brought their weapons, whereas the Danes who guarded the prisoners were exceedingly well-armed and had a fey look about them. Perhaps it would be best, absent orders, to let someone else decide the issue.

"Very well. I'll lead ye up to the fort. The garrison commander can decide to let ye in or no."

The parlay complete, Roland scrambled up the bank followed by Patch and Engard. Behind him on the bar, those Invalids dressed as Danes spoke gibberish commands to the woebegone men posing as prisoners, occasionally jabbing a man in the ribs with the butt of a spear to keep the line moving. It was a convincing display and none challenged them as they marched up through the largely abandoned encampment in the gathering gloom.

Two guards at the southern gate saw them coming and were soon joined by two more. A moment later, a broad-shouldered man appeared at the gate. He wore a fine cape and a polished steel helmet that marked him as a man of rank—no doubt the garrison commander. As the column neared, the man came forward to meet them with the four guards following close behind. He held up a hand to signal the oncoming column to halt. It was a signal understood in any language and Roland complied.

As the Welshman drew near, Roland once more pointed proudly to the bound men behind him and declared their status.

"Prisoners!" he said with a flourish.

The garrison commander scowled as he took a long look at this unexpected arrival. Iolyn stepped forward and cleared his throat. The garrison commander was a distant relative of Lord Daffyd and outranked him. For once, Iolyn appreciated that the man was his superior.

"My lord," he began, "this man here is from Haakon the Black. Says he's been told to bring these rebel prisoners to the fort to be held for Lord Roderic."

The garrison commander's scowl deepened.

"When did we begin taking prisoners?" he asked. "I've received no word of any prisoners to be brought here." The man pointed at Roland. "Tell him that Lord Roderic is not here!"

"Told him that already, my lord," Iolyn offered. "Didn't seem to make him any difference. Not sure he understands much Welsh."

The commander of the fortress at Deganwy was not known for his patience, and what little he had was at an end. It was almost completely dark now and he had been called away from his supper to deal with this unexpected arrival. Whatever this damned Dane said, Deganwy Castle was a fortress, not a gaol! He took two long strides forward until he stood at arm's length from this tall Dane who had upset an otherwise quiet evening.

"Understand this," he snarled, poking a finger at Roland's chest, "no prisoners in my fort!" The finger never reached its target. In one quick motion, Roland seized the man's wrist, pulled him forward and punched him beneath his breastbone. It was a trick he'd learned years ago from another Welshman, Alwyn Madawc, and it dropped the garrison commander to his knees, gasping for air. Roland slammed a fist into the man's temple and he toppled over and lay still

Near the head of the column, Seamus Murdo saw the fortress commander go down and needed no further signal. He thrust the concealed longbows he'd been carrying into Engard's arms and charged the guards. The big Scotsman let out a chilling howl as he came on, an old war cry born in the wild highlands of his home. It was a cry Roman legionnaires might have recognized defending Hadrian's wall a thousand years before.

Two of the guards stood their ground and lowered their spears to meet this sudden onslaught, while the other two fled back toward the gate, shouting an alarm to the men on the wall above. Murdo rumbled directly at the two men blocking his path and swept aside their spears with his long-handled axe as though they were twigs. He lowered his shoulder and bulled his way into them, hardly slowing his forward charge as the two guards were sent tumbling to either side of the path.

The few men in the camp who had trailed the Danes and their prisoners up the hill out of curiosity heard the big Scotsman's war cry and stood gawking as a ripple of movement ran down the length of the column. These Danes, who they thought to be allies, drew their weapons and turned toward them, while the bound hands of the prisoners, suddenly free, drew forth blades from tunics and cloaks all along the line.

Iolyn watched it all in horror. He started to draw his own sword, but saw Patch and two of the now-armed prisoners turn toward him. It suddenly occurred to him that someone would need to raise the alarm in the camp. He turned and ran. Those of his men who did the same lived. Those too slow to react did not.

Roland saw Murdo lurch past him and followed in the big man's wake. As they charged up the path toward the fort, they saw the two guards who had fled reach the thick oak door that served as the gate into the lower bailey. The two men dropped their spears and began frantically pushing the massive barrier shut. Two more guards joined them from the wall walk above and the gate began to swing toward them with a load groan.

"Seamus, the gate!" Roland screamed as he overtook and passed the Scotsman. At a sprint, he covered the final twenty paces to the rapidly closing gate and leapt through the gap. A startled guard picked up a spear and thrust it at his belly. He dodged the point and brought his short sword down in a quick slash that dented the man's helmet and opened up his cheek to the bone. Behind the fallen guard, he saw three men leaning into the gate in a panicked effort to close it. But there was an impediment. The huge bulk of Seamus Murdo was wedged in the opening.

With a roar, the giant Scot planted his feet and shoved. Men on the other side of the wooden barrier dug in their heels, but were slowly driven backwards as Murdo leaned a huge shoulder into the thick oak, forcing the gap wider an inch at a time. Roland swung around to see a score of men pouring out of a barracks on the other side of the bailey and coming at the run to defend the gate. He turned back in time to see one of the guards break and run as Murdo bulled the gate half open.

"Invalids," he screamed, "to me!"

The first man through the door was Sir John Blackthorne. Missing an arm, Fancy Jack carried no shield, but he did not need one. He took down one of the guards straining at the gate with a backhand slash as he passed. Murdo now stepped through the gap and clubbed the remaining guard senseless with the butt of his axe. The two reached Roland just as the wave of aroused garrison troops bore down on him.

Murdo stepped to the front and Roland ducked as the man swung his long, wicked axe behind him and brought it forward in a deadly arc. The head of the axe clove a spear in half without slowing and took one of the charging guards in the side, doubling the man over.

The headlong rush of the garrison troops hesitated before this disfigured giant, as he drew back the axe for another swing. Fancy Jack peeled off to the right, feinting convincingly at one defender who tripped over himself backing away. The man blundered into one of his comrades causing them both to go down. Still moving forward, Sir John disarmed a swordsman with a quick twisting motion of his blade—a manoeuvre Roland had never seen before.

Five men were down or disarmed in a blink of an eye, but more were coming. Roland could see another dozen streaming down from the hilltop forts as the men to his front pressed forward in a desperate attempt to throw them back and secure the gate.

But it was too late for that.

With the south gate now fully open, the Invalids and the Welsh archers began to pour into the bailey. The defenders saw them come and knew the lower bailey was lost. They turned and began to flee toward the two bastions on the hilltops.

Among the crush of men rushing in through the gate was Engard who began handing out longbows to his men as they pressed into the bailey. Beside him, Friar Cyril gave out bundles of arrows, a fistful at a time. A few crossbow bolts began to fall in amongst them, striking one man in the shoulder. The shot came from the wall walk on the far side of the bailey. The crossbowman belatedly saw longbows being strung and ran for his life. He did not reach safety.

Roland saw the garrison troops in the lower bailey fleeing to the left and right, seeking safety behind the timber walls that topped the hills on either side. He had counted on this. None of Llywelyn's spies had known how to gain entrance to either of the hilltop fortifications. Now the panicked garrison troops were pointing the way.

Roland looked over his shoulder and saw Patch charge through the gate looking for someone to kill. His second-in-command's sword was already streaked with blood and there was fire in his one good eye. That afternoon on the gravel bar, they had agreed that he would lead the assault on the smaller eastern hill. As Patch reached him, Roland pointed at the fleeing men who were streaming toward a single small door tucked into the southern end of the palisade.

"Go!" he shouted, and Patch did not hesitate. A score of picked men, including Jamie Finch and four of the Welsh archers, followed close on his heels as he charged after the garrison troops running for their lives from the growing rout in the lower bailey.

"Sir Roland!"

He turned to see Sergeant Billy lurch through the gate.

"The fellows in the camp are gatherin' down the hill. They'll be along very soon I reckon."

"Aye, Billy! Get the rest in and get that gate barred."

He turned back to Sir John, who was now surrounded by a score of Invalids and more of the Welsh archers. His orders were to lead the assault on the larger western fortification and he had now assembled his picked men, Seamus Murdo among them. Off to his left, desperate men were scrambling up a steep slope and disappearing on the other side, where a rocky outcrop concealed the entrance to the western fort. Sir John set off at a run after them, his picked men trailing behind.

Roland kept a dozen of Engard's bowmen with him and led them up a flight of wooden steps to the southern battlement. Down the hill Daffyd's men were milling about in the camp, but had not managed to organize a counterattack on the fort. He left the archers on the wall walk with orders to shoot anything that came within their range, then turned to see a knot of panicked defenders trying to force their way through the only entrance to the eastern fort. It was a narrow door that would only accommodate one man at a time, but many more than that tried to force their way through.

As Patch and his men fell on the rearmost of this mass, some turned to fight, but these were garrison troops and no match for men of the Invalid Company in full battle fury. They died where they stood. Other men at the rear of the crush began to throw down their weapons and beg for mercy.

Patch and Jamie Finch paid them no mind. They bulled their way through the surrendering troops until they reached the

191

doorway. The last man fighting to get in looked over his shoulder and saw them coming. He screamed at the men inside to let him through—to no avail. In desperation, he slashed at Patch and died for his trouble. In the narrow passage, his lifeless body had nowhere to fall, so Patch seized the corpse by the collar and jerked it out of the doorway. The passageway, built narrowly to make entry difficult, now worked against the defenders. In the crush, men had no room to turn about and shove the door closed behind them.

So death followed them inside.

Patch and Jamie Finch forced their way over the threshold and into the passageway. Others crowded in behind them. The fight in those close quarters was a nightmare. The defenders knew that if the entrance was lost, so was the fortress, but none could stand against the fury of Patch. It was as though he was washing away the stain of his dereliction in Chester with reckless courage.

One by one, defenders fell until those in the passage lost all heart. Patch, with Jamie Finch on his heels, stumbled over the bodies in the passage and out onto the rocky summit of the hill. Behind them came more of the Invalids. A few flickering torches revealed the last of the defenders scrambling over the timber walls to escape.

Once he saw Patch and Finch disappear through the door to the eastern fort, Roland looked to the west, but Fancy Jack and his men were out of sight behind the stone outcrop. By now it was almost fully dark. A bright quarter moon hung in the sky, but clouds had started racing up from the south, blocking the light for long stretches.

Roland looked down the hill toward the encampment below. It was as though an angry mass of fireflies had been unleashed in the night. Dozens of torches were lit and men were moving everywhere in the darkness. He heard Sergeant Billy's wooden peg thumping on the steps behind him and motioned the old veteran to join him. The man peered down toward the river.

"They'll try to force the gate, and soon."

"Aye, Billy, it looks that way. Make good use of Engard's archers when they are in range. As soon as the forts are secured, I'll be back with more men."

Then, to his left, Roland heard a cheer and turned toward the eastern fort. It was too dark to see faces, but he recognized the thin shape of Jamie Finch, standing on the parapet there, waving vigorously at him.

The eastern fort was theirs.

With Sergeant Billy organizing the defence of the lower bailey, Roland bounded down the steps and set off toward the hidden entrance to the western fort. He heard a crossbow bolt whiz by his head as he ran and saw a man on the wall above duck quickly down. Off to his right, on the level ground in the centre of the bailey, Sir John had placed his four Welsh archers. They waited with arrows nocked and longbows drawn for a target. When the man's head popped back up, he took one shaft in the shoulder and one in the neck.

As Roland came over the rock outcropping he saw a standoff in front of the small door to the western bastion. The defenders had almost completely closed the only entrance into the fort, but something had blocked the final two feet between door and frame. Spear points bristled inside the gap, ready to fend off any attempt to force it open from the outside. Though no defender showed himself, Roland could hear defiant curses coming from the men behind the door. His own men stood in a loose circle shouting back curses of their own.

As he drew near, Roland saw that one of the shields stolen from Haakon's men had been jammed between the heavy door and the jam, preventing the men inside from sealing the entrance. The man who had done the deed lay dead, his hand still on the shield. He could not tell who it was in the eerie flickering light cast by the torches in the bailey. Ten paces back from the gap in the door stood a trio of his archers with drawn bows waiting for anyone foolish enough to reach into the gap to dislodge the shield. None did.

Fancy Jack was standing with the archers near the door, beseeching them to find some target that might break the standoff. The sleeve that covered the man's one good arm was black with blood where one of the spears had ripped through the rich fabric of his tunic. Roland touched Sir John's shoulder and the man whirled around, a look, half fury and half despair, on his face.

"You're wounded!" Roland shouted over the din.

The one-armed knight glanced down at his sleeve and spat on the ground.

"Bastards won't break!" he shouted back. "What of the other fort?"

"The east fort is taken," Roland said, leaning in to be heard over the men hurling insults and defiant curses at each other. "But the men in the camp are gathering. They'll be at the bailey gate soon!"

Sir John Blackthorne shook his head. This had been his first test as a leader of the Invalids—and he was failing. Roland looked up at the palisade above the gate. He could see spear points showing above the wall and the occasional glint from the helmets of men crouched behind it. None dared stand and present a target to his Welsh longbowmen in the bailey below.

He looked north along the wall then back south and saw no sign of defenders. The men inside knew that this lone gate had to be held or they were lost. They had massed along the wall there—and no doubt behind the door itself—to repel any attempt to break through. The plan to force the door had failed. The words of Sir Roger came to Roland.

No plan survives its first encounter with the enemy.

It was time to change the plan.

***

In the darkness, a dozen men slipped quietly along the wooden palisade of the fort that topped the western hill, staying close to the wall. Roland led this silent band, followed by Sir John, Seamus Murdo, a handful of Invalids and two of the Welsh archers. Behind them another twenty men continued to pressure the defenders at the half-open door. Roland led them over the hump of the rock outcrop and down the far side, out of sight of the melee at the door and the defenders on the wall there. He looked up at the timber palisade and judged the height at no more than ten feet. He turned to Seamus.

"Here," he whispered.

The big Scotsman turned and braced his back against the logs of the wall with his knees bent. He cupped his huge hands, lacing his fingers together and nodded. Roland grasped the big man's shoulders and set his right foot in the cradle of Murdo's hands. He hoisted himself up and placed his left foot on the big man's right shoulder and lunged for the top of the wall, his arms outstretched.

Standing on the shoulders of a man who stood over six feet tall, he was easily able to grasp the top of the wall and hoist himself up and over the sharpened tops of the timbers. There was no one there to challenge him. He looked south and saw the length of wall in that direction was dark and deserted. To the north, a few guttering torches revealed defenders massed behind and above the gate. None seemed to notice this breach in their defences.

He leaned back into the wall and reached over the side. Murdo hoisted Sir John up. Roland grasped the one-armed knight by the wrist and pulled him over the top.

"Obliged," the man whispered, breathing a little heavily from the awkward scramble.

One by one, men used Seamus Murdo as a ladder until all save himself were inside the fort. Roland motioned the three archers to climb down from the wall and find a decent shooting angle on the rocky knoll summit of the hill fort that sat behind and above the lone gate. When the bowmen were in place, he turned back to the Invalids, who were gathered behind him in the darkness.

"No sound till we're on them," he whispered. He could barely see the men's faces but sensed their eagerness for the fight.

"With me now."

He turned and, in a crouch, padded quietly along the parapet toward the defenders at the gate. The attention of those men was riveted by the attackers outside who made one loud foray after another to threaten the vulnerable door. None noticed the line of men coming out of the darkness along the wall walk until it was too late.

A single defender caught motion in the corner of his eye when Roland was no more than ten paces from him. The archers already on station had waited for this moment. Before the man could cry out a warning, an arrow took him in the back and he toppled off the wall. Within seconds, two more men did the same. Roland leapt over a dead body and barrelled into a defender who was turning, too late, to bring his spear into play. The man pitched backwards off the wall walk into the mass of defenders below, scattering them.

Panic swept through the ranks of Daffyd's men as the Invalids let out a roar and fell upon the confused defenders. Half of Roland's band leapt down from the wall and attacked men who were defending the gate. Outside the wall, the eruption of noise within stirred the attackers to once more rush the oak door. Its defenders had turned away to meet the threat from their rear and that was all the opening they needed. They drove the door inward and poured into the last stronghold of Deganwy.

In minutes, it was over.

***

The prisoners from the garrison were herded into the centre of the bailey and guards were posted. Roland climbed wearily up to join Sergeant Billy on the parapet that overlooked the gate, trailed by Patch and Sir John. Engard had been checking the placement of his archers along the south wall and joined them as all looked down at the enemy camp below.

It had taken less time to take the fortress than a smith took to shoe a horse. Had the two hundred men in the camp acted boldly and assaulted the lower bailey in those first minutes, the outcome would likely have been different, but they had not. Surprise gave the attackers enough time to secure the fortress before they faced a serious challenge from the men below. But soon, it would be coming.

As they watched, fires in the camp were doused and dozens of torches that had been moving about like sparks from a bonfire among the tents and huts, winked out one by one. Roland looked up. The clouds blowing in from the south now blocked the moonlight and the breeze from that direction felt moist on the skin. A storm was coming.

"Douse the torches," he ordered. As the encampment at the bottom of the hill was plunged into darkness he saw little to be gained by illuminating his own position. The burning brands would not cast effective light much beyond the wall, but would make his men easily visible from below. The order was relayed from the south gate along the walls of the bailey and up to the hilltop forts.

When the last light was snuffed out, a deep darkness fell over Deganwy. Men all along the south wall strained to see as down the hill scuffling sounds could be heard moving up through the dark toward the south wall.

"Make ready!" Roland shouted, as a hail of arrows and a mass of men came hurtling out of the darkness straight for the gate.

Affair of the Heart

It was full night when Rhys Madawc reined in his horse and dismounted. His village was a mile away, but Talfryn's men sometimes patrolled this road and he could not risk being discovered. He led the animal into the woods where he found a small clearing with some feeble shoots of grass. He hobbled the horse and set off on a familiar game trail to approach the village unseen. It had been a long day in the saddle and it had not started well.

He'd awakened on a ridge overlooking the valley of the River Clwyd to find the sun already above the eastern horizon. He cursed himself for not stirring earlier and crept back to observe the trail behind him. His heart caught in his throat as he heard movement coming his way through the woods, but gave a sigh of relief when a doe bounded up the track then turned off onto a game trail. There was still no sign of pursuit from the east. He'd hurriedly mounted and headed west, toward the far side of the valley and home.

Rhys pushed his horse hard, anxious to make up the ground he'd lost by his late start in the morning, but the day had turned mild and the path had thawed into a sloppy mess. He'd stopped in the early afternoon to let the animal drink from one of the many streams flowing down from the hills and to feed it a few handfuls of grain he'd carried in a sack, but then pressed on westward as hard as he dared push his mount.

At midafternoon, he'd forded the Clwyd proper and, by nightfall, had reached country he knew by heart. He was relieved when he led his horse off the trail and into the woods. He'd feared pursuers from Shipbrook might overtake him, but there was no danger of that now as he hurried through the dark woods.

As he followed the trail, his hand went to the sword he had belted to his side. It was an old blade he'd spied that was waiting for repair by Shipbrook's smith, but the edge had seemed keen enough. He was not as much a fool as Sir Declan might think. He knew he was far from skilled with the weapon, but perhaps he would not need to be. Somewhere ahead he heard a dog bark. His heart began to pound—and not from the exertion.

Almost there.

***

The men from Shipbrook had risen before dawn and ridden hard all day in pursuit of the missing boy. Near noon, Sir Roger had reined in and pointed to a pile of horse turds by the trail. Declan slid out of the saddle and squatted down to get a closer look.

"Very fresh, my lord. Not more than an hour old."

They had closed the gap, but not enough. As darkness fell, they pushed on, picking their way slowly along the muddy path. They would have ridden right past this spot on the trail, had Declan not heard a horse whinny off in the woods to his right. He signalled to Sir Roger to dismount and together they walked slowly along the track until Declan found the faint signs of hoof prints.

"That looks like our boy," he said.

"It would appear," Sir Roger agreed. "At least he is smart enough not to just ride straight into a nest of vipers. He'll be coming at things quietly and on foot. His village must be close now."

Setting off on foot and leading their horses, they followed the tracks a quarter of a mile into the woods. There they found the missing Shipbrook horse, hobbled and contentedly munching weeds in the clearing. Quietly, they hobbled their own mounts and Declan slowly walked the perimeter of the small clearing looking for signs of Rhys' passing. He found a game trail with what might be a boot mark in the soft ground, but it had grown too dark to be sure if the boy had gone that way. Then he heard a dog bark off in the distance. The sound had come from the same direction the game trail was heading. He beckoned to his master.

"Can't be sure, but I think Rhys passed this way."

Sir Roger nodded and the two men set off down the track travelled by many deer and one Welsh boy. Here, the woods were thin and occasional shafts of moonlight penetrated to illuminate the path, but it was still slow going. The game trail was faint and the woods grew thicker the further they went. Finally, in frustration, Declan stopped.

"My lord," he whispered, "I can barely see the ground, much less our boy's tracks. I fear we've lost our way."

Just then, they heard a cow bellow off to their left. Sir Roger made a hand motion and bent into a crouch. Declan did the same and together they moved toward the sound. After a few hundred paces, they fetched up on the edge of the trees, with cleared land stretching away into the moonlight.

The large field to their front was well-tended, with stubble from last season's harvest standing atop neat rows of earth. A substantial dwelling sat alone in the middle of the open land, a wisp of smoke curling from the peak of the roof. Sir Roger carefully studied the soft ground at the forest's edge and scratched his chin.

"No tracks," he whispered.

"Aye," Declan said. "He's gone off this trail somewhere back a way. We must have missed it in the dark. It's too bad we don't have Roland with us. I'm no tracker. So, what now, my lord?"

Sir Roger sat down on a clear spot and did not speak for a time.

"It's certain enough it was his horse we found in the clearing," he said.

"Our horse," Declan added cheerfully.

"Aye, our horse. And we saw only one decent path from the clearing and it was heading this way."

"Aye, and I'm thinkin' that house yonder must be near the village," Declan said. "So, where is he?"

Sir Roger looked once more at the lay of the land in the dim light.

"Nothin' but two hundred yards of open ground ahead, but see how the house backs up to the wood line over there," he said, pointing to the south edge of the cleared land. "That's less than fifty paces, and, if I wanted to approach the house without being seen, that's where I would come from."

"I see yer point, my lord, but what if this is not the place he has been heading to? He may skirt this stead entirely and keep moving."

Sir Roger took another long look at the house.

"He very well may. Look at the house. I would not expect our friend Talfryn to dwell in a place this modest, though it is fairly grand for a simple farmer's place. I wish I knew what was in that damn boy's head!" he hissed in frustration. "Either way, he'd likely stay to cover as much as he can. If it were me, I'd circle around to the south, either to approach the house or bypass it."

Declan nodded.

"So would I."

Together they set off south, just inside the last rank of trees that formed the border of the cleared land. As they moved they kept watch on the house, as a quarter-moon climbed higher into the eastern sky. When they reached the place where the wood line swung back to the east, Sir Roger grasped Declan by the arm.

"There!"

Across the moonlit field, a figure had emerged from a neck of the woods and was moving toward the house. Declan stood, his hand going to his sword hilt.

"Wait!" Sir Roger commanded. "We do not know what the lad is up to. Best we watch a bit." They settled back and watched the boy creep carefully toward the back of the house, not more than a hundred paces from where they stood. At length, he reached the shadow of the dwelling and disappeared into the gloom. For a moment, there was a curious sound, then the boy stepped back into the moonlight. This time, there was someone with him.

It was a girl.

"What's this?" whispered Sir Roger.

"That doesn't look like Talfryn," Declan replied, dryly.

The two watched from the shadows as Rhys Madawc spoke urgently to the girl, who kept glancing back at the house. They were too distant to make out the words being spoken, but the tone was unmistakable. The boy opened his arms in supplication, but the girl crossed hers, unmoved by whatever plea he was making.

The big Norman knight shook his head in wonderment.

"We've had this all wrong. He's not come back for revenge at all. He's in love!"

Declan suppressed a rueful laugh.

"We've ridden half way across Wales for a lovesick pup, my lord!"

"By God, he is more like his father than any of us realized!" the big Norman knight said, with a touch of affection in his voice.

At that moment, the girl turned and started back toward the house. Rhys grasped her arm, but she pulled away and turned on him. Her words did not reach the watchers in the woods, but the heated tone in her voice was plain enough.

"It would appear, my lord, that the lady does not return the poor lad's affections," said Declan. "Shall we collect up the young suitor and get us all back to Shipbrook?"

"Aye," sighed Sir Roger. "This would be a jest, if it were not so damned dangerous!"

They watched as the girl hurried to the back of the house and disappeared within. For a long moment, the boy just stood there, illuminated by moonlight, his head hung low. Then he turned and headed straight toward where Sir Roger and Declan lay in hiding. In his despair, he paid little attention to his surroundings and walked right into their ambush.

Declan rose behind him, clapping a hand over the boy's mouth and twisting his right arm behind his back, as Sir Roger stepped out of the shadows.

"We've come to take ye back, lad," he whispered.

For a moment, the boy tried to pull away, but Declan held him firm. When he stopped struggling, the Irish knight lowered his hand, but kept a loose grip on the boy's arm.

"My lords, what are you doing here?" Rhys gasped.

"Chasin' a horse thief," Declan said.

"We thought ye'd come to do harm to Talfryn, lad, and feared ye'd get yerself killed," Sir Roger said. "But it seems we were wrong."

The boy hung his head in shame.

"I...I loved her, my lord, and she loved me. Or so she told me many times. But when I fled, there was no time to speak to her. So I had to come back. I was going to take her with me—back to Shipbrook."

"And she said no," prompted Declan.

"She was afraid, my lord. She said she could not leave her home—that England was an evil place filled with evil men."

"She had the right of it there!" Declan declared.

"I am done with women!" the boy said flatly.

Sir Roger smiled in the dark. Any boy who would ride across Wales and risk his life for love was not likely done with women.

"Fair enough, he said. "Now, let's be home to Shipbrook before word starts to spread of your presence here."

The words were hardly out of his mouth, when a new sound came from the direction of the house. It was the nicker of a horse. They all turned in time to see a man leading the animal from a small barn beside the house. In the bright moonlight, they saw him climb into the saddle and kick the horse into a trot, then a run.

"It's Mairwen's father!" Rhys whispered in alarm.

"He'll be goin' to fetch yer step-father I expect," said Sir Roger. "How far to Talfryn's place?"

"Not far," Rhys said mournfully.

"Then no time to waste," the big knight said. "We'd best run."

No further urging was needed as the three abandoned the cover of the woods and fled across the open ground. When they found the path that would lead them back to the horses, Sir Roger called a halt and bent over, sucking in lungfuls of air.

"I'm...getting too old...for this," he gasped.

Recovering a bit, he waved the two younger men forward. Under the trees, the darkness deepened and their pace slowed as they moved along the narrow and uneven game trail. Finally, a horse's snort in the distance led them to the clearing. They unhobbled their mounts and led them quickly back toward the road, but the journey through the woods had taken most of an hour.

As they reached the road and started to mount, the stillness of the night was shattered as a dozen armed and mounted men came thundering down the track from the village. The man at the head of the column shouted at them to halt, as half of his men swept past them, blocking the road in both directions. Cut off, Sir Roger and Declan drew their swords.

"It's Morgant," Rhys said mournfully.

Declan whispered an oath under his breath.

"That's the bastard I disarmed at the ford."

"Not our lucky day then," Sir Roger whispered back.

"Do we fight, my lord?"

Sir Roger nodded.

"We kill him first," the big Norman said grimly as he started to put the spurs to his mount. Declan laid a restraining hand on his arm.

"My lord..." he said and needed to say no more. For three of the riders had dismounted and were pointing longbows in their direction. Had it been swords on swords alone, a fight would have been worth the risk, but with no armour there was no chance against these archers. They would die before they struck a blow.

Morgant smiled grimly as he saw his quarry was snared. He rode up to Declan.

"You owe me a sword, English!" he growled.

"I told you, I'm Irish," he said and offered his weapon, hilt-first to the man. The Welshman took it, then urged his horse in close and struck Declan a hard blow to the face that almost unhorsed him.

"Yer English scum in these parts."

Sir Roger still held his broadsword in his hand and there was murder in his eyes as he saw Declan reel back in his saddle. It was Rhys who saved him. As the big man's sword arm drew back, the Welsh boy seized it and held tight.

"My lord!" he hissed, "the bows."

For a moment, Sir Roger reflexively fought to pull his arm free, but the Welsh archers had edged closer and only waited for a signal to bring down the knight. With a force of will, he let his arm fall to his side. Morgant rode up to him with a smirk on his face.

"Yer weapon."

Sir Roger handed his sword over.

"And who are you, old man?"

Declan had recovered himself enough to see his master go stiff.

"I am Sir Roger de Laval, master of Shipbrook and vassal of Earl Ranulf of Chester. What is yer name, pup?"

Morgant bristled at the insult, but did not strike Sir Roger. Perhaps the Norman's claim of connection to the powerful Earl of Chester gave him pause, or perhaps it was the murder that still lingered in the man's eyes. He turned instead to Rhys, who offered up his sword without complaint.

"Welcome home, Rhys," he said with a sneer. "Your father will be so pleased to see you!" Rhys made no reply and Morgant swung around in his saddle.

"Bind them!" he ordered.

Men leapt forward and quickly tied the hands of the three prisoners. With no further word, Morgant spurred his horse back along the trail as his men fell in around their new prisoners. The men from Shipbrook had no choice but to follow. They rode a half mile to the edge of the village and continued through the darkened hamlet. The road led up a long slope to a small timber palisade, with torches burning above the gate. Morgant led the troop inside and dismounted. Taking up most of the interior of the crude little fort was a rather grand hall. From the large arched door of the dwelling, a tall man emerged.

"Talfryn," Rhys whispered to Sir Roger, which brought a quick cuff to his head from the nearest guard.

Morgant gave his master a short bow and pointed to his prisoners.

"It seems your son, the thief, has returned and brought henchmen with him, my lord!" he said in triumph.

In the torchlight, it was hard to read the expression on Talfryn's face, but when he spoke there was grim satisfaction in his voice.

"So, the young snake I held close to my bosom has come back to bite me once more! Were the tithes you stole not rich enough for you, son, that you should return for more and bring these brigands with you?"

"You know well, I stole no tithes," Rhys snarled at the man. "Ask old Tomas. After your men waylaid me on the trail, I threw the bag to him as I passed through town."

Talfryn came down the short set of steps to the muddy courtyard and looked up at Rhys, shaking his head sadly.

"My men reported no such meeting with you on the trail, Rhys, but I did get a report of you galloping through the town on the day you were to deliver the silver to the fathers at St. Asaph's. Old Tomas swears you dropped an empty bag at his feet and fled onward.

"That's a lie," Rhys said bitterly.

Talfryn shrugged.

"Old Tomas, bless his soul, will testify otherwise."

"What did that cost you?" the boy shot back.

"Deny what you will, Rhys, you left with the money and it did not reach the church. You were seen fleeing and now you've returned in the dead of night, with these two, who are no doubt outlaws."

"I am no outlaw," Sir Roger interjected. "Nor do I believe this boy a thief. I am Sir Roger de Laval of Shipbrook, vassal of Earl Ranulf."

Talfryn turned away from Rhys and stared at the big knight.

"I know of Shipbrook and I've heard the name de Laval, but who's to say you are he? A man in your difficult position might claim to be anyone. And even if you are a vassal of Ranulf, I would remind you that the Earl of Chester does not rule in Gwynedd. Prince Daffyd does."

He paused as he looked at the prisoners.

"The punishment for stealing from the church is hanging," he said flatly and beckoned Morgant forward.

"Take them to the gallows tree at first light," he ordered, a note of triumph in his voice, "and hang them all."

Haakon the Black

It was past midnight when two scouts rode up to the column of Dub Gaill. The Danes had marched hard through the night and were only a mile from the camp at Deganwy. Haakon had sent the riders ahead to assess the state of things at the fortress and their report astonished him.

"Our boats are there, lord, pulled up on the gravel bar below the camp and undamaged!"

Haakon had not expected this. He had hoped that the thieves would be so untrained in handling the longships that they would run aground somewhere downstream. He had sent men to check the river every mile as they marched north, but they had found nothing. Now this! Why would these English who had stolen his boats put in at a Welsh encampment? He had expected them to make for the Irish Sea and perhaps take their trophies up the Dee to Chester, but they had not. Could his Welsh clients be betraying him? The thought had started to take root when the second rider spoke up.

"My lord, the Welsh are camped between the river and the fortress on the hill. They look to be in disarray. We rode right up to the edge of the camp and none challenged us. It appears the fortress has been taken by the same men who took our boats. We saw wounded in the camp, so there must have been a fight. If there was, the Welsh lost. There is much confusion among them."

None of this made much sense to Haakon, but two things did. His three remaining boats were safe and the men who had stolen them and burnt the others were only a mile away.

"Pick up the pace!" he roared at the men in the front ranks. He had scores to settle.

***

"Who commands here?" Haakon's words were a demand, not a question.

The mercenary leader had ridden into the camp unchallenged, as all around him men rushed about in no apparent order. Some tended to wounded comrades. Some argued with one another, while some simply sat and stared at the mud-spattered warriors who had come tramping out of the darkness.

At first, no one came forward to greet the new arrivals. Up the hill, three men were furiously arguing over which of them should be in command when word came that real Danes had arrived. They hurried down the slope to meet the leader of the Dub Gaill. Haakon swung out of the saddle and looked them over as though inspecting spavined horses. One man of the three was bold enough to step forward.

"Welcome, Lord Haakon. I am Mabon, oath man to Lord Daffyd. I command here at Deganwy." There was angry muttering behind the man, but he ignored it.

Haakon looked around at the chaos in the camp, then up at the barred gate of the castle.

"It does not look like you do!" Haakon snarled. "I command now."

Mabon looked as if he might protest, but behind him were two hundred beaten men. Behind Haakon were four hundred Dub Gaill warriors spoiling for a fight. Mabon bowed his head.

"As you wish, my lord."

"You've let yer fortress be taken. How?"

Mabon cleared his throat and told the humiliating story of how hardly more than a hundred men had arrived in the longships claiming to be sent by Haakon himself and had bluffed their way into the fortress.

"We stormed the gate twice trying to dislodge them, my lord," he added meekly, "but their archers killed a score of my men. We were preparing for a new assault when you arrived."

Haakon looked past Mabon at the demoralized men in the camp and saw the lie in that statement. He dropped his gaze and met the Welshman's eyes.

"There *is* going to be another assault this night and your men had best be ready to do as I order!" he growled.

Mabon bowed his head in acceptance.

"But first, I would know who has your fort and who burnt my boats!"

***

The watchers on the south wall saw the Danes arrive. After the failure of two half-hearted assaults on the gate, the Welsh had slunk back to their camp, leaving their dead where they lay. The beaten men had rekindled their fires and relit their torches—clearly done with attacks for the night. It was by the light of these fires that the men on the south wall of Deganwy Castle saw the Dub Gaill march out of the darkness and into the camp below.

There was no mistaking who these men were. Most carried the familiar red and black shields marking them as Haakon's mercenaries, but it was their bearing that set them apart. These men had marched nearly twenty miles over bad roads to get here and still moved with more purpose than the beaten Welsh. Sergeants issued quiet orders and men fanned out to set a defensive perimeter, while others rushed down to the gravel bar, clambering aboard to inspect the three surviving longships.

Jamie Finch counted heads as best he could by the light of the fires. He raised a finger as he counted each score of men emerging from the darkness into the light. He ran through three hands and half of another before the tail of the column came into view.

"Near four hundred," said Patch who had been watching the count. "It looks like he's brought his whole force with him."

"I'm not surprised," said Roland. "This Haakon would take the burning of his boats personally. They're worth more to him than whatever gold he's paid."

"He'll want revenge," said Sergeant Billy.

A Prince of Wales

"Aye, I expect he will, but we'll soon know," Roland said and pointed down the hill.

A single man came trudging up the hill carrying a torch and a shield. At a hundred paces from the gate he stopped and shouted up the hill.

"Lord Haakon seeks safe conduct to speak to those holding the fort!"

There was a low buzz along the wall at this news.

"Invite him to parlay, Sir Roland, and we'll kill the bastard with our bows," Engard snarled and his Welsh archers looked eager for the chance. Roland shook his head.

"That, I will not do. If I give my word, I will not break it, even to kill Haakon the Black. He comes to take our measure, and I would take his as well, but you must swear, Engard, you and all your bowmen must swear, you will not strike him unless I order it."

There was grumbling, but Engard raised an arm and it quieted.

"You've led us this far, Sir Roland. I would never have believed we could take Deganwy, but here we stand in possession of the place. You command here."

Roland swung around and called down to the herald.

"Tell your master he may come speak with us. He has my word we will not attack him."

The man with the shield wasted no time retreating to the camp. Within minutes he reappeared, trudging up toward the gate. Behind him came an unusually tall man who wore an expensive cloak over a beautiful knee-length mail shirt. Atop his head was a polished steel helmet with a long, jet-black raven feather affixed to one side. If his garb were not enough to mark him as a leader, his bearing surely did.

Haakon the Black had come to make their acquaintance.

When the two were fifty paces from the gate they stopped. Haakon casually took off his helmet and shook out his long black hair. He swept his gaze along the south wall of the fortress as though he owned the place. He seemed to have little regard for his safety, so close to his enemies.

A fine show of bravado, Roland thought, but he noticed the Dane stayed close behind his shield-bearer.

Completing his inspection of the walls, he called up to the fort. He spoke in Danish.

"Who commands here?" he asked with surprising politeness.

On the wall, men did not understand the words, but all knew who the mercenary leader was addressing.

"I command here," Roland answered in Danish without elaboration.

"Ah, the strange Dane who speaks with a poor accent and commands a host of Englishmen!" Haakon exclaimed, as though pleased with his deduction. "My men, the ones you left alive, they say you are called Sir Roland. It's an odd name for an Englishman and an odd title for a Dane."

"And you are Haakon the Black," Roland returned mildly, "a man who tortures prisoners to death."

"Yes, I am Haakon! And yes, I will make men suffer if they have information I want or if they have given me cause for grievance. And you, my English Dane, you and your men have given me much to grieve over! Why did you burn my boats?" This he asked in an almost plaintiff voice, as though baffled that anyone would have done such a thing.

"It was a cold night, Haakon, and they do burn nicely, do they not? I'd have torched them all, but I needed three to fool your allies down in the camp."

"Such a pity," Haakon said and his sorrow seemed almost genuine. Then his voice turned harsh.

"I do not know who you are or who you serve, but it matters not," the Dub Gaill leader snarled. "You burned my boats! For that you, and all your men, will die. You should have stayed in England, Sir Roland. You should not have meddled in Wales!"

"And you should have taken your own advice, Haakon," Roland shot back. "But here you are in Wales, a long way from home and without boats to get you back there."

For a long moment there was no response from the two men below. Then Haakon jammed his helmet back on his head and turned on his heel. The shield-bearer hurried to follow.

"He doesn't look happy," said Sergeant Billy, dryly.

"What did he say?" Sir John asked.

"He said he's going to kill us all," Roland answered, loud enough for all the men clustered along the south wall to hear.

"Let 'em try," growled Patch. "He'll find the Invalid Company is not that easy to kill!"

"Let them come," added Engard, grimly. "We have our own scores to settle. We haven't forgotten what the bastard did to Gwilyn and Caden!"

"They've got over five hundred men down there," said Fancy Jack. "If they get over the wall, there'll be hell to pay."

"Worried, Sir John?" Patch asked.

"Nay, I'm happy!" the one-armed knight replied. "I signed on with the Invalids to kill mercenaries and will finally have my chance. I'll be waiting for them on the wall."

Roland did not know where Haakon would choose to strike, but the weathered gate was the most vulnerable point. He ordered half of Engard's archers to the south wall to join the thirty English already manning it. He directed Sir John to station himself with twenty of the Invalids in the bailey behind the gate to defend it should the heavy doors be breached.

He sent Jamie Finch with a dozen men to watch over the north wall for any threat there. He gave the young Londoner a hunting horn to signal any trouble on the backside of the fortress. The rest of the Invalid Company would occupy the two hilltop redoubts.

Down below, they could hear crisp orders being given and watched as the dozen fires blazing in the camp were doused once more. A sprinkle of rain began to fall as the last fire winked out and the night turned ink black once more.

"They'll be coming before dawn," Roland said to the men who surrounded him. "Get back to your posts and keep a sharp eye."

***

In the Welsh camp, new orders were issued. An oak log was found washed up on the gravel bar and Mabon's men were ordered to haul it up on the bank and hoist it onto a wagon. It was lashed to the bed and its forward end tapered to form a ram.

Daffyd's men were ordered to form up around the ram and wait for a signal to move.

While the Welsh were grunting and hauling the heavy log up the bank, a large force of Danes gathered at the edge of camp and began securing anything on their persons that might rustle or rattle or gleam in the night. Haakon's senior lieutenants personally checked every man before leading them out of camp and into the night. As they disappeared into the darkness, the light sprinkle became a steady cold rain.

***

The men inside Deganwy Castle heard trouble coming before they could see it. At first, there was a low rumbling sound that came from the direction of the Welsh camp. Then, shouted orders could be heard in the darkness below. On the south wall, men drew their swords and archers nocked their arrows and waited.

Out of the gloom, a heavy-beamed wagon appeared just a hundred paces from the gate. Atop the wagon was the waterlogged trunk of an oak with two large limbs protruding on either side. The limbs had snapped half off somewhere in its journey down the Conwy. Six men leaned into each limb and pushed the makeshift ram toward the gate, while others pushed from behind. Four shield-bearers hurried along a few paces ahead of the wagon to protect those manning the ram from archers. Behind the ram, the rest of Daffyd's Welshman followed and behind them came Danes keeping a watchful eye on the zeal of their Welsh allies.

As soon as the ram came into view, Engard's archers began to pour arrows into the men manning it and those who followed behind. The shield-bearers stopped dozens of shafts, but not all. Men began to fall. As soon as a pusher was hit, a new man was shoved forward to take his place. With Haakon's men ready to strike down any man who wavered, none did.

Fifty paces from the gate, the path levelled and the wagon gained momentum. Men were dropping in bunches, some being crushed beneath the wagon's wheels, but on came the ram. With a thunderous crash, the tapered end of the oak log smashed into the weathered wood of the gate. The men who waited behind the barrier with drawn swords heard the wood crack and groan, but it held.

Now the run up had to be repeated. As the survivors of the first charge scrambled back down the slope, the Danes used ropes lashed to the rear of the wagon to pull it back into the darkness. On the wall, men cheered, but Roland did not. Two of his men had been struck by longbow shafts sent up by the attackers and were being tended by Friar Cyril. It was a small price to pay for repelling an attack—and that worried Roland. The assault had felt half-hearted. There were almost six hundred men gathered outside the fort and he'd seen barely half that many attack the gate.

He turned and tried to see what was happening elsewhere around the perimeter of the fortress, but the darkness and driving rain hid any new threat from view. Outside the gate, the rumble of wagon wheels could be heard over the growing roar of the storm as the ram began to move back up the hill. Then, from across the bailey, Roland heard the blast of a hunting horn, the signal for trouble on the north wall. He had stationed Jamie Finch there and knew, with frightening clarity, that here lay the real threat. He grabbed Patch by the sleeve.

"Tom, hold the gate!" he shouted, as he turned and bounded down the steps three at a time.

***

In the darkness below the north wall, the Dub Gaill waited for the sound of the ram slamming into the gate. A dozen of them had fanned out around the base of the wall and each held a wicked, three-pronged grappling hook. Every Danish longship had an ample supply of these hooks, essential tools for snagging other vessels and pulling them close for boarding. The three boats left on the gravel bar below the camp had supplied all that Haakon needed.

When the sound of the ram reached them, the Danes stepped forward and began to swing the iron hooks attached to long ropes in widening loops to gather momentum. With long practice, they released them at the top of the arc to sail over the north wall. The hooks bit deep into the wood of the palisades and now Deganwy Castle, like some ponderous trading cog, was ensnared. A dozen men began to climb up the ropes, hand over hand. Two hundred more stood ready to follow them.

From the bailey behind the south gate, Fancy Jack saw Roland coming down the stairs. He had heard the horn blast and recognized there was a new danger in that quarter. He and his men fell in behind Roland and sprinted across the open ground toward the north wall. They could already see men hoisting themselves over the top of the log parapet and onto the wall walk. Screams reached them, as the Invalids cut down half of the men who were first up the ropes. But the Danes kept coming, and Roland could see bodies sprawled in the dirt of the bailey below the wall—his men.

As he reached the base of the wooden steps that led up to the wall walk, a Dane came barrelling down at him, his shield still slung over his back. The man screamed a war cry and swung his sword wildly, striking nothing but air as Roland ducked beneath the blow, driving his shoulder into the man's gut and cartwheeling him into the air. The Dane landed hard and tried to rise, but Sir John drove his sword into the man's chest. He made an odd gulping sound and sat down. He dropped his sword and held both hands over the wound for a moment, but he was a veteran and knew it was mortal. He lay back, took his sword in hand and waited for the Valkyries to come.

Roland did not see the man's fate, as he bolted up the wooden steps to the wall walk just as a Dane with an axe heaved himself over and stumbled toward him. Before the man could regain his balance, Roland grasped him by the collar and sailed him screaming into space. He landed with a thud in the bailey, where he was dispatched by Sir John's men.

An arm's length away, a helmeted head rose above the sharpened timbers. Roland slashed the rope with his short sword. The Dub Gaill gave a startled cry as he plummeted downward. Ahead of him, he counted five Danes holding a thirty foot stretch of the wall, with another four hoisting themselves over the parapet. He peered over the side and saw a host of Danes massed below the wall with scores on the ropes or waiting their turn.

With nine mercenaries now on the wall, the Invalids still held the advantage in numbers, but they could only come at the Danes from either end of the narrow wall walk, one man at a time. If the Danes could hold the captured section of wall, the weight of numbers would swing rapidly in their favour. And if the north wall was lost, so too would be Deganwy Castle. There was no time now for plans or for strategies.

There was only time to fight.

Ten feet ahead of him, he saw Jamie Finch parry a vicious slash from a Dane and drive his blade up under the man's ribs. The blade lodged there and, as the man toppled off the wall walk, Finch had to grasp the palisade with his free hand to keep from being dragged along. He pulled his blade free just as another Dane swung over the wall and landed in front of him. The man was half a head taller and half again heavier than the young Invalid. Roland recognized him.

It was Haakon.

"Jamie!" Roland shouted, as the mercenary leader turned on Finch and swung his long broadsword in a backhand stroke at the young man's head. Finch ducked under the blade as a large chunk of the south wall went flying. For a moment the sword stuck in the wood and Finch uncoiled with his own blade, aimed at Haakon's groin. The big Dane did not retreat, but lunged forward, ramming his shield into Finch's head and sending the boy tumbling off the wall and into the bailey.

Alwyn Madawc had once worried that Roland Inness lacked the killing fury needed to win a desperate fight. He needn't have. As Roland watched Jamie Finch fall, he lost all concern for the defence of the castle, or the outcome of this war, or the fate of Llywelyn. He felt nothing but fury and the urgent need to kill this Dane.

"Haakon!" he screamed.

The Dub Gaill leader was already looking in his direction. He raised his sword in mock salute.

"Sir Roland? Is it you?" he jeered. "I was expecting a man, but I see it is another boy!" He waved his sword toward the bottom of the wall where Jamie Finch lay. "That's what happens to boys who fight Haakon!"

217

Roland did not reply. At his feet was one of the red and black shields, dropped there by the man he had pitched off the wall walk. He plucked it up and moved toward the Dane, who stood waiting. Over the man's shoulder, he could see more mercenaries hauling themselves over the wall.

Off to his right, he heard a thundering boom. He knew it was the ram smashing into the gate again, but ignored the sound. The men he'd ordered to throw back any breach of the gate were now fighting to save the north wall from being overrun. If they could not clear this wall, the gate would not matter.

Roland watched Haakon shift his shield arm up and draw back his long broadsword. And he saw something else—Haakon was right-handed and the parapet of the north wall rose almost to the man's right shoulder, hemming in his sword arm. He would have to keep his long blade clear of the wall.

Roland closed in and Haakon uncoiled with a lunge forward. Their shields met and the Dane made a straight thrust over the top at Roland's head, missing by inches. Roland jerked his shield up, hoping its edge would break the man's wrist or forearm, but the Dane was too quick. The shield caught only the blade of the broadsword as Haakon drew it back.

With both shields raised, Roland bent his knees and made a straight thrust at Haakon's groin. The man sensed it coming and twisted away as Roland's blade slid along the tightly linked mail at the Dane's hip. As Haakon twisted away, he swung his broadsword in a vicious overhead arc that caught the edge of Roland's shield and split it down to the boss. The long blade wedged there and Haakon cursed as he tried to free it. Finally, it jerked loose and the two men drew back, glaring at each other through the pouring rain.

At the far end of the section of wall the Danes occupied, Roland saw Seamus Murdo slowly forcing the intruders back with his vicious long-handled axe, but more of the mercenaries were gaining the wall behind Haakon. A few were beginning to leap from the wall walk down into the bailey, the first wave in what would soon be a deadly torrent pouring over the north wall.

With a cold certainty, Roland knew they were losing this battle. He went back on the attack, feinting low then slashing

218

high. Haakon slid his shield down to block the feint and Roland's blade struck the side of his helmet, slicing through the raven's wing and denting the steel. Haakon staggered backwards, but recovered quickly.

Behind him, four more Danes hoisted themselves up over the jagged timbers of the north wall. But they never reached the wall walk. All four froze at the top of the wall, then fell backwards into space. In the clamour of battle, Roland did not hear them cry out, but Haakon did. He looked over his shoulder and saw three of the men behind him on the wall tumble headfirst into the bailey. The big Dane swung his shield up as two longbow shafts imbedded in the oak.

It was Engard and six of his bowmen. They loosed another volley and three more Danes who had come over the wall without shields died.

The Dub Gaill were brave—recklessly so—but they were not suicidal and neither was Haakon the Black. The big Dane kept his shield between him and the archers, but pointed his sword at Roland.

"Another time, boy!" he snarled, then vaulted back over the wall. For a second Roland saw the man's hands gripping the top of the wall, white in the pounding rain. Then they were gone.

Along the wall walk, nothing but dead bodies now lay between Roland and Seamus Murdo. The two looked at each other, then over the palisade and saw the Danes streaming back down the slope, through the thick gorse and into the darkness.

The north wall had held.

Roland motioned for Sir John to take command of the wall and made his way back down to the bailey. He saw Engard standing with his longbowmen. He walked over and hugged the startled Welshman.

"You and your men saved us tonight, Engard," he said, drawing back. "We were losing the north wall."

Engard shrugged.

"After the south gate held, we had nothing left to shoot at on that side. So, we came looking for targets on this side of the bailey. Unlucky for the Danes."

"Not for this one," Roland said with a weary smile.

***

"Eight dead—six of ours and two of the Welsh archers, sir," Sergeant Billy reported. "A dozen wounded—all of them Invalids. Nine can still fight. One will probably not last the night."

Roland nodded wearily as he listened to the casualty figures. All things considered, a low butcher's bill for this night's work—unless you were one of the names on the bill. He'd already been told that Jamie Finch had survived his fall from the north wall with a broken arm. Friar Cyril had set the bone and splinted the arm.

When the Danes had broken off their attack in the north, he'd run across the bailey to find the gate intact, but beginning to splinter at the centre. Outside the south wall, the ground was littered with dead, more of the Welsh longbowmen's work.

The rain had stopped and a few stars could now be seen through gaps in the clouds as he stood with his leaders around him atop the south wall. Even in the dark, he could see that all were exhausted.

Roland turned to Patch.

"Where is your banner, Tom?"

For a moment, the old veteran did not take his meaning, then his tired eyes lit up. He looked to Sergeant Billy, who dug into his tunic and pulled forth a carefully folded piece of black cloth. He handed it to Patch.

"Hoist it," Roland ordered.

There was a tall pole over the gate that flew the banner of the House of Aberffraw, when Lord Daffyd was in residence. It was empty now and Patch secured the cloth by a rope attached to the pole and hauled it up. Roland watched it rise above the south gate as the sky began to lighten in the east. The black banner of the Invalid Company was nearly invisible against the predawn sky, but the silver wolf's head caught what little light there was. Men all over Deganwy Castle saw it and stood a little straighter.

"Thank you, sir," Patch said in a husky voice.

"You've earned it, Tom. You've all earned it."

The Gallows Tree

Thirty miles away from the embattled fortress of Deganwy, a tired man led his horse into a small barn and unsaddled the animal. It was hours until dawn, but it had already been an eventful and unsettling night.

The first sign of trouble had been the sound of his daughter's voice coming from outside the house, long past the girl's usual bedtime. He'd peeked through the shutters and seen her standing in the moonlight, arguing with a boy. The boy's face was in shadow, but there was no doubt who it was.

He was shocked that Rhys Einion had returned to the village after his own father had accused him of theft, but less shocked that the boy had come in the night to disturb his daughter's slumber. Anyone with eyes to see had known that Talfryn's son was sweet on his girl.

Not so long ago, he had encouraged the connection. Having his daughter joined to the son of the local chieftain would have been good for the family and Rhys had ties through his dead mother to another powerful family in the village. It would have been a very good match for his Mairwen, but alas, the boy had stolen money—and from the church no less!

He'd dressed hastily and hurried downstairs, only to see Mairwen march through the back door with tears in her eyes. Rushing to the door, he'd seen Rhys Einion trudging off into the night.

So, Mairwen had rebuffed him.

As he turned back from the door, his daughter had sobbed.

221

"He wanted me to run away with him!"

He'd put his arm around the girl.

"There now, stop yer tears. Ye did right sending the thief packing. He'll not be back to trouble ye again, girl. Once I tell Talfryn his son is back, the man will scour the country till he has him sure!"

This only made the girl bawl louder.

"No! You mustn't, father," the girl said, as she gulped for air between sobs. "I know he's no thief, but Talfryn will hang him anyway. I couldn't bear that! I wanted to go with him—I did, but he said it was to England and that made me afraid. So, I said no. But...but...I wanted to go...I love Rhys! Please don't tell Talfryn he was here!"

The man had realized long ago that he did not understand women, and particularly his wilful thirteen-year-old daughter. At some point, he had stopped trying.

"Yer talking nonsense, Mairwen. Now get to yer room and stay there!" he ordered.

Ignoring his daughter's pleas, he had fetched his horse. The girl would be cross with him, but that would pass and it was a small price to pay for the favour he would curry with the local chieftain. He'd mounted and galloped over to Talfryn's fort to alert him that his wayward son had returned.

Talfryn had been pleased to hear this news and within an hour, his man Morgant had returned with three prisoners in tow, Rhys among them. Satisfied that he had done his duty and gained favour in the eyes of the chieftain, he had ridden home.

With the horse safe in the barn, he slipped back into the house and stopped by Mairwen's room to see if the girl was asleep or awake and in a sulk. He cracked the door. The room was empty.

What now?

***

As soon as her father had ridden off to alert Talfryn, Mairwen had bolted out the back door. If her stubborn father would not listen to reason, she would have to take matters into her own hands and warn Rhys of the danger he was in. Rhys' tracks in the soft earth were easy to follow as she ran across the open field and into the wood line. Here things became confusing, for there were multiple tracks, but all led in the same direction, so she followed.

She saw tracks leave the woods and followed them across a large field her family owned. The trail led into another dense patch of trees she knew well. She had often walked in this glade as a girl, but only during the day. Now, in the darkness, it looked different and frightening, and the tracks were not so easy to see. But Mairwen was not a girl to be daunted when her back was up. As she pondered how to follow, she heard faint sounds ahead of her. It must be Rhys!

She plunged into the woods toward the sounds to her front, stopping now and again to listen. Bare branches and brambles along the trail clutched at the cape she had wrapped around her as she hurried along. She burst out into a clearing to find it empty, but off to the right she heard a horse whinny and felt her hopes rise. Perhaps Rhys had got clear away before her sire could bring down disaster on the poor boy!

She followed the sound of the horse, but then heard angry voices shouting. Creeping closer, she'd watched as Rhys and two other men were seized by Morgant. He'd taken them back toward the village as prisoners and she had followed as fast as she could. At this hour, there was no one about as she hurried past the darkened huts and on to Talfryn's timber fortress. By the time she reached it, the gate was closed and barred.

There was no point pounding on the gate. She knew Talfryn would no more listen to reason than her father, but she knew someone who might. She set off at a run back toward the village.

***

Inside Talfryn's stockade, the two knights from Shipbrook sat through the night in a horse pen with a runaway Welsh boy, their hands bound behind them. Talfryn's men had kept a careful watch over the prisoners, but otherwise left them alone. Now the sky over the eastern wall of the palisade was starting to brighten.

"I'll not be hung like a criminal," Sir Roger said, tugging for the hundredth time at the ropes that bound him.

"That would be my choice as well," Declan O'Duinne agreed.

The Welsh boy sniffed and spoke mournfully.

"Ye should never have come after me, my lords," he said, his voice cracking. "Now I've led ye to this! What will Lady Catherine think of me?"

Declan snorted.

"Lady Catherine? Yer worried over Lady Catherine? Why, I take second place to no man when it comes to avoidin' her censure, but at the moment, I think having our necks stretched is the more pressing concern!"

Rhys Madawc sniffed again.

"I loved her…"

"Well, lad, men have done stupider things for love," Sir Roger offered, touched by the boy's misery. "But forget about the wench. We need to find a way out of this."

"Up!" The command rang across the small courtyard as Talfryn and Morgant came striding across the packed earth of the small courtyard toward the pen. Behind them marched eight armed men, while two more unbarred the gate of the small fortress and pushed it open. The two guards who had watched them in the few hours since their capture rushed in and hauled the prisoners to their feet.

Talfryn turned to Morgant.

"You have your orders!" he said, loudly enough for the bound men to hear, a mirthless smile visible on his face even in the dim light.

"Aye, my lord," Morgant answered, obediently.

"Bring out the prisoners!" he ordered.

The two guards gave each of the condemned men a jab with the butt end of their spears to get them moving toward the gate. As they reached Talfryn, Sir Roger stopped abruptly and turned on the man.

"When word of this reaches Cheshire, men will come for you, Talfryn," he said with a snarl. "This little fort will not save you and if you run, they will find you. I know these men—and they will come."

"Ah, threats!" Talfryn said and clapped his hands. "I had expected begging, but no matter. Begging would not have helped you either. As for these men of Cheshire you speak of, none there will ever know what happened here, so your threats are..."

He was cut off by an outburst from Rhys.

"You are *not* my father!"

The man whirled to face the boy, his arrogant smile instantly replaced with a look of pure hatred in the gathering light of dawn. A curse was on his lips, but he bit it back. He knew the boy was goading him and he fought to control his rage.

That his young wife had been bedded by another man was an old rumour whispered around the village for years. Derryth had denied it, but the suspicion had lodged in his heart like a canker. And when their son arrived, he had seen nothing of himself in the child's countenance. Now he looked down at Rhys and saw what he had always seen there, the face of another man—the face of his own humiliation. With an effort of will he checked his anger.

"I wish that were so, Rhys, for you have dishonoured the name of Einion. Would that I had never sired a thief for a son," he said, affecting an air of sad resignation.

"You did not sire me! And I am no Einion! Madawc is my name."

"It's a lie!" Talfryn spat back.

"My mother told me otherwise!" the boy shouted.

"Your mother was a whore!" Talfryn roared, losing all control of his temper.

"What did you call my daughter?"

All heads turned as one to locate where this new voice had come from. Standing in the open gate was a bent old woman wrapped in a shawl with a young girl standing beside her.

"Grandmother!" Rhys exclaimed, in near shock. "Mairwen!"

Sir Roger and Declan exchanged quick glances. This drama had taken a new twist.

"Rhys, my sweet boy," the old woman purred. "I've missed you."

She then turned back to Talfryn.

"Now, what did you call my daughter?" she said again, with venom dripping from every word.

It had taken Talfryn a moment to recover from this unexpected appearance, but he managed it.

"Maeve, this is none of your affair. The boy stole the tithes for the church. He must hang."

"The boy is my grandson and that makes it my affair. What's more, your charge is a damned lie!" the old woman said. "I know Rhys and he would not do such a thing. I demand you release him!"

Talfryn chewed on his lip. His dead wife's mother was the matriarch of a local clan nearly as powerful as his own. There had once been hope that his marriage to Derryth would unite the families, but the rumours of her liaison with Alwyn Madawc had soured those hopes. He had been a dutiful husband in public, but in private he had behaved cruelly towards his new bride and no less so to the boy who came nine months after they wed—a boy he always suspected was not his own.

But the village was small and word of his treatment spread. It had made for bad blood between the families. This would make it worse, but Talfryn saw no other way. To back down now, in front of his men, would be a sign of weakness and his family had not ruled this small stretch of Wales for twenty years by being weak.

"Stand clear, Maeve!" he shouted at the old woman. "Morgant, carry out your orders!"

Morgant motioned to the phalanx of guards behind him and they moved to surround the prisoners. They levelled their spears and began to herd the three out the gate and into the lane that ran by the fortress. Morgant planted himself in front of Maeve and Mairwen, blocking them from any further mischief. It was light enough now to see the track stretching down a gentle hill toward the village.

The land between the fortress and the cluster of huts was cleared and cultivated, save for a huge old oak that had been allowed to grow in the centre of the field to provide shade for the peasants tending the crops through the summer heat. But over the years the tree had acquired a more sinister purpose. One limb

226

grew straight out from the trunk at about three times the height of a man—perfect for use by a hangman.

It was the gallows tree.

"You can't hang a man without Lord Daffyd's leave!" Maeve shouted as Talfryn strode past her. "He's just a boy!" Mairwen wailed.

"Lord Daffyd is occupied with hunting down the rebel Llywelyn these days and lets me do as I please here—as you well know, Maeve," he said to the old woman dismissively. He glanced over his shoulder at Mairwen as he started down the hill after the execution detail. "And this boy you are so concerned with was man enough to steal from the church, so he's man enough to hang. Your sire should take a willow switch to you for interfering in such things, girl."

The two trailed down the hill after the procession, futilely scolding, threatening and begging as they went. It took only a few minutes to reach the solitary tree in the middle of the field, its branches bare and stark in the thin light of the winter morning. One of the guards had a rope over his shoulder and heaved an end over the low limb. He expertly fashioned a noose in one end and looked toward Talfryn.

The chieftain nodded toward Sir Roger and two of the guards seized him by his bound arms and dragged him forward. The big man lunged hard to his left and sent one of his captors stumbling backward into the dirt. The man on his right arm tried to pull him back and received a vicious head butt for his trouble, his nose exploding in blood as he released his grip. As the man he'd dropped with his first lunge struggled to his feet, the Lord of Shipbrook kicked him in the side of the head and he dropped unconscious back to the ground.

It was signal enough for Declan to sweep a leg at the ankles of the man who had been restraining him. The man's feet shot out from beneath him, but he held his grip on the prisoner's arm. As he struggled to rise, Declan brought a knee up under his chin and the light went out in his eyes.

This unexpected explosion of violence froze Talfryn's men. Rhys, seeing his chance, twisted away from his guard. In three running steps, he reached Talfryn and kicked the man in the groin doubling him over. With a moan, he sank to the ground.

It was Morgant who recovered first. He smashed a fist into the side of Rhys' head and the boy went down hard. He turned to the seven men who stood gaping at the mayhem.

"Kill them!" he bellowed.

His order snapped the spell and the guards lowered their spears and fanned out. Together they moved toward the two bound men who edged backwards. Rhys shook his head and tried to get to his feet, but felt dizzy. As he placed both hands on the frozen ground and tried to rise, he felt a strange rumbling vibration in the palms of his hands. It took him a moment to realize what it was.

Horses. Lots of horses.

He staggered to his feet. Over the crest of the hill near Talfryn's small fort came a thick column of riders, moving fast. A man near the front of the column held a banner that caught the morning light. The boy recognized the red and yellow banner of the House of Aberffraw.

Talfryn groaned as he also struggled to stand. He saw his men frozen in place looking back up the hill. He turned and saw the riders coming. A good forty men had already crested the hill and there looked to be no end in sight, a formidable force in these parts. The shock of this sudden arrival was allayed by the sight of the banner at the head of the column. It was the symbol of his master, Daffyd ap Owain. He relaxed.

***

Griff Connah rode beside the flag bearer near the head of the column as they passed the small wooden stockade on the hill. It was an unremarkable little fort, not unlike a dozen others scattered through the wilder parts of Gwynedd. It most likely belonged to some minor vassal of Daffyd's, and had there been less need for haste, he would have had his men demolish it. But on this day, he could brook no delays.

He had rousted his men up well before dawn and they had been making good progress while the ground was still frozen. If it warmed during the day, these trails would turn to muck once more and his progress would slow. It was thirty more miles to Deganwy. If Roland Inness and his Invalids had taken the castle, they would have need of him and his four hundred men very soon.

But despite the urgency of the march, a scene down the hill caught his attention. There appeared to be an execution in process and it was not going well. He saw two bound men standing with their backs to an old oak tree. Near them, one man sat on the ground holding both hands on a nose that gushed blood, while another lay flat on his back and wasn't moving. A half dozen or so other men stood with spears levelled toward the bound men, but their heads had swivelled around toward the road. A little apart from all this were two women and a well-dressed man half bent at the waist.

He wondered idly why so many armed men were having difficulty with just two prisoners. He looked closer at the two—one tall and bald, the other with long red hair. Then he reined in his horse abruptly and gawked. Behind him, men had to jerk their reins to the right and left to keep from piling into their leader and trampling him.

By God...it was de Laval and O'Duinne!

Recovering himself, he signalled for the column to halt in place and dug his heels into The Grey's flanks. The horse nimbly jumped the ditch beside the road and trotted down to the gathering by the gallows tree. Talfryn had managed to pull himself erect and greeted this newcomer deferentially. He had never seen the tall man on the grey horse before, but he rode under the banner of Lord Daffyd and he had hundreds of men behind him—reason enough for caution.

"My lord, we did not mean to delay your march," Talfryn managed. "We were about to hang three thieves."

Griff did not dismount. He looked down at Talfryn with disdain.

"It looks like you've made a botch of it," he said idly. "Did Lord Daffyd approve of this execution?"

Talfryn squirmed.

"He has given me free rein in these matters, my lord." he said, with as much assurance as he could muster. But the crone who stood behind him would have none of it.

"He did not!" Maeve shrieked. "Lord Daffyd knows nothing of this."

"I'm not surprised," Griff said. "Even a man as stupid as Daffyd would never approve the hanging of the Earl of Chester's favourite vassal!"

Talfryn looked confused.

"You...you are not Lord Daffyd's man?" he managed to blurt out.

Griff gave him a cold look.

"I am not, sir."

"But...but...your banner..."

"It's the banner of the House of Aberffraw, you ass—the banner of the true Prince of Gwynedd—the banner of Llywelyn ap Iowerth!"

***

Declan was first to recognize Griff Connah, having spent six months encamped with Llywelyn's men before the taking of Chester. He turned to Sir Roger with a grin.

"We are saved, my lord."

Sir Roger squinted up the hill. His eyes were not as sharp as they once had been and there was a good bit of blood dripping down from his forehead—none of it his own. He saw naught but a tall man on a horse.

"Who?"

"Griff Connah, by God," said Declan. "God bless the Welsh!"

Sir Roger dropped his bloody head and leaned back against the gallows tree.

"God bless them indeed!"

***

Griff dismounted and, ignoring the local chieftain, bowed to the old woman and girl.

"My ladies, you may spread the word that the usurper Daffyd is finished. Prince Llywelyn rules Gwynedd now, and there will be no more of this," he said gesturing toward the gallows tree. Talfryn could only stand there, mouth agape, as Griff turned and snapped off crisp orders to his men.

The three prisoners had their bonds cut and their guards were disarmed without a struggle. Sir Roger and Declan walked up the hill to greet their rescuer, chafing their wrists where the bonds had dug into the flesh. Declan walked up to Morgant and punched the man in the nose. Blood spurted and the Welshmen staggered backwards. Declan pointed to the broadsword that hung at his hip.

"My sword."

All the fight had gone out of Talfryn's henchman. He meekly drew the sword and handed it over by the hilt. On Griff's orders, ten men rode up to the small fortress on the hill and within minutes smoke began to rise from the structure. Talfryn and Morgant were seized and their hands bound as they watched in despair as the weathered wood of their fortress became a roaring blaze. Maeve spit on the ground as the two men were led away.

Sir Roger turned to Griff.

"Our thanks," said Sir Roger simply, glancing up at the gallows tree. "I did not fancy dying like that."

Griff shook his head.

"A few minutes more and you would have! You Normans— you are lucky folk! Maybe that's why you seem to rule half the world. But what brought you here?"

Declan pointed to Rhys Madawc, who was in deep conversation with Mairwen.

"An affair of the heart."

Griff looked over at the boy and laughed.

"Well, she is a comely lass, but now is no time for wooing. I have urgent business in Deganwy this day. Your man, Inness, and his Invalids were to have taken the castle there last night. If he did, they will be in grave need of my help as soon as I can reach them."

"Roland? At Deganwy?" Sir Roger blurted.

"So I hope, my lord."

"Then we ride with you, sir. We'll need two mounts."

Griff looked at the old, blood-spattered warrior and the Irish knight. The one he knew by reputation. The other he'd seen fight.

"I'll be glad of your company!" he said and turned to one of his men.

"Bring up two spare mounts, quickly."

"Three, my lord."

It was Rhys Madawc.

Sir Roger turned and placed his big hands on the boy's shoulders.

"Yer not ready lad. It will likely be bloody work ahead."

Rhys was unmoved.

"I know I am not ready to fight beside you, my lord, but I will find ways to make myself useful—as any squire would."

Sir Roger sighed.

"But what of the girl?" he asked, nodding toward Mairwen, who stood by the boy's grandmother. "It will be safe for you to return now with Talfryn ruined. And that girl—had she not brought the old one there, we'd have been hung for certain."

"Aye, and I thanked her kindly for that, my lord. But I gave her a chance to come away with me last night and she would not," he said shaking his head. "For her sake, I almost got us all hung. I am done with women!"

Declan arched an eyebrow and Sir Roger barked a laugh.

"Well, I doubt they are done with you, lad," he said and turned to Griff.

"Three horses. I'll be bringing my squire."

The Uncles

As dawn broke over the mountains of Eryri, Lord Roderic's men began crossing the Strait of Menai. This being his domain, he had sent men to every village up and down the narrow strait to collect any boats that could carry more than five men across. A ferry had made the crossing here since Roman times. Now that craft was jammed with men and horses and smaller craft were being rowed across the turbulent waters.

The first men ashore paid no heed to the parchment nailed to an oak near the ferry landing. None of them could read. It wasn't until the third ferry run that a literate man took a curious look at it. His eyes widened when he saw the signature at the bottom. He ripped it down from the oak and hurried back to where the ferry was just pulling away from the shore for the return trip to the mainland. The man waded into the water and hauled himself aboard.

As the empty ferry made its way back to the other shore, he unfolded the parchment and read it through again. For a moment, he wondered if he should just cast the thing into the water and forget he'd seen it, but he was a man proud of his devotion to duty. Lord Roderic had to see this. He only hoped that his master wouldn't blame the messenger.

***

On the mainland shore, Daffyd's troops waited their turn. All had passed the night sleeping on the ground near the crossing site south of Bangor. They'd made a gruelling twenty-mile march over rough roads the day before and had been roused hours before dawn. Now, in the fashion of soldiers everywhere who have been hurried along only to wait, they dozed, threw dice, relieved themselves and complained.

Up the hill behind them, their master, Lord Daffyd, was still abed in his fine white campaign tent.

"Cleanest tent I've ever seen," one veteran muttered to his fellows, as the pristine white shelter reflected the morning sunlight.

"Never seen a night in the field, I'd wager," a man to his right offered, as he spit a wad of phlegm in the dirt.

"Nor has the man sleepin' in it," a third man added.

"Shut up—the lot of ye!" came a sharp command from behind them. It was their sergeant and, in the manner of sergeants everywhere, he had ignored their bellyaching up to a point. They had now reached that point.

"When yer lord of the land," he growled, "ye can sleep in a fine white tent, but fer now, yer nothing but shit stompers. Shut yer mouths or ye'll be carryin' the ration bags."

This silenced the men and, after a while, they turned back to telling tales and gambling as they waited their turn in the boats. But the tedium was broken when a rider galloped up on a lathered horse and reined in before the white tent. The foot soldiers watched as the man dismounted and made for the flap at the entrance. Daffyd's guards blocked his way and even at a distance they could hear him protest.

It was loud enough to wake the man inside, for soon the balding head of the man who ruled half of Gwynedd poked out of the flap. What was said did not carry down to the men below who watched with interest, but the guards drew back and the rider disappeared inside. The men wondered what news he brought, but went back to their pursuits. They knew they would find out soon enough.

***

"Deganwy taken? How can that be?"

Annoyed at being roused from a peaceful sleep, Daffyd had stumbled to the tent flap to give his guards a proper hiding for the disturbance. He now stood stunned by the news this rider had brought him.

"It was a ruse, my lord. Men came in Haakon's longships. They spoke Danish and said they had rebel prisoners to be taken to the fort. They...forced the gate."

Daffyd's strode back and forth inside the tent clenching and unclenching his fists. He had felt uncomfortable ever since crossing the ford on the Conwy and marching away from his own domains. Now this! He had left a full garrison to guard the damned fort and two hundred men camped below it. It would take an army to take the place by assault.

"They forced the gate? How many men did they have?" he demanded, barely able to control his fury.

"They came in three of the Dane's longships, my lord. Perhaps forty to a boat counting the prisoners."

Daffyd screwed up his face as he tried and failed to do the sum in his head. But he had seen these boats. Three of them could hardly hold enough men to take his fortress by storm.

"How could so few force the cursed gate?" he bellowed.

"It was...open, my lord."

Daffyd stopped pacing and sat down heavily on his cot.

"Open...dear God..."

"Aye, lord," the man said sheepishly. "Yer garrison commander came out to question these Danes. He ordered them back to their boats, but they struck him down. And these prisoners—they were but posing as such! They threw off their bonds and had hidden weapons. Prisoners and Danes alike rushed the gate. They took the lower bailey in a matter of minutes and not long after it looked as though they had gained control of both hilltops as well."

"What of Iolyn?" David raged as he stood once more. "I left that bastard in charge of the camp!"

The messenger hesitated a moment, but gathered himself.

"Iolyn is dead, my lord. We charged the gate twice, just minutes after the attack began, but they had barred it. Iolyn fell, along with a score of others, but we could not force the gate. They had archers, my lord—good ones!"

Daffyd shook his head in consternation.

235

"Three boatloads of men marched through two hundred of my own and took a fort garrisoned by eighty more. Who commands there now?" he asked wearily.

"When I left camp, my lord, they were arguing over who had command and what to do next. I thought the thing to do was bring you this news in all haste."

Daffyd had started to hurriedly dress as the messenger finished his tale of disaster at Deganwy. These men who had taken his fortress were likely Llywelyn's. Who else could it be, unless Haakon himself had turned on them? He had warned Roderic not to trust the Dub Gaill. But the archers…the Danes had not brought archers. He did not know who sat in his fortress. He only knew he had to kill them.

***

The men lounging below the white tent on the hill had watched events with great interest. After the early arrival of the rider, the top of the hill had erupted like a disturbed bed of ants. Guards had scurried in every direction. Messengers had been summoned and dispatched. Before long, Lord Roderic rode up to his brother's tent and dismounted as Daffyd emerged to meet him. Within a minute, the two men could be seen screaming at each other, though their words were too distant to be overheard. Daffyd was pointing back to the north and Roderic was waving some sort of parchment in his older brother's face.

"Brotherly love," said one soldier dryly.

Further comment was cut short as the contentious parlay at the tent ended. Roderic mounted his warhorse, said something clearly unpleasant to Daffyd and spurred back down the hill toward the ferry crossing. The men who commanded Daffyd's troops had watched things play out at a distance. None would have thought to intervene between the two brothers. When elephants contend, it's always best for mice to stand clear.

But once Roderic had made his hasty exit, they began moving up toward the white tent in ones and twos, thirsty for news. For three fortnights, there had been an alliance between the brothers—the east and the west of Gwynedd finally joining forces to snuff out Llywelyn's rebellion. Many of the men who trudged up toward the tent had been fighting the rebel prince for seven long years. The alliance between their master and his younger brother had given them hope that the end might be in sight and this new dispute worried them.

Just across the strait and a half day's march away was Aberffraw and Llywelyn. Anglesey was good open country where a larger force could easily crush a smaller one. Surely this opportunity would not be missed. But the scene at the tent had unsettled them. Something was amiss and, to a man, they approached the tent fearing the worst.

***

"Up, up, my shit stompers!" the sergeant roared. His men scrambled to their feet. "Form up on the road!"

Men stepped lively and began to line up on the rutted path facing down toward the ferry crossing where the last of Roderic's men were loading onto the boats. The sergeant stood off to the side with hands on his hips.

"Now—about face, lads. We're marching back home."

***

It was noon, when another rider from Deganwy reached the column of men marching along the coast road northeast of Bangor. He sought out Daffyd to make his report.

"My lord, Lord Haakon marched into the camp at midnight with near four hundred of his Dub Gaill, and took command. He straight away ordered an assault on the castle."

The news that the mercenary leader had taken command over his own men disturbed him, but at least he now knew the Dane had not betrayed them.

"And what of this attack?"

"The assault failed, my lord. Haakon's men gained the north wall, but could not hold it."

"And our men?"

"We lost another score attacking the gate, lord."

"Does Haakon know who these bastards are who took the fort?"

The messenger shook his head.

237

"It's a mystery to him, lord, though he said they might be English. After the last attack, they ran up a banner above the south wall."

"English? What sort of banner was it?" Daffyd asked, genuinely curious. He knew the banners favoured by the English Marcher Lords. His nearest neighbour amongst the border Earls was Ranulf of Chester, but he had been careful to keep the peace with him over the years. It could not be Ranulf! If these were Llywelyn's men, the banner would likely be the red and yellow lions of the House of Aberffraw—his own banner and that of his nephew.

"I got a good look at it after the last charge, lord. It was all of black, with the head of a wolf."

Daffyd blinked. A black banner with a wolf's head? He'd never seen the like. Feeling a headache coming on, he pressed two meaty fingers against each of his temples and rubbed.

Who had taken his fortress at Deganwy?

***

Through the morning, the defenders of Deganwy Castle anxiously watched the camp at the bottom of the hill. There was plenty of activity there, but no sign of a renewed assault. Half of the men, exhausted after two nights with no rest, slept at their posts, weapons at hand.

At noon, a watch was posted and men not on duty gathered in the centre of the bailey. Nine graves had been dug for the men who had not survived the taking of the fortress or the attempts by the Danes and Welsh to take it back. The bodies of the Danes who had died inside the stockade in the early morning attack were pitched over the north wall to join a dozen already lying there.

The seven Invalids and two Welshmen who had fallen were wrapped in shrouds and laid in their graves as Friar Cyril prayed over them, first in English, then in Welsh and finally in Latin. He prayed for the men's souls. He prayed for peace for the families, who would never see them again.

Roland watched the man with new respect. This odd, skinny little churchman, who had taken on the role of chaplain to the Invalid Company as penance for past sins, had seemed ridiculous when first he'd met him in Chester. But the man who had busied himself getting drunken soldiers safely abed in their barracks had acquitted himself well on the march to Dolwyddelan and on the journey down the River Conwy. Now, as he stood before the Invalids to honour their dead, he spoke to them with power and conviction and tenderness. Friar Cyril was proving to be a priest in full.

When the service was concluded, the friar walked back to the south wall with Roland and Sir John. It was a beautiful day with a near cloudless sky, but for a few dark smudges over the southern horizon. As they looked down on the enemy camp, Fancy Jack turned to the churchman.

"Father, you have a way with a prayer," he said earnestly. "Perhaps you could beseech God to grant us a victory here."

Friar Cyril shook his head.

"I can't do that, Sir John," he said softly. "I can ask God for strength to face our trials. I can ask Him to grant us peace, though we walk through the valley of the shadow of death, but those people down there," he said and pointed to the small figures moving about in the camp, "are his creations too. We must not ask God to pick between us. I don't think He likes it."

Sir John frowned.

"Well whose side are you on, sir?" he demanded.

"Oh, I am not God, Sir John," the little priest said with a grim smile. "I would prefer that we kill them."

The Storm

From a low hill, Llywelyn's scouts watched as Roderic's army began to gather itself on the west side of the Menai Strait. By noon, the last man and horse had reached Anglesey. Across the strait, they had seen another column of men march away—back toward Bangor. A courier had reached the Prince by late morning with news that the uncles had split their force.

Split they might be, but Roderic alone had a thousand men at his command. Three hundred were cavalry. If Llywelyn was foolish enough to abandon the Llys and fight on open ground, Roderic would unleash his mounted troops to make short work of the rebel foot soldiers. If Llywelyn chose to stay and defend the Llys, it would be Roderic's seven hundred infantry who would flush him out of that lightly fortified enclosure, to be ridden down and cut to pieces by his cavalry.

When his army had assembled, Roderic ordered scouts forward to probe Llywelyn's strength. The cavalry advanced an hour behind the screen of scouts, and the infantry began its day-long march to Aberffraw. Llywelyn's own scouts fell back as Roderic's men advanced. Couriers took word of the enemy's approach to the Prince throughout the morning.

By noon, Roderic's scouts were within sight of Aberffraw. They drew back after a hail of longbow shafts erupted from the walls of the royal Llys and fell in amongst their ranks. With the cavalry an hour behind and the infantry not expected to arrive until nightfall, the scouts settled in to watch.

***

"There's a man to see you outside, lord. One of the fishermen I believe."

Llywelyn set down the silver chalice he'd been examining and signalled the man to bring the visitor in. It was Caradog Priddy and he had a worried look on his face.

"Master Priddy, you look troubled," Llywelyn said, dispensing with preambles.

"Ye have the rights of that, lord. We've a problem."

"Well, spit it out, man. Bad news doesn't improve with age."

"It's the weather—it's not right. Too warm for mid-winter and that breeze blowin' in from the south—it feels wet to me."

"For God's sake, speak plainly, sir!" Llywelyn snapped. "Warm weather and a moist breeze seems nothing to worry overmuch about."

Priddy shook his head.

"Aye, it seems so, but it's what these signs foretell, lord. That is the trouble. I've seen it like this only once before, when I was a young man. Sunny day in the dead of winter, warm wet wind blowin' in hard from the south and behind it came a tempest the likes I've never seen. Six boats went down in Cardigan Bay that day. The rest of us were lucky to make it back into a sheltered harbour, but even there we lost two more boats to the wind and waves."

Llywelyn rose and started toward the entrance of the great hall, beckoning Priddy to follow. From the archway, he scanned the sky, which was a clear, pale blue, with hardly a cloud in sight. He lowered his eyes and looked toward the sea where Priddy's boats were beached. Above the southern horizon, the sky had a vaguely bruised look and there was a steady wind blowing in from that quarter that caused the Prince's cape to whip behind him. Llywelyn was no seaman, but he had lived out in the elements for seven long years and knew the signs of approaching bad weather.

"How soon, Master Priddy?"

Priddy rubbed his chin.

"I expect we'll feel the first of it in a few hours, my lord, and by evening it will be upon us in full fury."

241

Llywelyn took a moment to let the import of this news sink in. The plan had been to wait for the cover of darkness to slip out of the Llys and march down to the bay where they would load the men and set sail for Deganwy. If Priddy's tidings were true, that would be impossible now.

"So, what's to be done?"

"Can't leave the boats on the beach, lord. Storm'll smash 'em to kindlin'. Won't do ye any good then. Can't just lay out a ways either. In this kinda blow, ye can't be caught off a lee shore. We'll have to find a safe anchorage."

"And where would you find that," Llywelyn asked.

"Only two that I know of hereabouts, lord—Holyhead and Caenarfon, but Roderic's men control both. We could sail in, but not back out again."

"I think neither of us could afford that, sir."

Priddy nodded.

"Them boats all I got, lord," Priddy said flatly

The old sailor rubbed his chin, lost in thought for a moment, then spoke.

"My lord, our only safety will be finding refuge off a weather shore and the nearest of those is t'other side of Anglesey. If ye'd march yer lads down to the ships now, we might be able to clear the headland of Trwyn y Gadair 'fore we're driven up on the rocks. Then, we could run up the channel with the wind at our backs and make the north side of the island before we sink. We get there and we're off a weather shore with the wind blowin' out and comfy as home in bed. But ye'll need to have yer men take ship now, my lord, if we are to be safe away."

As the old shipmaster spoke, Llywelyn continued to stare at the southern horizon. The darkness there was slowly growing. He cursed under his breath at the ill luck. The scouts his men had chased away with their longbows lurked out of range but not out of sight and his own scouts had reported that the first units of Roderic's cavalry were arriving on the field. In six more hours he could have been safe away, but if they marched out now, in broad daylight, they would be caught in flat, open ground. The horsemen would fall on his men like wolves on the fold. It would be a slaughter.

Llywelyn turned to Priddy and gestured toward three riders off in the distance to the east.

"My scouts tell me there are over three hundred of those men gathering out there. We cannot move before dark."

Priddy shook his head sadly.

"By dark, the wind will be too strong for us to get far enough to sea to clear the lee side of the island. By midnight, there'll be rain blowin' in sideways from the south and breakers higher than a man's head down at the shore. My boats must go soon if they go at all."

Llywelyn gave a grim nod.

"If you sail now, how long to reach safe waters in the north?"

Priddy turned his face to the south, feeling the strength of the wind.

"In calm seas, it would take six hours, maybe seven, lord, but hard to judge in this weather, maybe twice that. Then, we ride out the storm."

"Then you sail back to us?"

"Aye, once the wind dies or shifts around to northerly. If it keeps blowing from the south, lord, I'll tell ye plain, we cannot sail against it." If the winds are favourable, we can return by dark tomorrow. Can you hold out here that long?"

Llywelyn still had his eyes on the three riders on the horizon.

"Yes," he said, and knew it was a lie.

***

Llywelyn ap Iowerth, Prince of Gwynedd, stood atop a high dune and watched as the boats that had transported him to Anglesey fought their way back out to sea. The southwesterly wind was growing stiffer by the hour and the faint bruising he had seen on the horizon in the early afternoon was now a menacing line of black clouds racing toward him.

Since he was a boy, he had been convinced that it was God's will that he rule Gwynedd—all of Gwynedd—but he had not thought it would take seven long years of living like a bandit in the wilderness to realize His will. He'd not complained to his Maker over the trials he had suffered, but wondered if he had offended the Almighty in some way as he watched the last of his thirty fishing boats disappear around a headland to the west. What was it Inness had said to him?

God is a fickle ally.

A stronger gust of wind blew sand up the hard-packed beach to add to the bulk of the dune as he clambered down its shifting surface and mounted his horse. The tide was ebbing now and he was able to ride up the bed of the Aberffraw River, hidden from the view of Roderic's scouts. As he neared the town, the first fat drops of rain began to pepper the sand around him.

By the time he reached the enclosure of the royal Llys, the rain was coming steady and the wind was picking up. He dismounted and scanned the walls. His men stood almost shoulder to shoulder on a raised earthen step, ready to defend every foot of the barrier—but it was only eight feet high, had no towers and no arrow loops. It was more a decoration than a defensive barrier. It would be a minor hindrance when the onslaught came.

A groom took his horse and he strode into the hall. Gruffydd was sitting at a table drinking ale, which had been found to be in great supply within the Llys. He looked morose. He and his brother had been told of the approaching storm and had strongly demanded that they march down to the coast immediately to take ship. Llywelyn had refused.

It had been many years since either of his cousins had ridden to war and he'd reminded them what cavalry could do to infantry in open ground. They had grumbled, but when he thought the two might abandon his cause, fear had won out, fear of being ridden down by cavalry and fear of Roderic.

Their uncle would know by now they had joined Llywelyn's rebellion. Backing out now would not save them if their cousin's cause failed. In the end, Maredudd had agreed to take command of the fleet and sailed with Priddy in the early afternoon. Gruffydd spent the remainder of the day drinking in the hall. Llywelyn ignored him as he walked through the huge room and into a smaller one that held a part of Roderic's treasury.

Above his head, could hear the rain drumming louder on the roof of the hall. Priddy had not exaggerated the ferocity of the storm and it was only just beginning. He looked at a table where a sampling of silver objects lay. His uncle's main trove was kept secure behind the formidable walls of Caenarfon Castle, but a small fortune had been locked away in this room as well. Some of it had been pulled from a vault and spread on a table.

Llywelyn sat down heavily and looked at the hoard. The day before, he had been surprised when delegations from a substantial number of the local barons of Anglesey had arrived in answer to his summons. Mostly, these were led by younger sons and, in a few cases, by bastard sons, none wishing to offend the new resident of the royal Llys, but none willing to upset the old ruler either.

Llywelyn greeted them all as though they were patriarchs and sent them home with generous gifts of silver from Roderic's own coffers. He had taken note of who had paid him respect and who had not. There would be an accounting for that at the end of all this.

Outside, there was a wailing sound as the wind began to twist around corners and sweep under the eaves of the hall. He felt bone weary, but knew he dare not show it. He walked back through the great hall where his cousin continued to down ale in silence and stepped back through the front entrance.

It was twilight, but nearly as dark as midnight, as the wind roared in from the south carrying sheets of rain with it. He could see his men hunkering down against the fury of the storm and wondered what shape they would be in by the morning when Roderic would have his entire force up. He had six hundred men. His uncle had a thousand. It was bad odds.

He was about to summon one of his lieutenants and order half the men to take shelter when he heard footsteps behind him. He turned to see the skinny poet, Benfras, approach. The man had been left at liberty in the hall and had sharp ears. He no doubt knew the dilemma Llywelyn faced.

"My lord! What shall you do?" he shouted above the growing roar of the wind.

"We will wait here for your old lord, master poet." Llywelyn shouted back. "I expect we will see him around first light."

The poet looked at the men huddled close to the wall with no way to shield themselves from the fury of wind and rain.

"But you will lose, my lord. Even a poet can see that!" the man cried.

Llywelyn shrugged.

"It's in God's hands now."

The poet tugged at his sleeve.

"Does not God help those that help themselves, lord? Step inside. I have a story about a saint I would tell you."

Llywelyn stared at the man. His sharp face was drenched and strands of his long, wet hair clung to his cheeks where the swirling wind had plastered them. The man's eyes were intense and he did not turn away from Llywelyn's gaze or release his grasp on the Prince's sleeve. Llywelyn shrugged. He would need more than a fanciful tale to survive through the morrow, but what harm could it do?

He let the poet lead him back inside the entrance to the hall.

"Is this to be another tale of Saint Daffyd?" Llywelyn asked wearily. He'd been raised on stories of Wales' patron saint, most of which seemed rather trivial and boring to him as a young man. The ancient churchman had supposedly advised Welsh warriors to put leeks in their bonnets before battle. The Welsh had triumphed, but Llywelyn had always been sceptical as to how the ornamental vegetables had helped.

"I've found no leeks in Roderic's larder," he said.

"No, no, my lord," the poet said, waving away the idea of Saint Daffyd as though shooing a fly. "I speak of Saint Dwynwen!"

Llywelyn screwed up his face.

"I can't say as I've heard of that one."

"She's our patron saint of lovers, my lord."

Llywelyn sighed.

"Perhaps we should stay with Saint Daffyd after all, lad. I'll not have much use for lovers when your old lord attacks at dawn."

Benfras shook his head vigorously.

"This has naught to do with lovers, my lord. It has to do with what Saint Dwynwen did when she lost hers. She became a hermit!"

"I know poets enjoy the sound of their own voices," Llywelyn said testily, "but get to the point!"

"Of course, my lord, of course," he answered hastily. "Dwynwen took up the hermit's life on an island, where she lived out her days alone. The place is called Ynys Llanddwyn, after the saint, lord. It is a very unusual island, inasmuch as it is not always surrounded by the sea. There is a thin finger of land that connects it to the shore. At each high tide, the sea rushes in and covers it completely. At low tide it can be crossed for a few hours, but the sand is deep and the path narrow. It's a hard place to approach, lord, and I think a better place to defend than this," he said, casting a sceptical eye at the low wall of the Llys.

Llywelyn arched an eyebrow. He had only been half listening to the poet, but this last part intrigued him. If such a place existed, it would indeed be more defensible than the Llys.

"And where is this saint's island, Benfras?" he asked, prepared to be disappointed.

The poet smiled broadly.

"It lies not three miles southeast along the coast. I've made a pilgrimage there myself."

Llywelyn stepped back across the entrance to the hall and looked at the dark shapes of his men crouched against the low wall. Tomorrow, they would be in the fight of their lives and they would lose if they stayed where they were. Perhaps it was time to put his faith in a heartbroken saint—and a poet. He swung around and strode back into the hall. There he found Gruffydd asleep on the table.

"Up, cousin!" he ordered. "Prepare your men to march!"

***

The men who survived the coming days would long remember the march from Aberffraw to Ynys Llanddwyn—Saint Dwynwen's Island. The night was dark as pitch and the rain swept over them in sheets. Shielded by the dark and the storm from the watchful eyes of Roderic's horsemen, they'd marched quietly out of the enclosure of the royal court, and down to the Ffraw River. They followed the gravel river bed toward the sea and watched as the small stream in the centre began to swell.

Before the rising river drove them from its course, the column of six hundred reached the bay where they had landed three days before. The ships that had brought them here were long gone. In their place were waves, higher than a horse's head and driven by a howling wind, that thundered as they crashed on the shore. The churning waters ran right up to the base of the dunes and, at times, men waded knee deep in the oncoming sea as they marched.

Llywelyn led the column with the spare little poet, Benfras, beside him to show the way. He wondered, as he looked at the heaving waters, whether Caradog Priddy had got his ships safe away. They'd covered a mile along the strand when the poet turned and called to Llywelyn over the wind.

"We must ford the River Cefni just ahead, my lord!" he shouted.

Llywelyn nodded. Whatever lay in their path, there could be no turning aside now. Ahead of him, he saw the dunes swing down toward the sea. He clambered up the wet shifting sand and looked down on a shallow river, frothed by the wind. Benfras struggled up beside him.

"It's only a mile beyond this river!" he screamed into the wind. Llywelyn did not reply. He simply started down the backside of the dune as his men began to climb the forward side. He reached the edge of the stream and edged into it. There was little current as the oncoming waves fought the river's flow to a standstill, but the river bottom was treacherous.

He leaned forward and started across. He was wearing mail and, if he lost his footing and went under, he would drown. But the water never rose more than chest high as he stumbled onto the far bank. He turned and saw Benfras and a long line of men, obediently following in his steps. He leaned down and extended a hand to the young poet and hauled him up on the bank.

"I don't know if we will survive this, poet," he shouted at the young man, "but if you do, you have the makings of an epic poem."

Benfras looked back on the line of men dutifully marching down the far dune and into the water.

"If I live, my lord, I will try to do it justice!"

***

For another hour, the cold and miserable men trudged along a narrow strip of white sand with high dunes to their left and a raging sea to their right. The wind slacked a little but the rain did not. As they neared a low headland where the dunes seemed to fall away to the east, Benfras cried out and pointed.

"Ynys Llanddwyn!"

Llywelyn peered through the pelting rain and saw a low hump of land just off shore. Huge breakers crashed on the rocky flanks sending up clouds of white spray. It was an island, indeed, as its near shore was separated from the mainland by a hundred yards of churning sea. He looked at Benfras.

"High tide, my lord," the man shouted, seeing the look of concern on his new patron's face. He stepped forward to observe the depth and the movement of the water. "It will turn soon. In a few hours, we can wade across."

Llywelyn nodded and sent word back along the column for men to take what shelter they could while they waited for the sea to subside. They collapsed in bunches on the sand, huddling together for warmth. The Prince stared across at the rocky knob of land rising out of the sea and wondered if this would be where his cause died.

"Have faith, lord." Benfras said. "You will be like Moses at the Red Sea. The waters *will* part!"

The Prince gave the eager young poet a weary smile, but said nothing. As he stared at the raging sea he had one thought.

Moses never reached the promised land.

***

Lord Roderic's best scout spit sand from his mouth and wiped the rain from his eyes as he stared across the Ffraw River at the royal Llys. He had crawled on his belly across the low dunes for two hours until he had reached this spot. He had come to count the men defending the walls, but had seen no one, not even a lookout. He waited for an hour and, seeing no activity across the river, he slid down the bank and ran in a crouch across the streambed, leaping the narrow river, barely wetting his feet.

He fetched up below the west bank and stayed still for a while. No alarm was raised, so he scrambled up the bank and ran to the wall itself. Still no sign of the rebel forces. Finally, he edged along the east wall and slid around the corner. The south gate to the court hung open. He cautiously peered inside. The place was empty!

He set off at a run back toward his own lines a mile away. He was still covered in grit when he was ushered into Roderic's campaign tent.

"They've gone, my lord!" he reported. "Not a soul can be found in the Llys. I could see where they marched down to the river bed, but the storm has washed away the trail there."

Roderic cursed. From the first, he had known that Llywelyn must have reached Anglesey by sea. A march through his domains, past Caenarfon and across the Menai Strait would not have gone unseen and unreported. Now it looked as though he might have escaped the same way, and if so, the chance to finally put an end to his nephew's pretensions had been lost.

But outside his tent, the wind still howled and the rain still roared, as it had since nightfall. That gave him hope. His scouts had confirmed that the rebels still held the Llys as darkness fell and the storm hit. No vessel he knew of could have taken off an army in Aberffraw Bay in such a gale. If they had, all would be at the bottom of the sea and his troubles would be over. But if they had not, then where was Llywelyn? He called for his courier.

"Order the scouts out at first light. I want every inch of this coast searched!"

* * *

Caradog Priddy had sailed due west out of Aberffraw Bay to gain distance from the coast before turning his little fleet to the northwest to catch the strengthening wind coming up from the south. It had taken all his skill at the steering oar to claw his way toward the deep water that separated Anglesey from Ireland. Two of his boats lost the battle with the rising gale and foundered on the rocks of Holyhead. Another was lost on an unseen reef in the dark of night as they made the turn to the northeast around the headland of Trwyn y Gadair.

Beyond that rocky promontory, the wind drove them north through whitecapping waves. Masts groaned and sails ripped. Priddy, slacked his sails, then reefed them before they were torn to tatters. He heaved heavy lines off the stern to slow his boat and keep it from driving its bow into a trough and pitchpoling. Occasional flashes of lightning revealed that others in the battered fleet were doing the same.

It was dawn before the fishing boats turned east and reached relative calm off the north shore of Anglesey. It had taken over half a day. The rain still fell in brief squalls, but the low island now shielded them from the brunt of the wind and waves. Priddy tossed out an anchor and let the surviving ships gather near. Looking at his own boat, he could see water sloshing knee-deep in his hold. He knew every one of his boat masters had leaks and frayed lines that needed attention after the battering they had taken.

He snapped off orders to his crew and handed off the steering oar to his youngest son. He could barely unclench his fingers after twelve hours, fighting to keep his boat off the rocks. He longed to sink down on a bench and rest, but made his way forward to where Lord Maredudd stood in the bow, drenched and exhausted.

The nobleman turned as he approached.

"Master Priddy," he said, his voice husky, "I swore ten times we would founder on the rocks, but each time you guided us safely past. You have my thanks."

Priddy just nodded. He was bone tired, but knew there was no time yet to rest.

"Your orders, my lord?"

Maredudd looked up at the sky.

"Can we sail back to Aberffraw Bay, sir?"

Priddy looked back to the west. Across that channel lay Dublin, but the waters in between still roiled, as deep swells rolled up from the south in the wake of the storm. He could see that the wind still blew strongly from the south.

He shook his head.

"No, my lord," he said, pointing back to the west. "These craft cannot sail against a wind such as that. We'll have to wait for it to shift."

Maredudd didn't speak, but turned back to the east.

"Then set a course for the mouth of the Conwy. If we can't sail back south to save my cousin, we shall see how his cause fares at Deganwy."

Priddy thought to protest. It was another three hours sailing time to the Conwy estuary. Once there, any chance of getting back to the stranded Prince at Aberffraw might be gone. But Maredudd was ruler of Meirionnydd and he let his protest die unspoken.

"Won't matter," he muttered to himself as he made his way aft to take up the steering oar once more. By his reckoning, it was likely too late to save Prince Llywelyn. He and his men would be long dead before they returned to Aberffraw Bay.

The Fifth Day

"**U**p, up, you shit stompers!" the sergeant shouted, as he rousted the men out of their blankets. They had reached the ford at the Conwy River after dark the day before and the tide had been high. There'd been no choice but to wait for dawn and low tide to cross. Then, to add to their misery, a sudden storm had burst upon them in the early evening with fierce wind and sheets of rain that soaked the men and doused their fires.

Their discomfiture only seemed to cheer the sergeant, who met the dawn with blustery good humour. Men grumbled and groaned, but moved with long-practiced habit to gather their kit and fall into ranks. Above them, the morning sky was blue and cloudless as they marched down to the ford and into the icy water of the Conwy.

Lord Daffyd had not waited for his foot to move, but had led four score of his mounted men across the ford as soon as the tide ebbed and set off for Deganwy. He rode into camp with his eldest son Owain beside him just as the sun came over the low hills to the east. In the morning light, his eyes were drawn upwards to the fortress on the two hills. He could see scores of bodies strewn beneath the south wall and above the gate flew the black banner his messenger had described. The sight made his stomach clinch, but no more so than the one that greeted him when he dropped his gaze to the camp.

The place had a sodden and dispirited look to it. A makeshift ram stood above the camp, its wood covered with longbow shafts. His Welsh troops stood about looking sullen and defeated, with a score of walking wounded among them. A few others, who looked beyond saving, were being tended to by a priest.

Daffyd turned to his son.

"See to this…mess," he ordered with a snarl and jerked his horse's head toward the river.

The scene on the gravel bar below the camp was very different. There were a few wounded among Haakon's men, but the Dub Gaill looked anything but defeated. Driftwood had been gathered and a dozen fires blazed along the banks of the Conwy. Some men were having breakfast and others were sharpening weapons or inspecting their recovered longships.

The sail of one of the boats had been fashioned into a makeshift tent. Daffyd could see men in deep discussion there, clustered around a tall striking figure. Haakon was Roderic's man and Daffyd had not met him, but there was no mistaking who was in command among the Danes. He guided his horse down the bank to the bar and rode over. Haakon saw him coming and stepped out of the tent to greet him.

"My lord, Daffyd," he said mildly, "welcome home."

Daffyd dismounted.

"My lord, Haakon, tell me what has happened here," he said. "Who holds my castle and why has it not been taken back?"

Haakon shrugged.

"It's a puzzle, my lord. My men claim they are Englishmen, but there is one Dane among them and at least a dozen or more Welsh longbowmen. Your men…" the mercenary leader hesitated, as though searching for words to describe the performance of Daffyd's troops. "Your men were as worthless as teats on a bull, my lord. They as much as gave away your fort." The big Dane gestured up the hill toward the palisade. "At least some tried to get it back and died for their trouble."

Daffyd bristled at the insult, but he had seen the sorry state of the camp. This mercenary's tone might be offensive, but his words rang true.

"What of your own men?" he countered.

Haakon shrugged.

"We attacked in the night. We gained the north wall, but could not hold it. Whoever sits up there," he said, gesturing again toward the fort, "knows their business. You'll have to take back your fort to solve this mystery, my lord."

Daffyd eyed the man suspiciously.

"And you?"

Haakon gave him a broad smile.

"Oh, we can help, my lord. In fact, I doubt you can take the place without us—but for that, you must pay."

Daffyd blinked.

"Pay? What do you mean?" he sputtered. "Roderic has paid you—and well!"

Haakon stepped closer to Daffyd and poked a finger in the man's chest.

"Your brother paid me to attack your troublesome nephew, my lord, not to help you get your fort back from a pack of brigands, whose loyalties, if any, are uncertain. I'm told you keep much of your silver in the fort. I will want a fourth part of whatever you have in your vaults up there.

Daffyd's face grew crimson.

"You jest, sir!"

"I do not, my lord. I have tested the strength of the men who hold your fort. You will not take it back without me."

Daffyd wanted to curse the man. He had ridden here at the head of eighty mounted men, with another two hundred foot soon to arrive. These troops would fight, but taking a well-defended fortress on a steep hill was no easy task, and he had seen the bodies sprawled beneath the southern wall and the beaten look of his men in the camp. With the Danes, he could muster near eight hundred swords to hurl at the castle. He might need them all.

Haakon stood there waiting, an indifferent look on his face. Finally, Daffyd gave him a grudging nod.

"One quarter—not one ounce more," he said through gritted teeth.

Haakon beamed and slapped the fat nobleman on his thick arm.

"Good! Now, here is how we do it."

***

In the fort on the hill, the weary defenders watched the arrival of Daffyd's troops. They had kept vigil through the long night as a strange winter tempest came slashing up from the south powered by fierce winds that left them sodden and cold. There had been no renewed attack from the Welsh or the Danes during the storm, but with the dawn, scores of mounted men had ridden into the camp under the proud banner of the House of Aberffraw. With Lord Daffyd's arrival, the lull in the battle would not last for long. By noon, a thick column of Welsh infantry had joined the mounted troops, as Jamie Finch once more kept count.

"Two hundred eighty in all," he announced as the last of the foot soldiers slogged into view. "With Haakon's men and what's left of the Welshmen in the camp, there'll be upwards of eight hundred men down there."

For the next hour, they kept watch on the road that ran from the ford on the Conwy up to the camp, but no more troops were sighted. Roland said nothing, but felt a rush of relief. Their bold capture of Deganwy Castle had served its purpose. Daffyd's arrival meant he had abandoned the effort to corner Llywelyn on Anglesey and had marched back alone to Deganwy. Roderic had not followed. The brother's forces were split.

Roland sent Jamie Finch up to the walls of the western hilltop fort to watch out to sea for the boats that would bring Llywelyn and his six hundred men from Anglesey. On the walls of the eastern fort, Friar Cyril watched the coast road that ran down from low hills to the east. Griff Connah would be coming that way with four hundred more.

It was the fifth day.

***

On Anglesey, the storm had blown through with only some lingering clouds and a gentle breeze left in its wake. At dawn, Roderic's scouts rode down to the coast in search of Llywelyn. They brought with them an old fisherman who'd sworn the invaders had come by boat. Hova Iwan had volunteered to show them where these boats had been beached on the sandy shore, but when they reached Aberffraw Bay, they only found a choppy sea, empty to the horizon. Whatever sign there might have been of a landing had long since been stripped away by the waves. But Hova Iwan knew what he'd seen.

"The boats were here, my lord, I'll swear to that," he stated emphatically. "But they had to be long gone when the storm blew in. No man who sails hereabouts would a left 'em on the beach to founder. There'd be wreckage on the sand if they had. But they went away empty! The men who came in those boats were still at the Llys late into the night while the storm still raged."

The commander of the scouts nodded. He'd seen a few signs that Llywelyn had come this way—down to the mouth of the Ffraw—but the rebel Prince had not marched into the sea. He must have turned and followed the coast, either southeast along the rolling dunes that swung off in that direction or southwest along a rocky arm of land that enclosed one side of the bay.

The man wasted no time in trying to divine which it was. He sent three riders in each direction along the coast and waited. Two hours later, the riders he'd sent southeast returned. They'd found Llywelyn.

***

"Ynys Llanddwyn?"

"Aye, my lord. You know it?"

"Of course, I know it," Roderic snapped at his scout. He pictured the tiny rocky islet only a few miles from where he now stood. He had ridden past it many times out hawking. He'd always thought Saint Dwynwen a bit daft for making that barren rock home, but it was a conveniently close pilgrimage site. On occasion, when there was a need for a show of piety, he would visit the ruins of an ancient church there to pay homage to the dead woman. But it wasn't the religious aspect of the place that concerned him, it was the narrow land bridge, submerged twice daily by the tides that connected the island to the shore.

"Where has he placed his men?"

"They're drawn up into three lines, lord, where the dunes slope up from the tidal neck. Couldn't see archers. They are likely placed behind the dunes."

257

Roderic rubbed his chin. It puzzled him that his rebel kin had not taken ship when he had the chance. Perhaps it was pride. His nephew had spent a busy few days issuing proclamations from the royal Llys. In these, he'd fashioned himself Lord of Aberffraw. To give up the place now would be a blow to his growing reputation, but it mattered not. Llywelyn had missed the chance to save himself and would now pay for it.

He had hoped to corner the rebels at the Llys, but wasn't surprised that his nephew had abandoned that indefensible compound when faced with superior numbers. He hadn't expected him to make a stand on Ynys Llanddwyn, but the move made sense. There were only a few hours each day when the strip of land that linked the island to the shore was free of water and firm enough to cross. His cavalry, which could have butchered infantry in the open, would not be able to get at the enemy flanks on the narrow land bridge.

But while Llywelyn's move to Ynys Llanddwyn negated many of his advantages, he still held one. Of his thousand men, two hundred were archers. No doubt Llywelyn had longbows of his own on the island, but not that many. It would be an unfair fight once the arrows flew and that suited him. He would thin out those three lines of rebels, then send in his men to crush them.

"Summons my captains," he ordered.

***

In the fortress of Deganwy, every second man kept watch on the enemy movements, while the rest tried to snatch a few moments of sleep—something they'd not done in two days. During the night, Sergeant Billy had found where the provisions were stored in the great hall and had passed out food and water to the defenders and the scores of prisoners huddled together in the centre of the bailey.

In his search for food, he'd also discovered Daffyd's treasury, hidden behind a concealed door and down a dozen steps to a crypt-like space beneath the floor of the hall. He sent for Roland, who had curled up on the wall walk to doze.

"What have you found, Billy?"

"Silver, sir. More than I've ever seen in one place."

Roland looked at the trove and gave a low whistle.

"It's a hoard—for certain!" He hefted a silver bar and examined a chalice with fine engravings. "Lord Daffyd has done well for himself."

Sergeant Billy laughed at that.

"He might not be thinking so at the moment!"

Roland gave the old soldier a smile.

"Jamie Finch reckons there must be eight hundred men down below," Roland said.

"Aye, I've heard," said Billy. "But when Griff Connah and Prince Llywelyn arrive, that'll even the odds!" here was just a note of scepticism in the man's voice, but no censure. "That's the plan, is it not?"

"Aye, Billy, that's the plan. Are you worried?"

At this, the one-legged sergeant shrugged.

"Not at all, sir. We all have to die sometime."

Fire on the Mountain

*T*he remains of the strange winter storm had swept over the rebel camp during the night, though most of the fury of it looked to be off to the west over the Irish Sea. Stars had appeared around midnight and the temperature had fallen. Griff Connah had his men up and in the saddle by the dim light of false dawn. It was the fifth day and the urgent need to reach Deganwy gnawed at him.

The cool air had firmed up the ground overnight, but the track was still slippery and they had fifteen miles to cover. He pushed the pace as much as he dared, but the going was slow. He glanced to his right at the big Norman knight who rode next to him and took a little comfort at the sight. The night before, they had sat beside a fire and talked about what was to happen when they reached Deganwy.

"So, what is yer plan, Master Connah?" Sir Roger had asked.

Griff did not answer at once. In truth, he had fretted over how to deploy his men since leading them west out of the camps. All were mounted, but over a hundred were archers riding the smaller Welsh ponies. *Those* he knew what to do with, but cavalry? On the few occasions when the rebel mounted forces had clashed with Daffyd's cavalry, it had been Llywelyn who led them, not he. He was a fighter and a proud man, but pride did not win battles.

Griff looked across the fire at Sir Roger de Laval. The Lord of Shipbrook's reputation as a hard man in a fight had long been known along the Welsh Marches. But it was not fighting cattle thieves that interested the Welshman. The tall, bald knight with the quick smile who sat across from him was the man who had commanded King Richard's heavy cavalry in Palestine. Here was a man who knew how to use mounted troops. Griff shook his head.

Pride be damned.

"I will confess, my lord, that I am an archer, not a knight, and more at home on the ground than in the saddle. I have a hundred longbowmen, but almost three hundred men on good horses. How would you use them?"

Sir Roger stirred some coals in the fire with a long stick and looked over the flames at the Welshman. He had not expected the rebel commander to ask his opinion and guessed that it had been a painful decision to do so. Connah had told him about the fortress on the two hills that overlooked the Conwy and the enemy camp that sat between the fortress and the river. What they would find once they reached Deganwy, the Welshman didn't know.

He took the stick from the coals and began to scratch on the dirt.

"This is what I would do…"

***

By early afternoon, the sky above Deganwy Castle had turned a bright blue. After days of wind and rain, the sun was dazzling and men turned up their faces to feel its warmth. Watchers on the walls of the castle had seen patrols leave the camp, circling the steep hills that cradled the wooden fortress. By early afternoon there were knots of troops in position, forming a complete cordon around the hills.

"Settling in for a siege?" asked Patch, as they watched the encirclement proceed from the north wall.

"Maybe," Roland replied, "though with eight hundred men, I would not expect them to be so patient. Have your lads keep a close eye. I'm going up to have a look to the west."

Roland did not have to explain what he was looking for. He crossed the bailey to the small door that was the only entrance to the western fort. He climbed over the rocky dome of the hill and up to the wall walk where Jamie Finch greeted him.

"You can see why they built their castle here," he said, nodding toward the view. Roland looked out on a scene of stunning beauty. Due north rose a huge dome of rock that formed a headland. The Welsh called it the Great Orme. To the northwest, the Irish Sea sparkled in the bright sun. Looking due west, he could see the Isle of Anglesey, still shrouded in low mists and below them, was the River Conwy, snaking its way from the mountains of Eryri to the sea. Some of those peaks could be seen through a golden haze in the distance.

He did not think he had ever seen a lovelier sight, but he had not climbed up here to admire the landscape. He swung his gaze back to the northwest, past a headland jutting out from Anglesey—out toward the Irish Sea. It was from that quarter that help would come, if it came.

Jamie followed his gaze.

"Been watching steady since I come up, sir. Nothing to be..."

He stopped in mid-sentence and leaned forward over the edge of the parapet. Had he seen something there at last?

Roland saw the boy straining to see through the morning haze and did the same. He pointed toward Anglesey.

"There! A hand's width to the right of the headland. Are those masts I see?"

Jamie Finch had the sharpest eyes in the Invalid Company, but not sharper than Roland's. He shifted his gaze from the last point of land he could see on Anglesey to the right and saw three thin, dark shapes dancing just above the horizon. With mounting excitement, they watched as the three masts became three ships with square sails heading directly toward the mouth of the river. Behind them, more masts began to peek over the curve of the horizon.

"Llywelyn," Roland said simply, and Jamie Finch pounded him on the back, heedless of rank in his excitement.

"Aye, sir. It's the Prince—just as he promised!"

Along the wall walk he saw more of the Invalids pointing out to sea. Word passed quickly and from the bailey below, a small cheer went up. As they watched, more and more ships joined the flotilla until they could count twenty-seven in all.

Roland hurried over to the south wall and looked down at the enemy camp. Some men were beginning to form into ranks there, but they seemed in no hurry and there was no sign that they had seen the approach of Llywelyn's fleet.

He ran back to the western wall as the boats grew nearer. It was a stirring sight—the dark hulls ploughing through cobalt seas to close the trap they had so carefully laid. He could see the lead boats start to reef their sails as the rest closed up only a mile offshore now. For long minutes he watched to see where they would make their landing, but the fleet came no closer. They appeared to have anchored near the mouth of the river.

"Why don't they land?" Finch asked.

"I don't know, Jamie," he said with a shake of his head.

Something isn't right, he thought, but held his tongue.

"Keep watch, and let me know if they move," he ordered, and climbed down from the west wall, making his way back to the bailey. Patch was there and Roland motioned for him to follow as he made his way into the eastern fort and joined Friar Cyril on the wall. From this vantage point, they could see two miles of the coast road coming down from a low ridge to the east, but nothing moved there. Patch nudged him and pointed to the enemy patrols that had set up a perimeter around the hill.

"Someone's coming in for a closer look!"

Roland dropped his eyes from the eastern horizon and saw three men moving in toward the base of the hill. Two carried large shields and a third could be seen following close behind. More movement caught his eye and he saw two more groups of three break away from the encircling cordon and move toward the fortress.

"What mischief is this?" Patch asked, a note of concern creeping into his voice.

"Archers!" Roland called. The men were not yet in bow range, but if they continued forward they soon would be. Engard and six of his Welsh longbowmen were stationed on the north wall and watched the men draw closer. At three hundred paces, they took aim and loosed at the first group. Their aim was true, but the large shields did their work and the men continued to advance. When they reached the base of the hill they halted and

263

crouched behind the shields. Roland ordered the archers to stand down as they were only wasting good arrows.

At first, nothing seemed to be happening, but then a thin wisp of grey smoke rose above the shields and it was a mystery no longer.

"They're firin' the gorse!" Patch cried as the smoke grew thicker. The men at the bottom of the hill began to back away, exposing a small blaze that grew in intensity by the second. Roland looked to his right and left and saw flames begin to blossom all around the foot of the hill.

He was no stranger to gorse fires. They were common in the Midlands. As a boy, he'd once seen a gorse fire race up a mountainside, driven by updrafts into a roaring wall of flame twenty feet high. He and his father had been hunting along the summit ridge of Kinder Scout when they'd seen a bit of smoke rising in the valley to the west. That fire had grown with frightening speed as it leapt up the steep sides of the mountain, driving deer, hares, grouse and all manner of moorland creatures ahead of it.

That day, Rolf Inness led his son down the opposite slope of the mountain to safety, and the fire had burnt itself out on the rocky summit of Kinder Scout. They'd gone back afterwards and seen the charred remains of the pitiful creatures who couldn't outrun the flames.

Here, atop the twin hills overlooking Deganwy, there would be no easy path to safety. Lord Daffyd's negligence had allowed the gorse to grow right up to the base of the fortress walls. The wood of the palisade was old and weathered and if the timbers caught, there would be only one way to turn to escape the inferno—out the south gate where steady traffic had kept the gorse at bay. He had seen the men starting to form up into lines there and now knew why. Out the south gate, Daffyd and Haakon would be waiting for them. He looked past the rising smoke toward the coast road. It was still empty.

Patch had seen the same thing. He turned to Roland.

"The boats?"

Roland shook his head.

"They are not landing, Patch. We are on our own. Gather the men."

***

As Caradog Priddy guided his fishing boat around a small teardrop of an island that lay off the eastern shore of Anglesey, the man in the bow got his first glimpse of Deganwy Castle. Maredudd had seen the place before, but never from the deck of a boat in the Irish Sea. From this vantage point, the timber fortress sat like a jagged brown crown circling the tops of the two knobby hills that looked down on the estuary of the Conwy.

At this distance, he could not tell who held the fort. For that they would need to get much closer. He looked back toward the stern and saw over a score of boats strung out behind Master Priddy's modest flagship. The old sailor stood impassively with his hands curled around the steering oar.

"Can you take her in close?" Maredudd shouted back to the man.

Priddy nodded.

"I'll bring us right into the mouth of the river, lord. You'll get a good look from there."

Maredudd turned back to watch, as off to his left the Great Orme loomed larger with each passing minute. Then he saw something odd. At the base of the hill, beneath the walls of the fort, some kind of haze seemed to be swirling. At first, he thought it was morning mist evaporating in the sun, but realized with a shock that it was smoke. In seconds the few thin wisps of grey became billowing clouds and bright red flames could be seen all along the base of the slope.

Someone had set fire to the mountain.

***

Lord Daffyd watched as the flames grew from a few burning clumps of gorse into a roaring inferno.

"My castle…," he whispered, mournfully, but Haakon heard him.

"You'll rebuild it, my lord—and keep the gorse cut back I expect."

Daffyd sighed.

"My treasure…"

"Silver won't burn, lord," the Dub Gaill leader said, pointedly. If the fire were hot enough all the pretty boxes and crucifixes and chalices would melt down into shapeless lumps, but Haakon would happily take one quarter of it, whatever its condition.

The two men stood on the track that led up to the south gate. They had deployed a thin cordon of troops to encircle the hill, though it was doubtful that the men in the castle could survive an attempt to flee in any direction but south. The flames would stop them.

Here, below the south gate, they had positioned over six hundred men in a tight arc at the base of the hill. Anyone fleeing the flames above would run right into a line of warriors four-deep. The outcome was not in doubt. On the hill above, the fire had swept up the slopes and now rose higher than the walls, with smoke billowing in choking clouds. The men up there would soon have to run, or die.

Thunder on the Plain

*T*here was a well in the bailey and a cistern atop each of the hills, but only four buckets could be found. Fighting the fire was impossible. Roland ordered his men down from the hilltop forts and into the centre of the bailey. To the north, the wall of flames overtopped the timber palisade. He stood beside Patch above the south gate and looked down on the only path left to escape the flames.

At the bottom of the hill, he could see thick lines of enemy warriors through the swirling smoke. At their centre stood a solid line of red and black shields—Haakon's Dub Gaill warriors, come to kill the men who'd burnt their boats. Off to the right, out toward the sea, the boats he'd seen clustered at the mouth of the river had not moved. None were putting in to shore.

"Damn, Llywelyn!" Patch growled bitterly. "Why isn't he landin' his troops?"

Roland shook his head.

"I don't know, Tom, but something has gone amiss." He looked down and saw the last of the Invalids come stumbling down through the choking clouds of smoke and gather behind the south gate. "I think it's time to take down your banner."

Patch nodded and hauled down the black banner with the wolf's head, folding it quickly and tucking it inside his coat. Together, they climbed down the stairs to join the men at the south gate.

The Invalids had gathered in a cluster behind the gate. Roland looked out at the familiar faces, some smeared with soot from the steady rain of ash, some with cloth tied over their nose and mouth to block the smoke. Jamie Finch, his arm in a splint, looked back at him with red rimmed eyes, but there was no hint of surrender there. He had his blade out and looked both eager and anxious.

Fancy Jack looked calm, but the broadsword in his hand twitched as though eager to draw blood. Seamus Murdo leaned on his long-handled axe with a placid look on his damaged face. Off to the side, he saw Friar Cyril cross himself. The priest had a dirk in his hand.

These men, veterans and newcomers alike, had followed him loyally and had never failed in a fight. Now he had led them to this place. He felt a sharp stab of guilt as he looked out on their faces. None would choose to stay here and burn, but all knew what waited for them on the other side of the gate. He thought of Millie, barely wed, and now so quickly to be widowed.

My fault, he thought.

He gathered himself. Whatever his guilt, these men deserved more from him than despair. He pointed to the gate and began to speak, his voice rasping from the smoke.

"They are four-deep at the bottom of the hill! The Danes, who fight for pay and torture prisoners, hold the centre of the line. They plan to stop us there and fold their line in upon us. Herd us like cattle to the slaughter. It's a good plan, but, by damned, we are the Invalid Company!"

There was a low growl from the men at that.

"No shield wall four-deep will stop us. We will form a tight column, like an arrow with a bodkin head. Six men only in front—the rest fall in behind, but stay close. We go down at the run and punch a hole right through their line! No one stops. No one turns to the side. If the man in front of you falters, you push! We keep moving straight down the hill to the river."

It took a moment for the import of Roland's words to sink in, then three men shouted at once.

"The boats!"

"Aye," Roland said with a grin. "We've three longships sitting on the gravel bar down there just waiting for us. We cut through those bastards at the bottom of the hill, push off and row. In a day's time, we could be tying up at the Shipgate in Chester!" He knew it was a lie and most of the men did as well, but men needed some shred of hope to cling to. It was all he had to give them.

"Shields to the front!" he screamed above the growing roar of the fire. A score of men pushed their way into the front ranks, presenting a wall of the red and black shields they had taken from Haakon. Roland took his place in the front rank. Beside him were Patch and Seamus Murdo. Behind him was Sir John Blackthorne. With but one arm, he could not carry a shield, but he took his place in the second rank and glared at any man who thought to displace him. Roland saw the leader of the Welsh bowmen striding forward to find his place at the front and stopped him.

"Engard, gather your archers behind us. There's an enemy line two hundred paces down the hill. Thin it out for us, if you please."

Engard raised his longbow in a salute and shouted orders to his men. Fifteen Welsh archers could still draw a bow and they formed a line behind the thick column of Invalids. At Engard's command, they drew and loosed a volley over the south wall. Jamie Finch had heard Roland's order and bounded back up to the wall to gauge the distance. He watched as a tight cluster of arrows arced over his head and dropped into the last two ranks at the bottom of the hill. He counted eight men hit.

"Drop ten paces," he called out, and the Welsh adjusted their angle of release. Another wave of longbow shafts slashed into the front ranks. Some there had reacted to the first volley by lifting shields, but not all. Another six men staggered out of ranks, though the disciplined Danes filled in the gaps quickly.

A ragged cloud of longbow shafts came arcing over the wall from below, as Daffyd's own archers responded, but they overshot the men huddled behind the gate and landed among the prisoners still clustered in the centre of the bailey. A dozen men toppled over, struck down by their own comrades. The rest began to scatter in a panic. Behind them, the north wall was now ablaze.

Jamie Finch bounded back down from the wall and Roland directed him and Sergeant Billy to the gate. An oak beam secured the heavy door. The two men hurried forward and stood ready to hoist it from its iron cradle on Roland's command. He looked back at the dense column of men, poised like a solid steel spike behind him.

He gave a hand signal to Sergeant Billy and Finch. They lifted the bar clear and swung the heavy door inwards on its massive hinges.

Roland gripped his shield and raised his sword.

"Invalids with me!" he roared and leapt through the gate, the Invalid Company howling behind him.

***

At the bottom of the hill, Lord Daffyd heard the howl. He'd been walking his dun-coloured charger nervously back and forth near the river bank and now reined in as he strained to see up the smoke-shrouded hill. Near him, Haakon sat, still as a statue, on a fine black stallion. To his front, the Dub Gaill formed a solid shield wall, four-deep. The front rank kneeled, the second rank stood above them with shields to the front and the third rank held their shields at an angle to the sky to fend off arrows. Those in the fourth row stood ready to step into any gap where a man might fall.

Together, they waited for the doomed men on the hill to come to them. To the left and right, Daffyd's Welsh troops curved up the hill like the horns of a bull and were lost to sight in the smoke. They would move in from the flanks once the Dub Gaill stopped any vain attempts to break through.

Haakon had insisted that he and his men be placed at the centre of the line. They had a personal score to settle with the bastards on the hill who'd burnt their boats. It had taken him years to acquire his fleet of longships and would take all the silver he'd been promised by Daffyd—and more—to replace them. But it was not the money that galled him. It was the insult. Word of his loss would spread and, in his business, reputation was all. Slaughtering the men that had burnt his boats would help remove the stain of that loss.

Smoke and ash swirled around the blazing fortress as the men at the base of the hill waited. Then they heard a sound that rose above the roar of the flames. It was half scream and half snarl, a low keening howl, more animal than human. They could see nothing through the billowing grey clouds to their front, but the sound grew louder and louder. Men braced themselves as dark forms erupted out of the smoke, only forty paces to their front.

***

Roland burst from the smoke and saw the Danes with their shields interlocked to his front. Behind them, he saw two mounted men, but had no time to concern himself with them. He made for the centre of the line. He did not look behind him. He had no need to. He could hear the howls of the Invalids close on his heels. They came on, shoulder to shoulder, in a tightly-packed column only six men wide, but twenty deep.

As they entered the trap laid for them, they paid no heed to the Welsh warriors on their flanks. They were a human spearhead with only one thought—to punch through the shield wall and reach the boats beyond. Drive through the Danes and the Welsh wouldn't matter.

A final hail of longbow shafts came from overhead and ripped gaps in the shield wall as Engard and his men fell in at the rear of the charging column. From behind the Danish line, return volleys came and Roland could hear arrows bury themselves into the wood of his shield as he ran.

At the very centre of the line, a big man with an axe in the second row locked eyes with him, his face contorted into a snarl. The Dane braced himself and drew back his axe, waiting for their shields to meet. Roland had seen this before. As soon as his shield was close enough, the man would come over the top with his axe to snag it and force it down. Then, his comrades on the right or left would make short work of him.

He ran faster.

There was no time to think, only time now for what Sir Alwyn had called the killing fury. The Dane raised his axe, ready for the collision. Roland lowered his shoulder as the man's blade flashed in the sun, but the Dane had misjudged his attacker's final burst of speed. Before the axe could fall, Roland jerked his shield up, ramming it into the warrior's wrist as his arm came over the top. The full weight of the heavy blade rotated forward, but the arm could not follow. The bones in the man's wrist snapped like twigs, as Roland ploughed into his shield. The Dane stumbled backwards, his axe hanging uselessly from a cord bound to his fractured wrist.

The impact of Roland's charge unbalanced the man kneeling in the front row and he too fell backwards. Roland stepped on his neck as he lunged after the man with the axe. As the big Dane staggered back into the third rank of men, the front rank of Invalids crashed into the shield wall.

The wall bowed inwards, but did not break. The force of the first impact had knocked many in the front rank backwards into their fellows. Any that could not keep their feet met a quick death. Patch climbed over the fallen Danes and drove his broadsword into a gap, found flesh, and pulled it back to look for another opening. Behind him men were beginning to lean into the backs of their comrades and push. To his right, Fancy Jack had somehow managed to fight his way to the front, though he had no shield. The man's blade slashed and thrust in a blur. All around, the sound was deafening—shield on shield, steel on steel, men hurling curses, men screaming in pain.

Roland bulled his way into the gap he'd hacked in the shield wall. The axe man had fallen backwards into the third row, but they would not open to let him through. Roland ignored him and lowered his shoulder once more. A man to his right jabbed at him with a spear, but missed. To his left, a fierce-looking man with blue rune marks on his face hacked at his shield. Then, a wicked, long-handled axe flashed past Roland's head and split the man's helmet straight through. Behind him, Roland heard a Scottish curse.

Seamus Murdo had followed Roland into the gap he had created, roaring his battle cries and swinging his murderous axe with abandon. A Dane struck the big Scot a glancing blow with his sword but Murdo hardly seemed to notice as he used his shield like a ram and kept his huge legs churning forward. As he

272

followed Roland deeper into the Dub Gaill lines, men rushed in to follow, hacking at Danes on either side of the small but growing crack in the solid shield wall.

Roland saw a man in the third row go down, felled by Murdo with the butt end of his long-handled axe. He plunged into the gap, driving his short sword in under the armpit of the man to his left. He felt pressure on his left side and twisted to see that Murdo had leaned into him as he hacked another gap in the line.

The men in the final row had expected nothing more than a good show this day. They'd been told there were no more than a hundred men coming down the hill to meet them. On a dozen battlefields, they'd seen far larger numbers hurl themselves at the Dub Gaill shield wall and die. The wall had never broken. Now, with alarming suddenness, a hole had been torn in the first three ranks and a wedge of men were pouring into it.

Behind the line, Haakon bawled at his men to close ranks and seal the gap, as the relentless pressure from the tight wedge of Invalids threatened to burst through the middle of his line. The Danes knew their business and, from the left and right, they turned inward to snuff out this penetration.

But the column that had slammed into the centre of the line was twenty men deep and had the impact of a battering ram. As the Dub Gaill turned, new gaps appeared in the solid barrier of the shield wall. Across a twenty-foot front, men forced their way into these gaps and the fight became a melee. The tight discipline of the Danes began to falter as men were attacked from front and sides.

To his right, Roland saw Patch strike down a man in the third row and climb over the fallen body to hack at the man behind. To his left, he saw two men leap backwards as Murdo's axe swept toward them. Beyond the spot where the two had stood, he saw—no one. He did not hesitate and prayed that Seamus would stay his axe as he burst through the opening and into the clear.

Roland ignored his own order and did not make straight for the longships, only fifty yards away. They'd gouged a small hole in the Dane shield wall, but most of the Invalids were still fighting their way through the narrow gap. He could hear

Haakon shouting at his men to close ranks and seal the breach. He could not let that happen.

He circled to his right and attacked the rear of the Danes' line and Patch followed him. Men who had turned to close the growing gap in the line now had to meet this new threat from the rear. On the other side of the breach, Seamus Murdo had also ignored his orders. He went after the rear of the Dub Gaill shield wall like a woodsman felling saplings. The gap grew, as the Invalid Company poured though and onto the gravel bar.

Roland watched them come. Friar Cyril, his robes and his dirk red with blood stumbled through along with Engard and the last of his archers. Men were streaming down the gravel bar, when the last man lurched free of the Danes. It was Sergeant Billy on his wooden leg, his sword slick with blood.

***

As Haakon saw his line ripped open, he felt his rage building. He would learn which of his mercenaries had run. They would regret that they hadn't died in the shield wall like men! But that was for later. Now he watched in near shock as these madmen sprinted across the bar toward the longships—his longships!

It had all happened too fast. The solid spike of the enemy column had burst out of the smoke and through his line before his men or the Welsh could fall on their flanks. Now they were loose in his rear! But he still had over three hundred warriors who had yet to strike a blow. He swung out of his saddle and drew his broadsword.

"Dub Gaill to me!" he shrieked. On the bank above the gravel bar, the mercenary Danes turned like a pack of hounds at their leader's command. Like a wave, they poured over the bank and onto the bar, following Haakon the Black after these men who had burnt their boats and broken their shield wall.

***

The riders on the coast road saw the smoke before they topped the final ridge that bounded the valley of the Conwy. As Griff Connah reached the crest of the ridge, he took in a sharp breath. A pall of smoke hung over the valley and, off to his right, an immense bonfire seemed to be consuming the hill upon which Deganwy Castle sat.

Roger de Laval reined in beside him and cursed. A pillar of dark smoke rose far into the sky above the castle. The walls could still be seen clinging to the rocky knolls, but sections had begun to burn along with the last of the gorse. If anyone still lived inside, they wouldn't for much longer. Sir Roger drew the broadsword from his belt and turned to Griff.

"See to your archers, sir," he said calmly. Beside him, Declan O'Duinne sat, sword in hand, waiting for the order to advance. Griff nodded and rode back down the column to join the bowmen who were bringing up the rear. As he passed his fellow Welshmen, the air was filled with the rasp of steel blades being unsheathed.

Three hundred men on good horses, armed with spears and swords had been given their instructions the night before. As the big Norman knight started down the ridge, he angled to the left and half the horsemen followed him. Declan O'Duinne led the other half to the right as they fanned out across the valley floor.

The men who had set the fires to the north and east of the fort had been idly watching the results of their handiwork, when they heard a low rumble of hooves behind them. They turned to see riders streaming down the ridge to the east and turning toward them as they reached level ground. Men started to run, but there was no sanctuary to be found, as the charge of Llywelyn's rebels thundered across the open ground and swept over them. They died in their scores.

As the right flank of the riders reached the burned over base of the hill, Declan slowed their charge. To his right, Sir Roger was leading the left wing forward at a gallop, swinging the line in an arc around the base of the hill toward the south. Like a scythe, the double line of horsemen left nothing standing in their wake as they swept down toward the river.

***

On the bank, Lord Daffyd had watched in shock as Haakon's shield wall bent and broke under the savage assault of the Invalid Company. For a moment, he felt panic start to grip him as these unknown warriors hacked their way through the Dub Gaill line and began to spill down onto the gravel bar. He edged his horse back, but saw with relief that none of the men turned toward him. They were running for the boats down by the river and that was not his concern. He could see there were hardly more than a hundred men fleeing across the bar and wondered how so few could have caused all this mischief. But the Danes had regrouped to chase them down.

It would all be over soon.

Then he heard a squeal behind him. He turned to see a horse plunge off the bank and onto the gravel bar. There was no rider in the saddle. The animal stumbled, regained its footing, and bolted down toward the river. A moment later a second horse appeared on the bank, with a rider aboard. The man reined in hard as he neared Daffyd, fear written on his face.

"My lord!" he screamed, pointing back into the blinding smoke. "Flee!"

Daffyd blinked and looked back toward where the man was pointing. He strained to see but there was nothing there but a grey haze. Then there were men running toward him—his men. Some were dropping their weapons as they fled. Others looked over their shoulder in terror. Daffyd needed no further prompting. He jerked savagely at his reins and spurred his horse into a gallop, fleeing south along the gravel bar and away from whatever was coming his way. Behind him, dark shapes began to appear. Then, a wall of charging horseflesh and flashing steel burst out of the swirling smoke.

Hell had come to the valley of the Conwy.

***

The Dub Gaill had been stunned by the breaching of their shield wall, but had not panicked. At Haakon's call, they turned and gave chase, as the Invalid Company sprinted for the longships at the river's edge. Roland was the last to leave the bank and he and Seamus Murdo each grabbed one of Sergeant Billy's arms to drag the old veteran along faster.

As men reached the line of boats at the river's edge they turned to see the Danes dropping down from the bank and forming up around Haakon. Sir John Blackthorn looked at the men beginning to cluster around the boats and at the Danes gathering less than a hundred yards away and knew the Dub Gaill would be upon them before they could launch the boats.

A longship was no fortress. Its sides are low, rising less than six feet from the keel, and they are thin. The hull is meant to hold back the sea, not men with swords and lances, but it was better than being swamped on the gravel bar. He did not wait for Roland to arrive. He bellowed for the Invalids to board the two nearest beached boats and stand ready to defend them. Men began to hoist themselves over the gunwale as the Dub Gaill closed on the boats.

Men saw Roland and Seamus coming with Sergeant Billy in tow and Haakon's men only fifty yards behind. Engard and a handful of his archers scrambled to the bow of the centre boat and sent shaft after shaft into the charging Danes, but they were few and the Danes were many.

Gasping for air, the last three men reached the boats. A half-dozen hands reached down to pull Sergeant Billy up and over the gunwales. With no time for niceties, Murdo set his hands on the man's rump and shoved. Billy fell gasping into the hull of the longship like a landed fish. More men leaned over the railing of the boat and dragged Roland and the big Scotsman aboard as the Dub Gaill wave surged around the beached ships.

***

As his Danes swarmed around the sides of the two longships, Haakon paced back and forth behind his warriors in mounting frustration. His men were aroused. Their shield wall had been broken and their longships again taken by these Englishmen. It was a blow to their pride that could not be tolerated. They pressed in on the sides of the boats with reckless bravery, but everywhere men waited for them with spears and axes and swords. Every attempt to climb up and over the gunwales was met with bristling steel and the number of dead that lay on the gravel bar grew.

Haakon winced as some of the Danes, in their rage, began to hack at the hull of the longships with their war axes, determined to get at the men who had tarnished their reputation. He was now losing boats *and* men and both were expensive to replace. He was about to order a withdrawal and have Daffyd's longbowmen finish the job from a safe distance when he heard a sound behind him.

He turned to see Daffyd's son, Owain, leading a mob of Welsh troops down toward the ships, no doubt coming to be in on the kill. He could use the man's archers, but the others would just be in the way. He started to hail the young Welsh noble when he saw a riderless horse gallop right off the edge of the bank and stumble as it landed on the gravel bar. Even at this distance, Haakon could see the animal's eyes were white with terror. Regaining its stride, the horse barrelled into the rear of the advancing Welshmen, trampling men in its path.

Behind the horse came men, leaping off the bank and onto the gravel bar. Most were weaponless and all were terrified. Haakon had seen routs before—had seen men run like this from his Dub Gaill. Something in the smoke had broken these men and it was coming his way.

***

Three hundred horsemen broke free of the choking smoke less than a furlong from the river. As they swept over the broken ground on the eastern side of the fortress their lines had frayed, but Declan O'Duinne managed to keep his right flank in check as Sir Roger led his wing in a long deadly arc off to his left. When it emerged from the smoke, the line of rebel cavalry was ragged, but intact. And for the first time, the mounted men could see more than a few dozen yards to the front.

And the sight was extraordinary.

Looking down the gentle slope to the river bank and the gravel bar beyond, Declan saw a mob. Hundreds of men were moving down toward a line of boats at the water's edge. Beyond them, hundreds more were swarming like ants around two of the boats. They were trying to board, but the men already there were beating them back. At this distance he couldn't tell who was friend or foe.

Sort them out when I get there, he thought.

Unprepared foot soldiers on open ground was the dream of every cavalryman and Declan could feel the eagerness of the men around him. Some started to surge forward. He stood in the saddle and shouted at them to hold formation. Off to his right he caught sight of Sir Roger as that flank caught up. The big knight had seen the disarray on the gravel bar and spurred his mount into a canter. As the right flank came even with the left, the two knights from Shipbrook led Llywelyn's rebels over the lip of the river bank and onto the gravel bar.

Men on the bar heard the pounding of hooves and the rattle of harness and turned, but it was far too late to save themselves.

***

Friar Cyril was first to see the line of horsemen drop down off the bank and plough into the rear of the Lord Daffyd's men, slaughtering many and scattering the rest. The churchman had staggered back from the stern of the longship where a knot of mercenary Danes had managed to force their way on board. The fighting there was savage—like a boarding at sea.

Men hacked at each other with swords, axes, grappling hooks and anything else that came to hand. Jamie Finch was in the thick of it, despite his broken arm. The young Londoner did not see a short, squat Dane with a milky eye swing a broken oar at him. He went down hard and did not move. The Dane stepped over a thwart to finish him and the friar drove his blade into the man's neck. He said a quick prayer for forgiveness—not his first this day.

As he looked up from his quick supplication, he saw the horsemen spilling over the bank. As they drove into the mass of Welsh troops on the bar, blades flashing in the afternoon sun, the churchman felt his heart soar. He looked around frantically and saw Sir Roland club a man trying to climb over the bow of the longship. He stumbled forward and reached out to touch his young commander's shoulder.

"Sir Roland," he croaked.

Roland whirled around, half expecting to find a Dane there.

Friar Cyril pointed.

"We are saved."

***

Haakon the Black had not survived twenty years of warfare across the northern seas by being slow to act. When he saw the rebel cavalry burst out of the smoke, he knew this battle was lost. He did not hesitate. He bulled his way in amongst his warriors and screamed at them to follow him. One longship sat empty on the bar not thirty yards away from the battle swirling around the other two and he turned and ran for it.

In the heat of battle, many of the Dub Gaill did not hear Haakon's command. Those who did not would be dead or captured within the hour. Those who followed Haakon, reached the longship and frantically shoved it into the river, hauling themselves aboard as the stern caught the current and swung downstream. Eighty men managed to crowd onto a boat meant for half that number as Llywelyn's rebel cavalry men fell on the rest.

Some of those left behind tried to form a hasty shield wall, but were ridden down. Others splashed into the river desperately trying to reach the longship. Two men who could swim were saved. Others drowned or were cut down in the shallows.

It was flood tide and the longship seemed to drift suspended between the flow of the river and the inrushing sea. With twice the usual number aboard, men cursed and shoved each other as they struggled to run out the oars and get underway. Haakon shouted orders and grasped the steering oar himself, trying to swing the bow around toward the mouth of the river.

Engard watched the boat spinning in the river with the tall Dane at the steering oar. He stumbled across a thwart and grabbed Roland by the arm.

"Haakon is fleeing!" he shouted in anguish.

Roland raised his head and saw the longship in the middle of the channel only a hundred yards away. There was no mistaking the big man in the stern fighting to control the boat. There was confusion on board, but oars were starting to be run out on each side and the bow was turning toward the sea.

The Welsh archer had set aside his longbow in favour of a spear as the battle for the beached longship turned into a melee.

He found it now and recovered two arrows from beneath a rowing bench.

"He must pay for Gwilyn and Caden," he said and nocked his arrow. Roland saw another of the Welsh archers retrieving his bow and took it from him. Engard handed him one of the shafts and, together, they drew. Roland released an instant after Engard. It was not a long shot, but Haakon stood at the helm in profile and the rowers had begun to find a rhythm. The longship lurched toward the sea, as the two shafts reached the top of their arc and plummeted down. One struck the Dane in the right shoulder and tore through muscle and sinew there. The second struck him in the neck. He sank to his knees and his hands slipped from the steering oar. A man took his place at the helm as other Dub Gaill cradled their fallen leader and eased him down to the deck. The crowded longship now surged forward against the flood tide and Haakon, dead or alive, was seen no more.

***

On the gravel bar, smoke drifted down from the burning fortress atop the two hills of Deganwy and hung over a scene gone strangely quiet. Hundreds of Daffyd's troops along with a few score Danes sat disarmed and morose on the rocks of the gravel bar. Griff Connah and his archers rode in through the smoke and gawked at the bodies and the prisoners crowding the bar.

Sir Roger and Declan gladly turned back command of the mounted host to Connah, who sent knots of rebel horsemen up and down the riverbank and through the Welsh encampment seeking any foes who had not been killed or captured on the bar. From the captured men, he learned that both Lord Daffyd and Owain had managed to flee the field. No doubt, they would be running for the safety of Rhuddlan.

Relieved of command, the two knights from Shipbrook rode up to the battered longships at the water's edge, fearful of what they would find there. It was a dreadful sight. The dead lay in heaps around the two boats and aboard each were more bodies that lay where they fell. The wounded were being tended to by men who barely had the strength left to stand.

As they drew near, both men reined in as they saw Roland climb down from the stern of one ship followed by an archer and the big Scot, Murdo. The young knight was barely recognizable. His face was soot smeared and his long dark hair was soaked with sweat. His eyes had a hollow look to them.

"He's alive, my lord," said Declan, his voice husky.

"Thank God for that," said Sir Roger, dismounting.

Roland looked up and saw his old master and old friend standing twenty feet away and gaped as though he'd seen phantoms. He stumbled toward the men from Shipbrook. His legs felt rubbery and he was suddenly aware of a raging thirst. There was something important he wanted to say to these two men, but he struggled to find the words. Then they came and he blurted them out.

"I… failed them, my lord," he croaked and waved an arm back toward the boats where the men of the Invalid Company were tending to their dead and wounded. "So many dead—my fault."

Sir Roger de Laval did not reply. He knew, when this much blood was spilt, words did not console. The big Norman had lost many men in his years of soldiering and still felt the pain of it— still sometimes saw their faces. Some men who led other men to war hardened their hearts to the losses and that hardened their hearts to much else. Others had their hearts broken by the men who died doing their bidding. Time would tell if Roland Inness could live with the losses. For now, he was dead on his feet and all used up. Sir Roger stepped forward and threw his arms around his old squire.

"Rest now, lad," he murmured. "It's a victory."

The Strait

*G*riff Connah watched as the south gate of Deganwy Castle collapsed in on itself, the final victim of the flames that had consumed the fortress. With patrols dispatched in pursuit of Lord Daffyd, he turned the head of The Grey back toward the river and looked out to sea. The sight made him rein in the horse and stare.

There were over a score of boats clustered together in the estuary of the Conwy. For a moment his heart soared. This could only be the fishing fleet promised to Llywelyn by Maredudd and Gruffydd—the fleet that was to deliver the Prince here, on this, the fifth day. But if the fleet had reached Deganwy, where was Llywelyn?

Connah did not know what the anchored boats meant, but feared the worst. He gave the spurs to The Grey and galloped down toward the gravel bar. He reined in when he reached the beached longships. Roland was drinking river water from an upturned helmet. Griff dismounted and embraced him.

"I don't know how ye did it, English, but ye did," he said, releasing his grasp, "but what of these damned boats," he added, pointing out to sea. "Why are they just sitting there?"

Roland shook his head.

"They sailed in before Daffyd fired the gorse. When we saw them, we thought we were saved, but not a man came ashore. Something's wrong there."

"To put it kindly," Griff said, with both fear and anger in his voice. He looked hard at Roland and could tell the young knight was exhausted, but a war and a throne were in the balance. "Can you handle one of these Viking boats?" he asked. "Are your men fit to row?"

Roland nodded wearily.

"Aye, fit enough, but we will see to my wounded before we put one in the river."

***

The longship shot out of the mouth of the River Conwy on the ebb tide current with hardly a need for oars to propel it toward the bobbing fleet of fishing boats anchored offshore. Roland stood a little unsteadily at the helm with Griff beside him. The approach of a longship had not gone unnoticed by the fleet. Men could be seen hurrying about the decks of the nearest boats. Some appeared to be hauling in anchors, while others were arming themselves with swords or spears.

"What's this?" Griff asked, his nerves raw.

"They don't know who we are, Griff, but they know these ships do not usually come in peace. Hail them."

The Welshman scrambled up to the bow and stood, waving his arms and shouting.

"It's Griff Connah, by God. If this be the fishermen from Meirionnydd, identify yerselves!"

For a moment, the only response from the nearest vessel was more scurrying around, but then a thin man in fine clothes appeared on deck. It was Lord Maredudd.

"Master Connah, thank God it is you and not some heathen Danes! Come alongside. We have much to relate."

Roland ordered his men to ship oars and the momentum of the longship took it close alongside the fishing boat. A grizzled old man with wild grey hair seemed to be master of the boat and he ordered men to secure lines between the two. Griff and Roland climbed up to greet Maredudd. It took no more than a glance to see that there were no troops on board, nor could any be seen on the nearby boats.

"Where is the Prince?" Griff asked, without preamble or formal address. Maredudd spread his hands, his lips drawn back in a grimace.

"Lord Llywelyn ordered the fleet to sail before the storm. Otherwise it would have been destroyed."

"And why did the Prince not sail with the fleet?"

"I pleaded with him to make the attempt, but he said he could not. It was still daylight and there was a mile of open ground between the Llys and the boats. Roderic's cavalry was already up and probing our defences. The Prince said to march out of the walls of the Llys without the cover of darkness would have invited a slaughter."

Griff's heart sank. He could see the truth in what Maredudd said, for he had just seen what three hundred of his own mounted troops had done to twice that number of infantry. Llywelyn would not risk exposing his men to rout and slaughter, but staying at the lightly fortified Llys would only delay an inevitable defeat. Roderic had a thousand men he could throw at the place.

"Roderic's infantry would have reached Aberffraw last night and attacked at first light today," he said, "but nothing is certain in war. Perhaps the storm delayed the assault. Perhaps the walls of the Llys have proven more of a defence than we thought. Perhaps the Prince is holding on there." He could see in Maredudd's eyes that he didn't believe it.

"Anything is possible," the nobleman said, with little conviction.

"Then we must go to his aid! My lord, bring your boats in close to shore. We will load my men and as many horses as we may and sail for Aberffraw."

Maredudd held up a hand in protest.

"Dark is coming on, Connah. It will take until midnight at least, to load these ships," he said flatly, "and it's a twelve-hour sail back around Anglesey to Aberffraw. I doubt we will like what we find there."

Griff Connah gave the nobleman a hard look.

"What are you suggesting, my lord?"

Maredudd shrugged.

"Until you hailed us, we did not know who had won the battle here. We saw the fort burn, but all else was obscured by smoke. Now we may rejoice that you have defeated Daffyd!"

"He has fled the field with his son, my lord," Griff said flatly. "He's probably making for Rhuddlan,"

"That will avail him nothing," Maredudd replied, with growing conviction. "His power here is broken. Half of Gwynedd is now at our mercy, if we are ready to take it!"

The half-ruler of tiny Meirionnydd paused and studied the tall Welsh archer closely.

"You must realize, Connah, that it is too late for Llywelyn. I grieve for him and for my own brother, but it is not too late for you and I! For seven years, you have fought and bled for this land. Be my strong right arm and we will take it for ourselves!" The man's eyes were shining as he finished.

Griff glanced at Roland, then turned back to Lord Maredudd.

"Bastard," Connah said, and punched him in the nose.

***

Lord Maredudd ap Cynan ap Owain leaned against a gunwale and held a wad of cloth to his face, trying to staunch the flow of blood from his nose. He had threatened to have Griff Connah disembowelled at the first opportunity. He reminded the tall archer that, whatever else he might be, he was still a commoner and that for such a one to strike a member of Gwynedd's ruling dynasty was a capital offense. He turned on the master of the vessel and threatened to hang the man if he took his boats into shore. Griff ignored the man and turned to the wiry old fisherman who had been leaning on the helm and watching events unfold.

"What is your name?" he inquired.

"Caradog Priddy, sir, master of this and other boats here."

"And this," Griff said, pointing at Maredudd with disgust, "is your master?"

The old fisherman looked at the nobleman and gave a weary nod.

"Lord Maredudd rules in Meirionnydd, sir, and that would include me and all the others here," he said, as though revealing some scandalous family secret.

A Prince of Wales

Griff walked over to Maredudd, grasped the man's fine tunic in two thick hands, dragged him to the railing of the boat and hung him over the water.

"Master Priddy, if this...man, were to fall overboard and drown, where then would your duty lie?"

The old sailor rubbed his chin.

"Why, Lord Gruffydd also rules in Meirionnydd sir, and he is still with the Prince. With Lord Maredudd dead, I would be bound to get myself back to aid Lord Gruffydd, of course. And, there is the matter of the silver."

"Silver?"

"Aye," said Caradog Priddy with a sly grin, "the Prince promised me a quarter my weight in silver to provide these ships and I always keep my bargains."

"Then the Prince will keep his," Griff replied and looked down at Maredudd, whose knuckles were white where they gripped the railing. There was pure hate in the man's eyes, but also defeat.

"What say you, Lord Maredudd?" Griff asked politely. "Are you with us?"

The man's eyes darted back to the water. He could not swim.

"Aye, aye," he managed through his mangled nose.

"Good!" said Griff as he hauled the frightened nobleman back onto the deck and sat him down on a small bench.

"That's settled then. Now, Master Priddy, bring in your boats."

***

Caradog Priddy ran his boat up on the sands that stretched along the coast north of the Conwy's mouth. The remainder of the fleet from Meirionnydd followed him in, until all twenty-seven were beached there. Exhausted men and skittish horses made their way across the exposed sand to the boats. Ramps were hastily constructed to bring the horses onboard and eighty were loaded on twelve of the boats. Four hundred men managed to jam into the remaining fifteen vessels by the time the tide turned.

As the fishing fleet from Meirionnydd took on its cargo of men and horses, Roland guided the longship back into the channel of the Conwy and beached the boat beside its mate on the gravel bar. When he dropped onto the gravel, he saw Sir Roger and Declan waiting for him there. Beside them was a boy. As he approached, Sir Roger nodded toward the lad.

"Sir Roland, meet Rhys Madawc, my new squire," he said, with more than his usual degree of formality. "Master Madawc, this is one of your predecessors, Sir Roland Inness."

The boy gave an energetic bow.

"Madawc?" asked Roland.

"Aye, Roland," said Declan, "it seems our Sir Alwyn left more behind than his heart when he fled Wales all those years ago."

"Sir Alywn—a son?" He stepped closer to the boy and stared.

"Aye, my lord," the boy said quietly, returning the stare without flinching. "Sir Alwyn was my sire, though I never knew the man and he never knew of me."

Roland looked from the boy to Declan to Sir Roger. "How…?"

"It is a long story," said Sir Roger, "and one you will appreciate, I think. Young Rhys came to Shipbrook looking for his father, but left a piece of his heart back in Wales." The big man paused and a half smile stole across his face. "He's not the first young man of my acquaintance to come to Shipbrook, then go traipsing off to Wales to bring back a girl."

Roland shook his head and managed a smile of his own.

"I will look forward to the tale when we are safe back in Cheshire, my lord, and as for you, Master Madawc, when this is over we will speak of your father, but mind you," he paused and pointed at Sir Roger, "this man has never failed to select fine squires. See that you do not ruin his record."

Rhys bobbed his head.

"Aye, sir."

Roland turned back to Sir Roger and Declan.

"I do not know what strange circumstances brought you two and the boy here, but what are your intentions?"

Sir Roger dropped a hand to his sword hilt.

"I've never left a fight half-finished. We go with you."

Roland exchanged a quick glance with Declan.

"Lady Catherine will not like it, my lord," said Declan.

Sir Roger shrugged.

"She is not here."

***

On the gravel bar beside the river, Sir Roger, Declan and Rhys joined Roland, as those Invalid's fit to fight crowded aboard the two longships. Seven men had been lost in the taking and holding of the fortress and another five had died in the mad charge through the Dub Gaill shield wall. Six men were too wounded to be of any use and would be left in the care of men assigned by Griff to defend Deganwy should Daffyd attempt to retake it.

One hundred seven men had ridden out of Chester just a fortnight before. Only eighty-nine effectives remained. Engard's archers had been reduced to sixteen and all joined the Invalids on the longships. With the last of the ebb tide, the boats cleared the mouth of the Conwy. The sun hung low in the western sky, as they waited for the tide to turn and float the rest of the fleet.

Griff Connah remained on Master Priddy's boat and signalled for Roland to bring his longship near as the tide rose. With its shallow draft, the longship eased up next to the fishing boat before that vessel's keel lifted off the sand. Roland scrambled over the rails to join the Welshman. He saw Lord Maredudd sitting disconsolately near the bow, still nursing his broken nose.

"How fares your Invalid Company?" Griff inquired as Roland dropped to the deck.

Roland wanted to tell this man that the Invalid Company was grievously damaged, that too many good men were dead—all in service to his Prince, but he bit those words back. He knew that he would long regret the men he had lost, but that he must set aside the regretting for another time. As Sir Roger had said, there was a fight to finish.

"A little over four score in fighting shape," he reported crisply.

Griff nodded. The losses were serious, but he had seen the burnt fort and the bodies littering the gravel bar where the Invalid Company had made their stand. He had guessed the casualties would be twice that. He looked at Roland and saw the pain in his eyes. Would these losses break him? He prayed not, for he needed the young knight.

"English, I need your help," he said bluntly. "I can lead men in a fight well enough, but I am no general to plan the battle. The tide will be at flood in another hour and I have no more thought of how to aid the Prince, than to sail away to Aberffraw and see what we find there. We need a plan."

Roland started to protest. He was weary down to his bones and wasn't sure he could think clearly. He'd hardly slept in four days and his last plan had been a near disaster. But sailing to Aberffraw with no plan was a certain way to get more of his men killed.

"Tell me about Anglesey," he said.

Griff rubbed his chin, then drew a knife from his boot and squatted on the deck. With the point of the blade, he scraped a three-quarter circle in the weathered wood, then carved a straight line to connect the two ends of the arc. He dug the tip of the blade into a spot a little inside the circle and pointed to the mark.

"Aberffraw."

Roland kneeled to look at the rough map.

"This flat side, then...that would be the strait?"

Griff nodded and drew a second straight line along the flat side of the circle to mark the mainland shore of the narrow waterway.

"Aye, that would be Menai."

"And where are we?"

Griff poked his knife a few inches above the beginning of the strait.

Roland stood and walked around the sketch on the deck. As he looked at it from different angles, he was joined by Caradog Priddy who had been keeping watch as his little fleet began to rise along with the tide. Roland looked up at the wiry old fisherman as he slowly circled the crude map.

"Master Priddy, I heard Lord Maredudd say it's twelve hours around the island to Aberffraw," he said, tracing a course along the coast of Anglesey to the point where Griff had marked the location of the royal court.

"Aye, if the wind is with us," the old sailor said and looked to the sky. "It's shifting to northerly now and that will help—if it holds."

Roland nodded as he continued to circle the map. Then he stopped and looked off toward Anglesey, easily visible across open water to the west. After a moment, he turned back to Priddy.

"Why don't we sail through the strait?"

Priddy blinked and didn't speak for a moment. Then he found his voice.

"The Menai? I've never done it," the old man said, "though I've met men, local men, who claim they have."

"And what did these locals tell you?"

"They say the Menai is narrow, hardly wider than a river in places. They say the tides are the worst of it. The flood tide sweeps in from both the north and south ends of the strait. Where they meet, there are whirlpools that will drive a boat right up onto rocky islands in the middle of the channel. They say it is a place to be feared."

"These local men who've sailed through the strait—how did they do it?"

Priddy scratched his head.

"Gently, I expect. As I recall, they enter the northern end two hours before high tide and run with the surge as far as they can. If their timing is right, they reach slack water halfway through and then run south to the open sea with the ebb."

"And how long would that take?"

"Running with the tide? Five hours at the most I would say."

Griff Connah had watched this exchange with growing excitement. He turned to Priddy.

"Can *you* do it?"

"It's too great a risk, my lord," the old man said sorrowfully. "The strait is treacherous, even in daylight, and we'd be going with the high tide after dark. These boats are our livelihood. Lose 'em and our families starve."

Griff looked hard at the man, but Caradog Priddy did not flinch.

"Very well, Master Priddy. Would another quarter of your weight in silver feed them awhile?"

Caradog Priddy grinned.

"Long enough, my lord, long enough!"

***

On Ynys Llanddwyn, the first attack across the land bridge came at midafternoon. Roderic's men had arrived on the dunes opposite the island an hour after dawn. They found the sea blocking their way and no sign of Llywelyn's rebels. Protected from attack by the tides, the Prince had drawn his men back to shelter behind a low bluff that overlooked the submerged land bridge.

As the tide ebbed through the morning, the men on the island kept watch. By an hour past noon, the last of the sea had retreated. Llywelyn ordered his archers to remain hidden, but marched the remainder of his force forward. They formed into three lines on the front slope of the bluff with their spearmen in the front rank. They did not have to wait long for Roderic's assault.

First came volley after volley of longbow shafts that fell in among the rebel lines. For an hour, men held their shields aloft and did their best to make themselves small, but the relentless rain of arrows had a way of finding flesh and the casualties mounted. The rebel archers returned the fire, but their volleys were feeble in comparison.

Llywelyn stood in the ranks with his men as the sand bridge to the island slowly emerged from the waves. From somewhere out of sight, a horn sounded and horsemen poured out of the dunes and the scrub trees on the Anglesey shore.

"Lock shields!" Llywelyn shouted.

With the cavalry advancing, the hail of arrows stopped. Men on the island dug in their heels and those with spears braced to meet the onslaught. A cavalry charge against infantry relies on shock, as thousands of pounds of horseflesh smash into men who try to turn it aside with spears and shields. Without speed, there is no shock, and Roderic's mounted attack was ill-timed for speed.

The tide had abated, but the coarse sand left behind was still sodden. As the first wave of horses reached the newly-exposed beach, first one then another plunged a hoof deep into the loose sand and snapped a foreleg. Horses and riders went down, flailing on the sand, and many that followed stumbled over the fallen. All the while, Llywelyn's archers poured longbow shafts into the men trying to extract themselves from the tangle.

On the treacherous sands, some riders managed to avoid the chaos to their front. These men, more brave than prudent, came on at a quarter of the speed customary for a mounted charge. A score of riders managed to make it to the base of the low rise where Llywelyn had set his defences, but there was no momentum behind their charge.

Sand that had so slowed the horses was more than firm enough for men to cross and Llywelyn ordered his front rank of spearmen to fall on them. Riders saw the line of men charging down the sandy slope and tried to turn away, but it was too late. They were swarmed under by men with spears and swords. Not a one made it back to their lines.

Less than an hour passed before movement was again seen on the enemy shore. Now, thick phalanxes of infantry marched out through the dunes and made straight for the rebel lines. Llywelyn glanced to his left and right. His men were on the verge of exhaustion after the long march through the storm and the wait for the enemy to appear, but none seemed ready to quit.

To his surprise, he saw Benfras, his new court poet, standing in the line a few feet away. He had ordered the young man to stay back with the archers, but the lad had scrounged a helmet, sword and shield from a fallen rebel and now stood near Llywelyn, his arm trembling with the strain of holding up the heavy shield.

"This is not like your poems," Llywelyn called to him as a new wave of arrows chewed into the wood of their shields.

The thin poet managed a weak smile.

"Well, my lord, it *is* like the beginning of a good battle poem—outnumbered hero, grave danger, little hope of victory."

"It is that," Llywelyn said dryly.

"But by the end of the poem, the hero always triumphs, lord!"

Llywelyn laughed.

"Well, let's hope we get to that part soon."

***

It was full dark as the lead longship approached the northern entrance to the Strait of Menai. At the helm was Caradog Priddy. The old sailor had insisted that the nimble longships should lead the flotilla and that he should be at the steering oar of the first boat. He brought with him his youngest son, who sat in the bow with a weighted line and called back the depths to his father. Men of the Invalid Company manned the oars.

The line of fishing boats, their square sails reefed, rode the flood tide south under a gentle northerly breeze. They followed in the wake of the longships like ducklings. Off to port, the outline of Bangor's grand cathedral came into view, rising above the dark streets of the town and shimmering under a brilliant full moon. Nothing stirred there as they moved past.

Two miles past Bangor, the strait curved round a rocky promontory and narrowed to no more than four hundred yards from one shore to the other. As the younger Priddy's soundings revealed, the narrow waterway was studded with submerged rocks and shoals. There was a deep channel, but it meandered from one side of the strait to the other and back again. The fishing boats needed deep water and Caradog Priddy's knuckles shone white on the steering oar as he eased through the treacherous passage.

***

Llywelyn spit sand from his mouth as he watched the flood tide sweep in to swamp the thin neck of land that separated Ynys Llanddwyn from the shore of Anglesey. Scores of bodies floated off the sand and bobbed there in the bright moonlight, a grim reminder of the carnage that had marked this long day.

Roderic's infantry had come at them in three separate attacks. Each had come dangerously close to breaking through the thinning ranks of rebel defenders before being beaten back. The final assault had come with seawater ankle-deep on the land bridge. The whole centre of his line had bulged inward under the relentless weight of the enemy and some of Roderic's men had managed to hack their way through, only to be cut down by Llywelyn's longbowmen.

When the rising tide halted further attacks, he ordered his men back over the bluff where they collapsed among the dunes and scrub brush. He had lost a third of his strength killed or wounded and knew that when the next low tide came, he could barely field a defensive line two deep.

Taking a final look at the human flotsam being taken away by the sea, Llywelyn trudged over the top of the rise and walked among his men. A few managed a weak salute to their prince, but most lay on the sand as though dead. Off to one side, the Prince saw Benfras sitting beneath a bush, his arms hugging his bent knees. The young poet rocked slowly back and forth, his head down, but he looked up at the sound of Llywelyn's approach. His eyes were wet.

"Are you injured?" the Prince asked gently.

The man shook his head.

"No, not a scratch, lord," he managed as he continued to rock. "Is it always like this—this butchery?"

"Yes," Llywelyn said flatly, "always."

"I see no glory in it," the poet said with a catch in his throat.

"There is none," said Llywelyn, "but men will make it so in the telling."

"Like the poets."

"Aye, like the poets, but they are not alone. Old men and boys love it best. It comforts the old and beguiles the young.

"And are you beguiled, my lord? You are young."

Llywelyn looked at the heaps of exhausted men laying all about him and shook his head.

"I cannot remember ever being young, poet."

***

A shudder ran though the hull of the longship as its starboard side scraped along a hidden shoal.

"Damn!" Caradog Priddy cursed as he heaved viciously on the steering oar to swing away from the obstruction.

"Still shallow to starboard," the younger Priddy sang out as he pulled in the weighted line and flung it twenty feet ahead. His father kept the steering oar hard over, searching for the way ahead like a blind man.

"Nine feet now," came the call and the old sailor eased off the oar a trifle.

For two hours they carefully picked their way down the turbulent strait. Three times they had almost run aground, but the shallow draft of the longship and Master Priddy's deft handling of the steering oar kept them afloat. Roland stood in the bow next to Declan and Priddy's son. Ahead he could see more rocks, laced with white foam from the rush of the tidal currents. He looked back over the stern and saw a half-dozen vessels, all carefully following in the wake of the boat ahead.

"Islands to port!" young Priddy sang out.

Roland turned back to the front and saw two low rocky islands near the middle of the strait. This was where the locals had warned of whirlpools and shifting currents. He made his way back to the stern where Priddy stood at the helm like some ancient sea spirit, with his jaw set and his tangled grey hair glowing in the moonlight.

"Oars up!" the old man shouted and the Invalids raised their blades from the water. The boat drifted silently forward. Priddy stared to the front as though trying to see beneath the water and Roland realized that the man did not know which channel to choose to safely pass the islands.

"The locals…?" Roland began.

"Never said which side of the damn islands was good water!" Priddy said. "Or, if they did, I've forgotten."

Roland looked astern and saw the second longship closing on them. He turned back to the man at the helm.

"Pick a side, Master Priddy, before the ducklings ram your stern."

Priddy gave a grim nod and slid the steering oar hard to port. "Row now, lads!" he shouted and the Invalids leaned into the oars. The longship slid toward the mainland shore skirting the islands in the middle of the strait. As they passed the first and neared the second, Roland looked off to starboard and saw movement in the water. He moved to the rail and strained his eyes.

It was a log—and other flotsam—swirling in a foaming circle between the islands and the Anglesey shore. As they glided far to port of the whirlpool he looked back at the helmsman and wondered if the old sailor had been wise or merely lucky. Either way, the man was earning his silver.

Safely past the islands, the longship reached slack water, as the tide turned from flood to ebb. If they could follow the retreating sea, they would reach open ocean in but two more hours. But if luck had helped them avoid the whirlpools, it failed them with the winds.

The voyage down the strait had been favoured by a light northerly breeze that gently drove the fishing boats southwards under reefed sails. Now the wind was turning southerly. Priddy was first to see the change.

"Wind's backing, lord," he called to Roland. "Have to put in 'fore my boats are blown back into those islands."

Roland made his way to the bow where Sir Roger, Declan and Griff were already gathered on the starboard side and staring at the Anglesey shore.

"There! Is that a pier?" Declan said and pointed a quarter-mile ahead. Griff leaned out over the rail and strained to see. He then whirled around and looked back to port. He pointed to the mainland side of the strait.

"Aye, and there's another—with a barge tied up. It's the ferry, by God!"

Priddy called for the men to raise their oars.

"My boats can't manoeuvre into this wind," he shouted at the men in the bow. "We'll have to tow 'em to the dock."

***

Put ashore on the ferry pier, Griff Connah summoned Roland, Sir Roger, Declan and Engard to a council of war, while Caradog Priddy used the two longships to deftly tow his fishing boats into the dock, one at a time.

"We cannot continue blindly," he said. "As soon as the horses are ashore, I will take Sir Roland, Sir Declan and two of my men who know Anglesey to see what has befallen the Prince. Sir Roger, if you please, get the mounted troops moving along the road to Aberffraw. I will leave you a guide who knows the way. Once we have found the Prince—for good or ill—we will meet you along the Aberffraw road."

As the gathering concluded, the first fishing boat reached the pier. Roland was relieved to see The Grey among the first horses unloaded and walked over to take the animal's reins. The big gelding nickered and pricked up its ears as Roland led him off the pier.

"What price would you put on that horse, English?" Griff asked.

Roland rubbed the animal's jaw.

"He's not for sale, Griff, but I appreciate you bringing him back sound."

"I guessed as much. Best horse I ever sat upon," the Welshman said and picked out another mount as it bounded up on the pier. They waited for Declan and the two local Anglesey men to find mounts. Once all were saddled, the big Welshman looked up at the full moon, now directly overhead. "It's good light for night riding, English," he said. "Let's go find my prince."

It was an hour before midnight.

***

Lord Roderic pulled on his boots and yawned. He had slept soundly in his own bed at the royal Llys. He had seen no need to spend an uncomfortable night in a tent this near to his own hall. As ordered, his Seneschal had awakened him an hour past midnight. Low tide at Ynys Llanddwyn would arrive in two more hours and this unpleasant episode would be over.

His men had taken heavy losses the previous afternoon, but the rebel lines had almost collapsed. Before the new dawn, he would crush Llywelyn. He wondered idly if his nephew would choose to die in battle or surrender. It hardly mattered. Llywelyn was too dangerous to let live.

As he pulled his mail jerkin on over his head, the Seneschal returned to the subject of the unfaithful barons he'd railed about the day before when Roderic had reclaimed the Llys. The old man had told him that many of his liege men had sent younger sons to bend the knee to his rebel kin. Llywelyn had welcomed them all and had liberally dispensed silver to the young nobles from Roderic's own treasury! Now the old man began reading off a list of offending barons he had compiled overnight. Roderic held up a hand. He would deal with the barons after he was finished with Llywelyn.

But the old counsellor now turned his venom on young Benfras, the court poet.

"That snivelling bastard exalted Llywelyn and made jest of you, my lord!" he railed.

"What jest?" Roderic had asked, mildly annoyed. He had liked the young poet's way with a rhyme.

"He...he called you a...horse turd, my lord!"

Roderic sighed. Could no one be trusted beyond this dried up old scribbler of a Seneschal? He buckled on his sword belt

"If the poet lives, Cadwalader, I will give him to you as a slave."

The old man bowed as Roderic walked out of the great hall. Four men of his bodyguard and his favourite horse waited for him there. He mounted and rode out of the Llys, following the main road to the east. Ynys Llanddwyn lay southeast along the coast, but the land between Aberffraw and the island was a treacherous stretch of high dunes and impassable marshes. It would be safer to keep to the main road east, then turn south a little past the bridge over the Cefni River.

As he rode, he looked up at the moon. Its light was bright enough to cast shadows as they followed the road east. It was a lovely night for a ride. In less than an hour, Roderic and his bodyguards clattered over the wooden bridge that spanned the small Cefni River, as a cloud blocked out the moonlight. The sudden loss of light slowed their pace to a walk as they searched for the smaller road that led down toward the army's encampment opposite Ynys Llanddwyn. Roderic's guards did not see the other riders until they were almost upon them.

Roderic reined in. He was surprised to see men on the road at this hour, but they could only be some of his own. Why they were heading toward Aberffraw and not encamped with the army puzzled him. Perhaps one of his commanders, in an excess of caution, was sending out patrols in all directions. Whatever their purpose or destination, their presence was fortunate. They could surely lead them back to the turnoff. Roderic sent one of his bodyguards ahead to meet the newcomers. The man urged his horse into a trot, raising his arm as he hailed the approaching riders.

"I ride with Lord Roderic." he called out. "We seek the road to the army's encampment." He watched as the approaching riders slowed for a moment. Then, as the moon slid from behind the cloud, he saw a flash of steel as swords were drawn from scabbards. He turned in horror to shout a warning as the riders spurred their horses straight at him.

***

Declan was the first to react when the rider identified his party. The Irishman spurred his horse forward as he drew his blade. He'd been told who the enemy was and this herald had as much as formally announced the man's presence. It was all he needed to know. As the rider to his front drew his own sword, Declan stood in his stirrups and unhorsed the man with a single crushing blow of his broadsword.

He did not stop, but plunged on toward the four riders still in the road ahead. One man turned his horse's head around and fled back down the road, while the others closed ranks to meet his charge. The young knight sensed movement to his right and saw Roland on his big grey gelding drawing even with him. He tried to urge more speed from his own mount, but the horse was no match for The Grey, and Roland was first to strike the line of riders.

It was here that his mount showed to best advantage. The Grey was no heavy warhorse, but the animal was taller and more muscular than most palfreys and would not shy away from contact if his rider did not. With Declan on his left, Roland aimed the horse to the right of the centre rider. The man seemed frozen as he watched these two unexpected enemies close on him. He swung his sword wildly at Roland's head, but his horse was spooked by the charging animals to his front and bolted off the road. The man struck nothing but air and barely kept his seat. Roland had bent forward until his cheek touched the neck of The Grey. As the rider to his right lurched off the road, he rose up and made a straight thrust with his short sword at the rider to his left. The blade went in under the man's armpit and he fell backwards from his saddle.

Roland wheeled The Grey around to see the rider he had forced off the road whipping his horse and escaping on firmer ground to the north. Declan was bludgeoning the man on the far left with his heavy sword. The rider parried with his own blade but the force of the blow drove the flat of the sword back into his face, stunning him. He managed to jerk his reins to the right and spurred his horse off the road. He made it only twenty yards before the animal became hopelessly bogged down.

With the road clear, Griff went pounding by in pursuit of the one man who had fled. Declan spurred after the Welshman, as the two men from Anglesey dismounted and closed in on the mired rider who was desperately trying to free his horse in the swamp. The man dismounted and flailed wildly at the two before losing his footing and falling backwards into the muck. He was not given a chance to regain his feet.

Roland set out to follow Griff and Declan and did not have to ride far. He saw Griff coming across a small bridge, leading a horse by its reins, its rider sitting slumped in the saddle. Declan brought up the rear.

The tall Welshman hailed him as they drew near.

"English! I know now why Llywelyn thinks you lucky. Had you not thought to sail down the Menai, we would not have been on this road at this hour to meet the Prince's favourite uncle!"

Roland sagged in the saddle. He did not feel lucky. He felt so tired he could hardly stay atop The Grey.

"Does this mean your war is over?" he asked

Griff looked back at Lord Roderic who sat with his head hung low.

"I believe it does, English."

***

Llywelyn rose slowly to his feet. It took an effort of will to do so, as duty overcame weariness. All around him men lay motionless on the sand. He looked up at the bright full moon and guessed from its position in the sky that it would be low tide in less than an hour. He had placed lookouts on the bluff, but he expected they were no more alert than the men scattered around him. He walked slowly through the sleeping mass of men, rousing his sergeants where he found them.

They rose, out of duty and habit, and began rousing the men around them. Slowly, men stumbled to their feet. Those up first helped others to rise. Llywelyn saw his poet, Benfras, shake himself and use his sword like a cane to rise shakily from the sand. He walked over to the young man.

"You can stay with the archers," he said.

Benfras shook his head.

"If your line breaks, Lord Prince, will the archers not die?"

"I expect they will," Llywelyn replied.

"Then why draw things out?" said the poet as he jammed on his helmet and hoisted his shield, its face studded with broken off longbow shafts.

"Do you have a rhyme for me, court poet?" Llywelyn asked as he slid his arm through the grip of his shield. "One to fit the occasion?"

Benfras cocked his head and squinted his eyes as though searching for words, any words, that might be worthy of what was about to happen. Then he straightened himself and spoke in that same clear high voice of his.

"A Prince and a poet marched down to the sea
To find in battle what glory there'd be

They found none at all, but the way that they fell
Gave poets and bards glorious tales for to tell"

For a moment, Llywelyn stood silent. Then he leaned in and touched his helmet to the poet's.

"It's a shame if the world should lose your rhymes, poet."

"It's a shame if Wales should lose its Prince, my lord."

The two men trudged over the bluff and took their place in the line to wait for the onslaught. Men sat down on the sand and leaned on their shields as they waited, in dread, for the last of the sea to ebb away. Little by little, the sand began to appear, as the waves retreated.

"Up!" Llywelyn shouted and his men rose to their feet staring at the far shore. Then a lone rider appeared, riding slowly toward the island.

It was Griff Connah.

***

In the aftermath of Lord Roderic's capture, resistance to Llywelyn collapsed. With their master in custody, many of Roderic's men happily came over to serve the Prince as did most of the Anglesey barons. In exchange for his life, Roderic agreed to abdicate his claim to the throne of Gwynedd and accept banishment. Within a day, he was put aboard a ship bound for the Isle of Man and exile.

Llywelyn did not dwell at Aberffraw long. He paid off Caradog Priddy who gladly transported the new ruler of Gwynedd and his troops across the Menai Strait to Caenarfon. After a few hours of dickering, that mighty fortress opened its gates and hailed their new Prince.

Having secured Llywelyn's crown, Roland led the Invalid Company back to Deganwy. He was joined there by the Prince, fresh from taking possession of Caenarfon Castle. Together, the two men walked alone through the ruins of the burnt fortress on the two hills.

"Your plan worked, Sir Roland," said the Prince. "I am grateful."

Roland stopped at the centre of what had been the bailey and felt a tightness in his chest. The turned-up earth from the graves there still looked fresh.

"By the end, it didn't much resemble my plan," he said and nodded toward the graves, "and the price was high."

Llywelyn squatted on his haunches and picked up a handful of the dirt.

"Your Invalids are hard men to kill, Sir Roland. I regret that some were lost, but ending this war will stop a great many other deaths."

Roland said nothing. He had heard others speak the same words, but had yet to decide if they were true.

"I will hope for that, my lord, most sincerely."

Llywelyn let the grave dirt slip through his fingers and stood up.

"Sir Roland, I have a new realm to rule and the barons here have, only lately, been forced to acknowledge my right to the crown. Time will tell which of these I can trust. At the moment, I trust none of them." Llywelyn turned and fixed Roland with a stare. "A prince needs men close to him he can rely on. Can I trust you, Sir Roland?"

Roland was startled by the question.

"I would not play you false, my lord, but I am Earl Ranulf's oath man."

Llywelyn nodded.

"Aye, and loyal, no doubt. But what if I make it worth Ranulf's while to release you from your oath? Would you join me—help me govern Wales, in peace if we can? If you will be my liege man, I will give you Deganwy and all the land attached to it. You would be a wealthy man, Sir Roland, and a trusted friend to a prince. What say you?"

Roland looked at Llywelyn. The man had only grown in stature since he had first met him as a young rebel in the wilderness. He was the kind of man that destiny smiled upon— a bit like England's own king—and a man that other men were drawn to. Were things different, he might gladly follow such a man, but he had his own star to guide on and that star was in a modest fort on the banks of the River Weaver.

"Thank you most kindly, my lord, but I have watched Earl Ranulf for many years and I have seen the things that trouble a baron's mind. Politics are not to my taste. I am content with my life and my lot. But I do wish you well. I think you will make a fine prince."

Llywelyn laughed at that.

"Ahh, Sir Roland, you lack ambition. This is why I wanted you for my own! But, alas, it seems it is not to be. Tell your Earl we are square."

The next day, Griff came to say his farewells as the Invalids mounted and sorted out their column.

"So, English, may I call upon you if I have a need for a brilliant, but complicated, plan in the future?"

Roland grinned.

"Aye, Griff, any time. Though next time you get to take the fort and I will ride to the rescue."

Griff reached up and took Roland's hand.

"Fair enough and Godspeed, my friend," he said and started to turn away, then stopped.

"Engard tells me you bested him with your bow."

"I would call it a draw."

Griff arched an eyebrow.

"That's not how he tells it, but remember one thing, English."

"Yes?"

"I'm better than Engard."

Roland laughed.

"Someday, Griff, when the two of us ride among the high peaks of Eryri, we must settle this."

"Someday, English, someday."

Roland gave a hand signal and the Invalid Company rode out of Deganwy and up the coast road toward Cheshire and home.

Home

A bright sun was shining, as Roland and the Invalid Company reached the border. The River Dee was deep and cold and never looked better. There was no hesitation as the riders plunged into the water and crossed back into England. Sir Roger, Declan and Rhys Madawc rode with Roland at the head of the column as they spurred their mounts up the familiar trail that led to Shipbrook.

On the high ground ahead, three riders appeared. One of the mounted men peeled off and galloped in the direction of the de Laval's small fortress. The other two rode down to greet the column.

"I expect Lady Catherine has had the lads out watching the ford from dawn till dusk," Declan said as they reined in at the riders' approach. "We are a bit overdue."

"Only by a week or so," Sir Roger grumbled. "And we *have* brought back the boy."

Declan stole a glance at Roland and gave him a wink. Sir Roger had fretted the entire ride back through Wales over the reception they would receive on their return to Shipbrook.

"Oh, aye, we have young Madawc in tow," Declan replied, "and that will count for something, to be sure."

"But were not the lot of you almost hung while collecting the lad?" Roland asked innocently.

The big knight scowled at his son-in-law.

"Catherine doesn't have to know everything."

"Things like you enlisting in a Welsh civil war and leading a cavalry charge, my lord?" Declan asked sweetly.

306

"Well, we saved *his* neck, did we not?" The Lord of Shipbrook said and jerked his thumb toward Roland.

"I can vouch for that, my lord," Roland said, "but what will you tell Lady Catherine of all this?"

Sir Roger shook his head sorrowfully and sighed.

"The truth. I never could lie to that woman," he said in resignation, as the rider drew near. It was Baldric.

"Welcome home, my lords!" he called out cheerfully and wondered why Sir Roger de Laval did not look at all happy to be back.

***

Of the one hundred seven men of the Invalid Company who rode out of Chester the month before, only eighty-seven returned to Shipbrook. Eight men remained in Wales recovering from wounds, and twelve more would never return. Friar Cyril had said a short mass for their souls before they rode away from Deganwy.

Roland and the Invalids tarried only a day at Shipbrook, but it was day to remember. The returning men somehow managed to crowd into the great hall of Shipbrook for a homecoming feast. Roland had never seen quite this kind of a banquet at Shipbrook. There was venison, wild boar and smoked salmon on the tables as well as a savoury rabbit stew. There were sweet tarts and meat pies and loaves of fresh-baked black bread. Barrels of ale were tapped and drained. It was a fitting welcome home for the men of Shipbrook and the Invalid Company as well.

To be sure, the de Lavals were not poor, but it took Lady Catherine's sharp eyes and good sense to make ends meet from the revenue of their lands. To her, money hard-earned was grudgingly spent and banquets were not a part of her household budget. But Prince Llywelyn had been generous to the men who had helped him win a throne and had favoured Sir Roger with enough silver to pay for a dozen such feasts.

Whatever complaints Lady Catherine might have had with her husband's adventures in Wales were aired in private. In public, she did not stray far from the big knight and did not complain when he pulled her close and kissed her cheek during the festivities.

***

The next morning, the Invalid Company made the half-day journey to Chester. Once inside the Northgate, Roland turned over command of the men to Sir John and rode on alone to Chester Castle. As he rode into the bailey, he saw that word of his return had already reached the Earl. Ranulf was standing on the steps of the keep, waiting for him. As Roland dismounted, the Earl hurried down to greet him.

"Sir Roland! I feared I would not see you until spring," he said with genuine warmth, "do you bring good tidings from Wales?"

Roland handed the reins of The Grey to a groom and bowed to the Marcher Lord.

"My lord, I bring news of Wales and of Llywelyn," Roland said gravely. "You can judge if these tidings are good or ill."

Ranulf furrowed his brow.

"Come then and join me inside. I'll want to know everything."

He led Roland to a small parlour on the second floor of the keep, where a blazing fire had banished the winter chill. For an hour, Roland recounted the events of the past month while Ranulf listened intently. He spoke of the trek through the towering peaks of Eryri in a blizzard and the fashioning of a plan to strike at Llywelyn's uncles. He told of the theft of Haakon the Black's longships and the defence of Deganwy Castle. He spoke of the courage of the Invalid Company and, sadly, of their losses.

When Roland finished his report, the nobleman rose and stood silently by the fire for a while. He had not missed the pain in the young knight's voice as he spoke of the men he'd lost.

"It's an extraordinary story, Sir Roland," he said, as he warmed his hands by the blaze. "In less than a month, you and the Invalids have wiped clean my debt of honour. That is well. Now that Llywelyn rules all of Gwynedd, it would not be wise to still be beholden to him." He paused and looked carefully at Roland.

"You are pained by your casualties—I can see that."

Roland blinked. He thought he had kept his personal feelings out of his report to the Earl.

"They were good men, my lord."

Ranulf nodded.

"Aye, aye, it is hard to lose good men, but you, more than most, know we live in a violent world, Sir Roland. And if the good are not prepared to fight, then…" The Earl let his advice trail off. He could see it would not do much good. Sir Roland would have to find his own way of dealing with leading men to their deaths.

"I've had news," he said, changing the subject, "a rumour really, that a party including Lord Daffyd was seen fording the Dee south of here a few days ago." The Earl gave a little sigh. "He was a man of limited vision. I will miss him."

"Aye, lord. I take your point. Llywelyn does not lack ambition, but for now I think our borders are safe from him."

"Why should that be so?"

"The Welsh love to fight each other, lord. It will be a while before they have time for us."

***

Lady Millicent Inness was talking with Cook about the evening meal, when the door to the small timber hall burst open. It was Sir Edgar Langdon, moving fast for a huge man with a bad leg. It took the big knight a moment to catch his breath as Millicent waited to hear his tidings.

"It's Roland, my lady! Down at the ford and headed this way."

Millicent rose, a little breathless herself. She had hoped her husband would be home in a few weeks, though she knew it could be much longer. Still as January came to an end, she had fretted and spent more time than was useful on the southern wall walk watching the ford over the Weaver. Now the wait was done.

"Are you sure, Edgar?"

"Well, the rider is bundled up so it's hard to tell, but I would know that big grey gelding anywhere."

Millicent broke into a relieved smile and quickly wrapped a heavy cloak around her shoulders. Sir Edgar hurried back out to gather the men-at-arms. Danesford was a modest place, but its lord was returning and that called for a proper reception. Millicent started for the door, then paused to pat her dress and run fingers through her hair. Then she almost laughed at herself. She knew this was vanity and that Roland would not care that her dress was wrinkled or her hair tangled, still…

When she reached the door, she heard footsteps behind her and turned to see Lorea coming down the steps from her bedchamber, a questioning look on her face.

"Come along, young miss. Your brother has come home!"

A huge smile split the girl's face. She ran down the stairs and took Millicent's hand. Together they walked out of the hall and waited by the gate.

***

As he rode up the road from the ford, Roland saw The Grey's ears prick up at the sight of home. The big horse broke into a trot with no urging from him. Atop the ridge was Danesford. He was struck by how raw and new the place looked after the time he'd spent in the aged and weathered fortress of Deganwy.

He could see the sentry in the lone watchtower. The man was leaning over and speaking to someone in the courtyard and paying no attention to whoever might be approaching the fort. He was making a mental note to speak to Sir Edgar about that when he rode through the gate of Danesford and saw that the big Saxon had turned out eight men-at-arms to greet him in the courtyard.

Roland barely saw them, his eyes going to Millicent who stood holding Lorea's hand a little way off.

"Welcome home!" Sir Edgar boomed.

"Good to be back," Roland replied, as he swung out of the saddle and handed the reins of The Grey to a waiting stable boy. He felt awkward as he walked between the men-at-arms flanking the gate. Such a formal reception seemed overdone, but Sir Edgar was his Master of the Sword and had his own way of doing things. He nodded at the men as he passed through their ranks, but his eyes were on Millie. Then he was through the cordon and standing before her.

He reached around her waist, pulling her close and lifting her off her feet. He buried his face in her neck and she gave a little shriek as he whirled her around.

"You smell like home," he murmured in her ear.

She laughed and drew back, still encircled by his arms.

"And you smell like horse, but I don't care."

Roland kissed her then and felt Lorea tugging at the edge of his cape. He sat Millicent back on her feet and threw an arm over the little girl's shoulder.

"Have you been good, Lorea?"

"Aye, Roland, I'm always good! I've done my chores and Lady Millicent is teaching me to do figures."

"A useful skill, sister."

"And I've kept the secret, as I've promised."

Roland raised an eyebrow and Millicent's eyes grew wide.

"Secret? What secret?"

Lorea stole a quick glance at Millicent, who gave her a little nod.

"I'm going to be an aunt, Roland!"

Dreams

*T*he riders came out of the trees. The weak winter sun glinted off armour and mail and sharpened lance heads. Horses snorted and stamped the frozen ground. Roland stood in the middle of the frost-covered field and saw them come. He did not hesitate. He turned and ran.

Behind him, he heard a command ring out and the sounds of warhorses lunging forward to give chase. He was a fast runner, but he was a hundred yards from the next wood line and he was not faster than a charging warhorse. He dared not look back, but he could hear them closing on him. Hooves pounded, leather groaned and metal clashed as death bore down on him.

And then he was in the woods. Saplings grew thick along the verge—too thick for horses to follow at speed. Roland could hear men shout and horses squeal as the thundering charge pulled up short in front of this barrier. He did not slack his flight. They would find gaps soon enough and be in the woods after him, but now they were on his ground.

Roland reached behind him to draw forth an arrow from his quiver. It was tipped with the wicked bodkin head—a spike of hard metal that could pierce chain mail at middle distance and plate armour in close quarters. He slowed, turning to look behind him. Only a few of the riders had made it into the trees.

They should have stayed in the field.

Roland stopped and drew his bow. The terror he had felt in the field was gone. He took a deep breath and woke up. He looked to see Millie sleeping soundly beside him. He must not have roused her. She had once said his nightmares would stop if he ever reached the trees before the riders.

He hoped she was right.

***

Four hundred miles south of Danesford, a man awoke to bright sunshine streaming through the high arched window of his bedchamber. His breathing was ragged and his nightshirt was soaked with sweat. He blinked at the light, confused. A moment before he had been running—running through a dark wood with death on his heels.

The woman beside him stirred and sat up in bed. He glanced at her and she tried to hide a questioning look. He must have cried out in his sleep again. He rubbed his temples. This was a new girl and perhaps it had frightened her. He didn't care.

"Leave me," he said dully. The girl scrambled to collect her clothes and hurried from the room.

William de Ferrers got up slowly and walked to the window. From this high perch, he looked out across his vast estate in Brittany. In the distance, fields turning green with the approach of spring extended to the horizon and beyond. The day was beautiful, the sky as blue as a robin's egg.

Below, he saw a small knot of his retainers gathering. Grooms were leading horses from the stables, in preparation for the day's hunt. The men all carried lances, so they would be seeking wild boar. He could hear them jesting with each, their spirits high. They were young men, around his own age, and full of the heedless confidence of young, well-born men everywhere. He envied them.

He had once been a skilled and relentless hunter, but the shadows in the forest now filled him with dread. For in the places he could not see—behind the tree, among the rocks, around the next bend in the trail, might be a man with a bow—a man who had promised to kill him.

He felt the heat rise in his face. He hated this bastard Dane who troubled his sleep. The man had already come dangerously close to making his threat a reality, beginning with a bloody day high on the slopes of Kinder Scout mountain. And after the disastrous battle at Towcester, he'd been ridden down and cornered by his tormentor. They'd crossed swords and he'd felt certain he could end this nightmare then. He had far more skill with a blade, but the ferocity of the man's attack had unnerved and finally exhausted him. Had it not been for the intervention of Earl William Marshall he would surely have died that day.

On that frozen field, he had looked into the eyes of the man who now haunted his dreams and saw no mercy there. Had he known then where it would all lead, he would have spared the life of the man's stubborn father, but he had not—and so the dreams came again and again.

He had lived that day, but always…always his sleep was troubled and he would make excuses for why he would not ride with his young retainers to the hunt.

It was intolerable.

He still had over two years left on his banishment from England, but he'd been generous in his financial support of King Richard's incessant wars with France. It was possible his return to Derbyshire might be sooner than many reckoned. But Derbyshire shared a border with Cheshire, which brought his nightmare all the closer. Something had to be done before that day came.

Something had to be done about Roland Inness.

A Prince of Wales

Historical Note

Many of the events depicted in *A Prince of Wales* are fictional, but this story was built around a core of documented history. It is a fictionalized account of the rise of Llywelyn ap Iowerth, later to be called Llywelyn the Great, in the months leading up to his first great victory over his uncles Daffyd and Roderic at the Battle of Aberconwy in 1194.

Other than its location near the mouth of the River Conwy, the details of that battle are sparse—a few lines from court poets being all historians have to go on. But certain events leading up to the clash and its aftermath are clear. For certain, Llywelyn allied himself with his cousins Gruffydd and Maredudd before this battle. What is less certain is where Roderic stood. Some accounts have him joining with Llywelyn for the battle and others have him on the losing side with his brother Daffyd. What is known is that Daffyd fled Gwynedd after the battle and Llywelyn went on to win two more engagements in Anglesey. Whether by violence or natural causes, Roderic was dead a year later.

The details in this book regarding the fratricidal competition to succeed Owain Gwynedd and rule northern Wales are factual. Before he died, Owain designated Hywel as his heir, but it appears that Roderic and Daffyd, the sons of Owain Gwynedd's second wife, had a well-developed plan to seize control of Gwynedd on Owain's death. Within a year, they had killed Hywel and driven off all other pretenders. They went on to divide Gwynedd and rule for almost twenty-five years.

Llywelyn was raised in Powys and, for a time, in England, to avoid the bloodbath that followed the death of Owain. He returned from that self-imposed exile at age fourteen to stake his claim to northern Wales, launching a long and bloody rebellion that lasted seven years. After defeating his uncles, he ruled

Gwynedd for forty-five years and was de facto ruler of most of Wales for much of that period—Llywelyn the Great, indeed!

As for this story, while there are historical records that show Llywelyn allied himself with Earl Ranulf of Chester later in his career, I've found nothing to suggest that the Earl supplied the rebel Prince with any men prior to his assumption of rule over Gwynedd. But we don't know that he didn't—do we? And if so, who better to send than Roland Inness and the Invalid Company?

Haakon the Black is a fictional character, but Roderic was wed to the daughter of the King of the Isles and did hire Gaelic/Danish mercenaries from Ireland on other occasions.

Some interesting geographic/historical facts:

- There was a fortress on the two rocky hills that still look down on the mouth of the River Conwy at Deganwy. It was probably of timber construction with some stonework around the foundation. It was built by a Norman, Robert of Rhuddlan, only a dozen years after the Conquest, but was later destroyed to keep it from falling into English hands.

- There is a fine ruin that can still be visited at Dolwyddelan, though it is what remains of a later castle that Llywelyn built after he became ruler of Gwynedd.

- Aberffraw still exists today as a sleepy little village in Anglesey. Save for the royal Llys, it was not much more than that in the 12th century.

- Ynys Llanddwyn, "Saint Dwynwen's Island" is still there today and still cut off from Anglesey at high tide. Saint Dwynwen is the Welsh patron saint of lovers.

- The Menai Strait has some of the most treacherous tidal action in Britain, particularly the stretch just west of Menai Bridge—known as "The Swellies."

- Legend does claim that 20,000 saints are buried on Ynys Enlli or Bardsey Island.

Books by Wayne Grant
The Saga of Roland Inness
Longbow
Warbow
The Broken Realm
The Ransomed Crown
A Prince of Wales

A Prince of Wales

Four years ago, I set out to tell the coming-of-age story of a fourteen-year-old boy with a longbow. The first four books in *The Saga of Roland Inness*—beginning with *Longbow* and concluding with *The Ransomed Crown*—encompass the coming-of-age story I set out to tell.

Having told that tale, I intended to move on to other stories, but something unexpected happened. Readers all over the world found something special in Roland Inness and his companions and wanted more. And I'll confess, I'd grown rather fond of my boy with the longbow as well. I also knew there were more stories to tell. So, the Saga continues with *A Prince of Wales*.

To learn more about The Saga of Roland Inness, visit my website at www.waynegrantbooks.com or the Longbow Facebook page.

ABOUT THE AUTHOR

I grew up in a tiny cotton town in rural Louisiana where hunting, fishing and farming are a way of life. Between chopping cotton, dove hunting and Little League ball I developed a love of great adventure stories like *Call It Courage* and *Kidnapped*.

Like most southern boys, I saw the military as an honourable career, so it was a natural step for me to attend and graduate from West Point. I just missed Vietnam, but served in Germany and Korea. I found that life as a Captain in an army broken by Vietnam was not what I wanted and returned to Louisiana and civilian life. I later served for four years as a senior official in the Pentagon and had the honour of playing a small part in the rebuilding of a great U.S. Army.

Through it all, I kept my love for great adventure stories. When I had two sons, I began making up stories for them about a boy and his longbow. Those stories grew to become my first novel, *Longbow*. The picture above was taken on Kinder Scout.

Wayne Grant

Printed in Great Britain
by Amazon